MASTER'S CHOICE

MASTER'S CHOICE

*Mystery Stories by Today's Top Writers
and the Masters Who Inspired Them*

Edited by
LAWRENCE BLOCK

BERKLEY PRIME CRIME, NEW YORK

MASTER'S CHOICE

A Berkley Prime Crime Book
Published by the Berkley Publishing Group
A Division of Penguin Putnam Inc.
375 Hudson Street, New York, New York 10014

The Penguin Putnam World Wide Web site address is
http://www.penguinputnam.com

Copyright © 1999 by Lawrence Block and Tekno-Books
Book design by Tiffany Kukec

First Edition: November 1999

Library of Congress Cataloging-in-Publication Data

Master's choice: mystery stories by today's top writers and the masters who inspired them / edited by Lawrence Block.
    p.   cm.
    ISBN 0-425-17031-4
    1. Detective and mystery stories, American.   I. Block, Lawrence.
PS648.D4M37   1999
813'.087208—dc21   99-30270
                                                                        CIP

Printed in the United States of America

10   9   8   7   6   5   4   3   2   1

Acknowledgments

"The Wedding Gig" copyright © 1980 by Stephen King. Reprinted by permission of the author.

"Murder-Two" copyright © 1998 by Joyce Carol Oates. Reprinted by permission of the author.

"The Crime of Miss Oyster Brown" copyright © 1991 by Peter Lovesey. Reprinted by permission of the author.

"Too Many Crooks" copyright © 1989 by Donald E. Westlake. Reprinted by permission of the author.

"Tired Old Man" copyright © 1975 by The Kilimanjaro Corporation. Reprinted by arrangement with, and permission of, the Author and the Author's agent, Richard Curtis Associates, Inc., New York, USA. All rights reserved.

"En Famille" copyright © 1996 by Ed Gorman. Reprinted by permission of the author.

"Another Room" copyright © 1990 by Joan Hess. Reprinted by permission of the author.

"Trick or Treat" copyright © 1975 by Judith Garner. Reprinted by permission of the author.

"High Stakes" copyright © 1984 by John Lutz. Reprinted by permission of the author.

"Souls Burning" copyright © 1991 by Bill Pronzini. Reprinted by permission of the author.

"Murder of the Frankfurter Man" copyright © 1934 by Benjamin Appel. Reprinted by permission of the Executors for the author's Estate, Carla Kunow, Willa Appel, and Marianne Appel Kunow.

"First Lead Gasser" copyright © 1993 by Tony Hillerman. Reprinted by permission of the author.

"Goodbye, Pops" copyright © 1969 by Joe Gores. Reprinted by permission of the author.

"How Far It Could Go" copyright © 1997 by Lawrence Block. Reprinted by permission of the author.

"In a Grove" copyright © 1960, 1961 by John O'Hara. Reprinted by permission of Random House, Inc.

Contents

MASTER'S CHOICE

INTRODUCTION

THERE COMES A time in the long and happy life of a writer when it occurs to him that he ought to edit an anthology. He looks at the ad card, that ever-lengthening list of titles appearing opposite the title page of each new book, and realizes there's an entire category missing from his own ad cards—to wit, *Anthologies (editor)*. By producing such a volume, he can add not only a book but a whole class of books, and may thereby increase, albeit minimally, his claim to be regarded not as a mere wordsmith but as a Man of Letters. And, *mirabile dictu*, he can accomplish all of this without having to sit down and actually *write* anything!

Remarkable that it's taken me this long.

But first, you see, I had to think of something for an anthology to be *about*. Anthologies are typically thematic. Locked-room murders, for instance. Unlocked-room murders. Stories set in the past, or in the afternoon, or in East Texas. Stories without cats.

It struck me that writers have an interesting perspective on the stories they read as well as those they write themselves. If I could convince ten or a dozen leading writers of short crime fiction to pick their favorite stories and explain their selections, I'd have not just another theme anthology but a book with enormous appeal.

And not only wouldn't I have to write anything, I wouldn't even have to pick the stories!

So the next time the incomparable Marty Greenberg pointed out that I really ought to do an anthology, I trotted out the idea for *Master's Choice*. He liked it at once, but wanted to make sure he knew just what I had in mind. "Do they pick their favorite from among the stories they've written?" he wondered. "Or is it the favorite story they've read?"

"Both," I said.

"That's two books," Marty pointed out. *"The Story I'm Proud I Wrote* and *The Story I Wish I'd Written."*

"Good," I said. "If I'm going to do a book without writing anything, I might as well do two of them. It doesn't sound like that much extra work."

As it turns out, *Master's Choice* is two books in one. The juxtaposition of the authors' selections from their own work and their favorites of stories they'd read was too interesting to lose. So the volume you hold in your hand contains two selections, each from a dozen of the finest writers of short crime fiction in the English-speaking world.

At the same time, you could say that *Master's Choice* is four books in two, because this is the first of at least two volumes. When I sent out invitations to pick a pair of stories for this project, I expected a strong positive response, but succeeded beyond my wildest dreams. I picked two dozen prominent crime writers, all of them particularly adept at short fiction. (I had to leave out some of my favorite writers because they write only novels.) I knew I was writing to busy people, men and women who get asked to participate in such projects all the time, and I calculated that even if fewer than half of them responded I'd have a book. And I figured that, with a little coaxing, I might get enough acceptances.

Well, go figure. Everybody wanted to play.

The lure, I suspect, is the chance to tell the world about a story one has always loved. Writers are great readers and have a special perspective on what they read. There were, as you'll see, some surprises in the stories they picked. Some lovely surprises.

I was unsure whether my own participation should be limited to the role of presenter, or master of ceremonies. Should I stand aside with uncharacteristic modesty? Or should I shove my way into the limelight?

What tipped the balance for me was the opportunity to include a short story by John O'Hara, a favorite author who is certainly not thought of as a writer of crime fiction. I love it, and, as far as I know, it's never been anthologized outside of the author's own collections. How could I pass up a chance to introduce it to you?

A second volume, with a lineup every bit as impressive as this one, is scheduled for publication a year from now. And if you folks out there like the result anywhere near as much as I do, *Master's Choice* may eventually run to quite a few volumes.

There's no limit to how many books I can produce if I don't have to write them.

LAWRENCE BLOCK
Greenwich Village

STEPHEN KING

"*The* Wedding Gig" isn't the sort of tale I ordinarily tell, and maybe that's why I like it so much. I was particularly fond of the story's tone and snappy slang; the narration almost seems to be coming from the horn of an old RCA gramophone, complete with groove-pops and needle hiss. Vo-do-dee-oh-do!

Joyce Carol Oates is a fine literary writer; she is also capable of writing paralyzing stories of horror and suspense. Her short novel Zombie *is a classic of this type; so is her story "Murder-Two." Its very quietness becomes part of its terrible final effect. Surely it is a tale Edgar Allan Poe would have enjoyed.*

The Wedding Gig

In THE YEAR 1927 we were playing jazz in a speakeasy just south of Morgan, Illinois, which is 70 miles from Chicago. It was real hick country, not another big town for 20 miles in any direction. But there were a lot of plowboys with a hankering for something stronger than Moxie after a hot day in the field, and a lot of young bucks out duding it up with their drugstore buddies. There were also some married men (you know them, friend, they might as well be wearing signs) coming far out of their way to be where no one would recognize them while they cut a rug with their not-quite-legit lassies.

That was when jazz was jazz, not noise. We had a five-man combination—drums, clarinet, trombone, piano, and trumpet—and we were pretty good. That was still three years before we made our first records and four years before talkies.

We were playing *Bamboo Bay* when this big fellow walked in, wearing a white suit and smoking a pipe with more squiggles in it than a French horn. The whole band was a little drunk but the crowd was positively blind and everyone was having a high old time. There hadn't been a single fight all night. All of us were sweating rivers and Tommy Englander, the guy who ran the place, kept sending up rye. Englander was a good fellow to work for, and he liked our sound.

The guy in the white suit sat down at the bar and I forgot him. We finished up the set with *Aunt Hagar's Blues*, which was what passed for racy out in the boondocks back then, and got a good round of applause. Manny had a big grin on his face as he put his horn down, and I clapped him on the back as we left the bandstand. There was a lonely-looking girl in a green evening dress that had been giving me the eye all night. She was a redhead, and I've always been partial to those. I got a signal from her eyes and the tilt of her head, so I started threading my way through the crowd to get to her.

Halfway there the man in the white suit stepped in front of me. Up close he looked tough, with bristly black hair and the flat, oddly shiny eyes that some deep-sea fish have. There was something familiar about him.

"Want to talk to you outside," he said.

The redhead was looking away. She seemed disappointed.

"It can wait," I said. "Let me by."

"My name is Scollay. Mike Scollay."

I knew the name. Mike Scollay was a small-time racketeer from Chicago who made his money running booze in from Canada. His picture had been in the paper a few times. The last time had been when another little Caesar tried to gun him down.

"You're pretty far from Chicago," I said.

"I brought some friends. Let's go outside."

The redhead looked over and I pointed to Scollay and shrugged. She sniffed and turned her back.

"You queered that," I said.

"Bimbos like that are a penny the bushel in Chi," he said. "Outside."

We went out. The air was cool on my skin after the smoky close atmosphere of the club, sweet with fresh-cut alfalfa grass. The stars were out, soft and flickering. The hoods were out too, but they didn't look a bit soft, and the only things flickering on them were their cigarettes.

"I've got some money for you," Scollay said.

"I haven't done anything for you."

"You're going to. It's two C's. Split it up with the band or hold back a hundred for yourself."

"What is it?"

"A gig," he said. "My sis is getting married. I want you to play for the reception. She likes Dixieland. Two of my boys say you play good Dixieland."

I told you Englander was good to work for. He was paying eighty a week split five ways, four hours a night. This guy was offering well over twice that for one gig.

"It's from five to eight, next Friday," Scollay said. "At the Grover Street Hall in Chi."

"It's too much," I said. "How come?"

"There's two reasons," Scollay said. He puffed on his pipe. It looked out of place in that yegg's face. He should have had a Lucky dangling from his mouth, or a Sweet Caporal. The pipe made him look sad and funny.

"First," he said, "maybe you heard the Greek tried to rub me out."

"I saw your picture in the paper," I said. "You were the guy trying to crawl into the sidewalk."

"Smart guy," he growled, but with no real force. "I'm getting too big for him. The Greek is getting old and he still thinks small. He ought to be back in the old country, drinking olive oil and looking at the Pacific."

"It's the Aegean," I said.

"An ocean's an ocean," he said. "Anyway, the Greek is still out to get me."

"In other words, you're paying two hundred because our last number might be arranged for Enfield rifle accompaniment."

Anger flashed on his face, and something else—sorrow? "I got the best protection money can buy. If anyone funny sticks his nose in, he won't get a chance to sniff twice."

"What's the other thing?"

Softly he said, "My sister's marrying an Italian."

"A good Catholic like you," I sneered softly.

The anger flashed again, white-hot, and I thought I'd pushed it too far. "A good *mick*! I'm a good mick, sonny, and you better not forget it!" To that he added, almost too low to be heard, "Even if I did lose most of my hair, it was red."

I started to say something, but he didn't give me the chance. He swung me around and pressed his face down until our noses almost touched. I never saw such anger and humiliation and rage and determination in a man's face. You never see that on a white face these days, the love-hate pressure of a man's race. But it was there then, and I saw it that night.

"She's fat," he breathed. "A lot of people have been laughing at me when my back is turned. They don't do it when I can see them, though. I'll tell you that, Mr. Cornet Player. Because maybe this little twerp was all she could get. But you're not gonna laugh at her and nobody else is either because you're gonna play too loud. No one is going to laugh at my sis."

I didn't know what to say. I didn't know why he told me or even why he thought a Dixieland band was his answer, but I didn't want to argue with him. You wouldn't have wanted to, either, funny clothes and pipe or not.

"We don't laugh at people when we play our gigs," I said. "Makes it too hard to pucker."

That relieved the tension. He laughed a short barking laugh. "You be there at five, ready to play. Grover Street Hall. I'll pay your expenses both ways."

I felt railroaded into the decision, but it was too late now. Scollay was already striding away, and one of his paid companions was holding open the back door of a Packard coupe.

They drove away. I stayed out awhile longer and had a smoke. The evening was soft and fine and Scollay seemed more and more like something I might have dreamed. I was just wishing we could bring the bandstand out to the parking lot and play when Biff tapped me on the shoulder.

"Time," he said.

"Okay."

We went back in. The redhead had picked up some salt-and-pepper sailor who looked twice her age. I don't know what a member of the U.S. Navy was doing in central Illinois, but as far as I was concerned, he could have her if her taste was that bad.

I didn't feel so hot. The rye had gone to my head, and Scollay seemed a lot more real in here, where the fumes of what his kind sold were strong enough to float on.

"We had a request for *Camptown Races*," Charlie said.

"Forget it," I said curtly. "None of that now."

I could see Billy-Boy stiffen just as he was sitting down to the piano, and then his face was smooth again. I could have kicked myself around the block.

"I'm sorry, Billy," I told him. "I haven't been myself tonight."

"Sure," he said, but there was no big smile and I knew he felt bad. He knew what I had started to say.

I TOLD them about the gig during our next break, being square with them about the money and how Scollay was a hood (although I didn't tell them there was another hood out to get him). I also told them that Scollay's sister was fat but nobody was to even crack a smile about it. I told them Scollay was sensitive.

It seemed to me that Billy-Boy Williams flinched again at that but you couldn't tell it from his face. It would be easier to tell what a walnut was thinking by reading the wrinkles on the shell. Billy-Boy was the best ragtime piano player we ever had and we were all sorry about the little ways it got taken out on him as we traveled from one place to another—the Jim Crow car south of the Mason-Dixon line, the balcony at the movies, the different hotel room in some towns—but what could I do? In those days you lived with those differences.

WE turned up at Grover Street on Friday at four o'clock just to make sure we'd have plenty of time to set up. We drove up from Morgan in a special Ford truck that Biff and Manny and I had put together. The back end was all enclosed, and there were two cots bolted to the floor. We even had an electric hotplate that ran off the battery, and the band's name was painted on the outside.

The day was just right—a ham-and-egg summer day if you ever saw one, with little white angel clouds floating over the fields. But it was hot and gritty in Chicago, full of the hustle and bustle you could get out of touch with in a place like Morgan. When we got there my clothes were sticking to my body and I needed to visit the comfort station. I could have used a shot of Tommy Englander's rye, too.

The hall was a big wooden building, sort of affiliated with the church where Scollay's sis was getting married, I guess. You know the kind of joint I mean—Ladies' Robert Browning Society on Tuesdays and Thursdays, Bingo on Wednesdays, and a sociable for the kids on Friday or Saturday night.

We trooped up the walk, each of us carrying his instrument in one hand and some part of Biff's drum-kit in the other. A thin lady with no breastworks to speak of was directing traffic inside. Two sweating men were hanging crepe paper. There was a bandstand at the front of the hall, and over it was a pair of pink-paper wedding bells and some tinsel lettering which said *BEST AL-WAYS MAUREEN AND RICO.*

Maureen and Rico. Damned if I couldn't see why Scollay was so upset. Maureen and Rico. Now wasn't that a combination!

The thin lady saw us and swooped down to our end of the hall. She looked like she had a lot to say, so I beat her to the punch. "We're the band," I said.

"The band?" She blinked at our instruments distrustfully. "Oh. I was hoping you were the caterers."

I smiled as if caterers always carried snare drums and trombone cases.

"You can—" she began, but just then a tough-looking boy of about 19 strolled over. A cigarette was dangling from the left corner of his mouth, but so far as I could see, it wasn't doing a thing for his image except making his left eye water.

"Open that stuff up," he said.

Charlie and Biff looked at me and I just shrugged. We opened our cases and he looked at the horns. Seeing nothing that looked lethal, he wandered back to his corner and sat down on a folding chair.

"You can set your things up right away," she went on, as if there had been no interruption. "There's a piano in the other room. I'll have my men wheel it in when we're done putting up our decorations."

Biff was already lugging his drum-kit up onto the little stage.

"I though you were the caterers," she said to me in a distraught way. "Mr. Scollay ordered a wedding cake and there are hors d'oeuvres and roasts of beef and—"

"They'll be here, ma'am," I said. "They get payment on delivery."

"—capons and roasts of pork and Mr. Scollay will be furious if—" She saw one of her men pausing to light a cigarette just below a dangling streamer and screamed, *HENRY!*" The man jumped as if he had been shot, and I escaped to the bandstand.

WE were all set up by a quarter to five. Charlie, the trombone player, was wah-wahing away into a mute and Biff was loosening up his wrists. The caterers had arrived at 4:20 and Miss Gibson (that was her name; she made a business out of such affairs) almost threw herself on them.

Four long tables had been set up and covered with white linen, and four black women in caps and aprons were setting places. The cake had been wheeled into the middle of the room for everyone to gasp over. It was six layers high, with a little bride and groom on top.

I walked outside to have a smoke and just about halfway through it I heard them coming, tooting away and making a general racket. When I saw the lead vehicle coming around the corner of the block below the church, I snubbed my smoke and went back inside.

"They're coming," I told Miss Gibson.

She went white as a sheet. That lady should have picked a different profession. "The tomato juice!" she screamed. "Bring in the tomato juice!"

I went back up to the bandstand and we got ready. We had played quite a few gigs like this before—what band hasn't?—and when the doors opened, we swung into a ragtime version of the *The Wedding March* that I had arranged myself. Most receptions we played for loved it.

Everybody clapped and yelled and then started gassing among themselves, but I could tell by the way some of them were tapping their feet that we were getting through. We were on—it was going to be a good gig.

But I have to admit that I almost blew the whole number when the groom and the blushing bride walked in. Scollay, dressed in a morning-coat and a ruffled shirt and striped trousers, shot me a hard look, and don't think I didn't see it. The rest of the band kept a poker face too, and we didn't miss a note. Lucky for us. The wedding party, which looked as if it were made up almost entirely of Scollay's goons and their molls, were wise already. They had to be, if they'd been at the church. But I'd only heard faint rumblings, you might say.

You've heard about Jack Sprat and his wife. Well, this was a hundred times worse. Scollay's sister had the red hair he was losing, and it was long and curly. But not that pretty auburn shade you may be imagining. It was as bright as a carrot and as kinky as a bedspring. She looked just awful. And had Scollay said she was fat? Brother, that was like saying you can buy a few things in Macy's. The woman was a dinosaur—350 if she was a pound. It had all gone to her bosom and hips and thighs like it does on fat girls, making her flesh grotesque and frightening. Some fat girls have pathetically pretty faces, but Scollay's sis didn't even have that. Her eyes were too close together, her mouth was too big, and her ears stuck out. Even thin, she'd have been as ugly as the serpent in the garden.

That alone wouldn't have made anybody laugh, unless they were stupid or just poison-mean. It was when you added the groom, Rico, to the combination that you wanted to laugh until you cried.

He could have put on a top hat and stood in the top half of her shadow. He was about five three and must have weighed all of 90 pounds soaking wet. He was skinny as a rail, and his complexion was darkly olive. When he grinned around nervously, his teeth looked like a picket fence in a slum neighborhood.

We just kept right on playing.

Scollay roared, "The bride and the groom! May they always be happy!"

Everyone shouted their approval and applauded. We finished our number with a flourish, and that brought another round. Scollay's sister Maureen smiled nervously. Rico simpered.

For a while everyone just walked around, eating cheese and cold cuts on crackers and drinking Scollay's best bootleg Scotch. I had three shots myself between numbers, and it was pretty smooth.

Scollay began to look a little happier, too—I imagine he was sampling his own wares pretty freely.

He dropped by the bandstand once and said, "You guys play pretty good." Coming from a music lover like him, I reckoned that was a real compliment.

Just before everyone sat down to the meal, Maureen came up herself. She was even uglier up close, and her white gown (there must have been enough white satin to cover three beds) didn't help her at all. She asked us if we could play *Roses of Picardy* like Red Nichols and His Five Pennies, because it was her very favorite song. Fat and ugly or not, she was very sweet about it, not a bit hoity-toity like some of the two-bitters that had been dropping by. We played it, but not very well. Still, she gave us a sweet smile that was almost enough to make her pretty, and she applauded when it was done.

They sat down to the meal around 6:15, and Miss Gibson's hired help rolled in the chow. They fell to it like a bunch of animals, which was not entirely surprising, and kept drinking it up all the time. I couldn't help noticing the way Maureen was eating, though. She made the rest of them look like old ladies in a roadside tearoom. She had no more time for sweet smiles or listening to *Roses of Picardy*. That lady didn't need a knife and a fork. She needed a steam shovel. It was sad to watch her. And Rico (you could just see his chin over the edge of the table where the bride's party was sitting) just kept handing her things, never changing that nervous simper.

We took a twenty-minute break while the cake-cutting ceremony was going on and Miss Gibson herself fed us out in the back part of the hall. It was hot as blazes with the cook stove on, and none of us was too hungry. Manny and Biff had brought some pastry boxes though, and were stuffing in slabs of roast beef and roast pork every time Miss Gibson turned her back.

By the time we returned to the bandstand, the drinking had begun in earnest. Tough-looking guys staggered around with silly grins on their mugs or stood in corners haggling over racing forms. Some couples wanted to Charleston, so we played *Aunt Hagar's Blues* (those goons ate it up) and *I'm Gonna Charleston Back to Charleston* and some other jazzy numbers like that. The molls rocked around the floor, flashing their rolled hose and sounding as shrill as macaws. It was almost completely dark outside, and millers and moths had come in through the open windows and were flitting around the light fixtures. And as the song says, the band played on. The bride and groom stood on the sidelines—neither of them seemed interested in slipping away early—

almost completely neglected. Even Scollay seemed to have forgotten them. He was pretty drunk.

It was almost 8:00 when the little fellow crept in. I spotted him immediately because he was sober and dressed better than the rest of them. And he looked scared. He looked like a near-sighted cat in a dog pound. He walked up to Scollay, who was talking with some floozie right by the bandstand, and tapped him on the shoulder. Scollay wheeled around, and I heard every word they said.

"Who the hell are you?" Scollay asked rudely.

"My name is *Katzenos*," the fellow said, and his eyes rolled whitely. "I come from the Greek."

Motion on the floor came to a dead stop. We kept on playing though, you bet. Jacket buttons were freed, and hands stole out of sight. I saw Manny looking nervous. Hell, I wasn't so calm myself.

"Is that right?" Scollay said ominously.

The guy burst out, "I din't want to come, Mr. Scollay—the Greek, he has my wife. He say he kill her if I doan' give you his message!"

"What message?" Scollay asked. His face was like a thundercloud.

"He say—" The guy paused with an agonized expression. His throat worked like the words were physical, and caught in there. "He say to tell you your sister is one fat pig. He say . . . he say . . ." His eyes rolled wildly at Scollay's expression. I shot a look at Maureen. She looked as if she had been slapped. "He say she's tired of going to bed alone. He say—you bought her a husband."

Maureen gave a great strangled cry and ran out, weeping. The floor shook. Rico pattered after her, his face bewildered and unhappy.

But Scollay was the frightening one. His face had grown so red it was purple and I half expected his brains to just blow out his ears. I saw that same look of mad agony. Maybe he was just a cheap hood, but I felt sorry for him. You would have, too.

When he spoke his voice was very quiet.

"Is there more?"

The little Greek wrung his hands with anguish. "Please doan' kill me, Mr. Scollay. My wife—the Greek, he got my wife! I doan' want to say these thing. He got my wife, my woman! He—"

"I won't hurt you," Scollay said, quieter still. "Tell me the rest."

"He say the whole town is laughing at you."

There was dead silence for a second. We had stopped playing. Then Scollay turned his eyes to the ceiling. Both his hands were shaking and held out clenched in front of him. He was holding them in fists so tight that it seemed his hamstrings ran all the way up his arms.

"*All right!*" He screamed. "*ALL RIGHT!*"

And he ran for the door. Two of his men tried to stop him, to tell him it was suicide, just what the Greek wanted, but Scollay was like a crazy man. He knocked them down and rushed out into the black summer night.

In the dead quiet that followed, all I could hear was the little man's tortured breathing and somewhere out back, the soft sobbing of the fat bride.

Just about then the young kid who had braced us when we came in uttered a curse and made for the door.

Before he could get there, automobile tires screeched on the pavement down the block and a car engine roared.

"It's him!" the kid screamed from the doorway. "Get down, boss! Get down!"

The next second we heard gunshots—maybe as many as ten, mixed calibres, close together. The car howled away. I could see all I wanted to reflected in that kid's horrified face.

Now that the danger was over, all the goons rushed out. The door to the back of the hall banged open and Maureen ran through again, everything jiggling. Her face was even more puffy, now with tears as well as weight. Rico came in her wake like a bewildered valet. They went out the door.

Miss Gibson appeared in the empty hall, her eyes wide. The man who had brought the message to Scollay had powdered.

"What happened?" Miss Gibson asked.

"I think Mr. Scollay just got rubbed out," Biff said. He looked green.

Miss Gibson stared at him for a moment and then just fainted dead away. I felt a little like fainting myself.

Just then, from outside, came the most anguished scream I have ever heard, then or since. You didn't have to go and peek to know who was tearing her heart out in that street, keening over her dead brother even while the cops and news photographers were on their way.

"Let's get out of here," I muttered. "Quick."

We had it packed in before five minutes had passed. Some of the goons came back, but they were too drunk and too scared to notice the likes of us.

We went out the back, each of us carrying part of Biff's drum-kit. Quite a parade we must have made, walking up the street, for anyone who saw us. I led the way, with my horn case tucked under my arm and a cymbal in each hand. When we got to the truck we threw everything in, willy-nilly, and hauled our butts out of there. We averaged 45 miles an hour going back to Morgan, back roads or not, and Scollay's goons must not have bothered to tip the cops to us, because we never heard from them.

We never got the 200 bucks, either.

SHE came into Tommy Englander's speak about ten days later, a fat girl in a black mourning dress. It didn't look any better than the white satin.

Englander must have known who she was (her picture had been in the Chicago papers, next to Scollay's) because he showed her to a table himself and shushed a couple of drunks at the bar who were sniggering.

I felt really bad for her, like I feel for Billy-Boy sometimes. It's tough to be on the outside. And she had been very sweet, the little I had talked to her.

When the break came, I went over.

"I'm sorry about your brother," I said, feeling awkward and hot in the face. "I know he really cared for you—"

"I might as well have fired those guns myself," she said. She was looking at her hands, which were really her best feature, small and well formed. She had a musician's fingers. "Everything that little man said was true."

"That's not so," I said uncomfortably, not knowing if it was so or not. I was sorry I'd come over, she talked so strangely. As if she were all alone, and crazy.

"I'm not going to divorce him, though," she went on. "I'd kill myself first."

"Don't talk that way," I said.

"Haven't you ever wanted to kill yourself?" she asked, looking up at me passionately. "Doesn't it make you feel like that when people use you and then laugh about it? Do you know what it feels like to eat and eat and hate yourself and then eat more? Do you know what it feels like to kill your own brother because you're *fat?*"

People were turning to look, and the drunks were sniggering again.

"I'm sorry," she whispered.

I wanted to talk to her, to tell her I was sorry too. I wanted to tell her something that would make her feel better, but I couldn't think of a single thing.

So I just said, "I have to go. The next set—"

"Of course," she said softly. "Of course you do. Or they'll start to laugh at *you*. But why I came was—will you play *Roses of Picardy*? I thought you played it very nicely at the reception. Will you?"

"Sure," I said. "Glad to."

And we did. But she left halfway through the number. And since it was sort of schmaltzy for a place like Englander's, we swung into a ragtime version of *The Varsity Drag*, which always tore them up. I drank too much the rest of the evening and by closing time I had forgotten all about it, almost.

Leaving for the night, it came to me that I should have told her that life goes on. That's what you say when someone's loved one dies. But, thinking about it, I was glad I hadn't. Maybe that's what she was afraid of.

OF course now everyone knows about Maureen Romano and her husband Rico, who survives her as the taxpayers' guest in the Illinois State Penitentiary. How she took over Scollay's two-bit organization and worked it into a Prohibition empire that rivaled Capone's. How she wiped out the Greek and two other North Side gang leaders, swallowing their operations. Rico, the bewildered valet, became her first lieutenant and was supposedly responsible for a dozen gangland hits himself.

I followed her exploits from the West Coast, where we were making some pretty successful records. Without Billy-Boy, though: He formed a band of his own after we left Englander's, an all-black Dixieland band, and they did real well down south. It was just as well. Lots of places wouldn't even audition us with a Negro in the group.

But I was telling you about Maureen. She made great news copy, not just because she was shrewd, but because she was a big operator in more ways than one. When she died of a heart attack in 1933, the papers said she weighed 500 pounds, but I doubt that. No one gets that big, do they?

Anyway, her funeral made the front pages—more than anyone could say for Scollay, who never got anyplace past page 4 in his whole miserable career. It took ten pallbearers to carry her coffin. There was a picture of that coffin in one of the tabloids. It was a horrible thing.

Rico wasn't bright enough to hold things together by himself, and he fell for assault with intent to kill the very next year.

I've never been able to get her out of my mind, or the agonized, hangdog way Scollay had looked that first night when he talked about her.

It's all very strange. I can't feel too sorry for her, looking back. Fat people can always stop eating. Poor guys like Billy-Boy Williams can only stop breathing. I still don't see any way I could have helped either of them, but I do feel sort of bad every now and then. Probably because I'm not so young as I once was. That's all it is, isn't it? Isn't it?

MURDER-TWO

Joyce Carol Oates

THIS, HE SWORE.

He'd returned to the town house on East End Avenue after eleven P.M. and found the front door unlocked and, inside, his mother lying in a pool of squid ink on the hardwood floor at the foot of the stairs. She'd apparently fallen down the steep length of the stairs and broken her neck, judging from her twisted upper body. She'd also been bludgeoned to death, the back of her skull caved in, with one of her own golf clubs, a two-iron, but he hadn't seemed to see that, immediately.

Squid ink?—well, the blood had looked black in the dim foyer light. It was a trick his eyes played on his brain sometimes when he'd been studying too hard, getting too little sleep. An *optic tic.* Meaning you see something more or less, and valid, but it registers surreally in the brain as something else. Like in your neurological programming there's an occasional bleep.

In Derek Peck, Jr.'s, case, confronted with the crumpled, lifeless body of his mother, this was an obvious symptom of trauma. Shock, the visceral numbness that blocks immediate grief—the unsayable, the unknowable. He'd last seen his mother, in that same buttercup-yellow quilted satin robe that had given her the look of an upright, bulky Easter toy, early that morning, before he'd left for school. He'd been away all day. And this abrupt, weird transition—from differential calculus to the body on the floor, from the anxiety-driven jokes of his Math Club friends (a hard core of them were meeting late, weekdays, preparing for upcoming SAT exams) to the profound and terrible silence of the town house that had seemed to him, even as he'd pushed open the mysteriously unlocked front door, a hostile silence, a silence that vibrated with dread.

He crouched over the body, staring in disbelief. "Mother? *Mother!*"

As if it was he, Derek, who'd done something bad, he the one to be punished.

He couldn't catch his breath. Hyperventilating! His heart beating so wildly he almost fainted. Too confused to think, *Maybe they're still here, upstairs?* for in his dazed state he seemed to lack even an animal's instinct for self-preservation.

Yes, and he felt to blame, somehow. Hadn't she instilled in him a reflex of guilt? If something was wrong in the household, it could probably be traced back to *him*. From the age of thirteen (when his father, Derek Senior, had divorced his mother, Lucille, same as divorcing *him*), he'd been expected by his mother to behave like a second adult in the household, growing tall, lank, and anxious as if to accommodate that expectation, and his sand-colored body hair sprouting, and a fevered grimness about the eyes. Fifty-three percent of Derek's classmates, girls and boys, at the Mayhew Academy, were from "families of divorce," and most agreed that the worst of it is you have to learn to behave like an adult yet at the same time a lesser adult, one deprived of his or her full civil rights. That wasn't easy even for stoic streetwise Derek Peck with an IQ of, what was it?—158, at age fifteen. (He was seventeen now.) So his precarious adolescent sense of himself was seriously askew: not just his *body image* (his mother had allowed him to become overweight as a small child, they say that remains with you forever, irremediably imprinted in the earliest brain cells), but more crucially his *social identity*. For one minute she'd be treating him like an infant, calling him her baby, her baby-boy, and the next minute she was hurt, reproachful, accusing him of failing, like his father, to uphold his *moral responsibility* to her.

This *moral responsibility* was a backpack loaded with rocks. He could feel it, first fucking thing in the morning, exerting gravity even before he swung his legs out of bed.

Crouched over her now, badly trembling, shaking as in a cold wind, whispering, "Mommy?—can't you wake up? Mom-*my*, don't be—" balking at the word *dead* for it would hurt and incense Lucille like the word *old*, not that she'd been a vain or frivolous or self-conscious woman for Lucille Peck was anything but, a woman of dignity it was said of her admiringly by women who would not have wished to be her and by men who would not have wished to be married to her. *Mommy, don't be old!* Derek would never have murmured aloud, of course. Though possibly to himself frequently this past year or so seeing her wan, big-boned and brave face in harsh frontal sunshine when they happened to descend the front steps together in the morning, or at that eerie position in the kitchen where the overhead inset lights converged in such a way as to cruelly shadow her face downward, bruising the eye sockets and the soft fleshy tucks in her cheeks. Two summers ago when he'd been away for six weeks at Lake Placid and she'd driven to Kennedy to pick him up, so eager to see him again, and he'd stared appalled at the harsh lines bracketing her mouth like a pike's, and her smile too happy and what he felt was pity, and this, too, made him feel guilty. *You don't pity your own mother, asshole.*

If he'd come home immediately after school. By four P.M. Instead of a quick call from his friend Andy's across the park, guilty mumbled excuse left on the answering tape, *Mother? I'm sorry guess I won't make dinner tonight okay?—Math Club—study group—calculus—don't wait up for me, please.* How relieved he'd been, midway in his message she hadn't picked up the phone.

Had she been alive, when he'd called? Or already . . . dead?

Last time you saw your mother alive, Derek? they'd ask and he'd have to invent for he hadn't seen her, exactly. No eye contact.

And what had he *said?* A rushed schoolday morning, a Thursday. Nothing special about it. No premonition! Cold and windy and winter-glaring and he'd been restless to get out of the house, snatched a Diet Coke from the refrigerator so freezing his teeth ached. A blurred reproachful look of Mother in the kitchen billowing in her buttercup-yellow quilted robe as he'd backed off smiling *'Bye, Mom!*

Sure she'd been hurt, her only son avoiding her. She'd been a lonely woman even in her pride. Even with her activities that meant so much to her; Women's Art League, East Side Planned Parenthood Volunteers, HealthStyle Fitness Center, tennis and golf in East Hampton in the summer, subscription tickets to Lincoln Center. And her friends: most of them divorced middle-aged women, mothers like herself with high-school or college-age kids. Lucille *was* lonely, how was that his fault?—as if, his senior year in prep school, he'd become a fanatic about grades, obsessed with early admission to Harvard, Yale, Brown, Berkeley, just to avoid his mother at that raw, unmediated time of day that was breakfast.

But, God, how he'd loved her! He had. Planning to make it up to her for sure, SAT scores in the highest percentile he'd take her to the Stanhope for the champagne brunch then across the street to the museum for a mother-son Sunday excursion of a kind they hadn't had in years.

How still she was lying. He didn't dare touch her. His breathing was short, ragged. The squid-inky black beneath her twisted head had seeped and co-agulated into the cracks of the floor. Her left arm was flung out in an attitude of exasperated appeal, the sleeve stained with red, her hand lying palm-up and the fingers curled like angry talons. He might have noted that her Movado watch was missing, her rings gone except Grandma's antique opal with the fluted gold setting—the thief, or thieves, hadn't been able to yank it off her swollen finger? He might have noted that her eyes were rolled up asymmet-rically in her head, the right iris nearly vanished and the left leering like a drunken crescent-moon. He might have noted that the back of her skull was smashed soft and pulpy as a melon but there are some things about your mother out of tact and delicacy you don't acknowledge seeing. *Mother's hair, though*—it was her only remaining good feature, she'd said. A pale silvery-brown, slightly coarse, a natural color like Wheaties. The mothers of his class-mates all hoped to be youthful and glamorous with bleached or dyed hair but not Lucille Peck, she wasn't the type. You expected her cheeks to be ruddy without makeup and on her good days they were.

By this time of night Lucille's hair should have been dry from her shower of so many hours ago Derek vaguely recalled she'd had, the upstairs bathroom filled with steam. The mirrors. Shortness of breath! Tickets for some concert or ballet that night at Lincoln Center?—Lucille and a woman friend. But Derek didn't know about that. Or if he'd known he'd forgotten. Like about the golf club, the two-iron. Which closet? Upstairs, or down? The drawers of Lucille's bedroom bureau ransacked, *his* new Macintosh carried from his desk, then dropped onto the floor by the doorway as if—what? They'd changed their minds about bothering with it. Looking for quick cash, for drugs. That's the motive!

What's Booger up to, now? What's going down with Booger, you hear?

He touched her—at last. Groping for that big artery in the throat—cater-oid?—car*toid*? Should have been pulsing but wasn't. And her skin clammy-cool. His hand leapt back as if he'd been burnt.

Jesus fucking Christ, was it possible—Lucille was *dead*?

And *he'd* be to blame?

That Booger, man! One wild dude.

His nostrils flared, his eyes leaked tears. He was in a state of panic, had to get help. It was time! But he wouldn't have noticed the time, would he?—

11:48 P.M. His watch was a sleek black-faced Omega he'd bought with his own cash, but he wouldn't be conscious of the time exactly. By now he'd have dialed 911. Except thinking, confused, the phone was ripped out? (*Was the phone ripped out?*) Or one of them, his mother's killers, waiting in the darkened kitchen by the phone? Waiting to kill *him*?

He panicked, he freaked. Running back to the front door stumbling and shouting into the street where a taxi was slowing to let out an elderly couple, neighbors from the adjoining brownstone and they and the driver stared at this chalk-faced grief-stricken boy in an unbuttoned duffel coat, barehead running into the street screaming, "Help us! Help us! Somebody's killed my mother!"

EAST SIDE WOMAN KILLED
ROBBERY BELIEVED MOTIVE

In a late edition of Friday's *New York Times*, the golf club-bludgeoning death of Lucille Peck, whom Marina Dyer had known as Lucy Siddons, was prominently featured on the front page of the Metro section. Marina's quick eye, skimming the page, fastened at once upon the face (middle aged, fleshy, yet unmistakable) of her old Finch classmate.

"Lucy! *No*."

You understood that this must be a *death photo*: the positioning on the page, upper center; the celebration of a private individual of no evident civic or cultural significance, or beauty. For *Times* readers the news value lay in the victim's address, close by the mayor's residence. The subtext being *Even here, among the sequestered wealthy, such a brutal fate is possible.*

In a state of shock, though with professional interest, for Marina Dyer was a criminal defense attorney, Marina read the article, continued on an inner page and disappointing in its brevity. It was so familiar as to resemble a ballad. *One of us* (Caucasian, middle aged, law abiding, unarmed) surprised and savagely murdered in the very sanctity of her home; an instrument of class privilege, a golf club, snatched up by the killer as the murder weapon. The intruder or intruders, police said, were probably looking for quick cash, drug money. It was a careless, crude, cruel crime; a "senseless" crime; one of a number of unsolved break-ins on the East Side since last September, though it was the first to involve murder. The teenaged son of Lucille Peck had returned home to find the front door unlocked and his mother dead, at about eleven P.M., at which time she'd been dead approximately five hours. Neighbors spoke of having heard no unusual sounds from the Peck residence, but several did speak of "suspicious" strangers in the neighborhood. Police were "investigating."

Poor Lucy!

Marina noted that her former classmate was forty-four years old, a year (most likely, part of a year) older than Marina; that she'd been divorced since 1991 from Derek Peck, an insurance executive now living in Boston; that she was survived by just the one child, Derek Peck, Jr., a sister, and two brothers. What an end for Lucy Siddons, who shone in Marina's memory as if beaming with life: unstoppable Lucy, indefatigable Lucy, good-hearted Lucy: Lucy, who was twice president of the Finch class of 1970, and a dedicated alumna: Lucy, whom all the girls had admired, if not adored: Lucy, who'd been so kind to shy stammering wall-eyed Marina Dyer.

Though they'd both been living in Manhattan all these years, Marina in a town house of her own on West Seventy-sixth Street, very near Central Park, it had been five years since she'd seen Lucy, at their twentieth class reunion; even longer since the two had spoken together at length, earnestly. Or maybe they never had.

The son did it, Marina thought, folding up the newspaper. It wasn't an altogether serious thought but one that suited her professional skepticism.

Boogerman! Fucking fan-tas-tic.

Where'd he come from?—the hot molten core of the Universe. At the instant of the Big Bang. Before which there was *nothing* and after which there would be *everything*: cosmic cum. For all sentient beings derive from a single source and that source long vanished, extinct.

The more you contemplated of origins the less you knew. He'd studied Wittgenstein—*Whereof one cannot speak, thereof one must be silent.* (A photocopied handout for Communication Arts class, the instructor a cool youngish guy with a Princeton Ph.D.) Yet he believed he could recall the circumstances of his birth. In 1978, in Barbados where his parents were vacationing, one week in late December. He was premature by five weeks and lucky to be alive, and though Barbados was an accident yet seventeen years later he saw in his dreams a cobalt-blue sky, rows of royal palms shedding their bark like scales, shriek-bright-feathered tropical birds; a fat white moon drooping in the sky like his mother's big belly, sharks' dorsal fins cresting the waves like the Death Raiders video game he'd been hooked on in junior high. Wild hurricane nights kept him from sleeping a normal sleep. Din of voices as of drowning souls crashing on a beach.

He was into Metallica, Urge Overkill, Soul Asylum. His heroes were heavy-metal punks who'd never made it to the Top Ten or if they did fell right back again. He admired losers who killed themselves ODing like dying's a joke, one final FUCK YOU! to the world. But he was innocent of doing what they'd claimed he'd done to his mother, for God's sake. Absolutely unbelieving fucking fantastic, *he, Derek Peck, Jr.*, had been arrested and would be tried for a crime perpetrated upon his own mother he'd loved! perpetrated by animals (he could guess the color of their skin) who would've smashed his skull in, too, like cracking an egg, if he'd walked in that door five hours earlier.

She wasn't prepared to fall in love, wasn't the type to fall in love with any client, yet here is what happened: just seeing him, his strange tawny-yearning eyes lifting to her face, *Help me! save me!*—that was it.

Derek Peck, Jr., was a Botticelli angel partly erased and crudely painted over by Eric Fischl. His thick stiffly moussed unwashed hair lifted in two flaring symmetrical wings that framed his elegantly bony, long-jawed face. His limbs were monkey-long and twitchy. His shoulders were narrow and high, his chest perceptibly concave. He might have been fourteen, or twenty-five. He was of a generation as distant from Marina Dyer's as another species. He wore a T-shirt stamped SOUL ASYLUM beneath a rumpled Armani jacket of the color of steel filings, and pinstriped Ralph Lauren fleece trousers stained at the crotch, and size-twelve Nikes. Mad blue veins thrummed at his temples. He was a preppy cokehead who'd managed until now to stay out of trouble, Marina had been warned by Derek Peck, Sr.'s, attorney, who'd arranged, through Marina's discreet urging, for her to interview for the boy's counsel: a probable psychopath-matricide who not only claimed complete innocence but seemed actually to believe it. He gave off a complex odor of the ripely organic and the chemical. His skin appeared heated, of the color and texture of singed oatmeal. His nostrils were rimmed in red like nascent fire and his eyes were a pale acetylene yellow-green, flammable. You would not want to bring a match too close to those eyes, still less would you want to look too deeply into those eyes.

When Marina Dyer was introduced to Derek Peck, the boy stared at her hungrily. Yet he didn't get to his feet like the other men in the room. He leaned forward in his chair, the tendons standing out in his neck and the strain of *seeing, thinking,* visible in his young face. His handshake was fumbling at first, then suddenly strong, assured as an adult man's, hurtful. Unsmiling, the boy shook hair out of his eyes like a horse rearing its beautiful brute head, and a painful sensation ran through Marina Dyer like an electric shock. She had not experienced such a sensation in a long time.

In her soft contralto voice that gave nothing away, Marina said, "Derek, *hi.*"

IT was in the 1980s, in an era of celebrity-scandal trials, that Marina Dyer made her reputation as a "brilliant" criminal defense lawyer; by being in fact brilliant, and by working very hard, and by playing against type. There was the audacity of drama in her positioning of herself in a male-dominated courtroom. There was the startling fact of her physical size: she was a "petite" size five, self-effacing, shy seeming, a woman easy to overlook, though it would not be in your advantage to overlook her. She was meticulously and unglamorously groomed in a way to suggest a lofty indifference to fashion, an air of timelessness. She wore her sparrow-colored hair in a French twist, ballerina style; her favored suits were Chanels in subdued harvest colors and soft dark cashmere wools, the jackets giving some bulk to her narrow frame, the skirts always primly to midcalf. Her shoes, handbags, briefcases, were of exquisite Italian leather, expensive but understated. When an item began to show signs of wear, Marina replaced it with an identical item from the same Madison Avenue shop. Her slightly askew left eye, which some in fact had found charming, she'd long ago had corrected with surgery. Her eyes were now direct, sharply focused. A perpetually moist, shiny dark-brown, with a look of fanaticism at times, but an exclusively professional fanaticism, a fanaticism in the service of her clients, whom she defended with a legendary fervor. A small woman, Marina acquired size and authority in public arenas. In a courtroom, her normally reedy, indistinct voice acquired volume, timbre. Her passion seemed to be aroused in direct proportion to the challenge of presenting a client as "not guilty" to reasonable jurors, and there were times (her admiring fellow professionals joked about this) that her plain, ascetic face shone with the luminosity of Bernini's St. Teresa in her ecstasy. Her clients were martyrs, their prosecutors persecutors. There was a spiritual urgency to Marina Dyer's cases impossible for jurors to explain afterward, when their verdicts were sometimes questioned. *You would have had to be there, to hear her, to know.*

Marina's first highly publicized case was her successful defense of a U.S. congressman from Manhattan who'd been charged with criminal extortion and witness tampering; her second was the successful, if controversial, defense of a black performance artist charged with rape and assault of a druggie-fan who'd come uninvited to his suite at the Four Seasons. There had been a prominent, photogenic Wall Street trader charged with embezzlement, fraud, obstruction of justice; there had been a woman journalist charged with attempted murder in the shooting-wounding of a married lover; there had been lesser-known but still meritorious cases, rich with challenge. Marina's clients were not invariably acquitted but their sentences, given their probable guilt, were considered lenient. Sometimes they spent no time in prison at all, only in halfway houses; they paid fines, did community service. Even as Marina Dyer shunned publicity, she reaped it. After each victory, her fees rose. Yet she was not avaricious, nor even apparently ambitious. Her life was her work, and her work her life. Of course, she'd been dealt a few defeats, in her early career when she'd sometimes defended innocent or quasi-innocent people, for modest fees. With the innocent you risk emotions, breakdown, stammering at crucial moments on the witness stand. You risk the eruption of rage, despair. With accomplished liars, you know you can depend upon a performance. Psychopaths are best: they lie fluently, but they believe.

Marina's initial interview with Derek Peck, Jr., lasted for several hours and was intense, exhausting. If she took him on, this would be her first murder trial; this seventeen-year-old boy her first accused murderer. And what a brutal murder: matricide. Never had she spoken with, in such intimate quarters, a client like Derek Peck. Never had she gazed into, for long wordless moments, any eyes like his. The vehemence with which he stated his innocence was compelling. The fury that his innocence should be doubted was mesmerizing. *Had* this boy killed, in such a way?—"transgressed"?—violated the law, which was Marina Dyer's very life, as if it were of no more consequence than a paper bag to be crumpled in the hand and tossed away? The back of Lucille Peck's head had literally been smashed in by an estimated twenty or more blows of the golf club. Inside her bathrobe, her soft naked-flaccid body had been pummeled, bruised, bloodied; her genitals furiously lacerated. An unspeakable crime, a crime in violation of taboo. A tabloid crime, thrilling even at second or third hand.

In her new Chanel suit of such a purplish-plum wool it appeared black as a nun's habit, in her crisp chignon that gave to her profile an Avedon-lupine sharpness, Marina Dyer gazed upon the boy who was Lucy Siddon's son. It excited her more than she would have wished to acknowledge. Thinking, I *am unassailable*, I *am untouched*. It was the perfect revenge.

*   *   *

LUCY Siddons. My best friend, I'd loved her. Leaving a birthday card and a red silk square scarf in her locker, and it was days before she remembered to thank me though it was a warm thank-you, a big-toothed genuine smile. Lucy Siddons who was so popular, so at ease and emulated among the snobbish girls at Finch. Despite a blemished skin, buck teeth, hefty thighs, and waddling-duck walk for which she was teased, so lovingly teased. The secret was, Lucy had *personality.* That mysterious X-factor which, if you lack it, you can never acquire it. If you have to ponder it, it's out of your reach forever. And Lucy was *good, good hearted.* A practicing Christian from a wealthy Manhattan Episcopal family famed for their good works. Waving to Marina Dyer to come sit with her and her friends in the cafeteria, while her friends sat stonily smiling; choosing scrawny Marina Dyer for her basketball team in gym class, while the others groaned. But Lucy was good, so good. Charity and pity for the despised girls of Finch spilled like coins from her pockets.

Did I love Lucy Siddons those three years of my life, yes I loved Lucy Siddons like no one since. But it was a pure, chaste love. A wholly one-sided love.

HIS bail had been set at $350,000, the bond paid by his distraught father. Since the recent Republican election-sweep it appeared that capital punishment would soon be reinstated in New York State, but at the present time there was no murder-one charge, only murder-two for even the most brutal and/or premeditated crimes. Like the murder of Lucille Peck, about which there was, regrettably, so much local publicity in newspapers, magazines, on television and radio, Marina Dyer began to doubt her client could receive a fair trial in the New York City area. Derek was hurt, incredulous: "Look, why would *I* kill her, *I* was the one who loved her!" he whined in a childish voice, lighting up another cigarette out of his mashed pack of Camels. "—*I was the only fucking one who loved her in the fucking universe!*" Each time Derek met with Marina he made this declaration, or a variant. His eyes flamed with tears of indignation, moral outrage. Strangers had entered his house and killed his mother and *he* was being blamed! Could you believe it! His life and his father's life torn up, disrupted like a tornado had blown through! Derek wept angrily, opening himself to Marina as if he'd slashed his breastbone to expose his raging palpitating heart.

Profound and terrible moments that left Marina shaken for hours afterward.

Marina noted, though, that Derek never spoke of Lucille Peck as *my mother* or *Mother* but only as *her, she.* When she'd happened to mention to him that she'd known Lucille, years ago in school, the boy hadn't seemed to hear. He'd been frowning, scratching at his neck. Marina repeated gently, "Lucille was an outstanding presence at Finch. A dear friend." But still Derek hadn't seemed to hear.

Lucy Siddons's son, who bore virtually no resemblance to her. His glaring eyes, the angular face, hard-chiseled mouth. Sexuality reeked about him like unwashed hair, solid T-shirt, and jeans. Nor did Derek resemble Derek Peck, Sr., so far as Marina could see.

In the Finch yearbook for 1970 there were numerous photos of Lucy Siddons and the other popular girls of the class, the activities beneath their smiling faces extensive, impressive; beneath Marina Dyer's single picture, the caption was brief. She'd been an honors student, of course, but she had not been a popular girl no matter her effort. Consoling herself, *I am biding my time. I can wait.*

And so it turned out to be, as in a fairy tale of rewards and punishments.

Rapidly and vacantly Derek Peck recited his story, his "alibi," as he'd recited it to the authorities numerous times. His voice resembled one simulated by computer. Specific times, addresses; names of friends who would "swear to it, I was with them every minute"; the precise route he'd taken by taxi, through Central Park, on his way back to East End Avenue; the shock of discovering *the body* at the foot of the stairs just off the foyer. Marina listened, fascinated. She did not want to think that this was a tale invented in a cocaine high, indelibly imprinted in the boy's reptile-brain. Unshakable. It failed to accommodate embarrassing details, enumerated in the investigating detectives' report: Derek's socks speckled with Lucille Peck's blood tossed down a laundry chute, wadded underwear on Derek's bathroom floor still damp at midnight from a shower he claimed to have taken at seven A.M. but had more plausibly taken at seven P.M. before applying gel to his hair and dressing in punk-Gap style for a manic evening downtown with certain of his heavy-metal friends. And the smears of Lucille Peck's blood on the very tiles of Derek's shower stall he hadn't noticed, hadn't wiped off. And the telephone call on Lucille's answering tape explaining he wouldn't be home for dinner he claimed to have made at about four P.M. but had very possibly made as late as ten P.M., from a SoHo club.

These contradictions, and others, infuriated Derek rather than troubled him, as if they represented glitches in the fabric of the universe for which he could hardly be held responsible. He had a child's conviction that all things must yield to his wish, his insistence. *What he truly believed, how could it not be*

so? Of course, as Marina Dyer argued, it *was* possible that the true killer of
Lucille Peck had deliberately stained Derek's socks with blood, and tossed
them down the laundry chute to incriminate him; the killer, or killers, had
taken time to shower in Derek's shower and left Derek's own wet, wadded
underwear behind. And there was no absolute, unshakable proof that the answering tape always recorded calls in the precise chronological order in which
they came in, not one hundred percent of the time, how could that be proven?
(There were five calls on Lucille's answering tape for the day of her death,
scattered throughout the day; Derek's was the last.)

The assistant district attorney who was prosecuting the case charged that
Derek Peck, Jr.'s motive for killing his mother was a simple one: money. His
$500 monthly allowance hadn't been enough to cover his expenses, evidently.
Mrs. Peck had canceled her son's Visa account in January, after he'd run up
a bill of over $6,000; relatives reported "tension" between mother and son;
certain of Derek's classmates said there were rumors he was in debt to drug
dealers and terrified of being murdered. And Derek had wanted a Jeep Wran-
gler for his eighteenth birthday, he'd told friends. By killing his mother he
might expect to inherit as much as $4 million and there was a $100,000 life-
insurance policy naming him beneficiary, there was the handsome four-story
East End town house worth as much as $2.5 million, there was a property in
East Hampton, there were valuable possessions. In the five days between
Lucille Peck's death and Derek's arrest he'd run up over $2,000 in bills—
he'd gone on a manic buying spree, subsequently attributed to grief. Derek
was hardly the model preppy student he claimed to be either: he'd been
expelled from the Mayhew Academy for two weeks in January for "disruptive
behavior," and it was generally known that he and another boy had cheated
on a battery of IQ exams in ninth grade. He was currently failing all his
subjects except a course in Postmodernist Aesthetics, in which films and com-
ics of Superman, Batman, Dracula, and *Star Trek* were meticulously decon-
structed under the tutelage of a Princeton-trained instructor. There was a
Math Club whose meetings Derek had attended sporadically, but he hadn't
been there the evening of his mother's death.

Why would his classmates lie about him?—Derek was aggrieved, wounded.
His closest friend, Andy, turning against him!

Marina had to admire her young client's response to the detectives' damn-
ing report: he simply denied it. His hot-flamed eyes brimmed with tears of
innocence, disbelief. The prosecution was the enemy, and the enemy's case
was just something they'd thrown together, to blame an unsolved murder on

him because he was a kid, and vulnerable. So he was into heavy metal, and he'd experimented with a few drugs, like everyone he knew, for God's sake. *He had not murdered his mother, and he didn't know who had.*

Marina tried to be detached, objective. She was certain that no one, including Derek himself, knew of her feelings for him. Her behavior was unfailingly professional, and would be. Yet she thought of him constantly, obsessively; he'd become the emotional center of her life, as if she were somehow pregnant with him, his anguished, angry spirit inside her. *Help me! Save me!* She'd forgotten the subtle, circuitous ways in which she'd brought her name to the attention of Derek Peck, Sr.'s, attorney and began to think that Derek Junior had himself chosen her. Very likely, Lucille had spoken of her to him: her old classmate and close friend Marina Dyer, now a prominent defense attorney. And perhaps he'd seen her photograph somewhere. It was more than coincidence, after all. She knew!

She filed her motions, she interviewed Lucille Peck's relatives, neighbors, friends; she began to assemble a voluminous case, with the aid of two assistants; she basked in the excitement of the upcoming trial, through which she would lead, like a warrior-woman, like Joan of Arc, her beleaguered client. They would be dissected in the press, they would be martyred. Yet they would triumph, she was sure.

Was Derek guilty? And if guilty, of what? If truly he could not recall his actions, was *he* guilty? Marina thought, *If I put him on the witness stand, if he presents himself to the court as he presents himself to me . . . how could the jury deny him?*

It was five weeks, six weeks, now ten weeks after the death of Lucille Peck and already the death, like all deaths, was rapidly receding. A late-summer date had been set for the trial to begin and it hovered at the horizon teasing, tantalizing, as the opening night of a play already in rehearsal. Marina had of course entered a plea of not guilty on behalf of her client, who had refused to consider any other option. Since he was innocent, he *could not* plead guilty to a lesser charge—first-degree, or second-degree, manslaughter, for instance. In Manhattan criminal law circles it was believed that going to trial with this case was, for Marina Dyer, an egregious error, but Marina refused to discuss any other alternative; she was as adamant as her client, she would enter into no negotiations. Her primary defense would be a systematic refutation of the prosecution's case, a denial seriatim of the "evidence"; passionate reiterations of Derek Peck's absolute innocence, in which, on the witness stand, he would be the star performer; a charge of police bungling and incompetence in failing to find the true killer, or killers, who had broken into other homes on the East Side; a hope of enlisting the jurors' sympathy. For Marina had learned long ago how the sympathy of jurors is a deep, deep well. You would not want to call these average Americans fools exactly, but they were strangely, almost magically, impressionable; at times, susceptible as children. They were, or would like to be, "good" people; decent, generous, forgiving, kind; not "condemning," "cruel." They looked, especially in Manhattan, where the reputation of the police was clouded, for reasons not to convict, and a good defense lawyer provides those reasons. Especially they would not want to convict, of a charge of second-degree murder, a young, attractive, and now motherless boy like Derek Peck, Jr.

Jurors are easily confused, and it was Marina Dyer's genius to confuse them to her advantage. For the wanting to be *good*, in defiance of justice, is one of mankind's greatest weaknesses.

"HEY: you don't believe me, do you?"

He'd paused in his compulsive pacing of her office, a cigarette burning in his fingers. He eyed her suspiciously.

Marina looked up startled to see Derek hovering rather close beside her desk, giving off his hot citrus-acetylene smell. She'd been taking notes even as a tape recorder played. "Derek, it doesn't matter what I believe. As your attorney, I speak for you. Your best legal—"

Derek said pettishly, "No! You have to believe me—*I didn't kill her.*"

It was an awkward moment, a moment of exquisite tension in which there were numerous narrative possibilities. Marina Dyer and the son of her old, now deceased, friend Lucy Siddons shut away in Marina's office on a late, thundery-dark afternoon; only a revolving tape cassette bearing witness. Marina had reason to know that the boy was drinking, these long days before his trial; he was living in the town house, with his father, free on bail but not "free." He'd allowed her to know that he was clean of all drugs, absolutely. He was following her advice, her instructions. But did she believe him?

Marina said, again carefully, meeting the boy's glaring gaze, "Of course I believe you, Derek," as if it was the most natural thing in the world, and he naive to have doubted. "Now, please sit down, and let's continue. You were telling me about your parents' divorce . . ."

" 'Cause if you don't believe me," Derek said, pushing out his lower lip so it showed fleshy red as a skinned tomato, "—I'll find a fucking lawyer who *does.*"

"Yes, but I do. Now sit down, please."

"You *do?* You *believe*—?"

"Derek, what have I been saying! Now, sit down."

The boy loomed above her, staring, For an instant, his expression showed fear. Then he groped his way backward, to his chair. His young, corroded face was flushed and he gazed at her, greeny-tawny eyes, with yearning, adoration.

DON'T touch me! Marina murmured in her sleep, cresting with emotion. *I couldn't bear it.*

MARINA Dyer. Strangers stared at her in public places. Whispered together, pointing her out. Her name and now her face had become media sanctioned, iconic. In restaurants, in hotel lobbies, at professional gatherings. At the New York City ballet, for instance, which Marina attended with a friend . . . for it had been a performance of this ballet troupe Lucille Peck had been scheduled to attend the night of her death. *Is that woman the lawyer? the one who . . . ? that boy who killed his mother with the golf club . . . Peck?*

They were becoming famous together.

HIS street name, his name in the downtown clubs, Fez, Duke's, Mandible, was "Booger." He'd been pissed at first, then decided it was affection not mockery. A pretty white uptown boy, had to pay his dues. Had to buy respect, authority. It was a tough crowd, took a fucking lot to impress them—money, and more than money. A certain attitude. Laughing at him, *Oh, you Booger-man!—one wild dude.* But now they *were* impressed. *Whacked his old lady? No shit! That Booger, man! One wild dude.*

Never dreamt of *it.* Nor of Mother, who was gone from the house as if traveling. Except not calling home, not checking on him. No more disappointing Mother.

Never dreamt of any kind of violence, that wasn't his thing. He believed in *passive-ism.* There was the great Indian leader, a saint. *Gandy.* Taught the ethic of *passive-ism,* triumphed over the racist-British enemies. Except the movie was too long.

Didn't sleep at night but weird times during the day. At night watching TV, playing the computer, "Myst" his favorite he could lose himself in for hours. Avoided violent games, his stomach still queasy. Avoided calculus, even the thought of it: the betrayal. For he hadn't graduated, class of ninety-five moving on without him, fuckers. His friends were never home when he called. Even girls who'd been crazy for him, never home. Never returned his calls. *Him, Derek Peck! Boooogerman.* It was like a microchip had been inserted in his brain, he had these pathological reactions. Not being able to sleep for, say, forty-eight hours. Then crashing, dead. Then waking how many hours later dry-mouthed and heart-hammering, lying sideways on his churned-up bed, his head over the edge and Doc Martens combat boots on his feet, he's kicking like crazy like somebody or something has hold of his ankles and he's gripping with both hands an invisible rod, or baseball bat, or club—swinging it in his sleep, and his muscles twitched and spasmed and veins swelled in his head close to bursting. *Swinging swinging swinging!*—and in his pants, in his Calvin Klein briefs, he'd *come.*

WHEN he went out he wore dark, very dark, glasses even at night. His long hair tied back rat-tail style and a Mets cap, reversed, on his head. He'd be getting his hair cut for the trial but just not yet, wasn't that like . . . giving in, surrendering . . . ? In the neighborhood pizzeria, in a place on Second Avenue he'd ducked into alone, signing napkins for some giggling girls, once a father and son about eight years old, another time two old women in their forties, fifties, staring like he was Son of Sam, sure okay! signing *Derek Peck, Jr.,* and dating it. His signature an extravagant red-ink scrawl. *Thank you!* and he knows they're watching him walk away, thrilled. Their one contact with fame.

His old man and especially his lady-lawyer would give him hell if they knew, but they didn't need to know everything. He was free on fucking bail, wasn't he?

IN the aftermath of a love affair in her early thirties, the last such affair of her life, Marina Dyer had taken a strenuous "ecological" field trip to the Galápagos Islands; one of those desperate trips we take at crucial times in our lives, reasoning that the experience will cauterize the emotional wound, make of its very misery something trivial, negligible. The trip was indeed strenuous, and cauterizing. There in the infamous Galápagos, in the vast Pacific Ocean due west of Equador and a mere ten miles south of the Equator, Marina had come to certain life-conclusions. She'd decided not to kill herself, for one thing. For why kill one*self*, when nature is so very eager to do it for you, and to gobble you up? The islands were rockbound, stormlashed, barren. Inhabited by reptiles, giant tortoises. There was little vegetation. Shrieking sea birds like damned souls except it was not possible to believe in "souls" here. *In no world but a fallen one could such lands exist*, Herman Melville had written of the Galápagos he'd called also the Enchanted Isles.

When she returned from her week's trip to hell, as she fondly spoke of it, Marina Dyer was observed to devote herself more passionately than ever, more single-mindedly than ever, to her profession. Practicing law would be her life, and she meant to make of her life a quantifiable and unmistakable success. What of "life" that was not consumed by law would be inconsequential. The law was only a game, of course: it had very little to do with justice, or morality; "right" or "wrong"; "common" sense. But the law was the only game in which she, Marina Dyer, could be a serious player. The only game in which, now and then, Marina Dyer might win.

THERE was Marina's brother-in-law who had never liked her but, until now, had been cordial, respectful. Staring at her as if he'd never seen her before. "How the hell can you defend that vicious little punk? How do you justify yourself, morally? He killed his *mother*, for God's sake!" Marina felt the shock of this unexpected assault as if she'd been struck in the face. Others in the room, including her sister, looked on, appalled. Marina said carefully, trying to control her voice, "But, Ben, you don't believe that only the obviously 'innocent' deserve legal counsel, do you?" It was an answer she had made numerous times, to such a question; the answer all lawyers make, reasonably, convincingly.

"Of course not. But people like you go too far."

" 'Too far'? 'People like me'—?"

"You know what I mean. Don't play dumb."

"But I don't. I don't know what you mean."

Her brother-in-law was by nature a courteous man, however strong his opinions. Yet how rudely he turned away from Marina, with a dismissive gesture. Marina called after him, stricken, "Ben, I don't know what you mean. Derek *is* innocent, I'm sure. The case against him is only circumstantial. The media . . ." Her pleading voice trailed off, he'd walked out of the room. Never had she been so deeply hurt, confused. Her own brother-in-law!

The bigot. Self-righteous bastard. *Never* would Marina consent to see the man again.

MARINA?—don't cry.

They don't mean it, Marina. Don't feel bad, please!

Hiding in the locker-room lavatory after the humiliation of gym class. How many times. Even Lucy, one of the team captains, didn't want her: that was obvious. Marina Dyer and the other last-choices, a fat girl or two, myopic girls, uncoordinated clumsy asthmatic girls laughingly divided between the red team and the gold. *Then, the nightmare of the game itself.* Trying to avoid being struck by thundering hooves, crashing bodies. Yells, piercing laughter. Swinging flailing arms, muscular thighs. How hard the gleaming floor when you fell! The giant girls (Lucy Siddons among them glaring, fierce) ran over her if she didn't step aside, she had no existence for them. Marina, made by the gym teacher, so absurdly, a "guard." *You must play, Marina. You must try. Don't be silly. It's only a game. These are all just games. Get out there with your team!* But if the ball was thrown directly at her it would strike her chest and ricochet out of her hands and into the hands of another. If the ball sailed toward her head she was incapable of ducking but stood stupidly helpless, paralyzed. Her glasses flying. Her scream a child's scream, laughable. It was all laughable. Yet it was her life.

Lucy, good-hearted repentant Lucy, sought her out where she hid in a locked toilet stall, sobbing in fury, a bloodstained tissue pressed against her nose. *Marina?—don't cry. They don't mean it, they like you, come on back, what's wrong?* Good-hearted Lucy Siddons she'd hated the most.

ON the afternoon of the Friday before the Monday that would be the start of his trial, Derek Peck, Jr., broke down in Marina Dyer's office.

Marina had known something was wrong, the boy reeked of alcohol. He'd come with his father, but had told his father to wait outside; he insisted that Marina's assistant leave the room.

He began to cry, and to babble. To Marina's astonishment he fell hard onto his knees on her burgundy carpet, began banging his forehead against the glass-topped edge of her desk. He laughed, he wept. Saying in an anguished choking voice how sorry he was he'd forgotten his mother's last birthday he hadn't known would be her last and how hurt she'd been like he'd forgotten just to spite her and that wasn't true, Jesus he loved her! the only person in the fucking universe who loved her! And then at Thanksgiving this wild scene, she'd quarreled with the relatives so it was just her and him for Thanksgiving she insisted upon preparing a full Thanksgiving dinner for just two people and he said it was crazy but she insisted, no stopping her when her mind was made up and he'd known there would be trouble, that morning in the kitchen she'd started drinking early and he was up in his room smoking dope and his Walkman plugged in knowing there was no escape. And it wasn't even a turkey she roasted for the two of them, you needed at least a twenty-pound turkey otherwise the meat dried out she said so she bought two ducks, yes *two dead ducks* from this game shop on Lexington and Sixty-sixth and that might've been okay except she was drinking red wine and laughing kind of hysterical talking on the phone preparing this fancy stuffing she made every year, wild rice and mushrooms, olives, and also baked yams, plum sauce, corn bread, and chocolate-tapioca pudding that was supposed to be one of his favorite desserts from when he was little that just the smell of it made him feel like puking. *He* stayed out of it upstairs until finally she called him around four P.M. and he came down knowing it was going to be a true bummer but not knowing how bad, she was swaying-drunk and her eyes smeared and they were eating in the dining room with the chandelier lit, all the fancy Irish linens and Grandma's old china and silver and she insisted *he* carve the ducks, he tried to get out of it but couldn't and Jesus! what happens!—he pushes the knife in the duck breast and there's actual blood squirting out of it!—and a big sticky clot of blood inside so he dropped the knife and ran out of the room gagging, it'd just completely freaked him in the midst of being stoned he couldn't take it running out into the street and almost hit by a car and her screaming after him *Derek come back! Derek come back don't leave me!* but he split from that scene and didn't come back for a day and a half. And ever after that she was drinking more and saying weird things to him like he was her baby, she'd felt him kick and shudder in her belly, under her heart, she'd talk to him inside her belly for months before he was born she'd lie down on the bed and stroke him, his head, through her skin and they'd talk together she said, it was the closest she'd ever been with any living creature and he was embarrassed not knowing what to say except *he* didn't remember, it was so long ago, and she'd say yes oh yes in your heart you remember in your heart you're still my baby boy *you do remember* and he was getting pissed saying

fuck it, no: he didn't remember any of it. And there was only one way to stop
her from loving him he began to understand, but he hadn't wanted to, he'd
asked could he transfer to school in Boston or somewhere living with his dad
but she went crazy, *no no no* he wasn't going, she'd never allow it, she tried
to hold him, hug and kiss him so he had to lock his door and barricade it
practically and she'd be waiting for him half-naked just coming out of her
bathroom pretending she'd been taking a shower and clutching at him and
that night finally he must've freaked, something snapped in his head and he
went for the two-iron, she hadn't had time even to scream it happened so fast
and merciful, him running up behind her so she didn't see him exactly—"It
was the only way to stop her loving me."

Marina stared at the boy's aggrieved, tearstained face. Mucus leaked alarm-
ingly from his nose. What had he said? He had said . . . *what?*

Yet even now a part of Marina's mind remained detached, calculating. She
was shocked by Derek's confession, but was she *surprised?* A lawyer is never
surprised.

She said, quickly, "Your mother Lucille was a strong, domineering woman.
I know, I knew her. As a girl, twenty-five years ago, she'd rush into a room
and all the oxygen was sucked up. She'd rush into a room and it was like a
wind had blown out all the windows!" Marina hardly knew what she was
saying, only that words tumbled from her; radiance played about her face like
a flame. "Lucille was a smothering presence in your life. She wasn't a normal
mother. What you've told me only confirms what I'd suspected. I've seen
other victims of psychic incest—I know! She hypnotized you, you were fighting for your life. It was your own life you were defending." Derek remained
kneeling on the carpet, staring vacantly at Marina. Tight little beads of blood
had formed on his reddened forehead, his snaky-greasy hair dropped into his
eyes. All his energy was spent. He looked to Marina now, like an animal who
hears, not words from his mistress, but sounds; the consolation of certain cadences, rhythms. Marina was saying, urgently, "That night, you lost control.
Whatever happened, Derek, it wasn't you. *You are the victim.* She drove you
to it! Your father, too, abrogated his responsibility to you—left you with *her,*
alone with *her,* at the age of thirteen. Thirteen! That's what you've been
denying all these months. That's the secret you haven't acknowledged. You
had no thoughts of your own, did you? For years? Your thoughts were *hers,* in
her voice." Derek nodded mutely. Marina had taken a tissue from the
burnished-leather box on her desk and tenderly dabbed at his face. He lifted
his face to her, shutting his eyes. As if this sudden closeness, this intimacy,

was not new to them but somehow familiar. Marina saw the boy in the court-room, her Derek: transformed: his face fresh scrubbed and his hair neatly cut, gleaming with health; his head uplifted, without guile or subterfuge. *It was the only way to stop her loving me.* He wore a navy-blue blazer bearing the elegant understated monogram of the Mayhew Academy. A white shirt, blue-striped tie. His hands clasped together in an attitude of Buddhistic calm. A boy, immature for his age. Emotional, susceptible. *Not guilty by reason of temporary insanity.* It was a transcendent vision and Marina knew she would re-alize it and that all who gazed upon Derek Peck, Jr., and heard him testify would realize it.

Derek leaned against Marina, who crouched over him, he'd hidden his wet, hot face against her legs as she held him, comforted him. What a rank animal heat quivered from him, what animal terror, urgency. He was sobbing, bab-bling incoherently, "—save me? Don't let them hurt me? Can I have im-munity, if I confess? If I say what happened, if I tell the truth—"

Marina embraced him, her fingers at the nape of his neck. She said, "Of course I'll save you, Derek. That's why you came to me."

PETER LOVESEY

*M*ost of my friends obey the law most of the time. A few free spirits once indulged in underage smoking or exceeded a speed limit. But I can think of certain people so sober, God-fearing, and honest that it would be hard to conceive of the crime they might have committed. This was the challenge for the story that follows: to construct a "crime" so footling that only a truly virtuous soul would be troubled by it. And to make that crime the first inexorable step to something more sinister.

For me, the charm of Donald E. Westlake's amiable crook Dortmunder is that I know things are going to go wrong from page one, but I never know how badly. I am conned each time by the logic behind the enterprise. The set-up here is particularly alarming; Dortmunder's in deep, deep trouble very soon. If you don't know Dortmunder, sample him now; this is as good an introduction as I can find. If you do know him, and you've read the story, can you resist reading it again? I couldn't.

THE CRIME OF MISS OYSTER BROWN

MISS OYSTER BROWN, a devout member of the Church of England, joined passionately each Sunday in every prayer of the Morning Service—except for the general Confession, when, in all honesty, she found it difficult to class herself as a lost sheep. She was willing to believe that everyone else in church had erred and strayed. In certain cases she knew exactly how, and with whom, and she would say a prayer for them. On her own account, however, she could seldom think of anything to confess. She tried strenuously, more strenuously—dare I say it?—than you or me to lead an untainted life. She managed conspicuously well. Very occasionally, as the rest of the congregation joined in the Confession, she would own up to some trifling sin.

You may imagine what a fall from grace it was when this virtuous woman committed not merely a sin, but a crime. She lived more than half her life before it happened.

She resided in a Berkshire town with her twin sister Pearl, who was a mere three minutes her senior. Oyster and Pearl—a flamboyance in forenames that owed something to the fact that their parents had been plain John and Mary Brown. Up to the moment of birth the Browns had been led to expect one child who, if female, was to be named Pearl. In the turmoil created by a second, unscheduled, daughter, John Brown jokingly suggested naming her Oyster. Mary, bosky from morphine, seized on the name as an inspiration, a delight to the ear when said in front of dreary old Brown. Of course the charm was never so apparent to the twins, who got to dread being introduced to people. Even in infancy they were aware that their parents' friends found the names amusing. At school they were taunted as much by the teachers as the children. The names never ceased to amuse. Fifty years on, things were still said just out of earshot and laced with pretended sympathy. "Here come Pearl and Oyster, poor old ducks. Fancy being stuck with names like that."

No wonder they faced the world defiantly. In middle age they were a formidable duo, stalwarts of the choir, the Bible-reading Circle, the Townswomen's Guild and the Magistrates' Bench. Neither sister had married. They lived together in Lime Tree Avenue, in the mock-Tudor house where they were born. They were not short of money.

There are certain things people always want to know about twins, the more so in mystery stories. I can reassure the wary reader that Oyster and Pearl were not identical; Oyster was an inch taller, more sturdy in build than her sister and slower of speech. They dressed individually, Oyster as a rule in tweed skirts and check blouses that she made herself, always from the same Butterick pattern, Pearl in a variety of mail-order suits in pastel blues and greens. No one confused them. As for that other question so often asked about twins, neither sister could be characterized as "dominant." Each possessed a forceful personality by any standard. To avoid disputes they had established a household routine, a division of the duties, that worked pretty harmoniously, all things considered. Oyster did most of the cooking and the gardening, for example, and Pearl attended to the housework and paid the bills when they became due. They both enjoyed shopping, so they shared it. They did the church flowers together when their turn came, and they always ran the bottle stall at the church fête. Five vicars had held the living at St Saviour's in the twins' time as worshippers there. Each new incumbent was advised by his predecessor that Pearl and Oyster were the mainstays of the parish. Better to fall foul of the diocesan bishop himself than the Brown twins.

All of this was observed from a distance, for no one, not even a vicar making his social rounds, was allowed inside the house in Lime Tree Avenue. The twins didn't entertain, and that was final. They were polite to their neighbours without once inviting them in. When one twin was ill, the other would transport her to the surgery in a state of high fever rather than call the doctor on a visit.

It followed that people's knowledge of Pearl and Oyster was limited. No one could doubt that they lived an orderly existence; there were no complaints about undue noise, or unwashed windows or neglected paintwork. The hedge was trimmed and the garden mown. But what really bubbled and boiled behind the regularly washed net curtains—the secret passion that was to have such a dire result—was unsuspected until Oyster committed her crime.

She acted out of desperation. On the last Saturday in July, 1991, her well-ordered life suffered a seismic shock. She was parted from her twin sister. The parting was sudden, traumatic and had to be shrouded in secrecy. The prospect of anyone finding out what had occurred was unthinkable.

So for the first time in her life Oyster had no Pearl to change the light bulbs, pay the bills and check that all the doors were locked. Oyster—let it be understood—was not incapable or dim-witted. Bereft as she was, she managed tolerably well until the Friday afternoon, when she had a letter to post, a letter of surpassing importance, capable—God willing—of easing her desolation. She had agonized over it for hours. Now it was crucial that the letter caught the last post of the day. Saturday would be too late. She went to the drawer where Pearl always kept the postage stamps and—calamity—not one was left.

Stamps had always been Pearl's responsibility. To be fair, the error was Oyster's; she had written more letters than usual and gone through the supply. She should have called at the Post Office when she was doing the shopping.

It was too late. There wasn't time to get there before the last post at five-fifteen. She tried to remain calm and consider her options. It was out of the question to ask a neighbour for a stamp; she and Pearl had made it a point of honour never to be beholden to anyone else. Neither could she countenance the disgrace of despatching the letter without a stamp in the hope that it would get by, or the recipient would pay the amount due.

This left one remedy, and it was criminal.

Behind one of the Staffordshire dogs on the mantel-piece was a bank statement. She had put it there for the time being because she had been too busy to check where Pearl normally stored such things. The significant point for Oyster at this minute was not the statement, but the envelope containing it. More precisely, the top right-hand corner of the envelope, because the first class stamp had somehow escaped being cancelled.

Temptation stirred and uncoiled itself.

Oyster had never in her life steamed an unfranked stamp from an envelope and used it again. Nor, to her knowledge, had Pearl. Stamp collectors sometimes removed used specimens for their collections, but what Oyster was contemplating could in no way be confused with philately. It was against the law. Defrauding the Post Office. A crime.

There was under twenty minutes before the last collection.

I couldn't, she told herself. *I'm on the Parochial Church Council. I'm on the Bench.*

Temptation reminded her that she was due for a cup of tea in any case. She filled the kettle and pressed the switch. While waiting, watching the first wisp of steam rise from the spout, she weighed the necessity of posting the letter against the wickedness of re-using a stamp. It was not the most heinous of crimes, Temptation whispered. And once Oyster began to think about the chances of getting away with it, she was lost. The kettle sang, the steam gushed and she snatched up the envelope and jammed it against the spout. Merely, Temptation reassured her, to satisfy her curiosity as to whether stamps could be separated from envelopes by this method.

Those who believe in retribution will not be in the least surprised that the steam was deflected by the surface of the envelope and scalded three of Oyster's fingers quite severely. She cried out in pain and dropped the envelope. She ran the cold tap and plunged her hand under it. Then she wrapped the sore fingers in a piece of kitchen towel.

Her first action after that was to turn off the kettle. Her second was to pick up the envelope and test the corner of the stamp with the tip of her fingernail. It still adhered to some extent, but with extreme care she was able to ease it free, consoled that her discomfort had not been entirely without result. The minor accident failed to deter her from the crime. On the contrary, it acted like a prod from Old Nick.

There was a bottle of gum in the writing desk and she applied some to the back of the stamp, taking care not to use too much, which might have oozed out at the edges and discoloured the envelope. When she had positioned the stamp neatly on her letter, it would have passed the most rigorous inspection. She felt a wicked frisson of satisfaction at having committed an undetectable crime. Just in time, she remembered the post and had to hurry to catch it.

There we leave Miss Oyster Brown to come to terms with her conscience for a couple of days.

We meet her again on the Monday morning in the local chemist's shop. The owner and pharmacist was John Trigger, whom the Brown twins had known for getting on for thirty years, a decent, obliging man with a huge moustache who took a personal interest in his customers. In the face of strong competition from a national chain of pharmacists, John Trigger had persevered with his old-fashioned service from behind a counter, believing that some customers still preferred it to filling a wire basket themselves.

But to stay in business he had been forced to diversify by offering some electrical goods.

When Oyster Brown came in and showed him three badly scalded fingers out in blisters, Trigger was sympathetic as well as willing to suggest a remedy. Understandably he enquired how Oyster had come by such a painful injury. She was expecting the question and had her answer ready, adhering to the truth as closely as a God-fearing woman should.

"An accident with the kettle."

Trigger looked genuinely alarmed. "An electric kettle? Not the one you bought here last year?"

"I didn't," said Oyster at once.

"Must have been your sister. A Steamquick. Is that what you've got?"

"Er, yes."

"If there's a fault . . ."

"I'm not here to complain, Mr Trigger. So you think this ointment will do the trick?"

"I'm sure of it. Apply it evenly, and don't attempt to pierce the blisters, will you?" John Trigger's conscience was troubling him. "This is quite a nasty scalding, Miss Brown. Where exactly did the steam come from?"

"The kettle."

"I know that. I mean was it the spout?"

"It really doesn't matter," said Oyster sharply. "It's done."

"The lid, then? Sometimes if you're holding the handle you get a rush of steam from that little slot in the lid. I expect it was that."

"I couldn't say," Oyster fudged, in the hope that it would satisfy Mr Trigger.

It did not. "The reason I asked is that there may be a design fault."

"The fault was mine, I'm quite sure."

"Perhaps I ought to mention it to the manufacturers."

"Absolutely not," Oyster said in alarm. "I was careless, that's all. And now, if you'll excuse me . . ." She started backing away and then Mr Trigger ambushed her with another question.

"What does your sister say about it?"

"My sister?" From the way she spoke, she might never have had one.

"Miss Pearl."

"Oh, nothing. We haven't discussed it," Oyster truthfully stated.

"But she must have noticed your fingers."

"Er, no. How much is the ointment?"

Trigger told her and she dropped the money on the counter and almost rushed from the shop. He stared after her, bewildered.

The next time Oyster Brown was passing, Trigger took the trouble to go to the door of his shop and enquire whether the hand was any better. Clearly she wasn't overjoyed to see him. She assured him without much gratitude that the ointment was working. "It was nothing. It's going to clear up in a couple of days."

"May I see?"

She held out her hand.

Trigger agreed that it was definitely on the mend. "Keep it dry, if you possibly can. Who does the washing up?"

"What do you mean?"

"You, or your sister? It's well known that you divide the chores between you. If it's your job, I'm sure Miss Pearl won't mind taking over for a few days. If I see her, I'll suggest it myself."

Oyster reddened and said nothing.

"I was going to remark that I haven't seen her for a week or so," Trigger went on. "She isn't unwell, I hope?"

"No," said Oyster. "Not unwell."

Sensing correctly that this was not an avenue of conversation to venture along at this time, he said instead, "The Steamquick rep was in yesterday afternoon, so I mentioned what happened with your kettle."

She was outraged. "You had no business."

"Pardon me, Miss Brown, but it is my business. You were badly scalded. I can't have my customers being injured by the products I sell. The rep was very concerned, as I am. He asked if you would be so good as to bring the kettle in next time you come, so that he can check if there's a fault."

"Absolutely not," said Oyster. "I told you I haven't the slightest intention of complaining."

Trigger tried to be reasonable. "It isn't just your kettle. I've sold the same model to other customers."

"Then they'll complain if they get hurt."

"What if their children get hurt?"

She had no answer.

"If it's inconvenient to bring it in, perhaps I could call at your house."

"No," she said at once.

"I can bring a replacement. In fact, Miss Brown, I'm more than a little concerned about this whole episode. I'd like you to have another kettle with my compliments. A different model. Frankly, the modern trend is for jug kettles that couldn't possibly scald you as yours did. If you'll kindly step into the shop, I'll give you one now to take home."

The offer didn't appeal to Oyster Brown in the least. "For the last time, Mr Trigger," she said in a tight, clipped voice, "I don't require another kettle." With that, she walked away up the high street.

Trigger, from the motives he had mentioned, was not content to leave the matter there. He wasn't a churchgoer, but he believed in conducting his life on humanitarian principles. On this issue, he was resolved to be just as stubborn as she. He went back into the shop and straight to the phone. While Oyster Brown was out of the house, he would speak to Pearl Brown, the sister, and see if he could get better co-operation from her.

Nobody answered the phone.

At lunchtime, he called in to see Ted Collins, who ran the garden shop next door, and asked if he had seen anything of Pearl Brown lately.

"I had Oyster in this morning," Collins told him.

"But you haven't seen Pearl?"

"Not in my shop. Oyster does all the gardening, you know. They divide the work."

"I know."

"I can't think what came over her today. Do you know what she bought? Six bottles of Rapidrot."

"What's that?"

"It's a new product. An activator for composting. You dilute it and water your compost heap and it speeds up the process. They're doing a special promotion to launch it. Six bottles are far too much, and I tried to tell her, but she wouldn't be told."

"Those two often buy in bulk," said Trigger. "I've sold Pearl a dozen tubes of toothpaste at a go, and they must be awash with Dettol."

"They won't use six bottles of Rapidrot in twenty years," Collins pointed out. "It's concentrated stuff, and it won't keep all that well. It's sure to solidify after a time. I told her one's plenty to be going on with. She's wasted her money, obstinate old bird. I don't know what Pearl would say. Is she ill, do you think?"

"I've no idea," said Trigger, although in reality an idea was beginning to form in his brain. A disturbing idea. "Do they get on all right with each other? Daft question," he said before Collins could answer it. "They're twins. They've spent all their lives in each other's company."

For the present he dismissed the thought and gave his attention to the matter of the electric kettle. He'd already withdrawn the Steamquick kettles from sale. He got on the phone to Steamquick and had an acrimonious conversation with some little Hitler from their public relations department who insisted that thousands of the kettles had been sold and the design was faultless.

"The lady's injury isn't imagined, I can tell you," Trigger insisted.

"She must have been careless. Anyone can hurt themselves if they're not careful. People are far too ready to put the blame on the manufacturer."

"People, as you put it, are your livelihood."

There was a heavy sigh. "Send us the offending kettle, and we'll test it."

"That isn't so simple."

"Have you offered to replace it?"

The man's whole tone was so condescending that Trigger had an impulse to frighten him rigid. "She won't let the kettle out of her possession. I think she may be keeping it as evidence."

"Evidence?" There was a pause while the implication dawned. "Blimey."

On his end of the phone, Trigger permitted himself to grin.

"You mean she might take us to court over this?"

"I didn't say that—"

"Ah."

"...but she does know the law. She's a magistrate."

An audible gasp followed, then: "Listen, Mr, er—"

"Trigger."

"Mr Trigger. I think we'd better send someone to meet this lady and deal with the matter personally. Yes, that's what we'll do."

Trigger worked late that evening, stocktaking. He left the shop about ten-thirty. Out of curiosity he took a route home via Lime Tree Avenue and stopped the car opposite the Brown sisters' house and wound down the car window. There were lights upstairs and presently someone drew a curtain. It looked like Oyster Brown.

"Keeping an eye on your customers, Mr Trigger?" a voice close to him said.

He turned guiltily. A woman's face was six inches from his. He recognized one of his customers, Mrs Wingate. She said, "She's done that every night this week."

"Oh?"

"Something fishy's going on in there," she said. "I walk my little dog along the verge about this time every night. I live just opposite them, on this side, with the wrought-iron gates. That's Pearl's bedroom at the front. I haven't seen Pearl for a week, but every night her sister Oyster draws the curtains and leaves the light on for half an hour. What's going on, I'd like to know. If Pearl is ill, they ought to call a doctor. They won't, you know."

"That's Pearl's bedroom, you say, with the light on?"

"Yes, I often see her looking out. Not lately."

"And now Oyster switches on the light and draws the curtains?"

"And pulls them back at seven in the morning. I don't know what you think, Mr Trigger, but it looks to me as if she wants everyone to think Pearl's in there, when it's obvious she isn't."

"Why is it obvious?"

"All the windows are closed. Pearl always opens the top window wide, winter and summer."

"That is odd, now you mention it."

"I'll tell you one thing," said Mrs Wingate, regardless that she had told him several things already. "Whatever game she's up to, we won't find out. Nobody ever sets foot inside that house except the twins themselves."

At home and in bed that night, Trigger was troubled by a gruesome idea, one that he'd tried repeatedly to suppress. Suppose the worst had happened a week ago in the house in Lime Tree Avenue, his thinking ran. Suppose Pearl Brown had suffered a heart attack and died. After so many years of living in that house as if it were a fortress, was Oyster capable of dealing with the aftermath of death, calling in the doctor and the undertaker? In her shocked state, mightn't she decide that anything was preferable to having the house invaded, even if the alternative was disposing of the body herself?

How would a middle-aged woman dispose of a body? Oyster didn't drive a car. It wouldn't be easy to bury it in the garden, nor hygienic to keep it in a cupboard in the house. But if there was one thing every well-bred English lady knew about, it was gardening. Oyster was the gardener.

In time, everything rots in a compost heap. If you want to accelerate the process, you buy a preparation like Rapidrot.

Oyster Brown had purchased six bottles of the stuff. And every night she drew the curtains in her sister's bedroom to give the impression that she was there.

He shuddered.

In the fresh light of morning, John Trigger told himself that his morbid imaginings couldn't be true. They were the delusions of a tired brain. He decided to do nothing about them.

Just after eleven-thirty, a short, fat man in a dark suit arrived in the shop and announced himself as the Area Manager of Steamquick. His voice was suspiciously like the one that Trigger had found so irritating when he had phoned their head office. "I'm here about this allegedly faulty kettle," he announced.

"Miss Brown's?"

"I'm sure there's nothing wrong at all, but we're a responsible firm. We take every complaint seriously."

"You want to see the kettle? You'll be lucky."

The Steamquick man sounded smug. "That's all right. I telephoned Miss Brown this morning and offered to go to the house. She wasn't at all keen on that idea, but I was very firm with the lady, and she compromised. We're meeting here at noon. She's agreed to bring the kettle for me to inspect. I don't know why you found her so intractable."

"High noon, eh? Do you want to use my office?"

Trigger had come to a rapid decision. If Oyster was on her way to the shop, he was going out. He had two capable assistants.

This was a heaven-sent opportunity to lay his macabre theory to rest. While Oyster was away from the house in Lime Tree Avenue, he would drive there and let himself into the back garden. Mrs Wingate or any other curious neighbour watching from behind the lace curtains would have to assume he was trying to deliver something. He kept his white coat on, to reinforce the idea that he was on official business.

Quite probably, he told himself, the compost heap will turn out to be no bigger than a cowpat. The day was sunny and he felt positively cheerful as he turned up the Avenue. He checked his watch. Oyster would be making mincemeat of the Steamquick man about now. It would take her twenty minutes, at least, to walk back.

He stopped the car and got out. Nobody was about, but just in case he was being observed he walked boldly up the path to the front door and rang the bell. No one came.

Without appearing in the least furtive, he stepped around the side of the house. The back garden was in a beautiful state. Wide, well-stocked and immaculately weeded borders enclosed a finely trimmed lawn, yellow roses on a trellis and a kitchen garden beyond. Trigger took it in admiringly, and then remembered why he was there. His throat went dry. At the far end, beyond the kitchen garden, slightly obscured by some runner beans on poles, was the compost heap—as long as a coffin and more than twice as high.

The flesh on his arms prickled.

The compost heap was covered with black plastic bin-liners weighted with stones. They lay across the top, but the sides were exposed. A layer of fresh green garden refuse, perhaps half a metre in depth, was on the top. The lower part graduated in colour from a dull yellow to earth-brown. Obvious care had been taken to conserve the shape, to keep the pressure even and assist the composting process.

Trigger wasn't much of a gardener. He didn't have the time for it. He did the minimum and got rid of his garden rubbish with bonfires. Compost heaps were outside his experience, except that as a scientist he understood the principle by which they generated heat in a confined space. Once, years ago, an uncle of his had demonstrated this by pushing a bamboo cane into his heap from the top. A wisp of steam had issued from the hole as he withdrew the cane. Recalling it now, Trigger felt a wave of nausea.

He hadn't the stomach for this.

He knew now that he wasn't going to be able to walk up the garden and probe the compost heap. Disgusted with himself for being so squeamish, he turned to leave, and happened to notice that the kitchen window was ajar, which was odd, considering that Oyster was not at home. Out of interest he tried the door handle. The door was unlocked.

He said, "Anyone there?" and got no answer.

From the doorway he could see a number of unopened letters on the kitchen table. After the humiliation of turning his back on the compost heap, this was like a challenge, a chance to regain some self-respect. This at least, he was capable of doing. He stepped inside and picked up the letters. There were five, all addressed to Miss P. Brown. The postmarks dated from the beginning of the previous week.

Quite clearly Pearl had not been around to open her letters.

Then his attention was taken by an extraordinary line-up along a shelf. He counted fifteen packets of cornflakes, all open, and recalled his conversation with Ted Collins about the sisters buying in bulk. If Collins had wanted convincing, there was ample evidence here: seven bottles of decaffeinated coffee, nine jars of the same brand of marmalade and a tall stack of boxes of paper tissues. Eccentric housekeeping, to say the least. Perhaps, he reflected, it meant that the buying of six bottles of Rapidrot had not, after all, been so sinister.

Now that he was in the house, he wasn't going to leave without seeking an answer to the main mystery, the disappearance of Pearl. His mouth was no longer dry and the gooseflesh had gone from his arms. He made up his mind to go upstairs and look into the front bedroom.

On the other side of the kitchen door more extravagance was revealed. The passage from the kitchen to the stairway was lined on either side with sets of goods that must have overflowed from the kitchen. Numerous tins of cocoa, packets of sugar, pots of jam, gravy powder and other grocery items were stored as if for a siege, stacked along the skirting boards in groups of at least half a dozen. Trigger began seriously to fear for the mental health of the twins. Nobody had suspected anything like this behind the closed doors. The stacks extended halfway upstairs.

As he stepped upwards, obliged to tread close to the banisters, he was gripped by the sense of alienation that must have led to hoarding on such a scale. The staid faces that the sisters presented to the world gave no intimation of this strange compulsion. What was the mentality of people who behaved as weirdly as this?

An appalling possibility crept into Trigger's mind. Maybe the strain of so many years of appearing outwardly normal had finally caused Oyster to snap. What if the eccentricity so apparent all around him were not so harmless as it first appeared? No one could know what resentments, what jealousies lurked in this house, what mean-minded cruelties the sisters may have inflicted on each other. What if Oyster had fallen out with her sister and attacked her? She was a sturdy woman, physically capable of killing.

If she'd murdered Pearl, the compost-heap method of disposal would certainly commend itself.

Come now, he told himself. This is all speculation.

He reached the top stair and discovered that the stockpiling had extended to the landing. Toothpaste, talcum powder, shampoos and soap were stacked up in profusion. All the doors were closed. It wouldn't have surprised him if when he opened one he was knee-deep in toilet-rolls.

First he had to orientate himself. He decided that the front bedroom was to his right. He opened it cautiously and stepped in.

What happened next was swift and devastating. John Trigger heard a piercing scream. He had a sense of movement to his left and a glimpse of a figure in white. Something crashed against his head with a mighty thump, causing him to pitch forward.

About four, when the Brown twins generally stopped for tea, Oyster filled the new kettle that the Steamquick Area Manager had exchanged for the other one. She plugged it in. It was the new-fangled jug type, and she wasn't really certain if she was going to like it, but she certainly needed the cup of tea.

"I know it was wrong," she said, "and I'm going to pray for forgiveness, but I didn't expect that steaming a stamp off a letter would lead to this. I suppose it's a judgement."

"Whatever made you do such a wicked thing?" her sister Pearl asked, as she put out the cups and saucers.

"The letter had to catch the post. It was the last possible day for the Kellogg's Cornflakes competition, and I'd thought of such a wonderful slogan. The prize was a fortnight in Venice."

Pearl clicked her tongue in disapproval. "Just because I won the Birds Eye trip to the Bahamas, it didn't mean you were going to be lucky. We tried for twenty years and only ever won consolation prizes."

"It isn't really gambling, is it?" said Oyster. "It isn't like betting."

"It's all right in the Lord's eyes," Pearl told her. "It's a harmless pastime. Unfortunately we both know that people in the church wouldn't take a charitable view. They wouldn't expect us to devote so much of our time and money to competitions. That's why we have to be careful. You didn't tell anyone I was away?"

"Of course not. Nobody knows. For all they know, you were ill, if anyone noticed at all. I drew the curtains in your bedroom every night to make it look as if you were here."

"Thank you. You know I'd do the same for you."

"I might win," said Oyster. "Someone always does. I put in fifteen entries altogether, and the last one was a late inspiration."

"And as a result we have fifteen packets of cornflakes with the tops cut off," said Pearl. "They take up a lot of room."

"So do your frozen peas. I had to throw two packets away to make some room in the freezer. Anyway, I felt entitled to try. It wasn't much fun being here alone, thinking of you sunning yourself in the West Indies. To tell you the truth, I didn't really think you'd go and leave me here. It was a shock." Oyster carefully poured some hot water into the teapot to warm it. "If you want to know, I've also entered the Rapidrot Trip of a Lifetime competition. A week in San Francisco followed by a week in Sydney. I bought six bottles to have a fighting chance."

"What's Rapidrot?"

"Something for the garden." She spooned in some tea and poured on the hot water. "You must be exhausted. Did you get any sleep on the plane?"

"Hardly any," said Pearl. "That's why I went straight to bed when I got in this morning." She poured milk into the teacups. "The next thing I knew was the doorbell going. I ignored it, naturally. It was one of the nastiest shocks I ever had hearing the footsteps coming up the stairs. I could tell it wasn't you. I'm just thankful that I had the candlestick to defend myself with."

"Is there any sign of life yet?"

"Well, he's breathing, but he hasn't opened his eyes, if that's what you mean. Funny, I would never have thought Mr Trigger was dangerous to women."

Oyster poured the tea. "What are we going to do if he doesn't recover? We can't have people coming into the house." Even as she was speaking, she put down the teapot and glanced out of the kitchen window towards the end of the garden. She had the answer herself.

Too Many Crooks

Donald E. Westlake

"Did you hear something?" Dortmunder whispered.

"The wind," Kelp said.

Dortmunder twisted around in his seated position and deliberately shone the flashlight in the kneeling Kelp's eyes. "What wind? We're in a tunnel."

"There's underground rivers," Kelp said, squinting, "so maybe there's underground winds. Are you through the wall there?"

"Two more whacks," Dortmunder told him. Relenting, he aimed the flashlight past Kelp back down the empty tunnel, a meandering, messy gullet, most of it less than three feet in diameter, wriggling its way through rocks and rubble and ancient middens, traversing 40 tough feet from the rear of the basement of the out-of-business shoe store to the wall of the bank on the corner. According to the maps Dortmunder had gotten from the water department by claiming to be with the sewer department, and the maps he'd gotten from the sewer department by claiming to be with the water department, just the other side of this wall was the bank's main vault. Two more whacks and this large, irregular square of concrete that Dortmunder and Kelp had been scoring and scratching at for some time now would at last fall away onto the floor inside, and there would be the vault.

Dortmunder gave it a whack.

Dortmunder gave it another whack.

The block of concrete fell onto the floor of the vault. "Oh, thank God," somebody said.

What? Reluctant but unable to stop himself, Dortmunder dropped sledge and flashlight and leaned his head through the hole in the wall and looked around.

It was the vault, all right. And it was full of people.

A man in a suit stuck his hand out and grabbed Dortmunder's and shook it while pulling him through the hole and on into the vault. "Great work, Officer," he said. "The robbers are outside."

Dortmunder had thought he and Kelp were the robbers. "They are?"

A round-faced woman in pants and a Buster Brown collar said, "Five of them. With machine guns."

"Machine guns," Dortmunder said.

A delivery kid wearing a mustache and an apron and carrying a flat cardboard carton containing four coffees, two decafs and a tea said, "We all hostages, mon. I gonna get fired."

"How many of you are there?" the man in the suit asked, looking past Dortmunder at Kelp's nervously smiling face.

"Just the two," Dortmunder said, and watched helplessly as willing hands dragged Kelp through the hole and set him on his feet in the vault. It was really very full of hostages.

"I'm Kearney," the man in the suit said. "I'm the bank manager, and I can't tell you how glad I am to see you."

Which was the first time any bank manager had said *that* to Dortmunder, who said, "Uh-huh, uh-huh," and nodded, and then said, "I'm, uh, Officer Diddums, and this is Officer, uh, Kelly."

Kearney, the bank manager, frowned. "Diddums, did you say?"

Dortmunder was furious with himself. Why did I call myself Diddums? Well, I didn't know I was going to need an alias inside a bank vault, did I? Aloud, he said, "Uh-huh. Diddums. It's Welsh."

"Ah," said Kearney. Then he frowned again and said, "You people aren't even armed."

"Well, no," Dortmunder said. "We're the, uh, the hostage-rescue team; we don't want any shots fired, increase the risk for you, uh, civilians."

"Very shrewd," Kearney agreed.

Kelp, his eyes kind of glassy and his smile kind of fixed, said, "Well, folks, maybe we should leave here now, single file, just make your way in an orderly fashion through—"

"They're coming!" hissed a stylish woman over by the vault door.

Everybody moved. It was amazing; everybody shifted at once. Some people moved to hide the new hole in the wall, some people moved to get farther away from the vault door and some people moved to get behind Dortmunder, who suddenly found himself the nearest person in the vault to that big, round, heavy metal door, which was easing massively and silently open.

It stopped halfway, and three men came in. They wore black ski masks and black leather jackets and black work pants and black shoes. They carried Uzi submachine guns at high port. Their eyes looked cold and hard, and their hands fidgeted on the metal of the guns, and their feet danced nervously, even when they were standing still. They looked as though anything at all might make them overreact.

"Shut up!" one of them yelled, though nobody'd been talking. He glared around at his guests and said, "Gotta have somebody to stand out front, see can the cops be trusted." His eye, as Dortmunder had known it would, lit on Dortmunder. "You," he said.

"Uh-huh," Dortmunder said.

"What's your name?"

Everybody in the vault had already heard him say it, so what choice did he have? "Diddums," Dortmunder said.

The robber glared at Dortmunder through his ski mask. "Diddums?"

"It's Welsh," Dortmunder explained.

"Ah," the robber said, and nodded. He gestured with the Uzi. "Outside, Diddums."

Dortmunder stepped forward, glancing back over his shoulder at all the people looking at him, knowing every goddamn one of them was glad he wasn't him—even Kelp, back there pretending to be four feet tall—and then Dortmunder stepped through the vault door, surrounded by all those nervous maniacs with machine guns, and went with them down a corridor flanked by desks and through a doorway to the main part of the bank, which was a mess.

The time at the moment, as the clock high on the wide wall confirmed, was 5:15 in the afternoon. Everybody who worked at the bank should have gone home by now; that was the theory Dortmunder had been operating from. What must have happened was, just before closing time at three o'clock (Dortmunder and Kelp being already then in the tunnel, working hard, knowing nothing of events on the surface of the planet), these gaudy showboats had come into the bank waving their machine guns around.

And not just waving them, either. Lines of ragged punctures had been drawn across the walls and the Lucite upper panel of the tellers' counter, like connect-the-dot puzzles. Wastebaskets and a potted Ficus had been over-turned, but fortunately, there were no bodies lying around; none Dortmunder could see, anyway. The big plate-glass front windows had been shot out, and two more of the black-clad robbers were crouched down, one behind the OUR LOW LOAN RATES poster and the other behind the OUR HIGH IRA RATES poster, staring out at the street, from which came the sound of somebody talking loudly but indistinctly through a bullhorn.

So what must have happened, they'd come in just before three, waving their guns, figuring a quick in and out, and some brown-nose employee look-ing for advancement triggered the alarm, and now they had a stalemate hos-tage situation on their hands; and, of course, everybody in the world by now has seen *Dog Day Afternoon* and therefore knows that if the police get the drop on a robber in circumstances such as these circumstances right here, they'll immediately shoot him dead, so now hostage negotiation is trickier than ever. This isn't what I had in mind when I came to the bank, Dortmunder thought.

The boss robber prodded him along with the barrel of his Uzi, saying, "What's your first name, Diddums?"

Please don't say Dan, Dortmunder begged himself. Please, please, some-how, anyhow, manage not to say Dan. His mouth opened. "John," he heard himself say, his brain having turned desperately in this emergency to that last resort, the truth, and he got weak-kneed with relief.

"OK, John, don't faint on me," the robber said. "This is very simple what you got to do here. The cops say they want to talk, just talk, nobody gets hurt. Fine. So you're gonna step out in front of the bank and see do the cops shoot you."

"Ah," Dortmunder said.

"No time like the present, huh, John?" the robber said, and poked him with the Uzi again.

"That kind of hurts," Dortmunder said.

"I apologize," the robber said, hard-eyed. "Out."

One of the other robbers, eyes red with strain inside the black ski mask, leaned close to Dortmunder and yelled, "You wanna shot in the foot first? You wanna *crawl* out there?"

"I'm going," Dortmunder told him. "See? Here I go."

The first robber, the comparatively calm one, said, "You go as far as the sidewalk, that's all. You take one step off the curb, we blow your head off."

"Got it," Dortmunder assured him, and crunched across broken glass to the sagging-open door and looked out. Across the street was parked a line of buses, police cars, police trucks, all in blue and white with red gumdrops on top, and behind them moved a seething mass of armed cops. "Uh," Dortmunder said. Turning back to the comparatively calm robber, he said, "You wouldn't happen to have a white flag or anything like that, would you?"

The robber pressed the point of the Uzi to Dortmunder's side. "Out," he said.

"Right," Dortmunder said. He faced front, put his hands way up in the air and stepped outside.

What a *lot* of attention he got. From behind all those blue-and-whites on the other side of the street, tense faces stared. On the rooftops of the red-brick tenements, in this neighborhood deep in the residential heart of Queens, sharpshooters began to familiarize themselves through their telescopic sights with the contours of Dortmunder's furrowed brow. To left and right, the ends of the block were sealed off with buses parked nose to tail pipe, past which ambulances and jumpy white-coated medics could be seen. Everywhere, rifles and pistols jittered in nervous fingers. Adrenaline ran in the gutters.

"I'm not with *them!*" Dortmunder shouted, edging across the sidewalk, arms upraised, hoping this announcement wouldn't upset the other bunch of armed hysterics behind him. For all he knew, they had a problem with rejection.

However, nothing happened behind him, and what happened out front was that a bullhorn appeared, resting on a police-car roof, and roared at him, *"You a hostage?"*

"I sure am!" yelled Dortmunder.

"What's your name?"

Oh, not again, thought Dortmunder, but there was nothing for it. "Diddums," he said.

"What?"

"Diddums!"

A brief pause: *"Diddums?"*

"It's Welsh!"

"Ah."

There was a little pause while whoever was operating the bullhorn conferred with his compatriots, and then the bullhorn said, *"What's the situation in there?"*

What kind of question was that? "Well, uh," Dortmunder said, and remembered to speak more loudly, and called, "kind of tense, actually."

"Any of the hostages been harmed?"

"Uh-uh. No. Definitely not. This is a . . . this is a . . . nonviolent confrontation." Dortmunder fervently hoped to establish that idea in everybody's mind, particularly if he were going to be out here in the middle much longer.

"Any change in the situation?"

Change? "Well," Dortmunder answered, "I haven't been in there that long, but it seems like—"

"Not that long? What's the matter with you, Diddums? You've been in that bank over two hours now!"

"Oh, yeah!" Forgetting, Dortmunder lowered his arms and stepped forward to the curb. "That's right!" he called. "Two hours! *More* than two hours! Been in there a long time!"

"Step out here away from the bank!"

Dortmunder looked down and saw his toes hanging ten over the edge of the curb. Stepping back at a brisk pace, he called, "I'm not supposed to do that!"

"Listen, Diddums, I've got a lot of tense men and women over here. I'm telling you, step away from the bank!"

"The fellas inside," Dortmunder explained, "they don't want me to step off the curb. They said they'd, uh, well, they just don't want me to do it."

"Psst! Hey, Diddums!"

Dortmunder paid no attention to the voice calling from behind him. He was concentrating too hard on what was happening right now out front. Also, he wasn't that used to the new name yet.

"Diddums!"

"Maybe you better put your hands up again."

"Oh, yeah!" Dortmunder's arms shot up like pistons blowing through an engine block. "There they are!"

"Diddums, goddamn it, do I have to shoot you to get you to pay attention?"

Arms dropping, Dortmunder spun around. "Sorry! I wasn't—I was—Here I am!"

"Get those goddamn hands up!"

Dortmunder turned sideways, arms up so high his sides hurt. Peering sidelong to his right, he called to the crowd across the street, "Sirs, they're talking to me inside now." Then he peered sidelong to his left, saw the comparatively calm robber crouched beside the broken doorframe and looking less calm than before, and he said, "Here I am."

"We're gonna give them our demands now," the robber said. "Through you."

"That's fine," Dortmunder said. "That's great. Only, you know, how come you don't do it on the phone? I mean, the way it's normally—"

The red-eyed robber, heedless of exposure to the sharpshooters across the street, shouldered furiously past the comparatively calm robber, who tried to restrain him as he yelled at Dortmunder, "You're rubbing it in, are ya? OK, I made a mistake! I got excited and I shot up the switchboard! You want me to get excited again?"

"No, no!" Dortmunder cried, trying to hold his hands straight up in the air and defensively in front of his body at the same time. "I forgot! I just forgot!"

The other robbers all clustered around to grab the red-eyed robber, who seemed to be trying to point his Uzi in Dortmunder's direction as he yelled, "I did it in front of everybody! I humiliated myself in front of everybody! And now you're making fun of me!"

"I *forgot!* I'm sorry!"

"You can't forget that! Nobody's ever gonna forget that!"

The three remaining robbers dragged the red-eyed robber back away from the doorway, talking to him, trying to soothe him, leaving Dortmunder and the comparatively calm robber to continue their conversation. "I'm sorry," Dortmunder said. "I just forgot. I've been kind of distracted lately. Recently."

"You're playing with fire here, Diddums," the robber said. "Now tell them they're gonna get our demands."

Dortmunder nodded, and turned his head the other way, and yelled, "They're gonna tell you their demands now. I mean, *I'm* gonna tell you their demands. *Their* demands. Not *my* demands. *Their* de—"

"*We're willing to listen, Diddums, only so long as none of the hostages get hurt.*"

"That's good!" Dortmunder agreed, and turned his head the other way to tell the robber, "That's reasonable, you know, that's sensible, that's a very good thing they're saying."

"Shut up," the robber said.

"Right," Dortmunder said.

The robber said, "First, we want the riflemen off the roofs."

"Oh, so do I," Dortmunder told him, and turned to shout, "They want the riflemen off the roofs!"

"*What else?*"

"What else?"

"And we want them to unblock that end of the street, the—what is it?— the north end."

Dortmunder frowned straight ahead at the buses blocking the intersection. "Isn't that east?" he asked.

"Whatever it is," the robber said, getting impatient. "That end down there to the left."

"OK." Dortmunder turned his head and yelled, "They want you to unblock the east end of the street!" Since his hands were way up in the sky somewhere, he pointed with his chin.

"*Isn't that north?*"

"I knew it was," the robber said.

"Yeah, I guess so," Dortmunder called. "That end down there to the left."

"*The right, you mean.*"

"Yeah, that's right. Your right, my left. *Their* left."

"*What else?*"

Dortmunder sighed, and turned his head. "What else?"

The robber glared at him. "I can *hear* the bullhorn, Diddums. I can *hear* him say 'What else?' You don't have to repeat everything he says. No more translations."

"Right," Dortmunder said. "Gotcha. No more translations."

"We'll want a car," the robber told him. "A station wagon. We're gonna take three hostages with us, so we want a big station wagon. And nobody follows us."

"Gee," Dortmunder said dubiously, "are you sure?"

The robber stared. "Am I *sure?*"

"Well, you know what they'll do," Dortmunder told him, lowering his voice so the other team across the street couldn't hear him. "What they do in these situations, they fix a little radio transmitter under the car, so then they don't have to *follow* you, exactly, but they know where you are."

Impatient again, the robber said, "So you'll tell them not to do that. No radio transmitters, or we kill the hostages."

"Well, I suppose," Dortmunder said doubtfully.

"What's wrong *now?*" the robber demanded. "You're too goddamn *picky*, Diddums; you're just the messenger here. You think you know my job better than I do?"

I know I do, Dortmunder thought, but it didn't seem a judicious thing to say aloud, so instead, he explained, "I just want things to go smooth, that's all. I just don't want bloodshed. And I was thinking, the New York City police, you know, well, they've got helicopters."

"Damn," the robber said. He crouched low to the littered floor, behind the broken doorframe, and brooded about his situation. Then he looked up at Dortmunder and said, "OK, Diddums, you're so smart. What *should* we do?"

Dortmunder blinked. "You want *me* to figure out your getaway?"

"Put yourself in our position," the robber suggested. "Think about it."

Dortmunder nodded. Hands in the air, he gazed at the blocked intersection and put himself in the robbers' position. "Hoo, boy," he said. "You're in a real mess."

"We *know* that, Diddums."

"Well," Dortmunder said, "I tell you what maybe you could do. You make them give you one of those buses they've got down there blocking the street. They give you one of those buses right now, then you know they haven't had time to put anything cute in it, like time-release tear-gas grenades or anyth—"

"Oh, my God," the robber said. His black ski mask seemed to have paled slightly.

"Then you take *all* the hostages," Dortmunder told him. "Everybody goes in the bus, and one of your people drives, and you go somewhere real crowded, like Times Square, say, and then you stop and make all the hostages get out and run."

"Yeah?" the robber said. "What good does that do us?"

"Well," Dortmunder said, "you drop the ski masks and the leather jackets and the guns, and *you* run, too. Twenty, thirty people all running away from the bus in different directions, in the middle of Times Square in rush hour, everybody losing themselves in the crowd. It might work."

"Jeez, it might," the robber said. "OK, go ahead and—What?"

"What?" Dortmunder echoed. He strained to look leftward, past the vertical column of his left arm. The boss robber was in excited conversation with one of his pals; not the red-eyed maniac, a different one. The boss robber shook his head and said, "Damn!" Then he looked up at Dortmunder. "Come back in here, Diddums," he said.

Dortmunder said, "But don't you want me to—"

"Come back in here!"

"Oh," Dortmunder said. "Uh, I better tell them over there that I'm gonna move."

"Make it fast," the robber told him. "Don't mess with me, Diddums. I'm in a bad mood right now."

"OK." Turning his head the other way, hating it that his back was toward this bad-mooded robber for even a second, Dortmunder called, "They want me to go back into the bank now. Just for a minute." Hands still up, he edged sideways across the sidewalk and through the gaping doorway, where the robbers laid hands on him and flung him back deeper into the bank.

He nearly lost his balance but saved himself against the sideways-lying pot of the tipped-over Ficus. When he turned around, all five of the robbers were lined up looking at him, their expressions intent, focused, almost hungry, like a row of cats looking in a fish-store window. "Uh," Dortmunder said.

"He's it now," one of the robbers said.

Another robber said, "But *they* don't know it."

A third robber said, "They will soon."

"They'll know it when nobody gets on the bus," the boss robber said, and shook his head at Dortmunder. "Sorry, Diddums. Your idea doesn't work anymore."

Dortmunder had to keep reminding himself that he wasn't actually *part* of this string. "How come?" he asked.

Disgusted, one of the other robbers said, "The rest of the hostages got away, that's how come."

Wide-eyed, Dortmunder spoke without thinking: "The tunnel!"

All of a sudden, it got very quiet in the bank. The robbers were now looking at him like cats looking at a fish with no window in the way. "The tunnel?" repeated the boss robber slowly. "You *know* about the tunnel?"

"Well, kind of," Dortmunder admitted. "I mean, the guys digging it, they got there just before you came and took me away."

"And you never mentioned it."

"Well," Dortmunder said, very uncomfortable, "I didn't feel like I should."

The red-eyed maniac lunged forward, waving that submachine gun again, yelling, "*You're* the guy with the tunnel! It's your tunnel!" And he pointed the shaking barrel of the Uzi at Dortmunder's nose.

"Easy, easy!" the boss robber yelled. "This is our only hostage; don't use him up!"

The red-eyed maniac reluctantly lowered the Uzi, but he turned to the others and announced, "*Nobody's* gonna forget when I shot up the switch-board. Nobody's *ever* gonna forget that. He wasn't *here!*"

All of the robbers thought that over. Meantime, Dortmunder was thinking about his own position. He might be a hostage, but he wasn't your normal hostage, because he was also a guy who had just dug a tunnel to a bank vault, and there were maybe 30 eyeball witnesses who could identify him. So it wasn't enough to get away from these bank robbers; he was also going to have to get away from the police. Several thousand police.

So did that mean he was locked to these second-rate smash-and-grabbers? Was his own future really dependent on *their* getting out of this hole? Bad news, if true. Left to their own devices, these people couldn't escape from a merry-go-round.

Dortmunder sighed. "OK," he said. "The first thing we have to do is—"

"We?" the boss robber said. "Since when are you in this?"

"Since you dragged me in," Dortmunder told him. "And the first thing we have to do is—"

The red-eyed maniac lunged at him again with the Uzi, shouting, "Don't you tell us what to do! *We* know what to do!"

"I'm your only hostage," Dortmunder reminded him. "Don't use me up. Also, now that I've seen you people in action, I'm your only hope of getting out of here. So this time, listen to me. The first thing we have to do is close and lock the vault door."

One of the robbers gave a scornful laugh. "The hostages are *gone*," he said. "Didn't you hear that part? Lock the vault door after the hostages are gone. Isn't that some kind of old saying?" And he laughed and laughed.

Dortmunder looked at him. "It's a two-way tunnel," he said quietly.

The robbers stared at him. Then they all turned and ran toward the back of the bank. They *all* did.

They're too excitable for this line of work, Dortmunder thought as he walked briskly toward the front of the bank. *Clang* went the vault door, far behind him, and Dortmunder stepped through the broken doorway and out again to the sidewalk, remembering to stick his arms straight up in the air as he did.

"Hi!" he yelled, sticking his face well out, displaying it for all the sharp-shooters to get a really *good* look at. "Hi, it's me again! Diddums! Welsh!"

"Diddums!" screamed an enraged voice from deep within the bank. "Come back here!"

Oh, no. Ignoring that, moving steadily but without panic, arms up, face forward, eyes wide, Dortmunder angled leftward across the sidewalk, shouting, "I'm coming out again! And I'm *escaping*!" And he dropped his arms, tucked his elbows in and ran hell for leather toward those blocking buses.

Gunfire encouraged him: sudden burst behind him of *ddrrritt, ddrrritt*, and then *kopp-kopp-kopp*, and then a whole symphony of *fooms* and *thug-thugs* and *padapows*. Dortmunder's toes, turning into high-tension steel springs, kept him bounding through the air like the Wright brothers' first airplane, swooping and plunging down the middle of the street, that wall of buses getting closer and closer.

"Here! In here!" Uniformed cops appeared on both sidewalks, waving to him, offering sanctuary in the forms of open doorways and police vehicles to crouch behind, but Dortmunder was *escaping*. From everything.

The buses. He launched himself through the air, hit the blacktop hard and rolled under the nearest bus. Roll, roll, roll, hitting his head and elbows and knees and ears and nose and various other parts of his body against any number of hard, dirty objects, and then he was past the bus and on his feet, staggering, staring at a lot of goggle-eyed medics hanging around beside their ambulances, who just stood there and gawked back.

Dortmunder turned left. *Medics* weren't going to chase him; their franchise didn't include healthy bodies running down the street. The cops couldn't chase him until they'd moved their buses out of the way. Dortmunder took off like the last of the dodoes, flapping his arms, wishing he knew how to fly.

The out-of-business shoe store, the other terminus of the tunnel, passed on his left. The getaway car they'd parked in front of it was long gone, of course. Dortmunder kept thudding on, on, on.

Three blocks later, a gypsy cab committed a crime by picking him up even though he hadn't phoned the dispatcher first; in the city of New York, only licensed medallion taxis are permitted to pick up customers who hail them on the street. Dortmunder, panting like a Saint Bernard on the lumpy back seat, decided not to turn the guy in.

HIS faithful companion May came out of the living room when Dortmunder opened the front door of his apartment and stepped into his hall. "*There* you are!" she said. "Thank goodness. It's all over the radio *and* the television."

"I may never leave the house again," Dortmunder told her. "If Andy Kelp ever calls, says he's got this great job, easy, piece of cake, I'll just tell him I've retired."

"Andy's here," May said. "In the living room. You want a beer?"

"Yes," Dortmunder said simply.

May went away to the kitchen and Dortmunder limped into the living room, where Kelp was seated on the sofa holding a can of beer and looking happy. On the coffee table in front of him was a mountain of money.

Dortmunder stared. "What's *that?*"

Kelp grinned and shook his head. "It's been too long since we scored, John," he said. "You don't even recognize the stuff anymore. This is money."

"But—From the vault? How?"

"After you were taken away by those other guys—they were caught, by the way," Kelp interrupted himself, "without loss of life—anyway, I told everybody in the vault there, the way to keep the money safe from the robbers was we'd all carry it out with us. So we did. And then I decided what we should do is put it all in the trunk of my unmarked police car in front of the shoe store, so I could drive it to the precinct for safekeeping while they all went home to rest from their ordeal."

Dortmunder looked at his friend. He said, "You got the hostages to carry the money from the vault."

"And put it in our car," Kelp said. "Yeah, that's what I did."

May came in and handed Dortmunder a beer. He drank, deep, and Kelp said, "They're looking for you, of course. Under that other name."

May said, "That's the one thing I don't understand. Diddums?"

"It's Welsh," Dortmunder told her. Then he smiled upon the mountain of money on the coffee table. "It's not a bad name," he decided. "I may keep it."

HARLAN ELLISON

*O*f all the peculiar questions asked of writers, particularly by lecture audiences comprised of readers and fans—two different lifeforms, trust me on this—I've always thought the least rational is: *"What's your favorite story?"*

I usually ask if the questioner means *"of all the stories I've ever read by anyone"* or *"the stories I myself have written."* Then, greedy little folk, he or she will reply, *"Er, uh . . . both!"* As if the answer meant anything like what the critic John Simon identified as being *"as vast and mysterious as the inside of a noodle."*

Yet here is an entire book in which each of us is asked that weird question. Not once, but twice.

This is a mug's game. I have hundreds of favorites. I've read a lot. But when I begged Larry Block to let me have at least three choices, the absolute minimum of favorites I could boil myself down to, he was ectothermic and vastly distant, implacable and hardly tolerable for a guy who owes me ten bucks from a long-time-ago afternoon on the corner of Christopher and Bleecker Streets. So, of my three all-time favorite stories in this vast and anything-but-distant category—"The Human Chair" by the great Japanese suspense writer Edogawa Rampo; "The Ears of Johnny Bear" by John Steinbeck; and "The Problem of Cell 13" by the immortal Jacques Futrelle, who went down with the Titanic, giving up his lifeboat seat to others—I have been forced to bite the bullet (in lieu of Block's earlobe), and I've gone with Futrelle. Because, well, because it's just so damned fine!

Which *brings me to the story of mine own creation I've picked from the 1,700+ I've had published here or there since my first sale in 1955. It has probably been in the top first percentile of my own favorites for a longer stretch of time than most of my "pets" sustain my admiration.*

"Tired Old Man" is 5,000 words long. I wrote it in June of 1975. It is a story with a peculiar history, which I'm inclined to take time to recount here.

First, however, let me warn you. I am not *the protagonist, Billy Landress, even though much of Billy's career parallels mine, and some of the things that happen to him in the story truly occurred . . . in a sorta kinda way; and some of his perceptions are ones I've come to hold as my own. Now, I suppose all that disclaiming will convince those of you who believe in the "he protesteth too much" philosophy that I am Billy. Well, that only goes to show how little some of you understand the art of creating fiction. A writer takes bits and pieces of himself—he cannibalizes himself—and he applies a little meat here and a little meat there, and he comes up with a character that bears a* resemblance *to himself (because, in all candor, who do I know* better *than myself?) but that is a new person entirely. So don't get all screwed up trying to fit me into Billy's shoes.*

Back to the story.

I was in New York on a visit. I went to dinner with Bob Silverberg and his then-wife Bobbie, and after dinner we went to a gathering of the old Hydra Club, the legendary writer's klatsch. It was at Willy Ley's apartment downtown. It was shortly before that great and wonderful man died, and it was good to see him again. The small apartment was jammed wall-to-wall. And I wandered around saying hello to this old friend or that seldom-seen fellow writer, and finally found myself sitting on a sofa next to a weary-looking old man in an easy chair. Marvelous conversationalist. We talked for almost an hour, until I got up and went to the kitchen to get a glass of water, where I found Bob with the now-late Hans Stefan Santesson, a dear friend and ex-editor of mine. I described the old man and asked who he was.

"That is Cornell Woolrich," Hans said.

My mouth must have fallen open. I had been sitting next to one of the giants of mystery fiction, a man whose work I'd read and admired for twenty years, since I'd been a kid and discovered a copy of Black Alibi *after seeing the 1946 Val Lewton film* The Leopard Man. *I was nine years old at the time, and the film made such an impression on me that I stayed at the Lake Theater in Painesville, Ohio, to see it three times on a Saturday. And it was the first time I ever really read those funny words that come at the beginning of the movie (I later learned those were "credits"), the words that said "Screenplay by Ardel Wray, based on the novel* Black Alibi *by Cornell Woolrich."*

How I got hold of the novel, I don't remember. But it was the first mystery fiction I'd ever read (excluding Poe, of course, all of whom I'd read by that time). Nine years old!

And in the rush of time as I grew up, voraciously devouring the works of every decent writer I could find, Woolrich (under his own name and his possibly even-more-famous pseudonym, William Irish) became a treasure-house of twists and turns in plotting, elegant writing style, misdirection, mood, setting, and suspense. Oh! the beautiful stories that man wrote. The "black book" series: The Black Angel, The Black Curtain, The Black Path of Fear, Rendezvous in Black, The Bride Wore Black *and (reread many more times)* Black Alibi. *And* Deadline at Dawn, Phantom Lady, Mightmare, Strangler's Serenade, Waltz into Darkness. *And all the short stories!*

Cornell Woolrich!

Jeeeezus, if Hans had said I was sitting next to Ernestfucking-Hemingway it couldn't have collapsed me more thoroughly. Bertrand Russell, Bob Feller, Dick Bong, Walt Kelly . . . all my heroes . . . it wouldn't have gotten to me half as much. Cornell Woolrich! I damn near fainted.

"But I thought he'd died years *ago," I said.*

They laughed at me. He was old, no doubt about that, *but he was very much alive. He wasn't writing anymore. His mother—whom he'd lived with all of his adult life, in a residential hotel in Man-hattan—had recently died; and he had only recently begun getting out and around.*

I was flabbergasted. I'd sat and talked *with Cornell Woolrich, one of my earliest writing heroes, and hadn't even* known *it. I wanted to find him in that crowded apartment and just be* near *him for a while longer.*

They were bemused by my goshwow attitude, but they were also a little perplexed. Hans said, "I do not remember seeing him here. Where is he?"

And I led them back to the easy chair in the far rear corner of the room. And he was gone. And he was nowhere in the apartment. And no one else had talked to him. And I never saw him again. And I learned later that he had died soon after that night.

To this day, I've felt there was something strange and pivotal in my meeting with Woolrich. He could not possibly have known who I was, nor could he have much cared. But we talked writing, and I was the only one *who saw or talked to him that night. I'm sure of that.*

I firmly do not *believe in ghosts or astrology or UFOs or much else of the nonsense gobbledygook that people substitute for the ability to handle reality. But from the time I left him in that easy chair till the moment I went back to find him, I was right in front of the only exit from that apartment, and* there was no way he could have gotten past me without my seeing him.

For years, I thought about that night in New York. And one afternoon, I sat down and wrote the first two pages of a story titled "Tired Old Man," in which I thought I would fictionalize that eve-ning and pay homage to a writer whose words had so deeply affected me.

But the two pages went into the idea file, unresolved. They stayed there for six years, until June of 1975. I was in the process of writing another story and had started on an idea I'd had a while back, and in looking for the note for that story I chanced upon the two pages of "Tired Old Man." And without my even knowing why, or realizing what I was doing, I resumed the writing on that six-year-old snippet of story as if it hadn't been years earlier and I'd never laid it aside.

And as impossible as it had been for me to write it years before, because I hadn't known how to write it years before, it was that easy for me to start with the very next sentence—as if I'd written the last word of the previous sentence only an instant earlier—and I drove through, all the way to the end, in one sitting.

Marki Strasser in the story is Cornell Woolrich. At least, in the impetus for the character. It isn't supposed to be Woolrich in the story, it's . . . well . . . that's what the story is about, as you'll see . . . but I wanted you to know how "Tired Old Man" came to be written; in memory of that long-ago night of ghosts, and by way of partial answer to the people who always ask me, "Where do you get your ideas?" and, "What's your favorite story?"

TIRED OLD MAN (An Homage to Cornell Woolrich)

THE HELL OF it is, you're never as tough as you think you are. There's always somebody with sad eyes who'll shoot you down when you're not even looking, when you're combing your hair, tying your shoelace. Down you go, like a wounded rhino, nowhere near as tough as you thought.

I came in from the Coast on a Wednesday, got myself locked up in the Warwick to finish the book, did it, called the messenger and had him take the manuscript over to Wyeth the following Tuesday, and I was free. Only nine months late, but it was an okay piece of work. It was going to be at least three days till I got the call telling me what alterations he wanted—there were three chapters dead in the middle I knew he'd balk at—I'd cheated on the psychiatric rationale for the brother-in-law's actions, had held back some stuff I knew Wyeth would demand I flesh out—and so I had time to kill.

I've got to remember to remind myself: if I ever use that phrase again, may my carbons always be reversed. Time to kill. Yeah, just the phrase.

I called Bob Catlett, thinking we'd get together for dinner with his wife, the psychiatrist, if he was still seeing her He said we could set it up for that night and by the way, why didn't I come along for the monthly meeting of The Cerberus Club. I choked back a string of uglies. "I don't think so, man. They give me a pain in the ass."

The Cerberus is a "writers' club" of old pros who've been around since Clarence Buddington Kelland was breaking in at Munsey's *Cavalier*. And what had been a fairly active group of working professionals in the Fifties and Sixties was now a gaggle of burnt-out cases and gossips, drinking too much and lamenting the passing of Ben Hibbs at the *Saturday Evening Post*. I was thirty years past that time, a young punk by their lights, and I saw no merit whatsoever in spending an evening up to my hips in dull chatter and weariness, gagging on cigarette smoke and listening to septuageneric penny-a-word losers comparing the merits of *Black Mask* to those of *Weird Tales*.

So he talked me into it. That's what friends are for.

We had dinner at an Argentinian restaurant off Times Square; and with my belly full of skirt steak and bread pudding I felt up to it. We arrived at the traditional meeting-place—the claustrophobic apartment of a sometime-editor who had once been a reader for Book-of-the-Month Club—around nine-thirty. It was packed from wall to wall.

I hadn't seen most of them in ten years, since I'd gone to the Coast to adapt my novel, *The Stalking Man*, for Paramount. It had been a good ten years for me. I'd left New York with a molehill of unpaid bills the creditors were rapidly turning into a mountain, and such despair both personally and professionally I'd half accepted the idea I'd never really make a decent living at writing. But doing four months' work each year in films and television had provided the cushion so I could spend eight months of the year working on books. I was free of debt, twenty pounds heavier, secure for the first time in my life, and reasonably happy. But walking into that apartment was like walking back into a corporeal memory of the dismal past. Nothing had changed. They were all there, and all the same.

My first impression was of lines of weariness.

Someone had superimposed a blueprint on the room and its occupants. In the background were all the moving figures, older and more threadbare than the last time I'd seen them gathered together in a room like this, moving (it seemed, oddly) a good deal more slowly than they should have been. As if they were embedded in amber. Not slow motion, merely an altered index of the light-admitting properties of the lenses of my eyes. Out of synch with their voices. But in the foreground, much sharper and brighter than the colors of the people or the room, was an overlay of lines of weariness. Gray and blue lines that were not merely topographically superimposed over faces and hands, and the elbows of the women, but over the entire room: lines rising off toward the ceiling, laid against the lamps and chairs, dividing the carpet into sections.

I walked through, between and among the blue and gray lines, finding it difficult to breathe as the oppressiveness of massed failure and dead dreams assaulted me. It was like breathing the dust of ancient tombs.

Bob Catlett and his wife had immediately wandered off to the kitchen for drinks. I would have scurried after them, but Leo Norris saw me, shoved between two ex-technical writers (each of whom had had brief commercial successes twenty years before with non-fiction popularizations of space science theory) and grabbed my hand. He looked exhausted, but sober.

"Billy! For God's sake, *Billy*! I didn't know you were in town. What a great thing! How long're you in for?"

"Only a few days, Leo. Book for Harper. I've been all locked up finishing it."

"Well, I'll say this for you, the Scott Fitzgerald Syndrome certainly hasn't hit you out there. How many books have you written since you left, three? Four?"

"Seven."

He smiled with embarrassment, but not enough embarrassment to slow the phony camaraderie. Leo Norris and I—despite his effusions—had never been close. When he had already been an established novelist, a fact one verified by getting one's name on the cover of *The Saint Detective Magazine*, I was banging off hammer murder novelettes for *Manhunt*, just to pay the rent in the Village. There had been no camaraderie in those days. But Leo was now on the slide, had been for the last six or eight years, had been reduced to writing a series of sex/spy/violence paperbacks: each one numbered (he was up to #27 the last time I looked), pseudonymous, featuring an unpleasant CIA thug named Curt Costener. Four of my last seven novels had been translated into successful films and one of them had become a television series. Camaraderie.

"Seven books in what—ten years?—that's damned good."

I didn't say anything. I was looking around; indicating I wanted to move on. He didn't pick up the message.

"Brett McCoy died, you know. Last week."

I nodded. I'd read him, but had never met him. Good writer. Police procedurals.

"Terminal. Inoperable. Lungs; really spread. Oh, he'd been on the way out for a long time. He'll be missed."

"Yeah. Well, excuse me, Leo, I have to find some people I came with."

I couldn't get through the press near the front door to join Bob in the kitchen. The only breeze was coming in from the hallway and they were jammed together in front of the passage. So I went the other way, deeper into the room, deeper into the inversion layer of smoke and monotoned chatter. He watched me go, wanting to say something, probably wanting to strengthen a bond that didn't exist. I moved fast. I didn't want any more obituary reports.

There were only five or six women in the crowd, as far as I could tell. One of them watched me as I edged through the bodies. I couldn't help noticing her noticing me. She was in her late forties, severely weathered, staring openly as I neared her. It wasn't till she spoke, "Billy?" that I recognized the voice. Not the face; even then, not the face. Just the voice, which hadn't changed.

I stopped and stared back. "Dee?"

She smiled no kind of smile at all, a mere stricture of courtesy. "How are you, Billy?"

"I'm fine. How're you? What's happening, what're you doing these days?"

"I'm living in Woodstock. Cormick and I got divorced; I'm doing books for Avon."

I hadn't seen anything with her name on it for some time. Those who haunt the newsstands and bookstores out of years of habit are like sidewalk cafe Greeks unable to stop fingering their worry beads. I would have seen her name.

She caught the hesitation. "Gothics. I'm doing them under another name."

This time the smile was nasty and it said: you've had the last laugh; yes, I'm selling my talent cheap; I hate myself for it; I'll slice my wrists in this conversation before I'll permit you to gloat. What's more offensive than being successful when they always dismissed you as the least of their set, and they've dribbled away all the promise and have failed? Nothing. They would eat the air you breathe. Bierce: Success, *n*. The one unpardonable sin against one's fellows. Unquote.

"Look me up if you get to Los Angeles," I said. She didn't even want to try that one. She turned back to the three-way conversation behind her. She took the arm of an elegant man with a thick, gray mop of styled Claude Rains hair. He was wearing aviator-style eyeglasses, wraparounds, tinted auburn. Dee hung on tight. That wouldn't last long. His suits were too well-tailored. She looked like a tattered battle flag. *When had they all settled for oblivion?*

Edwin Charrel was coming toward me from the opposite side of the room. He still owed me sixty dollars from ten years before. He wouldn't have forgotten. He'd lay a long, guilt-oozing story on me, and try to press a moist five bucks into my hand. Not now; *really*, not now; not on top of Leo Norris and

Dee Miller and all those crinkled elbows. I turned a hard right, smiled at a mom-and-pop writing team sharing the same glass of vodka, and worked my way to the wall. I kept to the outside and began to circumnavigate. My mission: to get the hell out of there as quickly as possible. Everyone knows, it's harder to hit a moving target.

And miles to go before I sleep.

The back wall was dominated by a sofa jammed with loud conversations. But the crowd in the center of the room had its collective back to the babble, so there was a clear channel across to the other side. I made the move. Charrel wasn't even in sight, so I made the move. No one noticed, no one gave a gardyloo, no one tried to buttonhole me. I made the move. I thought I was halfway home. I started to turn the corner, only one wall to go before the breeze, the door, and out. That was when the old man motioned to me from the easy chair.

The chair was wedged into the rear corner of the room at an angle to the sofa. Big, overstuffed, colorless thing. He was deep in the cushions. Thin, wasted, tired-looking, eyes a soft, watery blue. He was motioning to me. I looked behind me, turned back. He was motioning to *me*. I walked over and stood there above him.

"Sit down."

There wasn't anywhere to sit. "I was just leaving." I didn't know him.

"Sit down, we'll talk. There's time."

A spot opened at the end of the sofa. It would have been rude to walk away. He nodded his head at the open spot. So I sat down. He was the most exhausted-looking old man I'd ever seen. Just stared at me.

"So you write a little," he said. I thought he was putting me on. I smiled, and he said, "What's your name?"

I said, "Billy Landress."

He tested that for a moment, silently. "William. On the books it's William."

I chuckled. "That's right. William on the books. It's better for the lending libraries. Classier. Weightier." I couldn't stop smiling and laughing softly. Not to myself, right into his face. He didn't smile back, but I knew he wasn't taking offense. It was a bemusing conversation.

"And you're . . . ?"

"Marki," he said; he paused, then added, "Marki Strasser."

Still smiling, I said, "Is that the name you write under?"

He shook his head. "I don't write anymore. I haven't written in a long time."

"Marki," I said, lingering on the word, "Marki Strasser. I don't think I've read any of your work. Mystery fiction?"

"Primarily. Suspense, a few contemporary novels, nothing terribly significant. But tell me about you."

I settled back into the sofa. "I have the feeling, sir, that you're amused by me."

His soft, blue eyes stared back at me without a trace of guile. There was no smile anywhere in that face. Tired; old and terribly tired. "We're *all* amusing, William. Except when we get too old to take care of ourselves, when we get too old to keep up. Then we cease to be amusing. You don't want to talk about yourself?"

I spread my hands in surrender. I would talk about myself. He may have conceived of himself as too old to be amusing, but he was a fascinating old man nonetheless. He was a good listener. And the rest of the room faded, and we talked. I told him about myself, about life on the Coast, the plots of my books, in *précis*, what it took to adapt a suspense novel for the screen.

Body language is interesting. On the most primitive level, even those unfamiliar with the unconscious messages the positions of the arms and legs and torso give, can perceive what's going on. When two people are talking and one is trying to get across an important point to the other, the one making the point leans forward; the one resisting the point leans back. I realized I was leaning far forward and to the side, resting my chest on the arm of the sofa. He wasn't sinking too far back in the soft cushions of the easy chair; but he was back, in any event. He was listening to me, taking in everything I was saying, but it was as though he knew it was all past, all dead information, as though he was waiting to tell me some things I needed to know.

Finally, he said, "Have you noticed how many of the stories you've written are concerned with relationships of fathers to sons?"

I'd noticed. "My father died when I was very young," I said, and felt the usual tightness in my chest. "Somewhere, I don't remember where, I stumbled on a line Faulkner wrote once, where he said, something like, 'No matter what a writer writes about, if it's a man he's writing about the search for his father.' It hit me particularly hard. I'd never realized how much I missed him until one night just a few years ago, I was in a group encounter session and we were told by the leader of the group to pick one person out of the circle and to make that person someone we wanted to talk to, someone we'd never been able to talk to, and to tell that person everything we'd always wanted to say. I picked a man with a mustache and talked to him the way I'd never been able to talk to my father when I was a very little boy. After a little bit I was crying." I paused, then said very softly, "I didn't even cry at my father's funeral. It was a very strange thing, a disturbing evening."

I paused again, and collected my thoughts. This was becoming a good deal heavier, more personal, than I'd anticipated. "Then, just a year or two ago, I found that quote by Faulkner; and it all fitted into place."

The tired old man kept watching me. "What did you tell him?"

"Who? Oh, the man with the mustache? Hmmm. Well, it wasn't anything that potent. I just told him I'd made it, that he would be proud of me now, that I had succeeded, that I was a good guy and . . . he'd be proud of me. That was all."

"What *didn't* you tell him?"

I felt myself twitch with the impact of the remark. I went chill all over. He had said it so casually, and yet the force of the question jammed a cold chisel into the door of my memory, applied sudden pressure and snapped the lock. The door sprang open and guilt flooded out. How could Marki have known?

"Nothing. I don't know what you mean." I didn't recognize my voice.

"There must have been something. You're an angry man, William. You're angry at your father. Perhaps because he died and left you alone. But you didn't say something very important that you *needed* to say; you still need to say it. What was it?"

I didn't want to answer him. But he just waited. And finally I murmured, "He never said goodbye. He just died and never said goodbye to me." Silence. Then I shook, helplessly, trembled, reduced after so many years to a child, tried to shake it off, tried to dismiss it, and very quietly said, "It wasn't important."

"It wasn't important for him to hear it; but it was for you to say it." I couldn't look at him.

Then Marki said, "In the lens of time we are each seen as a diminishing mote. I'm sorry I upset you."

"You didn't upset me."

"Yes. I did. Let me try and make amends. If you have the time, let me tell you about a few books I wrote. You may enjoy this." So I sat back and he told me a dozen plots. He spoke without hesitations, fluidly, and they were awfully good. Excellent, in fact. Suspense stories, something in the vein of James M. Cain or Jim Thompson. Stories about average people, not private eyes or foreign agents; just people in stress situations where violence and intrigue proceeded logically from entrapping circumstances. I was fascinated. And what a talent he had for titles: *Dead by Morning, Cancel Bungalow 16, An Edge in My Voice, Whitemail, The Man Who Searched for Joy, The Diagnosis of Dr. D'arqueaAngel, Prodigal Father* and one that somehow struck me so forcibly I made a mental note to contact Andreas Brown at the Gotham Book Mart, to locate a used copy for me through his antiquarian book sources. I had to read it. it was titled *Lover, Killer*.

When he stopped talking, he looked even more exhausted than when he'd asked me to sit down. His skin was almost gray, and the soft, blue eyes kept closing for moments at a time. "Would you like a glass of water or something to eat?"

He looked at me carefully, and said, "Yes. I'd very much like a glass of water, thank you."

I got up, to force my way through to the kitchen.

He put his dry hand on mine. I looked down at him. "What do you want to be, eventually, William?"

I could have given a flip answer. I didn't. "Remembered," I said. Then he smiled, and removed his hand.

"I'll get that water; be right back."

I pushed through the crowd and got to the kitchen. Bob was still there, arguing with Hans Santesson about cracking the pro rata share of royalties problem for reprints of stories in college-level text-anthologies. Hans and I shook hands, and exchanged quick pleasantries while I drew a glass of water and put in a couple of ice cubes from the plastic sack half-filled with melted cubes in the sink. I didn't want to leave Marki for very long.

"Where the hell have you been tonight?" Bob asked.

"I'm sitting way at the back, with an old man; fascinating old man. Used to be a writer, he says. I don't doubt it. Jesus, he must have written some incredible books. Don't know how I could have missed them. I thought I'd read practically everything in the genre."

"What is his name?" Hans asked, with that soft lovely Scandinavian accent.

"Marki Strasser," I said. "What a goddam sensational story-sense he's got." They were staring at me.

"Marki Strasser?" Hans had frozen, his cup of tea halfway to his lips.

"Marki Strasser," I said again. "What's the matter?"

"The only Marki I know, who was a writer, was a man who used to come to these evenings thirty years ago. But he's been dead for at least fifteen, sixteen years."

I laughed. "Can't be the same one, unless you're wrong about his having died."

"No, I am certain about his death. I attended his funeral."

"Then it's someone else."

"Where's he sitting?" Bob asked.

I stepped out into the passage and motioned them to join me. I waited for the crowd to sway out of the way for a moment, and pointed. "There, back in the corner, in the big easy chair."

There was no one in the big easy chair. It was empty.

And as I stared, and they stood behind me, staring, a woman sat down in the chair and went to sleep, a cocktail in her hand. "He got up and moved somewhere else in the room," I said.

No, he hadn't. Of course.

WE were the last to go. I wouldn't leave. I watched each person pass out through the front door, standing right in front of the door so no one could get past me. Bob checked out the toilet. He wasn't in there. There was only one exit from the apartment, and I was in front of it. "Listen, goddammit," I said heatedly, to Hans and Bob and our host, who wanted desperately to vomit and go to bed, "I do *not* believe in ghosts; he *wasn't* a ghost, he *wasn't* a figment of my imagination, he *wasn't* a fraud; for God's sake I'm not *that* gullible I can't tell when I'm being put on; those stories he told me were too damned good; and if he was here, how the hell did he get out past me? I was right in front of the door even when I came to the kitchen to get the water. He was an *old* man, at least seventy-five, maybe older; he wasn't a goddam sprinter! *Nobody* could have gotten through that crowd fast enough to slip out into the hall behind me without banging into everyone, and *someone* would have remembered being pushed like that . . . so . . . ."

Hans tried to calm me. "Billy, we asked everyone who was here. No one else saw him. No one even saw you sitting on the sofa there, where you say you were sitting. No one else spoke to anyone like that, and many of the writers here tonight *knew* him. Why would a man tell you he was Marki Strasser if he was *not* Marki Strasser? He would have known that a room filled with writers who *knew* Marki Strasser would tell you if it was a joke."

I wouldn't let go of it. I was *not* hallucinating!

Our host went digging around in the back closet and came up with a bound file of old Mystery Writers of America programs from Edgar Award dinners;

he flipped through them, back fifteen years, and found a photograph of Marki Strasser. I looked at it. The photo was clear and sharp. It wasn't the same man. There was no way of confusing the two, even adding fifteen years to the face in the picture, even allowing for a severe debilitation from sickness. The Marki in the photograph was a round-faced man, almost totally bald, with thick eyebrows and dark eyes. The Marki I had talked to for almost an hour had had soft, blue eyes. Even if he had been wearing a hairpiece, those eyes couldn't be mistaken.

"It's not him, dammit!"

They asked me to describe him again. When that didn't connect, Hans asked me to tell him the stories and the titles. The three of them listened and I could see from their faces that they were as impressed with the books Marki had written as I was. But when I ran down and sat there, breathing hard, Hans and my host shook their heads. "Billy," Hans said, "I was the editor of the Unicorn Mystery Book Club for seven years; I edited *The Saint Detective Magazine* for more than ten. I have read as widely in the field of mystery fiction as anyone alive. No such books exist."

Our host, an authority on the subject, agreed.

I looked at Bob Catlett. He devoured them a book a day. Slowly, reluctantly, he nodded his head in agreement.

I sat there and closed my eyes.

After a while, Bob suggested we go. His wife had vanished an hour earlier with a group intent on getting cheesecake. He wanted to get to bed. I didn't know what to do. So I went back to the Warwick.

THAT night I pulled an extra blanket onto the bed, but still it was cold, very cold, and I shivered. I left the television set on, nothing but snow and a steady humming. I couldn't sleep.

Finally, I got up and got dressed and went out into the night. Fifty-fourth Street was empty and silent at three in the morning. Not even delivery trucks and, though I looked and looked for him, I couldn't find him.

I thought about it endlessly, walking, and for a while I imagined he had been my father, come back from the grave to talk to me. But it wasn't my father. I would have recognized him. I'm no fool, I would have recognized him. My father had been a much shorter man, with a mustache; and he had never spoken like that, in that way, with those words and those cadences.

It wasn't the almost-forgotten mystery novelist known as Marki Strasser.

Why he had used that name, I don't know; perhaps to get my attention, to lead me down a black path of fear that would tell me without question that he was someone else, because it had *not* been Marki Strasser. I didn't know who he was.

I came back to the Warwick and rang for the elevator. I stood in front of the mirrored panel between the two elevator doors, and I stared through my own reflection, into the glass, looking for an answer.

Then I went up to my room and sat down at the writing desk and rolled a clean sandwich of white bond, carbon, and yellow second sheet into the portable.

I began writing *Lover, Killer.*

It came easily. No one else could write that book.

But, like my father, he hadn't even said goodbye when I went to get him that glass of water. That tired old man.

The Problem of Cell 13

Jacques Futrelle

PRACTICALLY ALL THOSE letters remaining in the alphabet after Augustus S. F. X. Van Dusen was named were afterward acquired by that gentleman in the course of a brilliant scientific career, and, being honorably acquired, were tacked on to the other end. His name, therefore, taken with all that belonged to it, was a wonderfully imposing structure. He was a Ph.D., an LL.D., an F.R.S., an M.D., and an M.D.S. He was also some other things—just what he himself couldn't say—through recognition of his ability by various foreign educational and scientific institutions.

In appearance he was no less striking than in nomenclature. He was slender with the droop of the student in his thin shoulders and the pallor of a close, sedentary life on his clean-shaven face. His eyes wore a perpetual, forbidding squint—the squint of a man who studies little things—and when they could be seen at all through his thick spectacles, were mere slits of watery blue. But above his eyes was his most striking feature. This was a tall, broad brow, almost abnormal in height and width, crowned by a heavy shock of bushy, yellow hair. All these things conspired to give him a peculiar, almost grotesque, personality.

Professor Van Dusen was remotely German. For generations his ancestors had been noted in the sciences; he was the logical result, the mastermind. First and above all he was a logician. At least thirty-five years of the half century or so of his existence had been devoted exclusively to proving that two and two always equal four, except in unusual cases, where they equal three or five, as the case may be. He stood broadly on the general proposition that all things that start must go somewhere, and was able to bring the concentrated mental force of his forefathers to bear on a given problem. Incidentally it may be remarked that Professor Van Dusen wore a No. 8 hat.

The world at large had heard vaguely of Professor Van Dusen as The Thinking Machine. It was a newspaper catchphrase applied to him at the time of a remarkable exhibition at chess; he had demonstrated then that a stranger to the game might, by the force of inevitable logic, defeat a champion who had devoted a lifetime to its study. The Thinking Machine! Perhaps that more nearly described him than all his honorary initials, for he spent week after week, month after month, in the seclusion of his small laboratory from which had gone forth thoughts that staggered scientific associates and deeply stirred the world at large.

It was only occasionally that The Thinking Machine had visitors, and these were usually men who, themselves high in the sciences, dropped in to argue a point and perhaps convince themselves. Two of these men, Dr. Charles Ransome and Alfred Fielding, called one evening to discuss some theory which is not of consequence here.

"Such a thing is impossible," declared Dr. Ransome emphatically, in the course of the conversation.

"Nothing is impossible," declared The Thinking Machine with equal emphasis. He always spoke petulantly. "The mind is master of all things. When science fully recognizes that fact a great advance will have been made."

"How about the airship?" asked Dr. Ransome.

"That's not impossible at all," asserted The Thinking Machine. "It will be invented sometime. I'd do it myself, but I'm busy."

Dr. Ransome laughed tolerantly.

"I've heard you say such things before," he said. "But they mean nothing. Mind may be master of matter, but it hasn't yet found a way to apply itself. There are some things that can't be *thought* out of existence, or rather which would not yield to any amount of thinking."

"What, for instance?" demanded The Thinking Machine.

Dr. Ransome was thoughtful for a moment as he smoked.

"Well, say prison walls," he replied. "No man can *think* himself out of a cell. If he could, there would be no prisoners."

"A man can so apply his brain and ingenuity that he can leave a cell, which is the same thing," snapped The Thinking Machine.

Dr. Ransome was slightly amused.

"Let's suppose a case," he said, after a moment. "Take a cell where prisoners under sentence of death are confined—men who are desperate and, maddened by fear, would take any chance to escape—suppose you were locked in such a cell. Could you escape?"

"Certainly," declared The Thinking Machine.

"Of course," said Mr. Fielding, who entered the conversation for the first time, "you might wreck the cell with an explosive—but inside, a prisoner, you couldn't have that."

"There would be nothing of that kind," said The Thinking Machine. "You might treat me precisely as you treated prisoners under sentence of death, and I would leave the cell."

"Not unless you entered it with tools prepared to get out," said Dr. Ransome.

The Thinking Machine was visibly annoyed and his blue eyes snapped.

"Lock me in any cell in any prison anywhere at any time, wearing only what is necessary, and I'll escape in a week," he declared, sharply.

Dr. Ransome sat up straight in the chair, interested. Mr. Fielding lighted a new cigar.

"You mean you could actually *think* yourself out?" asked Dr. Ransome.

"I would get out," was the response.

"Are you serious?"

"Certainly I am serious."

Dr. Ransome and Mr. Fielding were silent for a long time.

"Would you be willing to try it?" asked Mr. Fielding, finally.

"Certainly," said Professor Van Dusen, and there was a trace of irony in his voice. "I have done more asinine things than that to convince other men of less important truths."

The tone was offensive and there was an undercurrent strongly resembling anger on both sides. Of course it was an absurd thing, but Professor Van Dusen reiterated his willingness to undertake the escape and it was decided upon.

"To begin now," added Dr. Ransome.

"I'd prefer that it begin tomorrow," said The Thinking Machine, "because—"

"No, now," said Mr. Fielding, flatly. "You are arrested, figuratively, of course, without any warning locked in a cell with no chance to communicate with friends, and left there with identically the same care and attention that would be given to a man under sentence of death. Are you willing?"

"All right, now, then," said The Thinking Machine, and he arose.

"Say, the death cell in Chisholm Prison."

"The death cell in Chisholm Prison."

"And what will you wear?"

"As little as possible," said The Thinking Machine. "Shoes, stockings, trousers, and a shirt."

"You will permit yourself to be searched, of course?"

"I am to be treated precisely as all prisoners are treated," said The Thinking Machine. "No more attention and no less."

There were some preliminaries to be arranged in the matter of obtaining permission for the test, but all three were influential men and everything was done satisfactorily by telephone, albeit the prison commissioners, to whom the experiment was explained on purely scientific grounds, were sadly bewildered. Professor Van Dusen would be the most distinguished prisoner they had ever entertained.

When The Thinking Machine had donned those things which he was to wear during his incarceration he called the little old woman who was his housekeeper, cook, and maid-servant all in one.

"Martha," he said, "it is now twenty-seven minutes past nine o'clock. I am going away. One week from tonight, at half past nine, these gentlemen and one, possibly two, others will take supper with me here. Remember Dr. Ransome is very fond of artichokes."

The three men were driven to Chisholm Prison, where the warden was awaiting them, having been informed of the matter by telephone. He understood merely that the eminent Professor Van Dusen was to be his prisoner, if he could keep him, for one week; that he had committed no crime, but that he was to be treated as all other prisoners were treated.

"Search him," instructed Dr. Ransome.

The Thinking Machine was searched. Nothing was found on him; the pockets of the trousers were empty; the white, stiff-bosomed shirt had no pocket. The shoes and stockings were removed, examined, then replaced. As he watched all these preliminaries, and noted the pitiful, childlike physical weakness of the man—the colorless face, and the thin, white hands—Dr. Ransome almost regretted his part in the affair.

"Are you sure you want to do this?" he asked.

"Would you be convinced if I did not?" inquired The Thinking Machine in turn.

"No."

"All right. I'll do it."

What sympathy Dr. Ransome had was dissipated by the tone. It nettled him, and he resolved to see the experiment to the end; it would be a stinging reproof to egotism.

"It will be impossible for him to communicate with anyone outside?" he asked.

"Absolutely impossible," replied the warden. "He will not be permitted writing materials of any sort."

"And your jailers, would they deliver a message from him?"

"Not one word, directly or indirectly," said the warden. "You may rest assured of that. They will report anything he might say or turn over to me, anything he might give them."

"That seems entirely satisfactory," said Mr. Fielding, who was frankly interested in the problem.

"Of course, in the event he fails," said Dr. Ransome, "and asks for his liberty, you understand you are to set him free?"

"I understand," replied the warden.

The Thinking Machine stood listening, but had nothing to say until this was all ended, then:

"I should like to make three small requests. You may grant them or not, as you wish."

"No special favors, now," warned Mr. Fielding.

"I am asking none," was the stiff response. "I should like to have some tooth powder—buy it yourself to see that it is tooth powder—and I should like to have one five-dollar and two ten-dollar bills."

Dr. Ransome, Mr. Fielding and the warden exchanged astonished glances. They were not surprised at the request for tooth powder, but were at the request for money.

"Is there any man with whom our friend would come in contact that he could bribe with twenty-five dollars?"

"Not for twenty-five hundred dollars," was the positive reply.

"Well, let him have them," said Mr. Fielding. "I think they are harmless enough."

"And what is the third request?" asked Dr. Ransome.

"I should like to have my shoes polished."

Again the astonished glances were exchanged. This last request was the height of absurdity, so they agreed to it. These things all being attended to,

The Thinking Machine was led back into the prison from which he had undertaken to escape.

"Here is Cell Thirteen," said the warden, stopping three doors down the steel corridor. "This is where we keep condemned murderers. No one can leave it without my permission; and no one in it can communicate with the outside. I'll stake my reputation on that. It's only three doors back of my office and I can readily hear any unusual noise."

"Will this cell do, gentlemen?" asked The Thinking Machine. There was a touch of irony in his voice.

"Admirably," was the reply.

The heavy steel door was thrown open, there was a great scurrying and scampering of tiny feet, and The Thinking Machine passed into the gloom of the cell. Then the door was closed and double-locked by the warden.

"What is that noise in there?" asked Dr. Ransome, through the bars.

"Rats—dozens of them," replied The Thinking Machine, tersely.

The three men, with final good nights, were turning away when The Thinking Machine called:

"What time is it exactly, Warden?"

"Eleven-seventeen," replied the warden.

"Thanks. I will join you gentlemen in your office at half past eight o'clock one week from tonight," said The Thinking Machine.

"And if you do not?"

"There is no 'if' about it."

CHISHOLM Prison was a great, spreading structure of granite, four stories in all, which stood in the center of acres of open space. It was surrounded by a wall of solid masonry eighteen feet high, and so smoothly finished inside and out as to offer no foothold to a climber, no matter how expert. Atop of this fence, as a further precaution, was a five-foot fence of steel rods, each terminating in a keen point. This fence in itself marked an absolute deadline between freedom and imprisonment, for, even if a man escaped from his cell, it would seem impossible for him to pass the wall.

The yard, which on all sides of the prison building was twenty-five feet wide, that being the distance from the building to the wall, was by day an exercise ground for those prisoners to whom was granted the boon of occasional semi-liberty. But that was not for those in Cell 13. At all times of the day there were armed guards in the yard, four of them, one patrolling each side of the prison building.

By night the yard was almost as brilliantly lighted as by day. On each of the four sides was a great arc light which rose above the prison wall and gave to the guards a clear sight. The lights, too, brightly illuminated the spiked top of the wall. The wires which fed the arc lights ran up the side of the prison building on insulators and from the top story led out to the poles supporting the arc lights.

All these things were seen and comprehended by The Thinking Machine, who was only enabled to see out his closely barred cell window by standing on his bed. This was on the morning following his incarceration. He gathered, too, that the river lay over there beyond the wall somewhere, because he heard faintly the pulsation of a motor boat and high up in the air saw a river bird. From that same direction came the shouts of boys at play and the occasional crack of a batted ball. He knew then that between the prison wall and the river was an open space, a playground.

Chisholm Prison was regarded as absolutely safe. No man had ever escaped from it. The Thinking Machine, from his perch on the bed, seeing what he saw, could readily understand why. The walls of the cell, though built he judged twenty years before, were perfectly solid, and the window bars of new iron had not a shadow of rust on them. The window itself, even with the bars out, would be a difficult mode of egress because it was small.

Yet, seeing these things, The Thinking Machine was not discouraged. Instead, he thoughtfully squinted at the great arc light—there was bright sunlight now—and traced with his eyes the wire which led from it to the building. That electric wire, he reasoned, must come down the side of the building not a great distance from his cell. That might be worth knowing.

Cell 13 was on the same floor with the offices of the prison—that is, not in the basement, nor yet upstairs. There were only four steps up to the office floor, therefore the level of the floor must be only three or four feet above the ground. He couldn't see the ground directly beneath his window, but he could see it further out toward the wall. It would be an easy drop from the window. Well and good.

Then The Thinking Machine fell to remembering how he had come to the cell. First, there was the outside guard's booth, a part of the wall. There were two heavily barred gates there, both of steel. At this gate was one man always on guard. He admitted persons to the prison after much clanking of keys and locks, and let them out when ordered to do so. The warden's office was in the prison building, and in order to reach that official from the prison yard one had to pass a gate of solid steel with only a peephole in it. Then coming from that inner office to Cell 13, where he was now, one must pass a heavy wooden door and two steel doors into the corridors of the prison; and always there was the double-locked door of Cell 13 to reckon with.

There were then, The Thinking Machine recalled, seven doors to be overcome before one could pass from Cell 13 into the outer world, a free man. But against this was the fact that he was rarely interrupted. A jailer appeared at his cell door at six in the morning with a breakfast of prison fare; he would come again at noon, and again at six in the afternoon. At nine o'clock at night would come the inspection tour. That would be all.

"It's admirably arranged, this prison system," was the mental tribute paid by The Thinking Machine. "I'll have to study it a little when I get out. I had no idea there was such great care exercised in the prisons."

There was nothing, positively nothing, in his cell, except his iron bed, so firmly put together that no man could tear it to pieces save with sledges or a file. He had neither of these. There was not even a chair, or a small table, or a bit of tin or crockery. Nothing! The jailer stood by when he ate, then took away the wooden spoon and bowl which he had used.

One by one these things sank into the brain of The Thinking Machine. When the last possibility had been considered he began an examination of his cell. From the roof, down the walls on all sides, he examined the stones and the cement between them. He stamped over the floor carefully time after time, but it was cement, perfectly solid. After the examination he sat on the edge of the iron bed and was lost in thought for a long time. For Professor Augustus S. F. X. Van Dusen, The Thinking Machine, had something to think about.

He was disturbed by a rat, which ran across his foot, then scampered away into a dark corner of the cell, frightened at its own daring. After a while The Thinking Machine, squinting steadily into the darkness of the corner where the rat had gone, was able to make out in the gloom many little beady eyes staring at him. He counted six pair, and there were perhaps others; he didn't see very well.

Then The Thinking Machine, from his seat on the bed, noticed for the first time the bottom of his cell door. There was an opening there of two inches between the steel bar and the floor. Still looking steadily at this opening, The Thinking Machine backed suddenly into the corner where he had seen the beady eyes. There was a great scampering of tiny feet, several squeaks of frightened rodents, and then silence.

None of the rats had gone out the door, yet there were none in the cell. Therefore there must be another way out of the cell, however small. The Thinking Machine, on hands and knees, started a search for this spot, feeling in the darkness with his long, slender fingers.

At last his search was rewarded. He came upon a small opening in the floor, level with the cement. It was perfectly round and somewhat larger than a silver dollar. This was the way the rats had gone. He put his fingers deep into the opening; it seemed to be a disused drainage pipe and was dry and dusty.

Having satisfied himself on this point, he sat on the bed again for an hour, then made another inspection of his surroundings through the small cell window. One of the outside guards stood directly opposite, beside the wall, and happened to be looking at the window of Cell 13 when the head of The Thinking Machine appeared. But the scientist didn't notice the guard.

Noon came and the jailer appeared with the prison dinner of repulsively plain food. At home The Thinking Machine merely ate to live; here he took what was offered without comment. Occasionally he spoke to the jailer who stood outside the door watching him.

"Any improvements made here in the last few years?" he asked.

"Nothing particularly," replied the jailer. "New wall was built four years ago."

"Anything done to the prison proper?"

"Painted the woodwork outside, and I believe about seven years ago a new system of plumbing was put in."

"Ah!" said the prisoner. "How far is the river over there?"

"About three hundred feet. The boys have a baseball ground between the wall and the river."

The Thinking Machine had nothing further to say just then, but when the jailer was ready to go he asked for some water.

"I get very thirsty here," he explained. "Would it be possible for you to leave a little water in a bowl for me?"

"I'll ask the warden," replied the jailer, and he went away.

Half an hour later he returned with water in a small earthen bowl.

"The warden says you may keep this bowl," he informed the prisoner. "But you must show it to me when I ask for it. If it is broken, it will be the last."

"Thank you," said The Thinking Machine. "I shan't break it."

The jailer went on about his duties. For just the fraction of a second it seemed that The Thinking Machine wanted to ask a question, but he didn't.

Two hours later this same jailer, in passing the door of Cell No. 13, heard a noise inside and stopped. The Thinking Machine was down on his hands and knees in a corner of the cell, and from that same corner came several frightened squeaks. The jailer looked on interestedly.

"Ah, I've got you," he heard the prisoner say.

"Got what?" he asked, sharply.

"One of these rats," was the reply. "See?" And between the scientist's long fingers the jailer saw a small gray rat struggling. The prisoner brought it over to the light and looked at it closely.

"It's a water rat," he said.

"Ain't you got anything better to do than to catch rats?" asked the jailer.

"It's disgraceful that they should be here at all," was the irritated reply. "Take this one away and kill it. There are dozens more where it came from."

The jailer took the wriggling, squirmy rodent and flung it down on the floor violently. It gave one squeak and lay still. Later he reported the incident to the warden, who only smiled.

Still later that afternoon the outside armed guard on the Cell 13 side of the prison looked up again at the window and saw the prisoner looking out. He saw a hand raised to the barred window and then something white fluttered to the ground, directly under the window of Cell 13. It was a little roll of linen, evidently of white shirting material, and tied around it was a five-dollar bill. The guard looked up at the window again, but the face had disappeared.

With a grim smile he took the little linen roll and the five-dollar bill to the warden's office. There together they deciphered something which was written on it with a queer sort of ink, frequently blurred. On the outside was this:

"Finder of this please deliver to Dr. Charles Ransome."

"Ah," said the warden, with a chuckle. "Plan of escape number one has gone wrong." Then, as an afterthought: "But why did he address it to Dr. Ransome?"

"And where did he get the pen and ink to write with?" asked the guard.

The warden looked at the guard and the guard looked at the warden. There was no apparent solution of that mystery. The warden studied the writing carefully, then shook his head.

"Well, let's see what he was going to say to Dr. Ransome," he said at length, still puzzled, and he unrolled the inner piece of linen.

"Well, if that—what—what do you think of that?" he asked, dazed.

The guard took the bit of linen and read this:

"Epa cseot d'net niiy awe htto n'si sih. T."

THE warden spent an hour wondering what sort of a cipher it was, and half an hour wondering why his prisoner should attempt to communicate with Dr. Ransome, who was the cause of his being there. After this the warden devoted some thought to the question of where the prisoner got writing materials, and what sort of writing materials he had. With the idea of illuminating this point, he examined the linen again. It was a torn part of a white shirt and had ragged edges.

Now it was possible to account for the linen, but what the prisoner had used to write with was another matter. The warden knew it would have been impossible for him to have either pen or pencil, and, besides, neither pen nor pencil had been used in this writing. What, then? The warden decided to investigate personally. The Thinking Machine was his prisoner; he had orders to hold his prisoners; if this one sought to escape by sending cipher messages to persons outside, he would stop it, as he would have stopped it in the case of any other prisoner.

The warden went back to Cell 13 and found The Thinking Machine on his hands and knees on the floor, engaged in nothing more alarming than catching rats. The prisoner heard the warden's step and turned to him quickly.

"It's disgraceful," he snapped, "these rats. There are scores of them."

"Other men have been able to stand them," said the warden. "Here is another shirt for you—let me have the one you have on."

"Why?" demanded The Thinking Machine, quickly. His tone was hardly natural, his manner suggested actual perturbation.

"You have attempted to communicate with Dr. Ransome," said the warden severely. "As my prisoner, it is my duty to put a stop to it."

The Thinking Machine was silent for a moment.

"All right," he said, finally. "Do your duty."

The warden smiled grimly. The prisoner arose from the floor and removed the white shirt, putting on instead a striped convict shirt the warden had brought. The warden took the white shirt eagerly, and then and there compared the pieces of linen on which was written the cipher with certain torn places in the shirt. The Thinking Machine looked on curiously.

"The guard brought *you* those, then?" he asked.

"He certainly did," replied the warden triumphantly. "And that ends your first attempt to escape."

The Thinking Machine watched the warden as he, by comparison, established to his own satisfaction that only two pieces of linen had been torn from the white shirt.

"What did you write this with?" demanded the warden.

"I should think it a part of your duty to find out," said The Thinking Machine, irritably.

The warden started to say some harsh things, then restrained himself and made a minute search of the cell and of the prisoner instead. He found absolutely nothing; not even a match or toothpick which might have been used for a pen. The same mystery surrounded the fluid with which the cipher had been written. Although the warden left Cell 13 visibly annoyed, he took the torn shirt in triumph.

"Well, writing notes on a shirt won't get him out, that's certain," he told himself with some complacency. He put the linen scraps into his desk to await developments. "If that man escapes from that cell I'll—hang it—I'll resign."

On the third day of his incarceration The Thinking Machine openly attempted to bribe his way out. The jailer had brought his dinner and was leaning against the barred door, waiting, when The Thinking Machine began the conversation.

"The drainage pipes of the prison lead to the river, don't they?" he asked.

"Yes," said the jailer.

"I suppose they are very small."

"Too small to crawl through, if that's what you're thinking about," was the grinning response.

There was silence until The Thinking Machine finished his meal. Then:

"You know I'm not a criminal, don't you?"

"Yes."

"And that I've a perfect right to be freed if I demand it?"

"Yes."

"Well, I came here believing that I could make my escape," said the prisoner, and his squint eyes studied the face of the jailer. "Would you consider a financial reward for aiding me to escape?"

The jailer, who happened to be an honest man, looked at the slender, weak figure of the prisoner, at the large head with its mass of yellow hair, and was almost sorry.

"I guess prisons like these were not built for the likes of you to get out of," he said, at last.

"But would you consider a proposition to help me get out?" the prisoner insisted, almost beseechingly.

"No," said the jailer, shortly.

"Five hundred dollars," urged The Thinking Machine. "I am not a criminal."

"No," said the jailer.

"A thousand?"

"No," again said the jailer, and he started away hurriedly to escape further temptation. Then he turned back. "If you should give me ten thousand dollars I couldn't get you out. You'd have to pass through seven doors, and I only have the keys to two."

Then he told the warden all about it.

"Plan number two fails," said the warden, smiling grimly. "First a cipher, then bribery."

When the jailer was on his way to Cell 13 at six o'clock, again bearing food to The Thinking Machine, he paused, startled by the unmistakable scrape, scrape of steel against steel. It stopped at the sound of his steps, then craftily the jailer, who was beyond the prisoner's range of vision, resumed his tramping, the sound being apparently that of a man going away from Cell 13. As a matter of fact he was in the same spot.

After a moment there came again the steady scrape, scrape, and the jailer crept cautiously on tiptoes to the door and peered between the bars. The Thinking Machine was standing on the iron bed working at the bars of the little window. He was using a file, judging from the backward and forward swing of his arms.

Cautiously the jailer crept back to the office, summoned the warden in person, and they returned to Cell 13 on tiptoes. The steady scrape was still audible. The warden listened to satisfy himself and then suddenly appeared at the door.

"Well?" he demanded, and there was a smile on his face.

The Thinking Machine glanced back from his perch on the bed and leaped suddenly to the floor, making frantic efforts to hide something. The warden went in, with hand extended.

"Give it up," he said.

"No," said the prisoner, sharply.

"Come, give it up," urged the warden. "I don't want to have to search you again."

"No," repeated the prisoner.

"What was it—a file?" asked the warden.

The Thinking Machine was silent and stood squinting at the warden with something very nearly approaching disappointment on his face—nearly, but not quite. The warden was almost sympathetic.

"Plan number three fails, eh?" he asked, good-naturedly. "Too bad, isn't it?"

The prisoner didn't say.

"Search him," instructed the warden.

The jailer searched the prisoner carefully. At last, artfully concealed in the waistband of the trousers, he found a piece of steel about two inches long, with one side curved like a half moon.

"Ah," said the warden, as he received it from the jailer. "From your shoe heel," and he smiled pleasantly.

The jailer continued his search and on the other side of the trousers waistband found another piece of steel identical with the first. The edge showed where they had been worn against the bars of the window.

"You couldn't saw a way through those bars with these," said the warden.

"I could have," said The Thinking Machine firmly.

"In six months, perhaps," said the warden, good-naturedly.

The warden shook his head slowly as he gazed into the slightly flushed face of his prisoner.

"Ready to give it up?" he asked.

"I haven't started yet," was the prompt reply.

Then came another exhaustive search of the cell. Carefully the two men went over it, finally turning out the bed and searching that. Nothing. The warden in person climbed upon the bed and examined the bars of the window where the prisoner had been sawing. When he looked he was amused.

"Just made it a little bright by hard rubbing," he said to the prisoner, who stood looking on with a somewhat crestfallen air. The warden grasped the iron bars in his strong hands and tried to shake them. They were immovable, set firmly in the solid granite. He examined each in turn and found them all satisfactory. Finally he climbed down from the bed.

"Give it up, Professor," he advised.

The Thinking Machine shook his head and the warden and jailer passed on again. As they disappeared down the corridor The Thinking Machine sat on the edge of the bed with his head in his hands.

"He's crazy to try to get out of that cell," commented the jailer.

"Of course he can't get out," said the warden. "But he's clever. I would like to know what he wrote that cipher with."

IT was four o'clock next morning when an awful, heart-racking shriek of terror resounded through the great prison. It came from a cell, somewhere about the center, and its tone told a tale of horror, agony, terrible fear. The warden heard and with three of his men rushed into the long corridor leading to Cell 13.

As they ran there came again that awful cry. It died away in a sort of wail. The white faces of prisoners appeared at cell doors upstairs and down, staring out wonderingly, frightened.

"It's that fool in Cell Thirteen," grumbled the warden.

He stopped and stared in as one of the jailers flashed a lantern. "That fool in Cell Thirteen" lay comfortably on his cot, flat on his back with his mouth open, snoring. Even as they looked there came again the piercing cry, from somewhere above. The warden's face blanched a little as he started up the stairs. There on the top floor he found a man in Cell 43, directly above Cell 13, but two floors higher, cowering in a corner of his cell.

"What's the matter?" demanded the warden.

"Thank God you've come," exclaimed the prisoner, and he cast himself against the bars of his cell.

"What is it?" demanded the warden again.

He threw open the door and went in. The prisoner dropped on his knees and clasped the warden about the body. His face was white with terror, his eyes were widely distended, and he was shuddering. His hands, icy cold, clutched at the warden's.

"Take me out of this cell, please take me out," he pleaded.

"What's the matter with you, anyhow?" insisted the warden, impatiently.

"I heard something—something," said the prisoner, and his eyes roved nervously around the cell.

"What did you hear?"

"I—I can't tell you," stammered the prisoner. Then, in a sudden burst of terror: "Take me out of this cell—put me anywhere—but take me out of here."

The warden and the three jailers exchanged glances.

"Who is this fellow? What's he accused of?" asked the warden.

"Joseph Ballard," said one of the jailers. "He's accused of throwing acid in a woman's face. She died from it."

"But they can't prove it," gasped the prisoner. "They can't prove it. Please put me in some other cell."

He was still clinging to the warden, and that official threw his arms off roughly. Then for a time he stood looking at the cowering wretch, who seemed possessed of all the wild, unreasoning terror of a child.

"Look here, Ballard," said the warden, finally, "if you heard anything, I want to know what it was. Now tell me."

"I can't, I can't," was the reply. He was sobbing.

"Where did it come from?"

"I don't know. Everywhere—nowhere. I just heard it."

"What was it—a voice?"

"Please don't make me answer," pleaded the prisoner.

"You must answer," said the warden, sharply.

"It was a voice—but—but it wasn't human," was the sobbing reply.

"Voice, but not human?" repeated the warden, puzzled.

"It sounded muffled and—and far away—and ghostly," explained the man.

"Did it come from inside or outside the prison?"

"It didn't seem to come from anywhere—it was just here, here, every-where. I heard it. I heard it."

For an hour the warden tried to get the story, but Ballard had become suddenly obstinate and would say nothing—only pleaded to be placed in another cell, or to have one of the jailers remain near him until daylight. These requests were gruffly refused.

"And see here," said the warden, in conclusion, "if there's any more of this screaming I'll put you in the padded cell."

Then the warden went his way, a sadly puzzled man. Ballard sat at his cell door until daylight, his face, drawn and white with terror, pressed against the bars, and looked out into the prison with wide, staring eyes.

That day, the fourth since the incarceration of The Thinking Machine, was enlivened considerably by the volunteer prisoner, who spent most of his time at the little window of his cell. He began proceedings by throwing another piece of linen down to the guard, who picked it up dutifully and took it to the warden. On it was written:

"Only three days more."

The warden was in no way surprised at what he read; he understood that The Thinking Machine meant only three days more of his imprisonment, and he regarded the note as a boast. But how was the thing written? Where had The Thinking Machine found this new piece of linen? Where? How? He carefully examined the linen. It was white, of fine texture, shirting material. He took the shirt which he had taken and carefully fitted the two original pieces of the linen to the torn places. This third piece was entirely superfluous; it didn't fit anywhere, and yet it was unmistakably the same goods.

"And where—where does he get anything to write with?" demanded the warden of the world at large.

Still later on the fourth day The Thinking Machine, through the window of his cell, spoke to the armed guard outside.

"What day of the month is it?" he asked.

"The fifteenth," was the answer.

The Thinking Machine made a mental astronomical calculation and satisfied himself that the moon would not rise until after nine o'clock that night. Then he asked another question:

"Who attends to those arc lights?"

"Man from the company."

"You have no electricians in the building?"

"No."

"I should think you could save money if you had your own man."

"None of my business," replied the guard.

The guard noticed The Thinking Machine at the cell window frequently during that day, but always the face seemed listless and there was a certain wistfulness in the squint eyes behind the glasses. After a while he accepted the presence of the leonine head as a matter of course. He had seen other prisoners do the same thing; it was the longing for the outside world.

That afternoon, just before the day guard was relieved, the head appeared at the window again, and The Thinking Machine's hand held something out between the bars. It fluttered to the ground and the guard picked it up. It was a five-dollar bill.

"That's for you," called the prisoner.

As usual, the guard took it to the warden. That gentleman looked at it suspiciously; he looked at everything that came from Cell 13 with suspicion.

"He said it was for me," explained the guard.

"It's a sort of a tip, I suppose," said the warden. "I see no particular reason why you shouldn't accept—"

Suddenly he stopped. He had remembered that The Thinking Machine had gone into Cell 13 with one five-dollar bill and two ten-dollar bills; twenty-five dollars in all. Now a five-dollar bill had been tied around the first pieces of linen that came from the cell. The warden still had it, and to convince himself he took it out and looked at it. It was five dollars; yet here was another five dollars, and The Thinking Machine had only had ten-dollar bills.

"Perhaps somebody changed one of the bills for him," he thought at last, with a sigh of relief.

But then and there he made up his mind. He would search Cell 13 as a cell was never before searched in this world. When a man could write at will, and change money, and do other wholly inexplicable things, there was something radically wrong with his prison. He planned to enter the cell at night—three o'clock would be an excellent time. The Thinking Machine must do all the weird things he did sometime. Night seemed the most reasonable.

Thus it happened that the warden stealthily descended upon Cell 13 that night at three o'clock. He paused at the door and listened. There was no sound save the steady, regular breathing of the prisoner. The keys unfastened the double locks with scarcely a clank, and the warden entered, locking the door behind him. Suddenly he flashed his dark lantern in the face of the recumbent figure.

If the warden had planned to startle The Thinking Machine he was mistaken, for that individual merely opened his eyes quietly, reached for his glasses, and inquired, in a most matter-of-fact tone:

"Who is it?"

It would be useless to describe the search that the warden made. It was minute. Not one inch of the cell or the bed was overlooked. He found the round hole in the floor, and with a flash of inspiration thrust his thick fingers into it. After a moment of fumbling there he drew up something and looked at it in the light of his lantern.

"Ugh!" he exclaimed.

The thing he had taken out was a rat—a dead rat. His inspiration fled as a mist before the sun. But he continued the search. The Thinking Machine, without a word, arose and kicked the rat out of the cell into the corridor.

The warden climbed on the bed and tried the steel bars in the tiny window. They were perfectly rigid; every bar of the door was the same.

Then the warden searched the prisoner's clothing, beginning at the shoes. Nothing hidden in them! Then the trousers waistband. Still nothing! Then the pockets of the trousers. From one side he drew out some paper money and examined it.

"Five one-dollar bills," he gasped.

"That's right," said the prisoner.

"But the—you had two tens and a five—what the—how do you do it?"

"That's my business," said The Thinking Machine.

"Did any of my men change this money for you—on your word of honor?"

The Thinking Machine paused just a fraction of a second.

"No," he said.

"Well, do you make it?" asked the warden. He was prepared to believe anything.

"That's my business," again said the prisoner.

The warden glared at the eminent scientist fiercely. He felt—he knew—that this man was making a fool of him, yet he didn't know how. If he were a real prisoner he would get the truth—but, then, perhaps, those inexplicable things which had happened would not have been brought before him so sharply. Neither of the men spoke for a long time, then suddenly the warden turned fiercely and left the cell, slamming the door behind him. He didn't dare to speak, then.

He glanced at the clock. It was ten minutes to four. He had hardly settled himself in bed when again came that heartbreaking shriek through the prison. With a few muttered words, which, while not elegant, were highly expressive, he relighted his lantern and rushed through the prison again to the cell on the upper floor.

Again Ballard was crushing himself against the steel door, shrieking, shrieking at the top of his voice. He stopped only when the warden flashed his lamp in the cell.

"Take me out, take me out," he screamed. "I did it, I did it, I killed her. Take it away."

"Take what away?" asked the warden.

"I threw the acid in her face—I did it—I confess. Take me out of here."

Ballard's condition was pitiable; it was only an act of mercy to let him out into the corridor. There he crouched in a corner, like an animal at bay, and clasped his hands to his ears. It took half an hour to calm him sufficiently for him to speak. Then he told incoherently what had happened. On the night before at four o'clock he had heard a voice—a sepulchral voice, muffled and wailing in tone.

"What did it say?" asked the warden, curiously.

"Acid—acid—acid!" gasped the prisoner. "It accused me. Acid! I threw the acid, and the woman died. Oh!" It was a long, shuddering wail of terror.

"Acid?" echoed the warden, puzzled. The case was beyond him.

"Acid. That's all I heard—that one word, repeated several times. There were other things, too, but I didn't hear them."

"That was last night, eh?" asked the warden. "What happened tonight—what frightened you just now?"

"It was the same thing," gasped the prisoner. "Acid—acid—acid!" He covered his face with his hands and sat shivering. "It was acid I used on her, but I didn't mean to kill her. I just heard the words. It was something accusing me—accusing me." He mumbled, and was silent.

"Did you hear anything else?"

"Yes—but I couldn't understand—only a little bit—just a word or two."

"Well, what was it?"

"I heard 'acid' three times, then I heard a long, moaning sound, then—then—I heard 'number eight hat.' I heard that twice."

"Number eight hat," repeated the warden. "What the devil—number eight hat? Accusing voices of conscience have never talked about number eight hats, so far as I ever heard."

"He's insane," said one of the jailers, with an air of finality.

"I believe you," said the warden. "He must be. He probably heard something and got frightened. He's trembling now. Number eight hat! What the—"

WHEN the fifth day of The Thinking Machine's imprisonment rolled around the warden was wearing a hunted look. He was anxious for the end of the thing. He could not help but feel that his distinguished prisoner had been amusing himself. And if this were so, The Thinking Machine had lost none of his sense of humor. For on this fifth day he flung down another linen note to the outside guard, bearing the words "Only two days more." Also he flung down half a dollar.

Now the warden knew—he *knew*—that the man in Cell 13 didn't have any half dollars—he *couldn't* have any half dollars, no more than he could have pen and ink and linen, and yet he did have them. It was a condition, not a theory; that is one reason why the warden was wearing a hunted look.

That ghastly, uncanny thing, too, about "acid" and "number eight hat" clung to him tenaciously. They didn't mean anything, of course, merely the ravings of an insane murderer who had been driven by fear to confess his crime, still there were so many things that "didn't mean anything" happening in the prison now since The Thinking Machine was there.

On the sixth day the warden received a postal stating that Dr. Ransome and Mr. Fielding would be at Chisholm Prison on the following evening, Thursday, and in the event Professor Van Dusen had not yet escaped—and they presumed he had not because they had not heard from him—they would meet him there.

"In the event he had not yet escaped!" The warden smiled grimly. Escaped!

The Thinking Machine enlivened this day for the warden with three notes. They were on the usual linen and bore generally on the appointment at half past eight o'clock Thursday night, which appointment the scientist had made at the time of his imprisonment.

On the afternoon of the seventh day the warden passed Cell 13 and glanced in. The Thinking Machine was lying on the iron bed, apparently sleeping lightly. The cell appeared precisely as it always did from a casual glance. The warden would swear that no man was going to leave it between that hour— it was then four o'clock—and half past eight o'clock that evening.

On his way back past the cell the warden heard the steady breathing again, and coming closer to the door, looked in. He wouldn't have done so if The Thinking Machine had been looking, but now—well, it was different.

A ray of light came through the high window and fell on the face of the sleeping man. It occurred to the warden for the first time that his prisoner appeared haggard and weary. Just then The Thinking Machine stirred slightly and the warden hurried on up the corridor guiltily. That evening after six o'clock he saw the jailer.

"Everything all right in Cell Thirteen?" he asked.

"Yes, sir," replied the jailer. "He didn't eat much, though."

It was with a feeling of having done his duty that the warden received Dr. Ransome and Mr. Fielding shortly after seven o'clock. He intended to show them the linen notes and lay before them the full story of his woes, which was a long one. But before this came to pass the guard from the river side of the prison yard entered the office.

"The arc light in my side of the yard won't light," he informed the warden.

"Confound it, that man's a hoodoo," thundered the official. "Everything has happened since he's been here."

The guard went back to his post in the darkness, and the warden phoned to the electric light company.

"This is Chisholm Prison," he said through the phone. "Send three or four men down here quick, to fix an arc light."

The reply was evidently satisfactory, for the warden hung up the receiver and passed out into the yard. While Dr. Ransome and Mr. Fielding sat waiting the guard at the outer gate came in with a special-delivery letter. Dr. Ransome happened to notice the address, and, when the guard went out, looked at the letter more closely.

"By George!" he exclaimed.

"What is it?" asked Mr. Fielding.

Silently the doctor offered the letter. Mr. Fielding examined it closely.

"Coincidence," he said. "It must be."

It was nearly eight o'clock when the warden returned to his office. The electricians had arrived in a wagon, and were now at work. The warden pressed the buzz-button communicating with the man at the outer gate in the wall.

"How many electricians came in?" he asked, over the short phone. "Four? Three workmen in jumpers and overalls and the manager? Frock coat and silk hat? All right. Be certain that only four go out. That's all."

He turned to Dr. Ransome and Mr. Fielding.

"We have to be careful here—particularly," and there was broad sarcasm in his tone, "since we have scientists locked up."

The warden picked up the special-delivery letter carelessly, and then began to open it.

"When I read this I want to tell you gentlemen something about how— Great Caesar!" he ended, suddenly, as he glanced at the letter. He sat with mouth open, motionless, from astonishment.

"What is it?" asked Mr. Fielding.

"A special-delivery letter from Cell Thirteen," gasped the warden. "An invitation to supper."

"What?" and the two others arose.

The warden sat dazed, staring at the letter for a moment, then called sharply to a guard outside in the corridor.

"Run down to Cell Thirteen and see if that man's in there."

The guard went as directed, while Dr. Ransome and Mr. Fielding examined the letter.

"It's Van Dusen's handwriting; there's no question of that," said Dr. Ransome. "I've seen too much of it."

Just then the buzz on the telephone from the outer gate sounded, and the warden, in a semitrance, picked up the receiver.

"Hello! Two reporters, eh? Let 'em come in." He turned suddenly to the doctor and Mr. Fielding. "Why, the man *can't* be out. He must be in his cell."

Just at that moment the guard returned.

"He's still in his cell, sir," he reported. "I saw him. He's lying down."

"There, I told you so," said the warden, and he breathed freely again. "But how did he mail that letter?"

There was a rap on the steel door which led from the jail yard into the warden's office.

"It's the reporters," said the warden. "Let them in," he instructed the guard; then to the two other gentlemen: "Don't say anything about this before them, because I'd never hear the last of it."

The door opened, and the two men from the front gate entered.

"Good evening, gentlemen," said one. That was Hutchinson Hatch; the warden knew him well.

"Well?" demanded the other, irritably. "I'm here."

That was The Thinking Machine.

He squinted belligerently at the warden, who sat with mouth agape. For the moment that official had nothing to say. Dr. Ransome and Mr. Fielding were amazed, but they didn't know what the warden knew. They were only amazed; he was paralyzed. Hutchinson Hatch, the reporter, took in the scene with greedy eyes.

"How—how—how did you do it?" gasped the warden, finally.

"Come back to the cell," said The Thinking Machine, in the irritated voice which his scientific associates knew so well.

The warden, still in a condition bordering on trance, led the way.

"Flash your light in there," directed The Thinking Machine.

The warden did so. There was nothing unusual in the appearance of the cell, and there—there on the bed lay the figure of The Thinking Machine. Certainly! There was the yellow hair! Again the warden looked at the man beside him and wondered at the strangeness of his own dreams.

With trembling hands he unlocked the cell door and The Thinking Machine passed inside.

"See here," he said.

He kicked at the steel bars in the bottom of the cell door and three of them were pushed out of place. A fourth broke off and rolled away in the corridor.

"And here, too," directed the erstwhile prisoner as he stood on the bed to reach the small window. He swept his hand across the opening and every bar came out.

"What's this in bed?" demanded the warden, who was slowly recovering.

"A wig," was the reply. "Turn down the cover."

The warden did so. Beneath it lay a large coil of strong rope, thirty feet or more, a dagger, three files, ten feet of electric wire, a thin, powerful pair of steel pliers, a small tack hammer with its handle, and—and a derringer pistol.

"How did you do it?" demanded the warden.

"You gentlemen have an engagement to supper with me at half past nine o'clock," said The Thinking Machine. "Come on, or we shall be late."

"But how did you do it?" insisted the warden.

"Don't ever think you can hold any man who can use his brain," said The Thinking Machine. "Come on; we shall be late."

IT was an impatient supper party in the rooms of Professor Van Dusen and a somewhat silent one. The guests were Dr. Ransome, Alfred Fielding, the warden, and Hutchinson Hatch, reporter. The meal was served to the minute, in accordance with Professor Van Dusen's instructions of one week before; Dr. Ransome found the artichokes delicious. At last the supper was finished and The Thinking Machine turned full on Dr. Ransome and squinted at him fiercely.

"Do you believe it now?" he demanded.

"I do," replied Dr. Ransome.

"Do you admit that it was a fair test?"

"I do."

With the others, particularly the warden, he was waiting anxiously for the explanation.

"Suppose you tell us how—" began Mr. Fielding.

"Yes, tell us how," said the warden.

The Thinking Machine readjusted his glasses, took a couple of preparatory squints at his audience, and began the story. He told it from the beginning logically; and no man ever talked to more interested listeners.

"My agreement was," he began, "to go into a cell, carrying nothing except what was necessary to wear, and to leave that cell within a week. I had never seen Chisholm Prison. When I went into the cell I asked for tooth powder, two ten and one five-dollar bills, and also to have my shoes blacked. Even if these requests had been refused it would not have mattered seriously. But you agreed to them.

"I knew there would be nothing in the cell which you thought I might use to advantage. So when the warden locked the door on me I was apparently helpless, unless I could turn three seemingly innocent things to use. They were things which would have been permitted any prisoner under sentence of death, were they not, warden?"

"Tooth powder and polished shoes, yes, but not money," replied the warden.

"Anything is dangerous in the hands of a man who knows how to use it," went on The Thinking Machine. "I did nothing that first night but sleep and chase rats." He glared at the warden. "When the matter was broached I knew I could do nothing that night, so suggested next day. You gentlemen thought I wanted time to arrange an escape with outside assistance, but this was not true. I knew I could communicate with whom I pleased, when I pleased."

The warden stared at him a moment, then went on smoking solemnly.

"I was aroused next morning at six o'clock by the jailer with my breakfast," continued the scientist. "He told me dinner was at twelve and supper at six. Between these times, I gathered, I would be pretty much to myself. So immediately after breakfast I examined my outside surroundings from my cell window. One look told me it would be useless to try to scale the wall, even should I decide to leave my cell by the window, for my purpose was to leave not only the cell, but the prison. Of course, I could have gone over the wall, but it would have taken me longer to lay my plans that way. Therefore, for the moment, I dismissed all idea of that.

"From this first observation I knew the river was on that side of the prison, and that there was also a playground there. Subsequently these surmises were verified by a keeper. I knew then one important thing—that anyone might approach the prison wall from that side if necessary without attracting any particular attention. That was well to remember. I remembered it.

"But the outside thing which most attracted my attention was the feed wire to the arc light which ran within a few feet—probably three or four—of my cell window. I knew that would be valuable in the event I found it necessary to cut off that arc light."

"Oh, you shut it off tonight, then?" asked the warden.

"Having learned all I could from that window," resumed The Thinking

Machine, without heeding the interruption, "I considered the idea of escaping through the prison proper. I recalled just how I had come into the cell, which I knew would be the only way. Seven doors lay between me and the outside. So, also for the time being, I gave up the idea of escaping that way. And I couldn't go through the solid granite walls of the cell."

The Thinking Machine paused for a moment and Dr. Ransome lighted a new cigar. For several minutes there was silence, then the scientific jailbreaker went on:

"While I was thinking about these things a rat ran across my foot. It suggested a new line of thought. There were at least half a dozen rats in the cell—I could see their beady eyes. Yet I had noticed none come under the cell door. I frightened them purposely and watched the cell door to see if they went out that way. They did not, but they were gone. Obviously they went another way. Another way meant another opening.

"I searched for this opening and found it. It was an old drain pipe, long unused and partly choked with dirt and dust. But this was the way the rats had come. They came from somewhere. Where? Drain pipes usually lead outside prison grounds. This one probably led to the river, or near it. The rats must therefore come from that direction. If they came a part of the way, I reasoned that they came all the way, because it was extremely unlikely that a solid iron or lead pipe would have any hole in it except at the exit.

"When the jailer came with my luncheon he told me two important things, although he didn't know it. One was that a new system of plumbing had been put in the prison seven years before; another that the river was only three hundred feet away. Then I knew positively that the pipe was a part of an old system; I knew, too, that it slanted generally toward the river. But did the pipe end in the water or on land?

"This was the next question to be decided. I decided it by catching several of the rats in the cell. My jailer was surprised to see me engaged in this work. I examined at least a dozen of them. They were perfectly dry; they had come through the pipe, and, most important of all, they were *not house rats, but field rats*. The other end of the pipe was on land, then, outside the prison walls. So far, so good.

"Then, I knew that if I worked freely from this point I must attract the warden's attention in another direction. You see, by telling the warden that I had come there to escape you made the test more severe, because I had to trick him by false scents."

The warden looked up with a sad expression in his eyes.

"The first thing was to make him think I was trying to communicate with you, Dr. Ransome. So I wrote a note on a piece of linen I tore from my shirt, addressed it to Dr. Ransome, tied a five-dollar bill around it, and threw it out the window. I knew the guard would take it to the warden, but I rather hoped the warden would send it as addressed. Have you that first linen note, Warden?"

The warden produced the cipher.

"What the deuce does it mean, anyhow?" he asked.

"Read it backward, beginning with the *T* signature and disregard the division into words," instructed The Thinking Machine.

The warden did so.

"*T-h-i-s*, this," he spelled, studied it a moment, then read it off, grinning: "This is not the way I intend to escape."

"Well, now what do you think o' that?" he demanded, still grinning.

"I knew that would attract your attention, just as it did," said The Thinking Machine, "and if you really found out what it was it would be a sort of gentle rebuke."

"What did you write it with?" asked Dr. Ransome, after he had examined the linen and passed it to Mr. Fielding.

"This," said the erstwhile prisoner, and he extended his foot. On it was the shoe he had worn in prison, though the polish was gone—scraped off clean. "The shoe blacking, moistened with water, was my ink; the metal tip of the shoelace made a fairly good pen."

The warden looked up and suddenly burst into a laugh, half of relief, half of amusement.

"You're a wonder," he said, admiringly. "Go on."

"That precipitated a search of my cell by the warden, as I had intended," continued The Thinking Machine. "I was anxious to get the warden into the habit of searching my cell, so that finally, constantly finding nothing, he would get disgusted and quit. This at last happened, practically."

The warden blushed.

"He then took my white shirt away and gave me a prison shirt. He was satisfied that those two pieces of the shirt were all that was missing. But while he was searching my cell I had another piece of that same shirt, about nine inches square, rolled into a small ball in my mouth."

"Nine inches of that shirt?" demanded the warden. "Where did it come from?"

"The bosoms of all stiff white shirts are of triple thickness," was the explanation. "I tore out the inside thickness, leaving the bosom only two thicknesses. I knew you wouldn't see it. So much for that."

There was a little pause, and the warden looked from one to another of the men with a sheepish grin.

"Having disposed of the warden for the time being by giving him something else to think about, I took my first serious step toward freedom," said Professor Van Dusen. "I knew, within reason, that the pipe led somewhere to the playground outside; I knew a great many boys played there; I knew that rats came into my cell from out there. Could I communicate with some one outside with these things at hand?

"First was necessary, I saw, a long and fairly reliable thread, so—but here," he pulled up his trousers legs and showed that the tops of both stockings, of fine, strong lisle, were gone. "I unraveled those—after I got them started it wasn't difficult—and I had easily a quarter of a mile of thread that I could depend on.

"Then on half of my remaining linen I wrote, laboriously enough I assure you, a letter explaining my situation to this gentleman here," and he indicated Hutchinson Hatch. "I knew he would assist me—for the value of the newspaper story. I tied firmly to this linen letter a ten-dollar bill—there is no surer way of attracting the eye of anyone—and wrote on the linen: 'Finder of this deliver to Hutchinson Hatch, *Daily American*, who will give another ten dollars for the information.'

"The next thing was to get this note outside on that playground where a boy might find it. There were two ways, but I chose the best. I took one of the rats—I became adept in catching them—tied the linen and money firmly to one leg, fastened my lisle thread to another, and turned him loose in the drain pipe. I reasoned that the natural fright of the rodent would make him run until he was outside the pipe and then out on earth he would probably stop to gnaw off the linen and money.

"From the moment the rat disappeared into that dusty pipe I became anxious. I was taking so many chances. The rat might gnaw the string, of which I held one end; other rats might gnaw it; the rat might run out of the pipe and leave the linen and money where they would never be found; a thousand other things might have happened. So began some nervous hours, but the fact that the rat ran on until only a few feet of the string remained in my cell made me think he was outside the pipe. I had carefully instructed Mr. Hatch what to do in case the note reached him. The question was: would it reach him?

"This done, I could only wait and make other plans in case this one failed. I openly attempted to bribe my jailer, and learned from him that he held the keys to only two of seven doors between me and freedom. Then I did something else to make the warden nervous. I took the steel supports out of the heels of my shoes and made a pretense of sawing the bars of my cell window. The warden raised a pretty row about that. He developed, too, the habit of shaking the bars of my cell window to see if they were solid. They were— then."

Again the warden grinned. He had ceased being astonished.

"With this one plan I had done all I could and could only wait to see what happened," the scientist went on. "I couldn't know whether my note had been delivered or even found, or whether the mouse had gnawed it up. And I didn't dare to draw back through the pipe that one slender thread which connected me with the outside.

"When I went to bed that night I didn't sleep, for fear there would come the slight signal twitch at the thread which was to tell me that Mr. Hatch had received the note. At half past three o'clock, I judge, I felt this twitch, and no prisoner actually under sentence of death ever welcomed a thing more heartily."

The Thinking Machine stopped and turned to the reporter.

"You'd better explain just what you did," he said.

"The linen note was brought to me by a small boy who had been playing baseball," said Mr. Hatch. "I immediately saw a big story in it, so I gave the boy another ten dollars, and got several spools of silk, some twine, and a roll of light, pliable wire. The professor's note suggested that I have the finder of the note show me just where it was picked up, and told me to make my search from there, beginning at two o'clock in the morning. If I found the other end of the thread I was to twitch it gently three times, then a fourth.

"I began the search with a small-bulb electric light. It was an hour and twenty minutes before I found the end of the drain pipe, half-hidden in weeds. The pipe was very large there, say twelve inches across. Then I found the end of the lisle thread, twitched it as directed and immediately I got an answering twitch.

"Then I fastened the silk to this and Professor Van Dusen began to pull it into his cell. I nearly had heart disease for fear the string would break. To the end of the silk I fastened the twine, and when that had been pulled in, I tied on the wire. Then that was drawn into the pipe and we had a substantial line, which rats couldn't gnaw, from the mouth of the drain into the cell."

The Thinking Machine raised his hand and Hatch stopped.

"All this was done in absolute silence," said the scientist. "But when the wire reached my hand I could have shouted. Then we tried another experiment, which Mr. Hatch was prepared for. I tested the pipe as a speaking tube. Neither of us could hear very clearly, but I dared not speak loud for fear of attracting attention in the prison. At last I made him understand what I wanted immediately. He seemed to have great difficulty in understanding when I asked for nitric acid, and I repeated the word 'acid' several times.

"Then I heard a shriek from a cell above me. I knew instantly that someone had overheard, and when I heard you coming, Mr. Warden, I feigned sleep. If you had entered my cell at that moment that whole plan of escape would have ended there. But you passed on. That was the nearest I ever came to being caught.

"Having established this improvised trolley it is easy to see how I got things in the cell and made them disappear at will. I merely dropped them back into the pipe. You, Mr. Warden, could not have reached the connecting wire with your fingers; they are too large. My fingers, you see, are longer and more slender. In addition I guarded the top of that pipe with a rat—you remember how."

"I remember," said the warden, with a grimace.

"I thought that if anyone were tempted to investigate that hole the rat would dampen his ardor. Mr. Hatch could not send me anything useful through the pipe until the next night, although he did send me change for ten dollars as a test, so I proceeded with other parts of my plan. Then I evolved the method of escape which I finally employed.

"In order to carry this out successfully it was necessary for the guard in the yard to get accustomed to seeing me at the cell window. I arranged this by dropping linen notes to him, boastful in tone, to make the warden believe, if possible, one of his assistants was communicating with the outside for me. I would stand at my window for hours gazing out, so the guard could see, and occasionally I spoke to him. In that way I learned that the prison had no electricians of its own, but was dependent upon the lighting company if anything should go wrong.

"That cleared the way to freedom perfectly. Early in the evening of the last day of my imprisonment, when it was dark, I planned to cut the feed wire which was only a few feet from my window, reaching it with an acid-tipped wire I had. That would make that side of the prison perfectly dark while the electricians were searching for the break. That would also bring Mr. Hatch into the prison yard.

"There was only one more thing to do before I actually began the work of setting myself free. This was to arrange final details with Mr. Hatch through our speaking tube. I did this within half an hour after the warden left my cell on the fourth night of my imprisonment. Mr. Hatch again had serious difficulty in understanding me, and I repeated the word 'acid' to him several times, and later on the words 'number eight hat'—that's my size—and these were the things which made a prisoner upstairs confess to murder, so one of the jailers told me next day. This prisoner heard our voices, confused of course, through the pipe, which also went to his cell. The cell directly over me was not occupied, hence no one else heard.

"Of course the actual work of cutting the steel bars out of the window and door was comparatively easy with nitric acid, which I got through the pipe in tin bottles, but it took time. Hour after hour on the fifth and sixth and seventh days the guard below was looking at me as I worked on the bars of the window with the acid on a piece of wire. I used the tooth powder to prevent the acid spreading. I looked away abstractedly as I worked and each minute the acid cut deeper into the metal. I noticed that the jailers always tried the door by shaking the upper part, never the lower bars; therefore I cut the lower bars, leaving them hanging in place by thin strips of metal. But that was a bit of daredeviltry. I could not have gone that way so easily."

The Thinking Machine sat silent for several minutes.

"I think that makes everything clear," he went on. "Whatever points I have not explained were merely to confuse the warden and jailers. These things in my bed I brought in to please Mr. Hatch, who wanted to improve the story. Of course, the wig was necessary in my plan. The special-delivery letter I wrote and directed in my cell with Mr. Hatch's fountain pen, then sent it out to him and he mailed it. That's all, I think."

"But your actually leaving the prison grounds and then coming in through the outer gate to my office?" asked the warden.

"Perfectly simple," said the scientist. "I cut the electric light wire with acid, as I said, when the current was off. Therefore when the current was turned on the arc didn't light. I knew it would take some time to find out what was the matter and make repairs. When the guard went to report to you the yard was dark, I crept out the window—it was a tight fit, too—replaced the bars by standing on a narrow ledge, and remained in a shadow until the force of electricians arrived. Mr. Hatch was one of them.

"When I saw him I spoke and he handed me a cap, a jumper, and overalls, which I put on within ten feet of you, Mr. Warden, while you were in the yard. Later Mr. Hatch called me, presumably as a workman, and together we went out the gate to get something out of the wagon. The gate guard let us pass out readily as two workmen who had just passed in. We changed our clothing and reappeared, asking to see you. We saw you. That's all."

There was silence for several minutes. Dr. Ransome was first to speak.

"Wonderful!" he exclaimed. "Perfectly amazing."

"How did Mr. Hatch happen to come with the electricians?" asked Mr. Fielding.

"His father is manager of the company," replied The Thinking Machine.

"But what if there had been no Mr. Hatch outside to help?"

"Every prisoner has one friend outside who would help him escape if he could."

"Suppose—just suppose—there had been no old plumbing system there?" asked the warden, curiously.

"There were two other ways out," said The Thinking Machine, enigmatically.

Ten minutes later the telephone bell rang. It was a request for the warden.

"Light all right, eh?" the warden asked, through the phone. "Good. Wire cut beside Cell Thirteen? Yes, I know. One electrician too many? What's that? Two came out?"

The warden turned to the others with a puzzled expression.

"He only let in four electricians; he has let out two and says there are three left."

"I was the odd one," said The Thinking Machine.

"Oh," said the warden. "I see." Then through the phone: "Let the fifth man go. He's all right."

ED GORMAN

Emile Zola is responsible for "En Famille." I went to college with the poet Mary Haines. A few years ago, she was editing a collection of literary stories, and called to reminisce about the coffee-and-cigarette college discussions we used to have about French writers. She asked me if I still read a lot of Zola and I said I hadn't in quite a few years. I went to the library shortly thereafter, and checked out a book of his stories. Not a bad one in the whole collection, and many of them powerful and unforgettable. I'd had the central idea for "En Famille" for years but couldn't get it right. Zola, with his emphasis on heredity and environment, showed me how to do it.

Stephen Crane was always able to capture the essential strangeness *of people, their isolation and quiet sorrow in even the most social of situations.* The Red Badge of Courage *is filled with such portraits, set against the society of an army at war. "The Blue Hotel" gives us another kind of society, that of hard, sly men dealing with an odd and somewhat disturbing stranger. Crane plays brilliantly with reality here—whose "truth" is the real truth, who is truly the victim? We think of hell as hot; here Crane shows us that hell can also be howling prairie winter.*

En Famille

By THE TIME I was eight years old, I'd fallen disconsolately in love with any number of little girls who had absolutely no interest in me. These were little girls I'd met in all the usual places: school, playground, neighborhood.

Only the girl I met at the racetrack took any interest in me. Her name was Wendy and, like me, she was brought to the track three or four times a week by her father, after school in the autumn months, during working hours in the summer.

Ours was one of those impossibly romantic relationships that only a young boy can have (all those nights of kissing pillows, pretending it was her, while my mind played one of those swelling romantic songs you hear in movies with Ingrid Bergman and Cary Grant: How vulnerable and true and beautiful she always was in my mind's perfect eye). I first saw her the spring of my ninth year, and not until I was fifteen did we even say hello to each other, even though we saw each other at least three times a week. But she was always with me, this girl I thought about constantly, and dreamed of nightly, the melancholy little blonde with the slow sad blue eyes and the quick sad smile.

I knew all about the sadness I saw in her. It was my sadness, too. Our fathers brought us to the track in order to make their gambling more palatable to our mothers. How much of a vice could it be if you took the little one along? The money lost at the track meant rent going unpaid, grocery-store credit cut off, the telephone frequently disconnected. It also meant arguing.

No matter how deeply I hid in the closet, no matter how many pillows I put over my head, I could still hear them shrieking at each other. Sometimes he hit her. Once he even pushed her down the stairs and she broke her leg. Despite all this, I wanted them to stay together. I was terrified they would split up. I loved them both beyond imagining. Don't ask me why I loved him so much. I have no idea.

The day we first spoke, the little girl and I, that warm May afternoon in my fifteenth year, a black eye spoiled her very pretty, very pale little face. So he'd finally gotten around to hitting her. My father had gotten around to hitting me years ago. They got so frustrated over their gambling, their inability to *stop* their gambling, that they grabbed the first person they found and visited all their despair on him.

She was coming up from the seats in the bottom tier where she and her father always sat. I saw her and stepped out into the aisle.

"Hi," I said after more than six years of us watching each other from afar.

"Hi."

"I'm sorry about your eye."

"He was pretty drunk. He doesn't usually get violent. But it seems to be getting worse lately." She looked back at their seats. Her father was glaring at us. "I'd better hurry. He wants me to get him a hot dog."

"I'd like to see you sometime."

She smiled, sad and sweet with her black eye. "Yeah, me too."

I saw her the rest of the summer but we never again got the chance to speak. Nor did we make the opportunity. She was my narcotic. I thought of no one else, wanted no one else. The girls at school had no idea what my home life was like, how old and worn my father's gambling had made my mother, how anxious and angry it had made me. Only Wendy understood.

Wendy Wendy Wendy. By now, my needs having evolved, she was no longer just the pure dream of a forlorn boy. I wanted her carnally, too. She'd become a beautiful young woman.

Near the end of that summer an unseasonable rainy grayness filled the skies. People at the track took to wearing winter coats. A few races had to be called off. Wendy and her father suddenly vanished.

I looked for them every day, and every night trudged home feeling betrayed and bereft. "Can't find your little girlfriend?" my father said. He thought it was funny.

Then one night, while I was in my bedroom reading a science fiction magazine, he shouted: "Hey! Get out here! Your girlfriend's on TV!"

And so she was.

"Police announce an arrest in the murder of Myles Larkin, who was found stabbed to death in his car last night. They have taken Larkin's only child, sixteen-year-old Wendy, into custody and formally charged her with the murder of her father."

I went twice to see her but they wouldn't let me in. Finally, I learned the name of her lawyer, lied that I was a shirt-tail cousin, and he took me up to the cold concrete visitors' room on the top floor of the city jail.

Even in the drab uniform the prisoners wore, she looked lovely in her bruised and wan way.

"Did he start beating you up again?" I asked.

"No."

"Did he start beating up your mother?"

"No."

"Did he lose his job or get you evicted?"

She shook her head. "No. It was just that I couldn't take it anymore. I mean, he wasn't losing any more or any less money at the track, it was just I—I snapped. I don't know how else to explain it. It was like I saw what he'd done to our lives and I—I snapped. That's all—I just snapped."

She served seven years in a minimum-security women's prison upstate, during which time my parents were killed in an automobile accident, I finished college, got married, had a child, and took up the glamorous and adventurous life of a tax consultant. My wife Donna knew about my mental and spiritual ups and downs. Her father had been an abusive alcoholic.

I didn't see Wendy until twelve years later, when I was sitting at the track with my seven-year-old son. He didn't always like going to the track with me—my wife didn't like me going to the track at all—so I'd had to fortify him with the usual comic books, candy, and a pair of "genuine" Dodgers sunglasses.

Between races, I happened to look down at the seats Wendy and her father usually took, and there she was. Something about the cock of her head told me it was her.

"Can we go, Dad?" my son Rob said. "It's so boring here."

Boring? I'd once tried to explain to his mother how good I felt when I was at the track. I was not the miserable, frightened, self-effacing owner of Advent Tax Systems (some system—me and my low-power Radio Shack computer and software). No. . . . When I was at the track I felt strong and purposeful and optimistic, and frightened of nothing at all. I was pure potential—potential for winning the easy cash that was the mark of men who were successful with women, and with their competitors, and with their own swaggering dreams.

"Please, Dad. It's really boring here. Honest."

But all I could see, all I could think about, was Wendy. I hadn't seen her since my one visit to the jail. Then I noticed that she, too, had a child with her, a very proper-looking little blonde girl whose head was cocked at the odd and fetching angle so favored by her mother.

We saw each other a dozen more times before we spoke.

Then: "I knew I'd see you again someday."

Wan smile. "All those years I was in prison, I wasn't so sure." Her daughter came up to her then and Wendy said: "This is Margaret."

"Hello, Margaret. Glad to meet you. This is my son Rob."

With the great indifference only children can summon, they nodded hellos.

"We just moved back to the city," Wendy explained. "I thought I'd show Margaret where I used to come with my father." She mentioned her father so casually, one would never have guessed that she'd murdered the man.

Ten more times we saw each other, children in tow, before our affair began.

April sixth of that year was the first time we ever made love, this in a motel where the sunset was the color of blood in the window, and a woman two rooms away wept inconsolably. I had the brief fantasy that it was my wife in that room.

"Do you know how long I've loved you?" she said.

"Oh, God, you don't know how good it is to hear that."

"Since I was eight years old."

"For me, since I was nine."

"This would destroy my husband if he ever found out."

"The same with my wife."

"But I have to be honest."

"I want you to be honest."

"I don't care what it does to him. I just want to be with you."

In December of that year, my wife Donna discovered a lump in her right breast. Two weeks later she received a double mastectomy and began chemotherapy.

She lived nine years, and my affair with Wendy extended over the entire time. Early on, both our spouses knew about our relationship. Her husband, an older and primmer man than I might have expected, stopped by my office one day in his new BMW and threatened to destroy my business. He claimed to have great influence in the financial community.

My wife threatened to leave me, but she was too weak. She had one of those cancers that did not kill her but that never left her alone, either. She was weak most of the time, staying for days in the bedroom that had become hers, as the guest room had become mine. Whenever she became particularly angry about Wendy, Rob would fling himself at me, screaming how much he hated me, pounding me with fists that became more powerful with each passing year. He hated me for many of the same reasons I'd hated my own father, my ineluctable passion for the track, and the way there was never any security in our lives, the family bank account wholly subject to the whims of the horses that ran that day.

Wendy's daughter likewise blamed her mother for the alcoholism that had stricken the husband. There was constant talk of divorce, but their finances were such that neither of them could quite afford it. Margaret constantly called Wendy a whore, and after a while Wendy realized that Margaret sincerely meant it.

Two things happened the next year. My wife was finally dragged off into the darkness, and Wendy's husband crashed his car into a retaining wall and was killed.

Even on the days of the respective funerals, we went to the track.

"He never understood."

"Neither did she," I said.

"I mean why I come here."

"I know."

"I mean how it makes me feel alive."

"I know."

"I mean how nothing else matters."

"I know."

"I should've been nicer to him, I suppose."

"I suppose. But we can't make a life out of blaming ourselves. What's happened, happened. We have to go on from here."

"Do you think Rob hates you as much as Margaret hates me?"

"More, probably," I said. "The way he looks at me sometimes, I think he'll probably kill me someday."

But it wasn't me who was to die.

All during Wendy's funeral, I kept thinking of those words. Margaret had murdered her mother just as Wendy had killed her father. The press made a lot of this.

All the grief I should have visited upon my dead wife I visited upon my dead lover. I went through months of alcoholic stupor. Clients fell away; rent forced me to move from our nice suburban home to a small apartment in a section of the city that always seemed to be on fire. I didn't have to worry about Rob anymore. He got enough loans for college and wanted nothing to do with me.

Years and more years, the track the only constant in my life. Many times I tried to contact Rob through the alumni office of his school but it was no use. He'd left word not to give his current address to his father.

There was the hospital, and, several times, the detox clinic. There was the church in which I asked for forgiveness, and the born-again rally at which I proclaimed my happiness in the Lord.

And then there was the shelter. Five years I lived there, keeping the place painted and clean for the other residents. The nuns seemed to like me.

My teeth went entirely, and I had to have dentures. The arthritis in my foot got so bad that I could not wear shoes for days at a time. And my eyesight, beyond even the magic of glasses, got so bad that when I watched the horse races on TV, I couldn't tell which horse was which.

Then one night I got sick and threw up blood and in the morning one of the sisters took me to the hospital where they kept me overnight. In the morning the doctor came in and told me that I had stomach cancer. He gave me five months to live.

There were days when I was happy about my death sentence. Looking back, my life seemed so long and sad, I was glad to have it over with. Then there were days when I sobbed about it, and hated the God the nuns told me to pray to. I wanted to live to go back to the track again and have a sweet, beautiful winner.

Four months after the doctor's diagnosis, the nuns put me in bed and I knew I'd never walk on my own again. I thought of Donna, and her death, and how I'd made it all the worse with the track and Wendy.

The weaker I got, the more I thought about Rob. I talked about him to the nuns. And then one day he was there.

He wasn't alone, either. With him was a very pretty dark-haired woman and a seven-year-old boy who got the best features of both his mother and father.

"Dad, this is Mae and Stephen."

"Hello, Mae and Stephen. I'm very glad to meet you. I wish I was better company."

"Don't worry about that," Mae said. "We're just happy to meet you."

"I need to go to the bathroom," Stephen said.

"Why don't I take him, and give you a few minutes alone with your Dad?" Mae said.

And so, after all these years, we were alone and he said, "I still can't forgive you, Dad."

"I don't blame you."

"I want to. But somehow I can't."

I took his hand. "I'm just glad you turned out so well, son. Like your mother and not your father."

"I loved her very much."

"I know you did."

"And you treated her very, very badly."

All his anger. All these years.

"That's a beautiful wife and son you've got."

"They're my whole life, everything that matters to me."

I started crying; I couldn't help it. Here at the end I was glad to know he'd done well for himself and his family.

"I love you, Rob."

"I love you, too, Dad."

And then he leaned down and kissed me on the cheek and I started crying harder and embarrassed both of us.

Mae and Stephen came back.

"My turn," Rob said. He patted me on the shoulder. "I'll be back soon."

I think he wanted to go somewhere alone to cry.

"So," Mae said, "are you comfortable?"

"Oh, very."

"This seems like a nice place."

"It is."

"And the nuns seem very nice, too."

"Very nice." I smiled. "I'm just so glad I got to see you two."

"Same here. I've wanted to meet you for years."

"Well," I said, smiling. "I'm glad the time finally came."

Stephen, proper in his white shirt and blue trousers and neatly combed dark hair, said, "I just wish you could go to the track with us sometime, Grandpa."

She didn't have to say anything. I saw it all in the quick certain pain that appeared in her lovely gray eyes.

"The racetrack, you mean?" I said.

"Uh-huh. Dad takes me all the time, doesn't he, Mom?"

"Oh, yes," she said, her voice toneless. "All the time."

She started to say more but then the door opened up and Rob came in and there was no time to talk.

There was no time at all.

THE BLUE HOTEL

Stephen Crane

I

THE PALACE HOTEL at Fort Romper was painted a light blue, a shade that is on the legs of a kind of heron, causing the bird to declare its position against any background. The Palace Hotel, then, was always screaming and howling in a way that made the dazzling winter landscape of Nebraska seem only a gray swampish hush. It stood alone on the prairie, and when the snow was falling, the town two hundred yards away was not visible. But when the traveler alighted at the railway station, he was obliged to pass the Palace Hotel before he could come upon the company of low clapboard houses which composed Fort Romper, and it was not to be thought that any traveler could pass the Palace Hotel without looking at it. Pat Scully, the proprietor, had proved himself a master of strategy when he chose his paints. It is true that on clear days, when the great transcontinental expresses, long lines of swaying Pullmans, swept through Fort Romper, passengers were overcome at the sight, and the cult that knows the brown reds and the subdivisions of the dark greens of the East expressed shame, pity, horror, in a laugh. But to the citizens of this prairie town and to the people who would naturally stop there, Pat Scully had performed a feat. With this opulence and splendor, these creeds, classes, egotisms, that streamed through Romper on the rails day after day, they had no color in common.

As if the displayed delights of such a blue hotel were not sufficiently enticing, it was Scully's habit to go every morning and evening to meet the leisurely trains that stopped at Romper and work his seductions upon any man that he might see wavering, gripsack in hand.

One morning, when a snow-crusted engine dragged its long string of freight cars and its one passenger coach to the station, Scully performed the marvel of catching three men. One was a shaky and quick-eyed Swede, with a great shining cheap valise; one was a tall bronzed cowboy, who was on his way to a ranch near the Dakota line; one was a little silent man from the East, who didn't look it and didn't announce it. Scully practically made them prisoners. He was so nimble and merry and kindly that each probably felt it would be the height of brutality to try to escape. They trudged off over the creaking board sidewalks in the wake of the eager little Irishman. He wore a heavy fur cap squeezed tightly down on his head. It caused his two red ears to stick out stiffly, as if they were made of tin.

At last, Scully, elaborately, with boisterous hospitality, conducted them through the portals of the blue hotel. The room which they entered was small. It seemed to be merely a proper temple for an enormous stove, which, in the center, was humming with godlike violence. At various points on its surface, the iron had become luminous and glowed yellow from the heat. Beside the stove Scully's son Johnnie was playing high-five with an old farmer who had whiskers both gray and sandy. They were quarreling. Frequently the old farmer turned his face toward a box of sawdust—colored brown from tobacco juice—that was behind the stove, and spat with an air of great impatience and irritation. With a loud flourish of words, Scully destroyed the game of cards and bustled his son upstairs with part of the baggage of the new guests. He himself conducted them to three basins of the coldest water in the world. The cowboy and the Easterner burnished themselves fiery red with this water, until it seemed to be some kind of metal polish. The Swede, however, merely dipped his fingers gingerly and with trepidation. It was notable that throughout this series of small ceremonies, the three travelers were made to feel that Scully was very benevolent. He was conferring great favors upon them. He handed the towel from one to another with an air of philanthropic impulse.

Afterward they went to the first room, and, sitting about the stove, listened to Scully's officious clamor at his daughters, who were preparing the midday meal. They reflected in the silence of experienced men who tread carefully amid new people. Nevertheless, the old farmer, stationary, invincible in his chair near the warmest part of the stove, turned his face from the sawdust

box frequently and addressed a glowing commonplace to the strangers. Usually he was answered in short but adequate sentences by either the cowboy
or the Easterner. The Swede said nothing. He seemed to be occupied in
making furtive estimates of each man in the room. One might have thought
that he had the sense of silly suspicion which comes to guilt. He resembled
a badly frightened man.

Later, at dinner, he spoke a little, addressing his conversation entirely to
Scully. He volunteered that he had come from New York where for ten years
he had worked as a tailor. These facts seemed to strike Scully as fascinating,
and afterward he volunteered that he had lived at Romper for fourteen years.
The Swede asked about the crops and the price of labor. He seemed barely
to listen to Scully's extended replies. His eyes continued to rove from man
to man.

Finally, with a laugh and a wink, he said that some of these Western com-
munities were very dangerous; and after his statement he straightened his
legs under the table, tilted his head and laughed again, loudly. It was plain
that the demonstration had no meaning to the others. They looked at him
wondering and in silence.

II

As the men trooped heavily back into the front room, the two little windows
presented views of a turmoiling sea of snow. The huge arms of the wind were
making attempts—mighty, circular, futile—to embrace the flakes as they
sped. A gatepost like a still man with a blanched face stood aghast amid this
profligate fury. In a hearty voice Scully announced the presence of a blizzard.
The guests of the blue hotel, lighting their pipes, assented with grunts of lazy
masculine contentment. No island of the sea could be exempt in the degree
of this little room with its humming stove. Johnnie, son of Scully, in a tone
which defined his opinion of his ability as a cardplayer, challenged the old
farmer of both gray and sandy whiskers to a game of high-five. The farmer
agreed with a contemptuous and bitter scoff. They sat close to the stove, and
squared their knees under a wide board. The cowboy and the Easterner
watched the game with interest. The Swede remained near the window, aloof,
but with a countenance that displayed signs of an inexplicable excitement.

The play of Johnnie and the graybeard was suddenly ended by another
quarrel. The old man arose while casting a look of heated scorn at his adversary. He slowly buttoned his coat, and then stalked with fabulous dignity from

the room. In the discreet silence of all the other men, the Swede laughed. His laughter rang somehow childish. Men by this time had begun to look at him askance, as if they wished to inquire what ailed him.

A new game was formed jocosely. The cowboy volunteered to become the partner of Johnnie, and they all then turned to ask the Swede to throw in his lot with the little Easterner. He asked some questions about the game, and, learning that it wore many names, and that he had played it when it was under an alias, he accepted the invitation. He strode toward the men nervously, as if he expected to be assaulted. Finally, seated, he gazed from face to face and laughed shrilly. This laugh was so strange that the Easterner looked up quickly, the cowboy sat intent and with his mouth open, and Johnnie paused, holding the cards with still fingers.

Afterward there was a short silence. Then Johnnie said, "Well, let's get at it. Come on, now!" They pulled their chairs forward until their knees were bunched under the board. They began to play, and their interest in the game caused the others to forget the manner of the Swede.

The cowboy was a board-whacker. Each time that he held superior cards he whanged them, one by one, with exceeding force, down upon the improvised table, and took the tricks with a glowing air of prowess and pride that sent thrills of indignation into the hearts of his opponents. A game with a board-whacker in it is sure to become intense. The countenances of the Easterner and the Swede were miserable whenever the cowboy thundered down his aces and kings, while Johnnie, his eyes gleaming with joy, chuckled and chuckled.

Because of the absorbing play none considered the strange ways of the Swede. They paid strict heed to the game. Finally, during a lull caused by a new deal, the Swede suddenly addressed Johnnie. "I suppose there have been a good many men killed in this room." The jaws of the others dropped and they looked at him.

"What in hell are you talking about?" said Johnnie.

The Swede laughed again his blatant laugh, full of a kind of false courage and defiance. "Oh, you know what I mean all right," he answered.

"I'm a liar if I do!" Johnnie protested. The card was halted, and the men stared at the Swede. Johnnie evidently felt that as the son of the proprietor he should make a direct inquiry. "Now, what might you be drivin' at, mister?" he asked. The Swede winked at him. It was a wink full of cunning. His fingers shook on the edge of the board. "Oh, maybe you think I have been to nowheres. Maybe you think I'm a tenderfoot?"

"I don't know nothin' about you," answered Johnnie, "and I don't give a damn where you've been. All I got to say is that I don't know what you're driving at. There hain't never been nobody killed in this room."

The cowboy, who had been steadily gazing at the Swede, then spoke. "What's wrong with you, mister?"

Apparently it seemed to the Swede that he was formidably menaced. He shivered and turned white near the corners of his mouth. He sent an appealing glance in the direction of the little Easterner. During these moments he did not forget to wear his air of advanced pot-valor. "They say they don't know what I mean," he remarked mockingly to the Easterner.

The latter answered after prolonged and cautious reflection. "I don't understand you," he said impassively.

The Swede made a movement then which announced that he thought he had encountered treachery from the only quarter where he had expected sympathy, if not help. "Oh, I see you are all against me. I see—"

The cowboy was in a state of deep stupefaction. "Say," he cried, as he tumbled the deck violently down upon the board, "say, what are you gittin' at, hey?"

The Swede sprang up with the celerity of a man escaping from a snake on the floor. "I don't want to fight!" he shouted. "I don't want to fight!"

The cowboy stretched his long legs indolently and deliberately. His hands were in his pockets. He spat into the sawdust box. "Well, who the hell thought you did?" he inquired.

The Swede backed rapidly toward a corner of the room. His hands were out protectingly in front of his chest, but he was making an obvious struggle to control his fright. "Gentlemen," he quavered, "I suppose I am going to be killed before I can leave this house! I suppose I am going to be killed before I can leave this house! I suppose I am going to be killed before I can leave this house!" In his eyes was the dying-swan look. Through the windows could be seen the snow turning blue in the shadow of dusk. The wind tore at the house, and some loose thing beat regularly against the clapboards like a spirit tapping.

A door opened, and Scully himself entered. He paused in surprise as he noted the tragic attitude of the Swede. Then he said, "What's the matter here?"

The Swede answered him swiftly and eagerly, "These men are going to kill me."

"Kill you!" ejaculated Scully. "Kill you! What are you talkin'?"

The Swede made the gesture of a martyr.

Scully wheeled sternly upon his son. "What is this, Johnnie?"

The lad had grown sullen. "Damned if I know," he answered. "I can't make no sense to it." He began to shuffle the cards, fluttering them together with an angry snap. "He says a good many men have been killed in this room, or something like that. And he says he's goin' to be killed here too. I don't know what ails him. He's crazy, I shouldn't wonder."

Scully then looked for explanation to the cowboy, but the cowboy simply shrugged his shoulders.

"Kill you?" said Scully again to the Swede. "Kill you? Man, you're off your nut."

"Oh, I know," burst out the Swede. "I know what will happen. Yes, I'm crazy—yes. Yes, of course, I'm crazy—yes. But I know one thing—" There was a sort of sweat of misery and terror upon his face. "I know I won't get out of here alive."

The cowboy drew a deep breath, as if his mind was passing into the last stages of dissolution. "Well, I'm doggoned," he whispered to himself.

Scully wheeled suddenly and faced his son. "You've been troublin' this man!"

Johnnie's voice was loud with its burden of grievance. "Why, good Gawd, I ain't done nothin' to 'im."

The Swede broke in. "Gentlemen, do not disturb yourselves. I will leave this house. I will go away, because"—he accused them dramatically with his glance—"because I do not want to be killed."

Scully was furious with his son. "Will you tell me what is the matter, you young devil? What's the matter, anyhow? Speak out!"

"Blame it!" cried Johnnie in despair, "don't I tell you I don't know? He—he says we want to kill him, and that's all I know. I can't tell what ails him."

The Swede continued to repeat, "Never mind, Mr. Scully; never mind. I will leave this house. I will go away, because I do not wish to be killed. Yes, of course, I am crazy—yes. But I know one thing! I will go away. I will leave this house. Never mind, Mr. Scully; never mind. I will go away"

"You will not go 'way," said Scully. "You will not go 'way until I hear the reason of this business. If anybody has troubled you, I will take care of him. This is my house. You are under my roof, and I will not allow any peaceable man to be troubled here." He cast a terrible eye upon Johnnie, the cowboy and the Easterner.

"Never mind, Mr Scully; never mind. I will go away. I do not wish to be killed." The Swede moved toward the door which opened upon the stairs. It was evidently his intention to go at once for his baggage.

"No, no," shouted Scully peremptorily; but the white-faced man slid by him and disappeared. "Now," said Scully severely, "what does this mean?"

Johnnie and the cowboy cried together, "Why, we didn't do nothin' to 'im!"

Scully's eyes were cold. "No," he said, "you didn't?"

Johnnie swore a deep oath. "Why, this is the wildest loon I ever see. We didn't do nothin' at all. We were just sittin' here playin' cards, and he—"

The father suddenly spoke to the Easterner. "Mr. Blanc," he asked, "what has these boys been doin'?"

The Easterner reflected again. "I didn't see anything wrong at all," he said at last slowly.

Scully began to howl. "But what does it mane?" He stared ferociously at his son. "I have a mind to lather you for this, me boy."

Johnnie was frantic. "Well, what have I done?" he bawled at his father.

III

"I think you are tongue-tied," said Scully finally to his son, the cowboy and the Easterner; and at the end of this scornful sentence, he left the room.

Upstairs the Swede was swiftly fastening the straps of his great valise. Once his back happened to be half turned toward the door, and, hearing a noise there, he wheeled and sprang up, uttering a loud cry. Scully's wrinkled visage showed grimly in the light of the small lamp he carried. This yellow effulgence, streaming upward, colored only his prominent features, and left his eyes, for instance, in mysterious shadow. He resembled a murderer.

"Man! man!" he exclaimed, "have you gone daffy?"

"Oh, no! Oh, no!" rejoined the other. "There are people in this world who know pretty nearly as much as you do—understand?"

For a moment they stood gazing at each other. Upon the Swede's deathly pale cheeks were two spots brightly crimson and sharply edged, as if they had been carefully painted. Scully placed the light on the table and sat himself on the edge of the bed. He spoke ruminatively. "By cracky, I never heard of such a thing in my life. It's a complete muddle. I can't, for the soul of me, think how you ever got this idea into your head." Presently he lifted his eyes and asked, "And did you sure think they were going to kill you?"

The Swede scanned the old man as if he wished to see into his mind. "I did," he said at last. He obviously suspected that this answer might precipitate an outbreak. As he pulled on a strap his whole arm shook, the elbow wavering like a bit of paper.

Scully banged his hand impressively on the footboard of the bed. "Why, man, we're goin' to have a line of ilictric streetcars in this town next spring."

" 'A line of electric streetcars,' " repeated the Swede stupidly.

"And," said Scully, "there's a new railroad goin' to be built down from Broken Arm to here. Not to mention the four churches and the smashin' big brick schoolhouse. Then there's the big factory, too. Why, in two years Romper'll be a met-tro-*pol*-is."

Having finished the preparation of his baggage, the Swede straightened himself. "Mr. Scully," he said, with sudden hardihood, "how much do I owe you?"

"You don't owe me anythin'," said the old man, angrily.

"Yes, I do," retorted the Swede. He took seventy-five cents from his pocket and tendered it to Scully; but the latter snapped his fingers in disdainful refusal. However, it happened that they both stood gazing in a strange fashion at three silver pieces on the Swede's open palm.

"I'll not take your money," said Scully at last. "Not after what's been goin' on here." Then a plan seemed to strike him. "Here," he cried, picking up his lamp and moving toward the door. "Here! Come with me a minute."

"No," said the Swede, in overwhelming alarm.

"Yes," urged the old man. "Come on! I want you to come and see a pic-ter—just across the hall—in my room."

The Swede must have concluded that his hour was come. His jaw dropped and his teeth showed like a dead man's. He ultimately followed Scully across the corridor, but he had the step of one hung in chains.

Scully flashed the light on the wall of his own chamber. There was revealed a ridiculous photograph of a little girl. She was leaning against a balustrade of gorgeous decoration, and the formidable bang to her hair was prominent. The figure was as graceful as an upright sled-stake, and, withal, it was of the hue of lead. "There," said Scully, tenderly, "that's the picter of my little girl that died. Her name was Carrie. She had the purtiest hair you ever saw. I was that fond of her, she—"

Turning then, he saw that the Swede was not contemplating the picture at all, but, instead, was keeping keen watch on the gloom in the rear.

"Look, man!" cried Scully, heartily. "That's the picter of my little gal that died. Her name was Carrie. And then here's the picter of my oldest boy,

Michael. He's a lawyer in Lincoln, an' doin' well. I gave that boy a grand eddication, and I'm glad for it now. He's a fine boy. Look at 'im now. Ain't he bold as blazes, him there in Lincoln, an honored an' respicted gintleman! An honored and respected gintleman," concluded Scully with a flourish. And, so saying, he smote the Swede jovially on the back.

The Swede faintly smiled.

"Now," said the old man, "there's only one more thing." He dropped suddenly to the floor and thrust his hand beneath the bed. The Swede could hear his muffled voice. "I'd keep it under me piller if it wasn't for that boy Johnnie. Then there's the old woman—Where is it now? I never put it twice in the same place. Ah, now come out with you!"

Presently he backed clumsily from under the bed, dragging with him an old coat rolled into a bundle. "I've fetched him," he muttered. Kneeling on the floor, he unrolled the coat and extracted from its heart a large yellow brown whisky bottle.

His first maneuver was to hold the bottle up to the light. Reassured, apparently, that nobody had been tampering with it, he thrust it with a generous movement toward the Swede.

The weak-kneed Swede was about to eagerly clutch this element of strength, but he suddenly jerked his hand away and cast a look of horror upon Scully.

"Drink," said the old man affectionately. He had risen to his feet, and now stood facing the Swede.

There was a silence. Then again Scully said, "Drink!"

The Swede laughed wildly. He grabbed the bottle, put it to his mouth; and as his lips curled absurdly around the opening and his throat worked, he kept his glance, burning with hatred, upon the old man's face.

IV

After the departure of Scully the three men, with the cardboard still upon their knees, preserved for a long time an astounded silence. Then Johnnie said, "That's the daddangedest Swede I ever see."

"He ain't no Swede," said the cowboy scornfully.

"Well, what is he then?" cried Johnnie. "What is he then?

"It's my opinion," replied the cowboy deliberately, "he's some kind of a Dutchman." It was a venerable custom of the country to entitle as Swedes all light-haired men who spoke with a heavy tongue. In consequence the idea of the cowboy was not without its daring. "Yes, sir," he repeated. "It's my opinion this feller is some kind of a Dutchman."

"Well, he says he's a Swede, anyhow," muttered Johnnie, sulkily. He turned to the Easterner. "What do you think, Mr. Blanc?"

"Oh, I don't know," replied the Easterner.

"Well, what do you think makes him act that way?" asked the cowboy.

"Why, he's frightened." The Easterner knocked his pipe against a rim of the stove. "He's clear frightened out of his boots."

"What at?" cried Johnnie and the cowboy together.

The Easterner reflected over his answer.

"What at?" cried the others again.

"Oh, I don't know, but it seems to me this man has been reading dime novels, and he thinks he's right out in the middle of it—the shootin' and stabbin' and all."

"But," said the cowboy, deeply scandalized, "this ain't Wyoming, ner none of them places. This is Nebrasker."

"Yes," added Johnnie, "an' why don't he wait till he gits *out West?*"

The traveled Easterner laughed. "It isn't different there even—not in these days. But he thinks he's right in the middle of hell."

Johnnie and the cowboy mused long.

"It's awful funny," remarked Johnnie at last.

"Yes," said the cowboy. "This is a queer game. I hope we don't git snowed in, because then we'd have to stand this here man bein' around with us all the time. That wouldn't be no good."

"I wish pop would throw him out," said Johnnie.

Presently they heard a loud stamping on the stairs, accompanied by ringing jokes in the voice of old Scully, and laughter, evidently from the Swede. The men around the stove stared vacantly at each other. "Gosh!" said the cowboy. The door flew open, and old Scully, flushed and anecdotal, came into the room. He was jabbering at the Swede, who followed him, laughing bravely. It was the entry of two roisterers from a banquet hall.

"Come now," said Scully sharply to the three seated men, "move up and give us a chance at the stove." The cowboy and the Easterner obediently sidled their chairs to make room for the newcomers. Johnnie, however, simply arranged himself in a more indolent attitude, and then remained motionless.

"Come! Git over there," said Scully.

"Plenty of room on the other side of the stove," said Johnnie.

"Do you think we want to sit in the draught?" roared the father.

But the Swede here interposed with a grandeur of confidence. "No, no. Let the boy sit where he likes," he cried in a bullying voice to the father.

"All right! All right!" said Scully, deferentially. The cowboy and the Easterner exchanged glances of wonder.

The five chairs were formed in a crescent about one side of the stove. The Swede began to talk; he talked arrogantly, profanely, angrily. Johnnie, the cowboy and the Easterner maintained a morose silence, while old Scully appeared to be receptive and eager, breaking in constantly with sympathetic ejaculations.

Finally the Swede announced that he was thirsty. He moved in his chair, and said that he would go for a drink of water.

"I'll git it for you," cried Scully at once.

"No," said the Swede, contemptuously. "I'll get it for myself." He arose and stalked with the air of an owner off into the executive parts of the hotel.

As soon as the Swede was out of hearing, Scully sprang to his feet and whispered intensely to the others, "Upstairs he thought I was tryin' to poison 'im."

"Say," said Johnnie, "this makes me sick. Why don't you throw 'im out in the snow?"

"Why, he's all right now," declared Scully. "It was only that he was from the East, and he thought this was a tough place. That's all. He's all right now."

The cowboy looked with admiration upon the Easterner. "You were straight," he said. "You were on to that there Dutchman."

"Well," said Johnnie to his father, "he may be all right now, but I don't see it. Other time he was scared, but now he's too fresh."

Scully's speech was always a combination of Irish brogue and idiom, western twang and idiom, and scraps of curiously formal diction taken from the storybooks and newspapers. He now hurled a strange mass of language at the head of his son. "What do I keep? What do I keep? What do I keep?" he demanded, in a voice of thunder. He slapped his knee impressively, to indicate that he himself was going to make reply, and that all should heed. "I keep a hotel," he shouted. "A hotel, do you mind? A guest under my roof has sacred privileges. He is to be intimidated by none. Not one word shall he hear that would prijudice him in favor of goin' away. I'll not have it. There's no place in this here town where they can say they iver took in a guest of mine because he was afraid to stay here." He wheeled suddenly upon the cowboy and the Easterner. "Am I right?"

"Yes, Mr. Scully," said the cowboy, "I think you're right."

"Yes, Mr. Scully," said the Easterner, "I think you're right."

V

At six o'clock supper, the Swede fizzed like a fire wheel. He sometimes seemed on the point of bursting into riotous song, and in all his madness he was encouraged by old Scully. The Easterner was encased in reserve; the cowboy sat in wide-mouthed amazement, forgetting to eat, while Johnnie wrathily demolished great plates of food. The daughters of the house, when they were obliged to replenish the biscuits, approached as warily as Indians, and, having succeeded in their purpose, fled with ill-concealed trepidation. The Swede domineered the whole feast, and he gave it the appearance of a cruel bacchanal. He seemed to have grown suddenly taller; he gazed, brutally disdainful, into every face. His voice rang through the room. Once when he jabbed out harpoon-fashion with his fork to pinion a biscuit, the weapon nearly impaled the hand of the Easterner, which had been stretched quietly out for the same biscuit.

After supper, as the men filed toward the other room, the Swede smote Scully ruthlessly on the shoulder. "Well, old boy, that was a good, square meal." Johnnie looked hopefully at his father; he knew that shoulder was tender from an old fall; and, indeed, it appeared for a moment as if Scully was going to flame out over the matter, but in the end he smiled a sickly smile and remained silent. The others understood from his manner that he was admitting his responsibility for the Swede's new viewpoint.

Johnnie, however, addressed his parent in an aside. "Why don't you license somebody to kick you downstairs?" Scully scowled darkly by way of reply.

When they were gathered about the stove, the Swede insisted on another game of high-five. Scully gently deprecated the plan at first, but the Swede turned a wolfish glare upon him. The old man subsided, and the Swede canvassed the others. In his tone there was always a great threat. The cowboy and the Easterner both remarked indifferently that they would play. Scully said that he would presently have to go to meet the 6:58 train, and so the Swede turned menacingly upon Johnnie. For a moment their glances crossed like blades, and then Johnnie smiled and said, "Yes, I'll play."

They formed a square, with the little board on their knees. The Easterner and the Swede were again partners. As the play went on, it was noticeable that the cowboy was not board-whacking as usual. Meanwhile, Scully, near the lamp, had put on his spectacles and, with an appearance curiously like an old priest, was reading a newspaper. In time he went out to meet the 6:58 train, and, despite his precautions, a gust of polar wind whirled into the room as he opened the door. Besides scattering the cards, it chilled the players to the marrow. The Swede cursed frightfully. When Scully returned, his entrance disturbed a cozy and friendly scene. The Swede again cursed. But presently they were once more intent, their heads bent forward and their hands moving swiftly. The Swede had adopted the fashion of board-whacking.

Scully took up his paper and for a long time remained immersed in matters which were extraordinarily remote from him. The lamp burned badly, and once he stopped to adjust the wick. The newspaper, as he turned from page to page, rustled with a slow and comfortable sound. Then suddenly he heard three terrible words. "You are cheatin'!"

Such scenes often prove that there can be little of dramatic import in environment. Any room can present a tragic front; any room can be comic. This little den was now hideous as a torture chamber. The new faces of the men themselves had changed it upon the instant the Swede held a huge fist in front of Johnnie's face, while the latter looked steadily over it into the blazing orbs of his accuser. The Easterner had grown pallid; the cowboy's jaw had dropped in that expression of bovine amazement which was one of his important mannerisms. After the three words, the first sound in the room was made by Scully's paper as it floated forgotten to his feet. His spectacles had also fallen from his nose, but by a clutch he had saved them in air. His hand, grasping the spectacles, now remained poised awkwardly and near his shoulder. He stared at the cardplayers.

Probably the silence was while a second elapsed. Then if the floor had been suddenly twitched out from under the men, they could not have moved quicker. The five had projected themselves headlong toward a common point. It happened that Johnnie, in rising to hurl himself upon the Swede, had stumbled slightly because of his curiously instinctive care for the cards and the board. The loss of the moment allowed time for the arrival of Scully, and also allowed the cowboy time to give the Swede a great push which sent him staggering back. The men found tongue together, and hoarse shouts of rage, appeal or fear burst from every throat. The cowboy pushed and jostled feverishly at the Swede, and the Easterner and Scully clung wildly to Johnnie; but through the smoky air, above the swaying bodies of the peace-compellers, the eyes of the two warriors ever sought each other in glances of challenge that were at once hot and steely.

Of course the board had been overturned, and now the whole company of cards was scattered over the floor, where the boots of the men trampled the fat and painted kings and queens as they gazed with their silly eyes at the war that was waging above them.

Scully's voice was dominating the yells. "Stop now! Stop, I say! Stop, now—"

Johnnie, as he struggled to burst through the rank formed by Scully and the Easterner, was crying, "Well, he says I cheated! He says I cheated! I won't allow no man to say I cheated! If he says I cheated, he's a ———!"

The cowboy was telling the Swede, "Quit, now! Quit, d'ye hear—"

The screams of the Swede never ceased. "He did cheat! I saw him! I saw him—"

As for the Easterner, he was importuning in a voice that was not heeded, "Wait a moment, can't you? Oh, wait a moment. What's the good of a fight over a game of cards? Wait a moment—"

In this tumult no complete sentences were clear. "Cheat"—"quit"—"he says"—these fragments pierced the uproar and rang out sharply. It was remarkable that, whereas Scully undoubtedly made the most noise, he was the least heard of any of the riotous band.

Then suddenly there was a great cessation. It was as if each man had paused for breath; and although the room was still lighted with the anger of men, it could be seen that there was no danger of immediate conflict, and at once Johnnie, shouldering his way forward, almost succeeded in confronting the Swede. "What did you say I cheated for? What did you say I cheated for? I don't cheat, and I won't let no man say I do!"

The Swede said, "I saw you! I saw you!"

"Well," cried Johnnie, "I'll fight any man what says I cheat!"

"No, you won't," said the cowboy. "Not here."

"Ah, be still, can't you?" said Scully, coming between them.

The quiet was sufficient to allow the Easterner's voice to be heard. He was repeating, "Oh, wait a moment, can't you? What's the good of a fight over a game of cards? Wait a moment!"

Johnnie, his red face appearing above his father's shoulder, hailed the Swede again. "Did you say I cheated?"

The Swede showed his teeth. "Yes."

"Then," said Johnnie, "we must fight."

"Yes, fight," roared the Swede. He was like a demoniac. "Yes, fight! I'll show you what kind of a man I am! I'll show you who you want to fight!

Maybe you think I can't fight! Maybe you think I can't! I'll show you, you skin, you cardsharp. Yes, you cheated! You cheated! You cheated!"

"Well, let's go at it, then, mister," said Johnnie coolly.

The cowboy's brow was beaded with sweat from his efforts in intercepting all sorts of raids. He turned in despair to Scully. "What are you goin' to do now?"

A change had come over the Celtic visage of the old man. He now seemed all eagerness; his eyes glowed.

"We'll let them fight," he answered, stalwartly. "I can't put up with it any longer. I've stood this damned Swede till I'm sick. We'll let them fight."

VI

The men prepared to go out of doors. The Easterner was so nervous that he had great difficulty in getting his arms into the sleeves of his new leather coat. As the cowboy drew his fur cap down over his ears, his hands trembled. In fact, Johnnie and old Scully were the only ones who displayed no agitation. These preliminaries were conducted without words.

Scully threw open the door. "Well, come on," he said. Instantly a terrific wind caused the flame of the lamp to struggle at its wick, while a puff of black smoke sprang from the chimney top. The stove was in mid-current of the blast, and its voice swelled to equal the roar of the storm. Some of the scarred and bedabbled cards were caught up from the floor and dashed helplessly against the farther wall. The men lowered their heads and plunged into the tempest as into a sea.

No snow was falling, but great whirls and clouds of flakes, swept up from the ground by the frantic winds, were streaming southward with the speed of bullets. The covered land was blue with the sheen of an unearthly satin, and there was no other hue save where, at the low black railway station—which seemed incredibly distant—one light gleamed like a tiny jewel. As the men floundered into a thigh-deep drift, it was known that the Swede was bawling out something. Scully went to him, put a hand on his shoulder and projected an ear. "What's that you say?" he shouted.

"I say," bawled the Swede again, "I won't stand much show against this gang. I know you'll all pitch on me."

Scully smote him reproachfully on the arm. "Tut, man!" he yelled. The wind tore the words from Scully's lips and scattered them far alee.

"You are all a gang of—" boomed the Swede, but the storm also seized the remainder of this sentence.

Immediately turning their backs upon the wind, the men had swung around a corner to the sheltered side of the hotel. It was the function of the little house to preserve here, amid this great devastation of snow, an irregular V-shape of heavily encrusted grass, which crackled beneath the feet. One could imagine the great drifts piled against the windward side. When the party reached the comparative peace of this spot, it was found that the Swede was still bellowing.

"Oh, I know what kind of a thing this is! I know you'll all pitch on me. I can't lick you all!"

Scully turned upon him panther-fashion. "You'll not have to whip all of us. You'll have to whip my son Johnnie. An' the man what troubles you durin' that time will have me to deal with."

The arrangements were swiftly made. The two men faced each other, obedient to the harsh commands of Scully, whose face, in the subtly luminous gloom, could be seen set in the austere impersonal lines that are pictured on the countenances of the Roman veterans. The Easterner's teeth were chattering, and he was hopping up and down like a mechanical toy. The cowboy stood rocklike.

The contestants had not stripped off any clothing. Each was in his ordinary attire. Their fists were up, and they eyed each other in a calm that had the elements of leonine cruelty in it.

During this pause, the Easterner's mind, like a film, took lasting impressions of three men—the iron-nerved master of the ceremony; the Swede, pale, motionless, terrible; and Johnnie, serene yet ferocious, brutish yet heroic. The entire prelude had in it a tragedy greater than the tragedy of action, and this aspect was accentuated by the long, mellow cry of the blizzard as it sped the tumbling and wailing flakes into the black abyss of the south.

"Now!" said Scully.

The two combatants leaped forward and crashed together like bullocks. There was heard the cushioned sound of blows, and of a curse squeezing out from between the tight teeth of one.

As for the spectators, the Easterner's pent-up breath exploded from him with a pop of relief, absolute relief from the tension of the preliminaries. The cowboy bounded into the air with a yowl. Scully was immovable as from supreme amazement and fear at the fury of the fight which he himself had permitted and arranged.

For a time the encounter in the darkness was such a perplexity of flying arms that it presented no more detail than would a swiftly revolving wheel. Occasionally, a face, as if illumined by a flash of light, would shine out, ghastly and marked with pink spots. A moment later, the men might have been known as shadows if it were not for the involuntary utterance of oaths that came from them in whispers.

Suddenly a holocaust of warlike desire caught the cowboy, and he bolted forward with the speed of a bronco. "Go it, Johnnie! Go it! Kill him! Kill him!"

Scully confronted him. "Kape back," he said; and by his glance the cowboy could tell that this man was Johnnie's father.

To the Easterner there was a monotony of unchangeable fighting that was an abomination. This confused mingling was eternal to his sense, which was concentrated in a longing for the end, the priceless end. Once the fighters lurched near him, and as he scrambled hastily backward he heard them breathe like men on the rack.

"Kill him, Johnnie! Kill him! Kill him! Kill him!" The cowboy's face was contorted like one of those agony masks in museums.

"Keep still," said Scully icily.

Then there was a sudden loud grunt, incomplete, cut short, and Johnnie's body swung away from the Swede and fell with sickening heaviness to the grass. The cowboy was barely in time to prevent the mad Swede from flinging himself upon his prone adversary. "No, you don't," said the cowboy, interposing an arm. "Wait a second."

Scully was at his son's side. "Johnnie! Johnnie, me boy!" His voice had a quality of melancholy tenderness. "Johnnie! Can you go on with it?" He looked anxiously down into the bloody, pulpy face of his son.

There was a moment of silence, and then Johnnie answered in his ordinary voice. "Yes, I—it—yes."

Assisted by his father he struggled to his feet. "Wait a bit now till you git your wind," said the old man.

A few paces away the cowboy was lecturing the Swede. "No, you don't! Wait a second!"

The Easterner was plucking at Scully's sleeve. "Oh, this is enough," he pleaded. "This is enough! Let it go as it stands. This is enough!"

"Bill," said Scully, "git out of the road." The cowboy stepped aside. "Now." The combatants were actuated by a new caution as they advanced toward collision. They glared at each other, and then the Swede aimed a lightning blow that carried with it his entire weight. Johnnie was evidently half stupid from weakness, but he miraculously dodged, and his fist sent the overbalanced Swede sprawling.

The cowboy, Scully and the Easterner burst into a cheer that was like a chorus of triumphant soldiery, but before its conclusion the Swede had scuffed agilely to his feet and come in berserk abandon at his foe. There was another perplexity of flying arms, and Johnnie's body again swung away and fell, even as a bundle might fall from a roof. The Swede instantly staggered to a little wind-waved tree and leaned upon it, breathing like an engine, while his savage and flame-lit eyes roamed from face to face as the men bent over Johnnie. There was a splendor of isolation in his situation at this time which the Easterner felt once when, lifting his eyes from the man on the ground, he beheld that mysterious and lonely figure, waiting.

"Are you any good yet, Johnnie?" asked Scully in a broken voice.

The son gasped and opened his eyes languidly. After a moment he answered, "No—I ain't—any good—any—more." Then from shame and bodily ill, he began to weep, the tears furrowing down through the bloodstains on his face. "He was too—too—heavy for me."

Scully straightened and addressed the waiting figure. "Stranger," he said, evenly, "it's all up with our side." Then his voice changed into that vibrant huskiness which is commonly the tone of the most simple and deadly announcements. "Johnnie is whipped."

Without replying, the victor moved off on the route to the front door of the hotel.

The cowboy was formulating new and unspellable blasphemies. The Easterner was startled to find that they were out in a wind that seemed to come direct from the shadowed arctic floes. He heard again the wail of the snow as it was flung to its grave in the south. He knew now that all this time the cold had been sinking into him deeper and deeper, and he wondered that he had not perished. He felt indifferent to the condition of the vanquished man.

"Johnnie, can you walk?" asked Scully.

"Did I hurt—hurt him any?" asked the son.

"Can you walk, boy? Can you walk?"

Johnnie's voice was suddenly strong. There was a robust impatience in it. "I asked you whether I hurt him any!"

"Yes, yes, Johnnie," answered the cowboy, consolingly, "he's hurt a good deal."

They raised him from the ground, and as soon as he was on his feet, he went tottering off, rebuffing all attempts at assistance. When the party rounded the corner, they were fairly blinded by the pelting of the snow. It burned their faces like fire. The cowboy carried Johnnie through the drift to the door. As they entered, some cards rose from the floor and beat against the wall.

The Easterner rushed to the stove. He was so profoundly chilled that he almost dared to embrace the glowing iron. The Swede was not in the room. Johnnie sank into a chair and, folding his arms on his knees, buried his face in them. Scully, warming one foot and then the other at the rim of the stove, muttered to himself with Celtic mournfulness. The cowboy had removed his fur cap, and with a dazed and rueful air he was running one hand through his tousled locks. From overhead they could hear the creaking of boards as the Swede tramped here and there in his room.

The sad quiet was broken by the sudden flinging open of a door that led toward the kitchen. It was instantly followed by an onrush of women. They precipitated themselves upon Johnnie amid a chorus of lamentation. Before they carried their prey off to the kitchen, there to be bathed and harangued with that mixture of sympathy and abuse which is a feat of their sex, the mother straightened herself and fixed old Scully with an eye of stern reproach. "Shame be upon you, Patrick Scully!" she cried. "Your own son, too. Shame be upon you!"

"There, now! Be quiet, now!" said the old man weakly to this slogan, sniffed disdainfully in the direction of those trembling accomplices, the cowboy and the Easterner. Presently they bore Johnnie away, and left the three men to dismal reflection.

VII

"I'd like to fight this here Dutchman myself," said the cowboy, breaking a long silence.

Scully wagged his head sadly. "No, that wouldn't do. It wouldn't be right. It wouldn't be right."

"Well, why wouldn't it?" argued the cowboy. "I don't see no harm in it."

"No," answered Scully, with mournful heroism. "It wouldn't be right. It was Johnnie's fight, and now we mustn't whip the man just because he whipped Johnnie."

"Yes, that's true enough," said the cowboy, "but—he better not get fresh with me, because I couldn't stand no more of it."

"You'll not say a word to him," commanded Scully, and even then they heard the tread of the Swede on the stairs. His entrance was made theatric. He swept the door back with a bang and swaggered to the middle of the room. No one looked at him. "Well," he cried, insolently, at Scully, "I s'pose you'll tell me now how much I owe you?"

The old man remained stolid. "You don't owe me nothin'."

"Huh!" said the Swede. "Huh! Don't owe 'im nothin'."

The cowboy addressed the Swede. "Stranger, I don't see how you come to be so gay around here."

Old Scully was instantly alert. "Stop!" he shouted, holding his hand forth, fingers upward. "Bill, you shut up!"

The cowboy spat carelessly into the sawdust box. "I didn't say a word, did I?" he asked.

"Mr. Scully," called the Swede, "how much do I owe you?" It was seen that he was attired for departure, and that he had his valise in his hand.

"You don't owe me nothin'," repeated Scully in the same imperturbable way.

"Huh!" said the Swede. "I guess you're right. I guess if it was any way at all, you'd owe me somethin'. That's what I guess." He turned to the cowboy. " 'Kill him! Kill him! Kill him!' " he mimicked, and then guffawed victoriously. " 'Kill him!' " He was convulsed with ironical humor.

But he might have been jeering the dead. The three men were immovable and silent, staring with glassy eyes at the stove.

The Swede opened the door and passed into the storm, giving one derisive glance backward at the still group.

As soon as the door was closed, Scully and the cowboy leaped to their feet and began to curse. They trampled to and fro, waving their arms and smashing into the air with their fists. "Oh, but that was a hard minute!" wailed Scully. "That was a hard minute! Him there leerin' and scoffin'! One bang at his nose was worth forty dollars to me that minute! How did you stand it, Bill?"

"How did I stand it?" cried the cowboy in a quivering voice. "How did I stand it? Oh!"

The old man burst into sudden brogue. "I'd loike to take that Swade," he wailed, "and hould 'im down on a shtone flure and bate 'im to a jelly wid a shtick!"

The cowboy groaned in sympathy. "I'd like to git him by the neck and ha-ammer him"—he brought his hand down on a chair with a noise like a pistol shot—"hammer that there Dutchman until he couldn't tell himself from a dead coyote!"

"I'd bate 'im until he—"

"I'd show *him* some things—"

And then together they raised a yearning, fantastic cry—"Oh-o-oh! if we only could—"

"Yes!"

"Yes!"

"And then I'd—"

"O-o-oh!"

VIII

The Swede, tightly gripping his valise, tacked across the face of the storm as if he carried sails. He was following a line of little naked, grasping trees which, he knew, must mark the way of the road. His face, fresh from the pounding of Johnnie's fists, felt more pleasure than pain in the wind and the driving snow. A number of square shapes loomed upon him finally, and he knew them as the houses of the main body of the town. He found a street and made travel along it, leaning heavily upon the wind whenever, at a corner, a terrific blast caught him.

He might have been in a deserted village. We picture the world as thick with conquering and elate humanity, but here, with the bugles of the tempest pealing, it was hard to imagine a peopled earth. One viewed the existence of man then as a marvel, and conceded a glamour of wonder to these lice which were caused to cling to a whirling, fire-smitten, ice-locked, disease-stricken, space-lost bulb. The conceit of man was explained by this storm to be the very engine of life. One was a coxcomb not to die in it. However, the Swede found a saloon.

In front of it an indomitable red light was burning, and the snowflakes were made blood color as they flew through the circumscribed territory of the lamp's shining. The Swede pushed open the door of the saloon and entered. A sanded expanse was before him, and at the end of it four men sat about a table drinking. Down one side of the room extended a radiant bar, and its guardian was leaning upon his elbows listening to the talk of the men at the table. The Swede dropped his valise upon the floor and, smiling fraternally upon the barkeeper, said, "Gimme some whisky, will you?" The man placed a bottle, a whisky glass, and a glass of ice-thick water upon the bar. The

Swede poured himself an abnormal portion of whisky and drank it in three gulps. "Pretty bad night," remarked the bartender indifferently. He was making the pretension of blindness which is usually a distinction of his class; but it could have been seen that he was furtively studying the half-erased bloodstains on the face of the Swede. "Bad night," he said again.

"Oh, it's good enough for me," replied the Swede hardily as he poured himself some more whisky. The barkeeper took his coin and maneuvered it through its reception by a highly nickeled cash-machine. A bell rang; a card labeled "20 cts." had appeared.

"No," continued the Swede, "this isn't too bad weather. It's good enough for me."

"So?" murmured the barkeeper languidly.

The copious drams made the Swede's eyes swim, and he breathed a trifle heavier. "Yes, I like this weather. I like it. It suits me." It was apparently his design to impart a deep significance to these words.

"So?" murmured the bartender again. He turned to gaze dreamily at the scroll-like birds and birdlike scrolls which had been drawn with soap upon the mirrors in back of the bar.

"Well, I guess I'll take another drink," said the Swede presently. "Have something?"

"No, thanks; I'm not drinkin'," answered the bartender. Afterward he asked, "How did you hurt your face?"

The Swede immediately began to boast loudly. "Why, in a fight. I thumped the soul out of a man down here at Scully's hotel."

The interest of the four men at the table was at last aroused.

"Who was it?" said one.

"Johnnie Scully," blustered the Swede. "Son of the man what runs it. He will be pretty near dead for some weeks, I can tell you. I made a nice thing of him, I did. He couldn't get up. They carried him in the house. Have a drink?"

Instantly the men in some subtle way encased themselves in reserve. "No, thanks," said one. The group was of curious formation. Two were prominent local business men; one was the district attorney; and one was a professional gambler of the kind known as "square." But a scrutiny of the group would not have enabled an observer to pick the gambler from the men of more reputable pursuits. He was, in fact, a man so delicate in manner when among people of fair class, and so judicious in his choice of victims, that in the strictly masculine part of the town's life he had come to be explicitly trusted and admired. People called him a thoroughbred. The fear and contempt with which his craft was regarded were undoubtedly the reason why his quiet dignity shone conspicuous above the quiet dignity of men who might be merely hatters, billiard markers or grocery clerks. Beyond an occasionally unwary traveler who came by rail, this gambler was supposed to prey solely upon reckless and senile farmers, who, when flush with good crops, drove into town in all the pride and confidence of an absolutely invulnerable stupidity. Hearing at times in circuitous fashion of the despoilment of such a farmer, the important men of Romper invariably laughed in contempt of the victim, and if they thought of the wolf at all, it was with a kind of pride at the knowledge that he would never dare think of attacking their wisdom and courage. Besides, it was popular that this gambler had a real wife and two real children in a neat cottage in a suburb, where he led an exemplary home life; and when any one even suggested a discrepancy in his character, the crowd immediately vociferated descriptions of this virtuous family circle. Then men who led exemplary home lives, and men who did not lead exemplary home lives, all subsided in a bunch, remarking that there was nothing more to be said.

However, when a restriction was placed upon him—as, for instance, when a strong clique of members of the new Polywog Club refused to permit him, even as a spectator, to appear in the rooms of the organization—the candor and gentleness with which he accepted the judgment disarmed many of his foes and made his friends more desperately partisan. He invariably distinguished between himself and a respectable Romper man so quickly and frankly that his manner actually appeared to be a continual broadcast compliment.

And one must not forget to declare the fundamental fact of his entire position in Romper. It is irrefutable that in all affairs outside his business, in all matters that occur eternally and commonly between man and man, this thieving cardplayer was so generous, so just, so moral, that in a contest he could have put to flight the consciences of nine-tenths of the citizens of Romper.

And so it happened that he was seated in this saloon with the two prominent local merchants and the district attorney.

The Swede continued to drink raw whisky, meanwhile babbling at the barkeeper and trying to induce him to indulge in potations. "Come on. Have a drink. Come on. What—no? Well, have a little one, then. By gawd, I've whipped a man tonight, and I want to celebrate. I whipped him good, too. Gentlemen," the Swede cried to the men at the table. "Have a drink?"

"Ssh!" said the barkeeper.

The group at the table, although furtively attentive, had been pretending to be deep in talk, but now a man lifted his eyes toward the Swede and said shortly, "Thanks. We don't want any more."

At this reply the Swede ruffled out his chest like a rooster. "Well," he exploded, "it seems I can't get anybody to drink with me in this town. Seems so, don't it? Well!"

"Ssh!" said the barkeeper.

"Say," snarled the Swede, "don't you try to shut me up. I won't have it. I'm a gentleman, and I want people to drink with me. And I want 'em to drink with me now. *Now*—do you understand?" He rapped the bar with his knuckles.

Years of experience had calloused the bartender. He merely grew sulky. "I hear you," he answered.

"Well," cried the Swede, "listen hard then. See those men over there? Well they're going to drink with me, and don't you forget it. Now you watch."

"Hi!" yelled the barkeeper, "this won't do!"

"Why won't it?" demanded the Swede. He stalked over to the table, and by chance laid his hand upon the shoulder of the gambler. "How about this?" he asked wrathfully. "I asked you to drink with me."

The gambler simply twisted his head and spoke over his shoulder. "My friend, I don't know you."

"Oh, hell!" answered the Swede, "come and have a drink."

"Now, my boy," advised the gambler kindly, "take your hand off my shoulder and go 'way and mind your own business." He was a little, slim man, and it seemed strange to hear him use this tone of heroic patronage to the burly Swede. The other men at the table said nothing.

"What! You won't drink with me, you little dude? I'll make you, then! I'll make you!" The Swede had grasped the gambler frenziedly at the throat, and was dragging him from his chair. The other men sprang up. The barkeeper dashed around the corner of his bar. There was a great tumult, and then was seen a long blade in the hand of the gambler. It shot forward, and a human body, this citadel of virtue, wisdom, power, was pierced as easily as if it had been a melon. The Swede fell with a cry of supreme astonishment.

The prominent merchants and the district attorney must have at once tumbled out of the place backward. The bartender found himself hanging limply to the arm of a chair and gazing into the eyes of a murderer.

"Henry," said the latter as he wiped his knife on one of the towels that hung beneath the bar rail, "you tell 'em where to find me. I'll be home, waiting for 'em." Then he vanished. A moment afterward the barkeeper was in the street, dinning through the storm for help and, moreover, companionship.

The corpse of the Swede, alone in the saloon, had its eyes fixed upon a dreadful legend that dwelt atop of the cash-machine: "This registers the amount of your purchase."

IX

Months later the cowboy was frying pork over the stove of a little ranch near the Dakota line when there was a quick thud of hoofs outside, and presently the Easterner entered with the letters and the papers.

"Well," said the Easterner at once, "the chap that killed the Swede has got three years. Wasn't much, was it?"

"He has? Three years?" The cowboy poised his pan of pork while he ruminated upon the news. "Three years. That ain't much."

"No. It was a light sentence," replied the Easterner as he unbuckled his spurs. "Seems there was a good deal of sympathy for him in Romper."

"If the bartender had been any good," observed the cowboy thoughtfully, "he would have gone in and cracked that there Dutchman on the head with a bottle in the beginnin' of it and stopped all this here murderin'."

"Yes, a thousand things might have happened," said the Easterner tartly.

The cowboy returned his pan of pork to the fire, but his philosophy continued. "It's funny, ain't it? If he hadn't said Johnnie was cheatin', he'd be alive this minute. He was an awful fool. Game played for fun, too. Not for money. I believe he was crazy."

"I feel sorry for that gambler," said the Easterner.

"Oh, so do I," said the cowboy. "He don't deserve none of it for killin' who he did."

"The Swede might not have been killed if everything had been square."

"Might not have been killed?" exclaimed the cowboy. "Everythin' square? Why, when he said that Johnnie was cheatin' and acted like such a jackass? And then in the saloon he fairly walked up to git hurt?" With these arguments the cowboy browbeat the Easterner and reduced him to rage.

"You're a fool!" cried the Easterner, viciously. "You're a bigger jackass than the Swede by a million majority. Now let me tell you one thing. Let me tell you something. Listen! Johnnie *was* cheating!"

" 'Johnnie,' " said the cowboy, blankly. There was a minute of silence, and then he said, robustly, "Why, no. The game was only for fun."

"Fun or not," said the Easterner, "Johnnie was cheating. I saw him. I know it. I saw him. And I refused to stand up and be a man. I let the Swede fight it out alone. And you—you were simply puffing around the place and wanting to fight. And then old Scully himself! We are all in it! This poor gambler isn't even a noun. He is kind of an adverb. Every sin is the result of a collaboration. We, five of us, have collaborated in the murder of this Swede. Usually there are from a dozen to forty women really involved in every murder, but in this case it seems to be only men—you, I, Johnnie, old Scully and that fool of an unfortunate gambler came merely as a culmination, the apex of a human movement, and gets all the punishment."

The cowboy, injured and rebellious, cried out blindly into this fog of mysterious theory, "Well, I didn't do anythin', did I?"

JOAN HESS

The inspiration for this story came with all the subtlety of a sonic boom. On an airplane from somewhere to Fayetteville, I read an editorial in the New York Times that contained the line: ". . . as strange as coming back to your apartment and discovering you have another room . . ." For reasons I can never explain, this analogy had an overwhelming impact on me. The following morning, I wrote "Another Room" and put it in the mail that afternoon, unable to deal with the quiet horror of an ending left entirely to the reader's imagination. Judith Garner's story "Trick or Treat" will leave you stunned, I hope, in a similar fashion.

Another Room

I COME IN, tired, frumpy, and disheveled, with my purse, my briefcase, a newspaper, the mail, a sack of groceries, another sack with several bottles of booze, everything all clutched in my arms or in my coat pockets or in my hands, along with my keys. But this is pretty much how I come home every night to my new apartment, and, as far as I can see into the future, the way I always will.

The day has been worse than a nightmare. I am delayed on the subway—not my fault—but this makes me late, and then I can't find the folder with the demographic data before the conference. I know it's on or in my desk, but I can't put my hands on it and my boss gives me this grim look and shakes his head and I feel like a sorority girl who missed curfew. I'm so rattled I spill coffee on my beige suit.

Then my secretary starts in on her personal problems and ends up sobbing in the ladies room most of the morning while I field the telephone. My first client shows up late, which means my second client has to wait, and all this results in a log jam in the reception room—by noon every last person in the office is snickering and I feel like a damned fool. They're lucky I don't have an assault weapon and a lot of ammunition.

But the thing is, I stagger into the apartment, dump my briefcase and the sacks on the sofa, throw my coat on the chair, and automatically hit the play button on the answering machine because I'm supposed to have drinks and dinner with Eddie unless he has to cancel. This is when I see the door.

The problem is that I've never seen this door before. I rented the apartment about a month ago. It's not "condo," but it's all I can afford, this one-room number in the Village. The neighborhood's relatively safe and has a lot of character. The building's old, which means the radiators are balky antiques, but I had to find something after the divorce and opted to pay too much for something trendy so the ex would know I was doing fine on my own.

I blink, but the door doesn't go away. I push everything aside, sink down on the sofa, and rub my forehead. The wall's been there all along, naturally, holding up the ceiling and blocking the view into my neighbors' bedroom. I can hear them, though. They fight, they make up, and then they do a lot of things that make me uncomfortable, but I can't bang on the wall and tell them they're disgusting. There's no law that says you can't behave like mindless animals, that you can't grunt and groan and shriek things that should not be overheard by disinterested parties lying on a murphy bed all of ten inches away.

But I digress. I'm sitting in the middle of the living room, a bunch of bills in my hand, my machine grinding out messages, and I'm staring at this door. Wood, with top and bottom panels, a doorknob—your basic door. But I'm renting an efficiency apartment in a renovated building and this door is not supposed to be there.

It looks as if it's always been there, right between the bookcase and the television. A really logical location for a door. If there were a separate bedroom, it would be in this precise location. I try to think. I'm fairly certain I'd hung a print there—nothing great, just a Cezanne that I'd picked up years ago. The table with the telephone is now to one side, but it had been centered along the wall as recently as this morning when I rushed out to the subway.

So I'm just sitting, staring at this door. I feel silly, but I look at the baseboards to check for signs of sawdust. I see ten years of dust. My ex used to complain about our baseboards, as if all I did every day was lie on the couch, stuff my face with chocolates, and think of ways to aggravate him when he came home from his hard day at the office. The only thing he forgot was that I'd had a hard day at the office, too. I'm as driven as he, and a damn sight smarter, although that was an issue I tactfully left unexplored.

I'm still staring at this door. Now I think of all sorts of people to call, but I'm having an awkward time with the imagined conversations. It's well past noon, so the super's drunk. My ex is in the Bahamas with his child bride. If I call my mother and say, "Hey, Mom, guess what I found?" she'll be on the next bus from Jersey City, commitment papers in her hot little hand. The more I imagine the announcement that I've just discovered a new room in my apartment, the more I can feel the coarse cotton straitjacket and see the solicitous smiles behind the hypodermics.

I need to think about it. I pour myself a stiff drink of Scotch, move the groceries to the kitchen area, empty the ashtrays, gather up the newspapers from last week, stuff dirty laundry in the closet, and sort of wander around keeping an eye on the door.

It's beginning to get dark, and I seem to think Eddie's going to show up soon. I don't remember making the date, but he called yesterday to remind me, which was rather clever of him. He knows I forget things, especially when I'm under all this pressure at the office and not delighted that the ex is remarried and hating to answer the telephone because I'm afraid it's my mother and I simply don't have the energy to deal with her steady stream of criticism. My shrink gave me a relaxation tape and a prescription refill, but I don't really want to relax and I can't take the pills when I'm drinking.

Okay, I tell myself. Open the door and see what's there.

After a minute, I pour myself another drink and sit down directly across from the door. I decide to count to one hundred, then just get up, walk across the room, and open it.

When I get to fifty, I consider waiting until Eddie shows up so we can open the door together. At seventy-five, I consider calling my shrink, but I know from experience I'll get the damn answering service.

Ninety-eight, ninety-nine, one hundred.

My knees aren't at their steadiest, and my hand is shaking as I pour myself another drink, but I go over and make myself try the doorknob. I don't know what I'm expecting—maybe a jolt of electricity or for the door to fly open and a bunch of people from the office to shout, "Surprise!" even though it's not my birthday and we all know I'm not going to see a promotion anytime soon, not after this morning's disastrous conference.

The door isn't locked. I turn the knob very slowly, for some reason feeling it's important not to make a sound, and ease the door open.

THE room is dark. I'm not about to set foot inside a dark room that wasn't there nine hours ago. I let go of the knob and feel for a switch.

I find one and flip it up. A light fixture on the ceiling goes on and I'm standing in the doorway of a bedroom. I take one step inside, then stop to study the room. It's small and cozy. There are no windows. There is a single bed, neatly made, and beside it a table with a lamp. A dresser, its surface pristine and well polished, and a mirror above it. A wardrobe. An easy chair. An old-fashioned braided rug.

I feel a rush of iciness as it occurs to me that someone might be crouched behind the door. I take a deep breath, let it out slowly, and then look behind the door. All I see is a print on the wall. The Cezanne, oddly enough.

I have to finish the drink before I can go any farther. A little courage—or is it bravado?—sinks in, and I tiptoe to the middle of the room. Although it is exceedingly tidy, there is a sense that it is occupied, although not by a slob like myself. The cushion on the armchair has a slight indentation—someone sits in it, perhaps reading or gazing pensively at the Cezanne.

I'm certain this room doesn't belong to the perverts. There is no other door, not even a closet door, so the only entrance is from my apartment. I get this really bizarre scenario about the previous tenant refusing to leave and vowing to live with me, but without my knowledge. I can almost see her sneaking in and out at night when I'm asleep not ten feet away on my bed, using her front-door key so very cautiously that there's not so much as a tiny click to awaken me.

Yes, the room belongs to a woman. The bedspread isn't ruffly but it has a pleasantly feminine appearance, and now I notice that the chair is upholstered in matching material. On the dresser, there's a vase with an artful arrangement of silk flowers.

I approach the dresser. Unlike mine, there is no dust or scattering of blonde hairs, no jumbled makeup or junk jewelry or bills and work from the office and that sort of accumulation that grows day by day.

I open the top drawer. Here is makeup, but in a compartmentalized tray. Scarves, each folded into a neat bundle. Several small jewelrystore boxes. An unused wallet, still in a box. A few odds and ends of jewelry in yet another compartmentalized box.

She is compulsive about order, I deduce in my best Sherlockian manner. I close that drawer and open the one below it. The sweaters are folded in uniform stacks. I continue to open the drawers and find that each is orderly. Unlike myself, she doesn't have to dig through a drawer every morning to find clean underwear and usable pantyhose. My shrink tells me almost every session that I'll experience less stress if I attempt a degree of organization, both in my apartment and in my mind. I always laugh and assure him that even in the midst of the chaos I know where everything is and that I prefer it that way.

Suddenly I want to burrow through all this neatness, and even pull the drawers out and dump their contents on the floor. Throw the scarves in the air and let them flutter to the floor in a rainbow puddle. Let the makeup clatter on the floor and roll under the chair and dresser. Jump up and down on the bed as if I were a naughty child. Yell profanities to disrupt the ambience of utter serenity.

I quickly close the drawer before I give way to the urge to undo this compulsive woman's handiwork. I am sweating, though, and in the mirror I notice my paleness as I drain the last few drops in the bottom of the glass, wishing for more.

If I leave the room and go to the kitchen to replenish my drink, will the room still be here when I return? If I stay here, will she come back and find me in her bedroom? If she does return, she'll be displeased to find an intruder in her tidy, compartmentalized world. Especially an intruder with dirty hair, a coffee splotch on her skirt, sweat stains on her blouse, a run in her pantyhose. An intruder who battles urges with Scotch.

I abruptly go out of the room and into the kitchen, where the sight of the bottle helps ease my uneven breathing and my anger. I manage to splash whisky into the glass without spilling it and gulp it down. I put the glass in the sink. Will the room still be there?

YES, I go to the wardrobe and open its doors. Of course everything hangs neatly and the shoes are aligned in precise rows. The woman dresses well, although with modest discretion. She doesn't stuff dirty clothes in the dark corners and then forget to take them to the laundromat. She is too fine a gentlewoman to wad up sweatshirts and jeans. Her shoes have no mud on them. Her purses, arranged on the shelf, don't have broken zippers and torn straps.

I'm beginning to like her less and less, this trespasser. For that is what she is. It is my apartment, my lease, my extra locks on the door, and my continual fight with the super to fix the leak in the bathroom. Who is she to hide in this orderliness? Why shouldn't she share my frustration when the radiator goes cold and the dripping faucet reverberates and the animals next door begin to groan?

Who she is is what I intend to find out. I slam the wardrobe door and go to the bedside table. Maybe I'll find an envelope with her name, or a perfectly balanced checkbook with her name—and our shared address beneath it. I yank open the drawer with enough anger to make it screech.

There is a Bible. She is pious and self-righteous, I think hotly. She knows I stopped going to church years ago, when I found the confession box claustrophobic and the platitudes nauseating. I can almost see her kneeling in a pew, her gloved hands clasped together, her face aglow with the inner radiance of a madonna.

I snatch up the Bible and open it to the first page to see if her name is written there in perfect script. Nothing. I throw the Bible on the bed and don't give it a second glance as it falls to the floor. She can pick it up and replace it herself.

I feel in the back of the drawer and blink as my hand withdraws, holding a small gun. I have a gun that resembles this one very closely. I bought it when I first moved to the neighborhood. I think it's in the bottom drawer of my dresser, under the sweaters and scarves. Or maybe in the back of a kitchen cabinet.

At least she's worried about being mugged, I think as I examine the gun to determine that it's loaded. Like me, she must lie awake at night listening to the horns blaring and the occasional arguments in the street below, or to the rhythmic squeals of the bed in the next apartment. Like me, she has nights when she can't sleep, when the sheets become damp and the blanket is twisted like a snake around her legs.

I feel better as I imagine her fear. She may not live in a chaos of dirty clothes, unpaid bills, dishes in the sink, dustballs on the floor, and calls from nosy relatives, but she still has a malignancy that swells in the dark and evokes demons.

I decide to steal her gun. Then she'll be even more frightened. After a few nights of insomnia, she'll be clumsy and scatter powder on her dresser. She'll leave clothes on the chair, forget to replace her makeup in the tray, decide it's easier to leave the bed unmade.

I start for the door, smiling to myself. Then I glance at the dresser, and above it I see her. I halt, catch my breath, and move cautiously forward until I'm facing her. Her hair color is much like mine, but she is wearing it in a stylish cut and it shines in the light. She is at least twenty pounds slimmer. Her face is not bloated. Her eyes are clear, with no trace of the redness that greets me every morning.

The worst thing is that she's smiling. It speaks of contempt, and I know that she compares my hair, my face, my body, and my clothes with hers and that she feels superior. She sees the ugly clutter in my room beyond the doorway.

I decide to show her just how messy life can be. I put the barrel of the gun in my mouth. Now I'm going to wait just a minute until I can see that she's beginning to comprehend what I'm about to do. Then I'm going to splatter brains and blood all over the ceiling and walls of her perfect, tidy bedroom.

TRICK OR TREAT

Judith Garner

I WAS SITTING with my American friend Bambi in our basement kitchen when the front doorbell rang. As the caretaker, I immediately rose to answer it, not for the first time cursing the necessity of taking on this job for the rent-free quarters.

It was October 30, and Mrs. Adams, my niggardly employer, had forbidden fires so early in the season. But already the chill and damp promised a fierce winter. I opened the street door to a grotesque little figure outlined against the yellow fog.

It was a small girl, about eight or nine years old, dressed as a witch in a long black university gown and pointed Welsh hat. She was not one of the tenants of our service flats, but I vaguely thought I had seen her playing in the Gardens with her Nanny and a pram. I had an idea she was an American, that her father had something to do with the Embassy. Not a pretty child, she had an old-fashioned rubber doll in a very dilapidated push-chair.

"Trick or treat?" she asked.

"Treat," I said firmly, thinking I was being offered a choice.

She looked at me expectantly, but when I made no move, she inquired, "Well, where is it then?"

"What?"

"My treat," she said patiently. "If you don't give me a treat, I'll play a trick on you."

"You be off now," I said crossly. "Why, it's extortion! You Americans are all gangsters at heart!"

I closed the door in her hostile little face and went down to the basement, where Bambi was lighting yet another of her cigarettes.

"Trick or treat," I explained.

"Oh!" she exclaimed. "I didn't know you had that custom in England."

"We don't. What is it, American?"

"Yes, indeed. We always used to go out in costumes trick-or-treating in New York."

"What kind of trick can I expect?"

"Well, my mother used to let us take a sockful of flour. If you hit it against the door it leaves a lovely mark."

"I thought I heard some sort of thud as I came downstairs," I said, "but it didn't sound like a sockful of flour, more like a kick."

"Well, they say things are very unpleasant in the States at Halloween nowadays. How gangs will break your windows or slash your tires if you don't give them at least a dollar."

I thought the custom simply encouraged hooliganism and I said so. "Anyhow, Halloween isn't until tomorrow."

Bambi looked put out at my unfriendliness about her national customs. "Good lord!" she said. "I've been giving away pennies for the Guy for the last month. I do think Guy Fawkes is just as peculiar. Fancy burning a human figure!"

I couldn't see it that way, but I held my tongue. Tonight I resented Bambi; poor though she was personally, I envied her the affluence of her background. Besides, I had always wanted to travel myself.

I poured her another cup of tea, and she reverted to her show-business anecdotes. Then Ron, my husband, joined us, and we played dominoes with the gas money until eleven.

I was up at six the next morning, bringing Ron his tea and stoking up the boiler for the hot water. At 7:30 I went up to the ground floor for the milk. The milkman was just leaving.

"Curious decorations you have around here," he said, gesturing at our front door. It certainly was odd. Nailed to the door was a doll's hand. It had a rubber skin filled with cotton; the stuffing was coming out. It looked ugly and perverted.

"If I'd seen that in Brixton or Camden Town," the man said, "you know what I would have thought? That someone was practicing voodoo. But you don't get that sort of thing around here. Not in Gloucester Road, you don't."

I pulled the dirty thing off the door and chucked it into an open dustbin.

"It's all up and down the Gardens," he continued. "Bits of a doll, nailed to the doors."

Not being superstitious, I just shrugged and went upstairs to distribute the milk. Later, having got my son off to school, I began cleaning the flats and the halls.

I did not associate the mutilated doll with my small visitor of the previous evening until, Mrs. Adams having sent me out shopping, I saw the torso just being removed from Professor Newton's door.

"Creepy, isn't it?" I greeted him.

"It's that wretched Halloween child who did it. Trick or treat indeed! Something disturbing about that family. Too much sibling rivalry is my diagnosis. I shall make a formal protest to the parents. Better yet, I shall write a letter to the *Times*, protesting about the importing of foreign customs—noxious foreign customs!" Having with some difficulty removed the nails, the Professor took the grisly souvenir into the house with him and indignantly slammed the door.

The head of the doll was impaled on the railings at the corner. There I found Lady Arthwaite studying it with interest. "I wonder what the poor thing has done to be decapitated," she murmured to me as I passed. "Positively medieval, isn't it? Or, to be precise, it's—well, I haven't seen a doll like that since before the war. The skin texture is so much more lifelike than this disgusting plastic you get nowadays. I would have liked one like it for my little granddaughter."

But as it was chilly I could not wait around. Nevertheless, her homely words took something of the horror out of the incident. I did my shopping, and made Mrs. Adams' lunch. I worked until it became dark, which was very early.

A storm was brewing. The sky was very dark and threatening. My son got home from school just in time, but I made him a nice cup of hot cocoa anyhow, in case the chill had entered his bones. He is a delicate boy.

The rain came pelting down just after five. Ron was drenched when he came in half an hour later. "Halloween," he said. "I need a drink." I mixed the whiskey and hot lemonade the way he liked it.

He sat crouching over the newly stoked boiler in his second-hand smoking jacket. I began preparing the dinner—chops, chips, and peas, with fruit salad and custard for dessert.

We began to eat. Suddenly the front doorbell sounded again. Muttering angrily, I climbed the stairs.

The little American stood there, dressed like a pirate this time.

"Trick or treat?" she said.

This time she had her baby brother in the push-chair.

JOHN LUTZ

*L*ike most good short stories, "August Heat" is about one thing. It hooks the reader, then never reveals too much too soon, and in heightening stages poses its fascinating question. The concept is simple and brilliant, and the execution spare and suspenseful. This deceptive simplicity and spareness lends it the power of a parable. Everything in the story belongs. Everything in the story works. While the ending provides sudden revelation like the punch line of some dark, celestial joke, it bores deep into the brain and lingers because it's delivered with a reserve that sets the reader's mind ticking. This is the perfectly balanced work of talent with tight control, of a miniaturist by nature diligently going about his craft. If "August Heat" were a watch, it would have a jeweled Swiss movement, it would keep precise time, and it would tick softly.

There's a subcategory in mystery short fiction that I think of as the man-on-a-ledge story. It's easy to understand why it exists. When your main character is poised on a narrow ledge a fatal number of floors above hard pavement, there's built-in suspense galore. In "High Stakes" I wanted to write the most effective story I could to add to that body of mystery literature. Fear of falling is one of our earliest terrors. It stays with us. The best of the man-on-a-ledge stories finds and manipulates that basic, breathless fear. The reader identifies with the poised protagonist, secure for now but perhaps a second away from plunging into oblivion. Maybe these stories work because in a way we're all on a ledge, with the odds on survival changing with the wind. Some of us like to feel the desperation, then find a safe way down.

High Stakes

ERNIE FOLLOWED THE bellhop into the crummy room at the Hayes Hotel, was shown the decrepit bathroom with its cracked porcelain, the black-and-white TV with its rolling picture. The bellhop, who was a teenager with a pimply complexion, smiled and waited. Ernie tipped him a dollar, which, considering that Ernie had no luggage other than the overnight bag he carried himself, seemed adequate. The bellhop sneered at him and left.

After the click of the door latch, there was thick silence in the room. Ernie sat on the edge of the bed, his ears gradually separating the faint sounds outside from the room's quietude—the thrumming rush of city traffic, a very distant siren or occasional honking horn, the metallic thumping and strumming of elevator cables from the bowels of the building. Someone dropped something heavy in the room upstairs. A maid pushed a linen cart with a squeaky wheel along the hall outside Ernie's door. Ernie bowed his head, cupped his face in his hands, and stared at the worn pale-blue carpet. Then he closed his eyes and sought the temporary anonymity of interior darkness.

Ernie's luck was down. Almost as low as Ernie himself, who stood a shade over five-foot-four, even in his boots with the built-up heels. Usually a natty dresser, tonight he'd disgraced his slender frame with a cheap off-the-rack brown suit, a soiled white shirt, and a ridiculous red clip-on bow tie. He'd had to abandon his regular wardrobe at his previous hotel in lieu of settling the bill. Ernie had a face like a conniving ferret's, with watery pinkish eyes and a long bent nose. His appearance wasn't at all deceptive. Ernie ferreted and connived.

He had spent most of his forty years in the starkly poor neighborhood of his birth; and if he wasn't the smartest guy around, he did possess a kind of gritty cunning that had enabled him to make his own erratic way in the world. And he had instinct, hunches, that led to backing the right horse sometimes, or playing the right card sometimes. Sometimes. He got by, anyway. Getting by was Ernie's game, and he just about broke even. He was not so much a winner as a survivor. There were people who resented even that.

One of those people was Carl Atwater. Ernie thought about Carl, opened his eyes, and stood up from the sagging bed. He got the half-pint of rye out of his overnight bag and went into the bathroom for the glass he'd seen on the basin. He tried not to think about Carl and the thousand dollars he owed Carl from that card game the last time he'd been here in his hometown. He poured himself a drink, sat at the nicked and scarred plastic-topped desk, and glanced around again at the tiny room.

Even for Ernie this was a dump. He was used to better things; he didn't always slip into town on the sly and sign into a fleabag hotel. If he hadn't needed to see his sister Eunice to borrow some money—not the thousand he owed Carl, just a couple of hundred to see him down to Miami—he wouldn't be here now, contemplating on how he would be on the roaches climbing the wall behind the bed if someone else were here to lay down some money on which one they thought would be first to reach the ceiling.

He smiled. What would Eunice think of him betting on cockroaches? She wouldn't be surprised; she'd told him for years that gambling was a sickness, and he had it bad. Maybe she was right, harping at him all the time to quit betting. But then she'd never hit the big one at Pimlico. She'd never turned up a corner of a hole card and seen a lovely third queen peeking out. She'd never . . .

The hell with it. Ernie got two decks of cards from a suitcoat pocket. He squinted at the decks, then slipped the marked one back into the pocket. Ernie always made it a point to carry a marked deck. A slickster in Reno had shown him how to doctor the cards so that only an expert could tell, and then only by looking closely. He broke the seal on the straight deck and dealt himself a hand of solitaire. He always played fair with himself. Two minutes after he'd switched on the desk lamp, tilting the yellowed shade to take the glare off the cards, he was lost in that intensity of concentration that only a devout gambler can achieve.

After losing three games in a row, he pushed the cards away and rubbed his tired eyes.

That was when someone knocked on the door.

Ernie sat paralyzed, not only by fear of Carl Atwater but by fear of what all gamblers regard as their enemy—the unexpected. The unexpected was what gave the dice a final unlikely tumble, what caused the favorite horse to stumble on the far turn, what filled inside straights for novice poker players. This time what the unexpected did was the worst it had ever done to Ernie; it delivered two very large business-like individuals to his hotel room. They had a key, and when their knock wasn't answered they had opened the door and walked right in.

They were big men, all right, but in the tiny room—and contrasted with Ernie's frailness—they appeared gigantic. The larger of the two, a lantern-jawed ex-pug type with a pushed-in nose and cold blue eyes, smiled down at Ernie. It wasn't the sort of smile that would melt hearts. His partner, a handsome dark-haired man with what looked like a knife scar down one cheek, stood wooden-faced. It was the smiling man who spoke.

"I guess you know that Carl Atwater sent us," he said. He had a deep voice that suited his immensity.

Ernie swallowed a throatful of marbles. His heart ran wild. "But . . . how could anyone know I was here? I just checked in."

"Carl knows lots of desk clerks in hotels all over the city," the smiler said. "Soon as you checked in, we heard about it and Carl thought you rated a visit." He grinned wider and lazily cracked his knuckles. The sound in the small room was like a string of exploding firecrackers. "Don't dummy up on us, Ernie. You know what kind of visit this is."

Ernie stood up without thinking about it, knocking his chair over backward. "Hey, wait a minute! I mean, Carl and I are old buddies, and all I owe him is an even thousand bucks. I mean, you got the wrong guy! Check with Carl— just do me that favor!"

"It's precisely because you only owe a thousand dollars that we're here," the dark-haired one said. "Too many people owe Carl small sums, welshers like yourself. You're going to be an example for the rest of the petty four-flushers, Ernie. It will be a bad example. They won't want to follow it. They'll pay their debts instead, and that will add up to a lot of money."

"There ain't no good ways to die," the smiler said, "but some ways is worse than others."

Both men moved toward Ernie, slowly, as if wanting him to fully experience his dread. Ernie glanced at the door. Too far away. "Just check with Carl! Please!" he pleaded mindlessly, backpeddling on numbed legs. He was trembling. The bonecrushers kept advancing. The window was behind Ernie, but he was twelve stories above the street. The fleabag room wasn't air-conditioned, so the window was open about six inches. Corner a rat and watch it instinctively choose the less immediate danger. Ernie whirled and flung himself at the window. He snagged a fingernail in the faded lace curtain, felt the nail rip as he hurled the window all the way open. The smiler grunted and lunged at him, but Ernie scampered outside onto the ledge with speed that amazed.

A gargantuan hand emerged from the open window. Ernie shuffled side-ways to avoid it. He pressed his quaking body back against the brick wall and stared upward at the black night sky, the stiff summer breeze whipping at his unbuttoned suitcoat.

The smiler stuck his huge head out the window. He studied the narrowness of the ledge on which Ernie was balanced, stared down at the street twelve stories below. He exposed a mouthful of crooked teeth and laughed a rolling, phlegmy rumble. The laugh was vibrant with emotion, but not humor.

"I told you some ways to die was worse than others," he said. "You're part worm, not part bird." He pulled his head back inside and shut the window. Ernie got a glimpse of sausage-sized fingers turning the lock.

Be calm, he told himself, be *calm*! He was trapped on the ledge, but his situation was much improved over what it had been a few minutes ago.

Then he really began to analyze his predicament. The concrete ledge he was poised on was only about six inches wide—not the place to go for a walk in his dress boots with their built-up slick leather heels. And just to his right, the ledge ended four feet away where the side of the building jutted out, and there were no other windows Ernie might be able to enter. To his left, beyond the locked window to his room, was a window to a room that did have an air conditioner. The old rusted unit extended from the window about three feet. Not only would that window be firmly fastened closed against the top of the unit, but there was no way to get around or over the bulky sloping steel squareness of the air conditioner to reach the next window.

Ernie glanced upward. There was no escape in that direction, either.

Then he looked down.

Vertigo hit him with hammer force. Twelve stories seemed like twelve miles. He could see the tops of foreshortened streetlights, a few toylike cars turning at the intersection. His mind whirled, his head swam with terror. The ledge he was on seemed only a few inches wide and was barely visible, almost behind him, from his precarious point of view. His legs quivered weakly; his boots seemed to become detached from them, seemed to be stiff, awkward creatures with their own will that might betray him and send him plunging to his death. He could see so far—as if he were flying. Ernie clenched his eyes shut. He didn't let himself imagine what happened to flesh and bone when it met the pavement after a twelve-story drop.

He shoved himself backward against the security of the wall with what strength he had left, his hands at his sides, his fingernails clawing into the mortar. That rough brick wall was his mother and his lover and every high card he had ever held. It was all he had. He was hypocrite enough to pray.

But the terror seeped into his pores, into his brain and soul, became one with him. A thousand bucks, a lousy thousand bucks! He could have gone to a loan shark, could have stolen something and pawned it, could have begged. He could have . . .

But he had to do something now. *Now!* He had to survive.

Not looking down, staring straight ahead with fear-bulged eyes, he chanced a hesitant, shuffling sideways step to his left, back toward his window. He dug his fingertips into the bricks as he moved, wishing the wall were soft so he could sink his fingers deep into it. Then he was assailed by an image of the wall coming apart like modeling clay in his hands, affording no support at all, sending him in a horrifyingly breathless arc into the night. He tried not to think about the wall, tried not to think about anything. It was a time for the primal raw judgment of fear.

Ernie made himself take another tentative step. Another. He winced each time his hard leather heels scraped loudly on the concrete. The material of his cheap suit kept snagging on the rough wall at his seat and shoulders, the backs of his legs. Once, the sole of his left boot slid on something small and rounded—a pebble, perhaps—with a rollerlike action that almost caused him to fall. The panic that washed over him was a cold dark thing that he never wanted to feel again.

Finally, he was at the window. He contorted his body carefully, afraid that the night breeze might snatch it at any second, craned his neck till it hurt, and peered into his room.

It was empty. The bonecrushers had left. The threadbare furniture, the bed, the hard, worn carpet, had never looked so sweet. One of Ernie's hands curled around the window frame, came in contact with the smooth glass. He could see the tarnished brass latch at the top of the lower frame, firmly lodged in the locked position.

He struck at the window experimentally. The backward force of the blow separated him from the brick wall. Air shrieked into his lungs in a shrill gasp, and he straightened his body and slammed it backward, cracking his head on the wall, making him dizzy and nauseated. He stood frozen that way for a full minute.

Gradually, he became aware of a coolness on his cheeks—the high breeze drying his tears. He knew he couldn't strike the glass hard enough to break it without sending himself in an unbalanced tilt out over the street to death waiting below.

Carl's bonecrushers were probably already having a beer somewhere, counting Ernie as dead. They were right. They were professionals who knew about such things, who recognized death when they saw it. Ernie's lower lip began to tremble. He wasn't an evil person; he'd never deliberately done anything to harm anyone. He didn't deserve this. *No one deserved this!*

He decided to scream. Maybe somebody—one of the other guests, a maid, the disdainful bellhop—would hear him.

"Help! Help!"

He almost laughed maniacally at the hopelessness of it. His choked screams were so feeble, lost on the wind, absorbed by the vast night. He could barely hear them himself.

As far back as he could remember, desperation had been with him as a dull ache in the pit of his stomach, like an inflamed appendix threatening to burst. If it wasn't a friend, it was surely a close acquaintance. He should be able to deal with it if anyone could.

Yet he couldn't. Not this time. Maybe it inevitably had to come to this, to the swift screaming plunge that had so often awoken him from dark dreams. But tonight there would be no awakening, because he wasn't dreaming.

Ernie cursed himself and all his ancestry that had brought him to this point. He cursed his luck. But he would not let himself give up; his gameness was all he had. There was always, for the man with a feel for the angles, some sort of edge against the odds.

His pockets! What was in his pockets that he might use to break the window?

The first object he drew out was a greasy comb. He fumbled it, almost instinctively lunged for it as it slipped from his fingers and dropped. He started to bow his head to watch the comb fall, then remembered the last time he'd looked down. He again pressed the back of his head against the bricks. The world rocked crazily.

Here was his wallet. He withdrew it from his hip pocket carefully, squeezing it as if it were a bird that might try to take flight. He opened it, and his fingers groped through its contents. He explored the wallet entirely by feel, afraid to look down at it. A few bills, a credit card, a driver's license, a couple of old IOUs that he let flutter into the darkness. He kept the stiff plastic credit card and decided to drop the wallet deliberately. Maybe someone below would see it fall and look up and spot him. The odds were against it, he knew. This was a bad neighborhood; there were few people on the sidewalks. What would happen is that somebody would find the wallet, stick it in his pocket, and walk away. Ernie started to work the bills, a ten and two ones, out of the wallet, then decided it wasn't worth the effort and let the wallet drop. Money wouldn't help him where he was.

There was a slight crack between the upper and lower window frames. Ernie tried to insert the credit card, praying that it would fit.

It did! A break! He'd gotten a break! Maybe it would be all he'd need!

He craned his neck sideways to watch as he slid the credit card along the frame and shoved it against the window latch. He could feel warmer air from the room rising from the crack and caressing his knuckles. He was so close, so close to being on the other side of that thin pane of glass and safe!

The latch moved slightly—he was sure of it! He pressed harder with the plastic card, feeling its edge dig into his fingers. He could feel or see no movement now. Desperately, he began to work the card back and forth. His hands were slick with perspiration.

The latch moved again!

Ernie almost shouted with joy. He would beat this! In a minute or five minutes the window would be unlocked and he would raise it and fall into the room and hug and kiss the worn carpet. He actually grinned as he manipulated his weakened fingers to get a firmer grip on the card.

And suddenly the card wasn't there. He gasped and snatched frantically, barely feeling the card's plastic corner as it slipped all the way through the crack into the room. He saw it slide to the bottom of the window pane, bounce off the inside wooden frame, and drop to the floor. From where he stood, he could see it lying on the carpet. Lying where it could no longer help him.

Ernie sobbed. His body began to tremble so violently that he thought it might shake itself off the ledge. He tried to calm himself when he realized that might actually happen. With more effort than he'd ever mustered for anything, he controlled himself and stood motionless.

He had to think, think, think! . . .

What else did he have in his pockets?

His room key!

He got it out and grasped it in the palm of his hand. It was affixed to no tag or chain, simply a brass key. He tried to fit it into the narrow crack between the upper and lower window frames, but it was far wider than the credit card; he couldn't even insert the tip.

Then he got an idea. The putty holding the glass in its frame was old and chipped, dried hard from too many years and too many faded layers of paint.

Ernie began to chip at the putty with the tip of the key. Some of it came loose and crumbled, dropping to the ledge. He dug with the key again and more of the dried putty broke away from the frame. He would have to work all the way around the pane, and that would take time. It would take concentration. But Ernie would do it, because there was no other way off the ledge, because for the first time he realized how much he loved life. He flexed his knees slightly, his back still pressed to the hard bricks, and continued to chip away at the hardened putty.

After what seemed like an hour, a new problem developed. He'd worked more than halfway around the edges of the window pane when his legs began to cramp painfully. And his knees began trembling, not so much from fear now as from fatigue. Ernie stood up straight, tried to relax his calf muscles.

When he bent to begin work again, he found that within a few minutes the muscles cramped even more painfully. He straightened once more, felt the pain ease slightly. He would work this way, in short shifts, until the pain became unbearable and his trembling legs threatened to lose all strength and sensation. He would endure the pain because there was no other way. He didn't let himself consider what would happen if his legs gave out before he managed to chip away all the putty. Cautiously he flexed his knees, scooted lower against the wall, and began wielding the key with a frantic kind of economy of motion.

Finally, the putty was all chipped away, lying in triangular fragments on the ledge or on the sidewalk below.

Ernie ran his hand along the area where the glass met the wood frame. He felt a biting pain as the sharp edge of the glass sliced into his finger. He jerked the hand back, stared at his dark blood. The finger began to throb in quick rhythm with his heart, a persistent reminder of mortality.

His problem now was that the pane wouldn't come out. It was slightly larger than the perimeter of the window frame opening, set in a groove in the wood, so it couldn't be pushed inward. It would have to be pulled out toward the street.

Ernie tried fitting the key between the wood and the glass so he could lever the top of the pane outward. The key was too wide.

He pressed his back against the bricks and began to cry again. His legs were rubbery; his entire body ached and was racked by occasional cramps and spasms. He was getting weaker, he knew; too weak to maintain his precarious perch on the narrow ledge. If only he still had the credit card, he thought, he would be able to pry the glass loose, let it fall to the sidewalk, and he could easily get back inside. But then if he'd held onto the card he might have been able to force the latch. The wind picked up, whipped at his clothes, threatened to fill his suitcoat like a sail and pluck him from the ledge.

Then Ernie remembered. His suitcoat pocket! In the coat's inside pocket was his deck of marked cards! His edge against the odds!

He got the cards out, drew them from their box, and let the box arc down and away in the breeze. He thumbed the top card from the deck and inserted it between the glass and the wooden frame. He gave it a slight twist and pulled. The glass seemed to move outward.

Then the card tore almost in half and lost all usefulness.

Ernie let it sail out into the night. He thumbed off the next card, bent it slightly so that it formed a subtle hook when he inserted it. This time the glass almost edged out of its frame before the card was torn. Ernie discarded that one and worked patiently, almost confidently. He had fifty more chances. The odds were with him now.

The tenth card, the king of diamonds, did the trick. The pane fell outward top first, scraped on the ledge, and then plummeted to shatter on the street below.

On uncontrollably shaking legs, Ernie took three shuffling sideways steps, gripped the window frame, and leaned backward in a stooped position, toward the room's interior.

Then he lost his grip.

His left leg shot out and his shoulder hit the wooden frame. Gravity on both sides of the window fought over him for a moment while his heart blocked the scream in his throat.

He fell into the room, bumping his head on the top of the window frame as he dropped, hitting the floor hard. A loud sob of relief escaped his lips as he continued his drop, whirling into unconsciousness.

HE awoke terrified. Then he realized he was still lying on his back on the scratchy, worn carpet, on the motionless, firm floor of his hotel room, and the terror left him.

But only for a moment.

Staring down at him was Carl Atwater, flanked by his two bonecrushers.

Ernie started to get up, then fell back, supporting himself on his elbows. He searched the faces of the three men looming over him and was surprised to see a relaxed smile on Carl's shrewd features, deadpan indifference on those of his henchmen. "Look, about that thousand dollars . . ." he said, trying to ride the feeble ray of sunshine in Carl's smile.

"Don't worry about that, Ernie, old buddy," Carl said. He bent forward, offering his hand.

Ernie gripped the strong, well-manicured hand, and Carl helped him to his feet. He was still weak, so he moved over to lean on the desk. The eyes of the three men followed him.

"You don't owe me the thousand anymore," Carl said.

Ernie was astounded. He knew Carl; they lived by the same unbreakable code. "You mean you're going to cancel the debt?"

"I never cancel a debt," Carl said in an icy voice. He crossed his arms, still smiling. "Let's say you worked it off. When we heard you checked in at the Hayes, we got right down here. We were in the building across the street ten minutes after you were shown to this room."

"You mean the three of you . . . ?"

"Four of us," Carl corrected.

That was when Ernie understood. The two bonecrushers were pros; they would never have allowed him to escape, even temporarily, out the window. They had let him get away, boxed him in so that there was no place to go but out onto the ledge. The whole thing had been a set-up. After locking the window the two bonecrushers had gone across the street to join their boss. Ernie knew who the fourth man must be.

"You're off the hook," Carl told him, "because I bet a thousand dollars that you'd find a way off that ledge without getting killed." There was a sudden genuine flash of admiration in his smile, curiously mixed with contempt. "I had faith in you, Ernie, because I know you and guys like you.

You're a survivor, no matter what. You're the rat that finds its way off the sinking ship. Or off a high ledge."

Ernie began to shake again, this time with rage. "You were watching me from across the street. The three of you and whoever you placed the bet with. . . . All the time I was out there you were watching, waiting to see if I'd fall."

"I never doubted you, Ernie," Carl told him.

Ernie's legs threatened to give out at last. He staggered a few steps and sat slumped on the edge of the mattress. He had come so close to dying; Carl had come so close to backing a loser. "I'll never place another bet," he mumbled. "Not on a horse, a football game, a roulette wheel, a political race . . . nothing! I'm cured, I swear it!"

Carl laughed. "I told you I know you, Ernie. Better than you think. I've heard guys like you talk that way hundreds of times. They always gamble again, because it's what keeps them alive. They have to believe that a turn of a card or a tumble of the dice or a flip of a coin might change things for them, because they can't stand things the way they are. You're like the rest of them, Ernie. I'll see you again sooner or later, and I'll see your money."

Carl walked toward the door. The bonecrusher with the knife scar was there ahead of him, holding the door open. Neither big man was paying the slightest attention to Ernie now. They were finished with him, and he was of no more importance than a piece of the room's worn-out furniture.

"Take care of yourself, Ernie," Carl said, and they went out.

Ernie sat for a long time staring at the floor. He remembered how it had been out on that ledge; it had changed him permanently, he was convinced. It had wised him up as nothing else could. Carl was wrong if he thought Ernie wasn't finished gambling. Ernie knew better. He was a new man and a better man. He wasn't all talk like those other guys. Carl was mistaken about him. Ernie was sure of it.

He would bet on it.

AUGUST HEAT

W. F. Harvey

PHENISTONE ROAD, CLAPHAM,
AUGUST 20TH, 190—.

I HAVE HAD what I believe to be the most remarkable day in my life, and while the events are still fresh in my mind, I wish to put them down on paper as clearly as possible.

Let me say at the outset that my name is James Clarence Withencroft.

I am forty years old, in perfect health, never having known a day's illness.

By profession I am an artist, not a very successful one, but I earn enough money by my black-and-white work to satisfy my necessary wants.

My only near relative, a sister, died five years ago, so that I am independent.

I breakfasted this morning at nine, and after glancing through the morning paper I lighted my pipe and proceeded to let my mind wander in the hope that I might chance upon some subject for my pencil.

The room, though door and windows were open, was oppressively hot, and I had just made up my mind that the coolest and most comfortable place in the neighborhood would be the deep end of the public swimming bath, when the idea came.

I began to draw. So intent was I on my work that I left my lunch untouched, only stopping work when the clock of St. Jude's struck four.

The final result, for a hurried sketch, was, I felt sure, the best thing I had done.

It showed a criminal in the dock immediately after the judge had pronounced sentence. The man was fat—enormously fat. The flesh hung in rolls about his chin; it creased his huge, stumpy neck. He was clean shaven (perhaps I should say a few days before he must have been clean shaven) and almost bald. He stood in the dock, his short, clumsy fingers clasping the rail, looking straight in front of him. The feeling that his expression conveyed was not so much one of horror as of utter, absolute collapse.

There seemed nothing in the man strong enough to sustain that mountain of flesh.

I rolled up the sketch, and without quite knowing why, placed it in my pocket. Then with the rare sense of happiness which the knowledge of a good thing well done gives, I left the house.

I believe that I set out with the idea of calling upon Trenton, for I remember walking along Lytton Street and turning to the right along Gilchrist Road at the bottom of the hill where the men were at work on the new tram lines.

From there onwards I have only the vaguest recollections of where I went. The one thing of which I was fully conscious was the awful heat, that came up from the dusty asphalt pavement as an almost palpable wave. I longed for the thunder promised by the great banks of copper-coloured cloud that hung low over the western sky.

I must have walked five or six miles, when a small boy roused me from my reverie by asking the time.

It was twenty minutes to seven.

When he left me I began to take stock of my bearings. I found myself standing before a gate that led into a yard bordered by a strip of thirsty earth, where there were flowers, purple stock and scarlet geranium. Above the entrance was a board with the inscription—

CHS. ATKINSON   MONUMENTAL MASON
WORKER IN ENGLISH AND ITALIAN MARBLES

From the yard itself came a cheery whistle, the noise of hammer blows, and the cold sound of steel meeting stone.

A sudden impulse made me enter.

A man was sitting with his back towards me, busy at work on a slab of curiously veined marble. He turned round as he heard my steps and stopped short.

It was the man I had been drawing, whose portrait lay in my pocket.

He sat there; huge and elephantine, the sweat pouring from his scalp, which he wiped with a red silk handkerchief. But though the face was the same, the expression was absolutely different.

He greeted me smiling, as if we were old friends, and shook my hand.

I apologised for my intrusion.

"Everything is hot and glary outside," I said. "This seems an oasis in the wilderness."

"I don't know about the oasis," he replied, "but it certainly is hot, as hot as hell. Take a seat, sir!"

He pointed to the end of the gravestone on which he was at work, and I sat down.

"That's a beautiful piece of stone you've got hold of," I said.

He shook his head. "In a way it is," he answered; "the surface here is as fine as anything you could wish, but there's a big flaw at the back, though I don't expect you'd ever notice it. I could never make really a good job of a bit of marble like that. It would be all right in the summer like this; it wouldn't mind the blasted heat. But wait till the winter comes. There's nothing quite like frost to find out the weak points in stone."

"Then what's it for?" I asked.

The man burst out laughing.

"You'd hardly believe me if I was to tell you it's for an exhibition, but it's the truth. Artists have exhibitions: so do grocers and butchers; we have them too. All the latest little things in headstones, you know."

He went on to talk of marbles, which sort best withstood wind and rain, and which were easiest to work; then of his garden and a new sort of carnation he had bought. At the end of every other minute he would drop his tools, wipe his shining head, and curse the heat.

I said little, for I felt uneasy. There was something unnatural, uncanny, in meeting this man.

I tried at first to persuade myself that I had seen him before, that his face, unknown to me, had found a place in some out-of-the-way corner of my memory, but I knew that I was practicing little more than a plausible piece of self-deception.

Mr. Atkinson finished his work, spat on the ground, and got up with a sigh of relief.

"There! What do you think of that?" he said, with an air of evident pride. The inscription which I read for the first time was this—

SACRED TO THE MEMORY
OF
JAMES CLARENCE WITHENCROFT.
BORN JAN. 18TH, 1860.
HE PASSED AWAY VERY SUDDENLY
ON AUGUST 20TH, 190—
"In the midst of life we are in death."

For some time I sat in silence. Then a cold shudder ran down my spine. I asked him where he had seen the name.

"Oh, I didn't see it anywhere," replied Mr. Atkinson. "I wanted some name, and I put down the first that came into my head. Why do you want to know?"

"It's a strange coincidence, but it happens to be mine."

He gave a long, low whistle.

"And the dates?"

"I can only answer for one of them, and that's correct."

"It's a rum go!" he said.

But he knew less than I did. I told him of my morning's work. I took the sketch from my pocket and showed it to him. As he looked, the expression of his face altered until it became more and more like that of the man I had drawn.

"And it was only the day before yesterday," he said, "that I told Maria there were no such things as ghosts!"

Neither of us had seen a ghost, but I knew what he meant.

"You probably heard my name," I said.

"And you must have seen me somewhere and have forgotten it! Were you at Clacton-on-Sea last July?"

I had never been to Clacton in my life. We were silent for some time. We were both looking at the same thing, the two dates on the gravestone, and one was right.

"Come inside and have some supper," said Mr. Atkinson.

His wife is a cheerful little woman, with the flaky red cheeks of the country-bred. Her husband introduced me as a friend of his who was an artist. The result was unfortunate, for after the sardines and watercress had been removed, she brought me out a Doré Bible, and I had to sit and express my admiration for nearly half an hour.

I went outside, and found Atkinson sitting on the gravestone smoking.

We resumed the conversation at the point we had left off.

"You must excuse my asking," I said, "but do you know of anything you've done for which you could be put on trial?"

He shook his head.

"I'm not a bankrupt, the business is prosperous enough. Three years ago I gave turkeys to some of the guardians at Christmas, but that's all I can think of. And they were small ones, too," he added as an afterthought.

He got up, fetched a can from the porch, and began to water the flowers. "Twice a day regular in the hot weather," he said, "and then the heat sometimes gets the better of the delicate ones. And ferns, good Lord! They could never stand it. Where do you live?"

I told him my address. It would take an hour's quick walk to get back home.

"It's like this," he said. "We'll look at the matter straight. If you go back home tonight, you take your chance of accidents. A cart may run over you, and there's always banana skins and orange peel, to say nothing of fallen ladders."

He spoke of the improbable with in intense seriousness that would have been laughable six hours before. But I did not laugh.

"The best thing we can do," he continued, "is for you to stay here till twelve o'clock. We'll go upstairs and smoke; it may be cooler inside."

To my surprise I agreed.

We are sitting in a long, low room beneath the eaves. Atkinson has sent his wife to bed. He himself is busy sharpening some tools at a little oilstone, smoking one of my cigars the while.

The air seems charged with thunder. I am writing this at a shaky table before the open window. The leg is cracked, and Atkinson, who seems a handy man with his tools, is going to mend it as soon as he has finished putting an edge on his chisel.

It is after eleven now. I shall be gone in less than an hour.

But the heat is stifling.

It is enough to send a man mad.

BILL PRONZINI

*M*ore *than a few critics have hung and continue to hang a hard-boiled label on the "Nameless Detective" series. (One even went so far as to call it "retro noir," whatever the hell that means.) Not so. None of the twenty-six "Nameless" novels to date is anything other than humanist crime fiction with an edge—my personal definition. In fact, just one "Nameless" short story can legitimately be tagged hardboiled, "Souls Burning," and that only because its edge is razor-honed. One reason I've selected it for inclusion here is that it's the exception that proves my point. The other reason, ironically enough, is that I consider it the best of all the "Nameless" shorts.*

Although much of his work was labeled hardboiled, Benjamin Appel was a prototypical writer of humanist crime fiction with an edge—a much sharper edge, fine-gritted with far more skill, nuance, and raw power than anything I could ever generate. His 1934 novel, Brain Guy, *is a better gangster story than Burnett's* Little Caesar; The Dark Stain *and* The Raw Edge *are brilliant dissections of urban race relations and waterfront corruption, respectively. Dark, mordant, and a model of concision, "Murder of the Frank-furter Man" addresses the same central theme as "Souls Burning" in a wholly dissimilar fashion. It was written in the early years of the Depression, sixty years before my story. Proving, perhaps, that there is little fundamental difference between the mean streets of then and now.*

Souls Burning

HOTEL MAJESTIC, SIXTH street, downtown San Francisco. A hell of an address—a hell of a place for an ex-con not long out of Folsom to set up housekeeping. Sixth Street, south of Market—South of the Slot, it used to be called—is the heart of the city's Skid Road and has been for more than half a century.

Eddie Quinlan. A name and a voice out of the past, neither of which I'd recognized when he called that morning. Close to seven years since I had seen or spoken to him, six years since I'd even thought of him. Eddie Quinlan. Edgewalker, shadow-man with no real substance or purpose, drifting along the narrow catwalk that separates conventional society from the underworld. Information seller, gofer, small-time bagman, doer of any insignificant job, legitimate or otherwise, that would help keep him in food and shelter, liquor and cigarettes. The kind of man you looked at but never really saw: a modern-day Yehudi, the little man who wasn't there. Eddie Quinlan. Nobody, loser—fall guy. Drug bust in the Tenderloin one night six and a half years ago; one dealer setting up another, and Eddie Quinlan, small-time bagman, caught in the middle; hard-assed judge, five years in Folsom, goodbye Eddie Quinlan. And the drug dealers? They walked, of course. Both of them.

And now Eddie was out, had been out for six months. And after six months of freedom, he'd called me. Would I come to his room at the Hotel Majestic tonight around eight? He'd tell me why when he saw me. It was real important—would I come? All right, Eddie. But I couldn't figure it. I had bought information from him in the old days, bits and pieces for five or ten dollars; maybe he had something to sell now. Only I wasn't looking for anything and I hadn't put the word out, so why pick me to call?

If you're smart you don't park your car on the street at night South of the Slot. I put mine in the Fifth and Mission Garage at 7:45 and walked over to Sixth. It had rained most of the day and the streets were still wet, but now the sky was cold and clear. The kind of night that is as hard as black glass, so that light seems to bounce off the dark instead of shining through it; lights and their colors so bright and sharp reflecting off the night and the wet surfaces that the glare is like splinters against your eyes.

Friday night, and Sixth Street was teeming. Sidewalks jammed—old men, young men, bag ladies, painted ladies, blacks, whites, Asians, addicts, pushers, muttering mental cases, drunks leaning against walls in tight little clusters while they shared paper-bagged bottles of sweet wine and cans of malt liquor; men and women in filthy rags, in smart new outfits topped off with sunglasses, carrying ghetto blasters and red-and-white canes, some of the canes in the hands of individuals who could see as well as I could, carrying a hidden array of guns and knives and other lethal instruments. Cheap hotels, greasy spoons, seedy taverns, and liquor stores complete with barred windows and cynical proprietors that stayed open well past midnight. Laughter, shouts, curses, threats; bickering and dickering. The stenches of urine and vomit and unwashed bodies and rotgut liquor, and over those like an umbrella, the subtle effluvium of despair. Predators and prey, half hidden in shadow, half revealed in the bright, sharp dazzle of fluorescent lights and bloody neon.

It was a mean street, Sixth, one of the meanest, and I walked it warily. I may be fifty-eight but I'm a big man and I walk hard too; and I look like what I am. Two winos tried to panhandle me and a fat hooker in an orange wig tried to sell me a piece of her tired body, but no one gave me any trouble.

The Majestic was five stories of old wood and plaster and dirty brick, just off Howard Street. In front of its narrow entrance, a crack dealer and one of his customers were haggling over the price of a baggie of rock cocaine; neither of them paid any attention to me as I moved past them. Drug deals go down in the open here, day and night. It's not that the cops don't care, or that they don't patrol Sixth regularly; it's just that the dealers outnumber them ten to one. On Skid Road any crime less severe than aggravated assault is strictly low priority.

Small, barren lobby: no furniture of any kind. The smell of ammonia hung in the air like swamp gas. Behind the cubbyhole desk was an old man with dead eyes that would never see anything they didn't want to see. I said, "Eddie Quinlan," and he said, "Two-oh-two" without moving his lips. There was an elevator but it had an *Out of Order* sign on it; dust speckled the sign. I went up the adjacent stairs.

The disinfectant smell permeated the second floor hallway as well. Room 202 was just off the stairs, fronting on Sixth; one of the metal 2s on the door had lost a screw and was hanging upside down. I used my knuckles just below it. Scraping noise inside, and a voice said, "Yeah?" I identified myself. A lock clicked, a chain rattled, the door wobbled open, and for the first time in nearly seven years I was looking at Eddie Quinlan.

He hadn't changed much. Little guy, about five-eight, and past forty now. Thin, nondescript features, pale eyes, hair the color of sand. The hair was thinner and the lines in his face were longer and deeper, almost like incisions where they bracketed his nose. Otherwise he was the same Eddie Quinlan.

"Hey," he said, "thanks for coming. I mean it, thanks."

"Sure, Eddie."

"Come on in."

The room made me think of a box—the inside of a huge rotting packing crate. Four bare walls with the scaly remnants of paper on them like psoriatic skin, bare uncarpeted floor, unshaded bulb hanging from the center of a bare ceiling. The bulb was dark; what light there was came from a low-wattage reading lamp and a wash of red-and-green neon from the hotel's sign that spilled in through a single window. Old iron-framed bed, unpainted night-stand, scarred dresser, straight-backed chair next to the bed and in front of the window, alcove with a sink and toilet and no door, closet that wouldn't be much larger than a coffin.

"Not much, is it," Eddie said.

I didn't say anything.

He shut the hall door, locked it. "Only place to sit is that chair there. Unless you want to sit on the bed? Sheets are clean. I try to keep things clean as I can."

"Chair's fine."

I went across to it; Eddie put himself on the bed. A room with a view, he'd said on the phone. Some view. Sitting here you could look down past Howard and up across Mission—almost two full blocks of the worst street in the city. It was so close you could hear the beat of its pulse, the ugly sounds of its living and its dying.

"So why did you ask me here, Eddie? If it's information for sale, I'm not buying right now."

"No, no, nothing like that. I ain't in the business anymore."

"Is that right?"

"Prison taught me a lesson. I got rehabilitated." There was no sarcasm or irony in the words; he said them matter-of-factly.

"I'm glad to hear it."

"I been a good citizen ever since I got out. No lie. I haven't had a drink, ain't even been in a bar."

"What are you doing for money?"

"I got a job," he said. "Shipping department at a wholesale sporting goods outfit on Brannan. It don't pay much but it's honest work."

I nodded. "What is it you want, Eddie?"

"Somebody I can talk to, somebody who'll understand—that's all I want. You always treated me decent. Most of 'em, no matter who they were, they treated me like I wasn't even human. Like I was a turd or something."

"Understand what?"

"About what's happening down there."

"Where? Sixth Street?"

"Look at it," he said. He reached over and tapped the window; stared through it. "Look at the people . . . there, you see that guy in the wheelchair and the one pushing him? Across the street there?"

I leaned closer to the glass. The man in the wheelchair wore a military camouflage jacket, had a heavy wool blanket across his lap; the black man manipulating him along the crowded sidewalk was thick-bodied, with a shiny bald head. "I see them."

"White guy's name is Baxter," Eddie said. "Grenade blew up under him in 'Nam and now he's a paraplegic. Lives right here in the Majestic, on this floor down at the end. Deals crack and smack out of his room. Elroy, the black dude, is his bodyguard and roommate. Mean, both of 'em. Couple of months ago, Elroy killed a guy over on Minna that tried to stiff them. Busted his head with a brick. You believe it?"

"I believe it."

"And they ain't the worst on the street. Not the worst."

"I believe that too."

"Before I went to prison I lived and worked with people like that and I never saw what they were. I mean I just never saw it. Now I do, I see it clear—every day walking back and forth to work, every night from up here. It makes you sick after a while, the things you see when you see 'em clear."

"Why don't you move?"

"Where to? I can't afford no place better than this."

"No better room, maybe, but why not another neighborhood? You don't have to live on Sixth Street."

"Wouldn't be much better, any other neighborhood I could buy into. They're all over the city now, the ones like Baxter and Elroy. Used to be it was just Skid Road and the Tenderloin and the ghettos. Now they're everywhere, more and more every day. You know?"

"I know."

"Why? It don't have to be this way, does it?"

Hard times, bad times: alienation, poverty, corruption, too much government, not enough government, lack of social services, lack of caring, drugs like a cancer destroying society. Simplistic explanations that were no explanations at all and as dehumanizing as the ills they described. I was tired of hearing them and I didn't want to repeat them, to Eddie Quinlan or anybody else. So I said nothing.

He shook his head. "Souls burning everywhere you go," he said, and it was as if the words hurt his mouth coming out.

Souls burning. "You find religion at Folsom, Eddie?"

"Religion? I don't know, maybe a little. Chaplain we had there, I talked to him sometimes. He used to say that about the hardtimers, that their souls were burning and there wasn't nothing he could do to put out the fire. They were doomed, he said, and they'd doom others to burn with 'em."

I had nothing to say to that either. In the small silence a voice from outside said distinctly, "Dirty bastard, what you doin' with my pipe?" It was cold in there, with the hard bright night pressing against the window. Next to the door was a rusty steam radiator but it was cold too; the heat would not be on more than a few hours a day, even in the dead of winter, in the Hotel Majestic.

"That's the way it is in the city," Eddie said. "Souls burning. All day long, all night long, souls on fire."

"Don't let it get to you."

"Don't it get to *you*?"

". . . Yes. Sometimes."

He bobbed his head up and down. "You want to do something, you know? You want to try to fix it somehow, put out the fires. There has to be a way."

"I can't tell you what it is," I said.

He said, "If we all just did *something*. It ain't too late. You don't think it's too late?"

"No."

"Me neither. There's still hope."

"Hope, faith, blind optimism—sure."

"You got to believe," he said, nodding. "That's all, you just got to believe."

Angry voices rose suddenly from outside; a woman screamed, thin and brittle. Eddie came off the bed, hauled up the window sash. Chill damp air and street noises came pouring in: shouts, cries, horns honking, cars whispering on the wet pavement, a Muni bus clattering along Mission; more shrieks. He leaned out, peering downward.

"Look," he said, "look."

I stretched forward and looked. On the sidewalk below, a hooker in a leopard-skin coat was running wildly toward Howard; she was the one doing the yelling. Chasing behind her, tight black skirt hiked up over the tops of net stockings and hairy thighs, was a hideously rouged transvestite waving a pocket knife. A group of winos began laughing and chanting "Rape! Rape!" as the hooker and the transvestite ran zigzagging out of sight on Howard.

Eddie pulled his head back in. The flickery neon wash made his face seem surreal, like a hallucinogenic vision. "That's the way it is," he said sadly. "Night after night, day after day."

With the window open, the cold was intense; it penetrated my clothing and crawled on my skin. I'd had enough of it, and of this room and Eddie Quinlan and Sixth Street.

"Eddie, just what is it you want from me?"

"I already told you. Talk to somebody who understands how it is down there."

"Is that the only reason you asked me here?"

"Ain't it enough?"

"For you, maybe." I got to my feet. "I'll be going now."

He didn't argue. "Sure, you go ahead."

"Nothing else you want to say?"

"Nothing else." He walked to the door with me, unlocked it, and then put out his hand. "Thanks for coming. I appreciate it, I really do."

"Yeah. Good luck, Eddie."

"You too," he said. "Keep the faith."

I went out into the hall, and the door shut gently and the lock clicked behind me.

Downstairs, out of the Majestic, along the mean street and back to the garage where I'd left my car. And all the way I kept thinking: There's something else, something more he wanted from me . . . and I gave it to him by going there and listening to him. But what? What did he really want?

I found out later that night. It was all over the TV—special bulletins and then the eleven o'clock news.

Twenty minutes after I left him, Eddie Quinlan stood at the window of his room-with-a-view, and in less than a minute, using a high-powered semi-automatic rifle he'd taken from the sporting goods outfit where he worked, he shot down fourteen people on the street below. Nine dead, five wounded, one of the wounded in critical condition and not expected to live. Six of the victims were known drug dealers; all of the others also had arrest records, for crimes ranging from prostitution to burglary. Two of the dead were Baxter, the paraplegic ex-Vietnam vet, and his bodyguard, Elroy.

By the time the cops showed up, Sixth Street was empty except for the dead and the dying. No more targets. And up in his room, Eddie Quinlan had sat on the bed and put the rifle's muzzle in his mouth and used his big toe to pull the trigger.

My first reaction was to blame myself. But how could I have known or even guessed? Eddie Quinlan. Nobody, loser, shadow-man without substance or purpose. How could anyone have figured him for a thing like that?

Somebody I can talk to, somebody who'll understand—that's all I want.

No. What he'd wanted was somebody to help him justify to himself what he was about to do. Somebody to record his verbal suicide note. Somebody he could trust to pass it on afterward, tell it right and true to the world.

You want to do something, you know? You want to try to fix it somehow, put out the fires. There has to be a way.

Nine dead, five wounded, one of the wounded in critical condition and not expected to live. Not that way.

Souls burning. All day long, all night long, souls on fire.

The soul that had burned tonight was Eddie Quinlan's.

MURDER OF THE FRANKFURTER MAN

Benjamin Appel

READING THE NEWSPAPER how Paddy Quayne died in the chair, my life hooked up again with things and times forgotten. I used to know Paddy Quayne. A big kid even then with a flat white face and the huge raw wrists of a meat chopper. Dead, now. I shoved the paper down on my desk and made the sign of the cross, and the finger that described the four holy points was blunt and a little twisted, not used to such devotions. I'd forgotten many things: religion was one of them, and Paddy another, so that thinking about him was a sort of confessional. Long ago, Paddy and I had lived down on the west side.

I said to myself: you big fat slob with a wife and kids, you're a murderer as much as Paddy, and it isn't all heredity and environment either, don't palm it off on any tripe like that. It was luck, the luck of the wind just stopping dead when another puff'd cut the leaf off. Paddy'd been blown out to hell while I had married and gotten wealth and family. The murder of the frankfurter man'd been my last but Paddy's first.

Now, my kid days in the west side were alive in me. It was as if I'd climbed halfway up a ladder, my face fixed on more climbing, and suddenly I'd looked down at the rungs I'd passed—there were my kid days before me, the earth from which I'd begun, I saw the people that made up this earliest earth of mine. They came from my heart and brain: girls, Anne, Mary, school teachers, old Mrs. Keenan with her faint respectable mustache, the hot-cross buns in the Dutch bakeries on Ninth Avenue.

It was hard to sit still. The blood of my kid days was hot in me, and again I felt that terrible wish to rise up, to rise tall as God, to front something unseen, something in my blood, to close my fist on the ache and the joy of the streets I'd run in, to grip the city and my youth, and hold fast. I sat up and said to myself: what the hell's wrong with you, you fat slob with your hair thinning out and such things done with forever.

I went to the outer office and told the secretary I wasn't in that day. I had a big deal to think over. I shut myself in, reread the notice about Paddy's murder. It didn't say whether he'd turned the priest down, but I'd bet anything he hadn't . . . So he'd gone on to other crimes. Christ, I was lucky . . .

First, was the big peppermint building. How big it was. They used to make peppermint candies on the top two floors. When the men were feeling good, they'd come out on the fire-escapes facing our backyard and chuck handfuls to us kids. Those we didn't catch we picked up in hard little fragments like bits of meteors that hardly ever hit and stayed intact. We were always hungry. We swiped stuff from the stationery stores where they kept their candy under glass in neat trays full of chocolate pins, merrywells, lafayettes, tootsie rolls. Sneaking from behind the El pillars down on Ninth, any guy could fetch bananas or apples out of Paddy's market. When we got bigger and were getting ready to graduate from public school, we started to raid the Greek frankfurter men.

Hunger got us in dutch even though we were the better families down in Hell's Kitchen. My father owned the tenement my family lived in. He was a contractor and vowed all of us were going to Fordham. Paddy's old man was a cop; his two brothers became cops. There was Angelo whose old man ran a fancy wop grocery full of expensive bologna in silver wrappings like they used for cigars; Smitty, Bigthumb, others.

Paddy started our club in a shed in our backyard. My shed was chosen so that the club members could be near the peppermints hailing down like manna from the sky. We put in benches, and had a lock inside and out. It'd be dark as soot. We'd sit there and smoke and talk, but mostly it would be Paddy spieling about what he could do, Paddy whiter than any girl, the rest of us squatting down, listening. What did we say? He made a ship of wood and painted it coal black with some stolen shoe-polish. This pirate ship bore the club name 1-4-ALL. We made stinkbombs of rolled-up movie film which we'd light and throw into the doors of the Greek coffee houses. The Greeks were the meat for our pogroms.

Paddy was sore at the frankfurter man. The greaser was a bum sport. He was a dark, sad-looking man, blowing on his cold hands as he waited for customers. The skinny long franks, sauerkraut, mustard, sold for 2¢ each. "We want old franks," Paddy hollered. "Hey, Greekie, you got old franks, no good to you?" The frankfurter man shook his head. He sold the best quality: "Come on boys, nice frankfooters, two pennies, plenty sourkrout." He smiled at the five of us bunched up hard against him. Me and Angelo dug out some pennies and bought franks. We piled on the sauerkraut until he grabbed for the fork, Paddy yelling, "The hell with the greaser, pile it on, gwan, you're paying good dough for it." Angelo glanced at me, let go of the fork. He was a good kid, a fat strong boy who used to go to the library with me. We walked off, the crowd wolfing at us. "Gimme a hunk." "Don't be cheap." Paddy, bellowing the loudest, and chiseling the most.

That winter the gutters were piled high with snow hills, across the tops of which the smaller kids tramped paths. No stranger was safe in the west side. After school, we'd hang around our snow forts and let fly at anybody whose looks we didn't like. Paddy made the Greek an offer. For two cents every day, we were to get five old franks. No use bulling. The Greek had old franks. The Greek complained to a cop, and we watched the bluecoat laughing at him, heard him saying: "Kids down here gotta make jokes. They chuck snowballs, Chris? It won't hurt you." The cop rolled down frosty Ninth, swinging his club. The Greek turned pale at the sight of us. It seemed there was no protection for him. "It's a tough country, the U.S.A.," Paddy hollered. "Tough for grease-balls."

He moved his wagon from corner to corner, but we hunted him down with our snowballs. Bang. They were always walloping his hand-wagon. We got to be good aimers. Once, Paddy smacked him plunk in the eye. He had a blinker, but still he didn't take up our offer on old franks, shaking his fist. "I'm a poor man," he cried; "let me alone, boys."

Angelo and I got sick of the fun, but Paddy was set: "You got old franks, and a frank a day for a guy ain't much."

The Greek cried. I'd never seen a big man, even a greaseball, cry in the open street. It was a bright winter day, the windows laced with frost, a day where all our faces were red, our eyes clear, the El cut sharp out of the sky, everything clean-looking as ice. And there was the Greek bawling, his breath freezing.

Paddy called a meeting about that bum sport. First, he led us on a sweet mickey raid. A shawled old Jewish woman carried her own wood in a little tin wagon to bake her sweet potatoes. She gave us one each, and we let her alone. "See," said Paddy, "that sheeny's not a bad sport." We ate the mickeys in our club, the sweet smell, the clean dense brown taste in our mouths. Angelo said Paddy was too tough on the Greek. Whyn't he let the poor guy alone? Paddy blew on his hot mickey. Angelo was a dope. The guy was only a greaseball, and betcha he's got a thousand bucks saved. All them bum sports had. All we wanted was a free frank a day. Gee, that showed you how cheap the greaseball was.

After school the next day, Paddy soaked our snowballs in water. When they froze he put them in paper bags he'd weedled out of the grocer. It was fun hunting somebody; we spread out, each fellow covering a few blocks. The Brooks and Bigthumb found the Greek. We joined forces, charged down on him, hollering, yelling like Indians in the movies circling a covered wagon, letting fly with all our might. Bang. He got hit hard and plenty, staggering against his wagon like a murdered man. Paddy yelled for us to hook the franks. We rushed in, grabbing the hot dogs and handfuls of sauerkraut, dumping them into our mouths. On the cold lonely corner nobody interfered, the store-keepers observing inside their doors with no guts to butt in because if they did we might come round and smash their windows. Seeing us eating up his stock, the frankfurter man came to life. We couldn't believe it. Greeks were yellow, you could do anything you wanted to them; and now this bum we'd been shellacking reached out and gripped Paddy. He was bleeding at the mouth from some of the snowballs, but he didn't let go of Paddy's collar, hollering for the cops. Paddy walloped him in the gut, shouting for us to fix the lousy—We piled in then. The Greek got wild and was pounded some more. We kicked him in the groin, mad as hell, Paddy the worst because his collar was ripped and he'd get sloughed from his old man. We charged the frankfurter man off his feet, booting him in the head and body. We had to pull Paddy away. The Greek was out. Paddy upset the wagon and we ran away. Ducking around the corner I looked back. The storekeepers had come out at last, a woman was screaming.

If ever a fellow needed a secret bunk and locked door, it was that time. We huddled in the club, sweating from the hard run. Paddy said, "That'll teach the greaseball a lesson." We said nothing to him because it was all done and over with, but when the meeting broke up, I took Angelo up to my house, in my room, kicking out my kid brother who slept in the same bed with me. Angelo began to cry. It was awful what we'd done. Angelo said he'd never see Paddy again and he was through with the club for keeps. Then he went home, and I wondered how I was going to tell Paddy the club was washed up and there'd be no more meetings.

That Greek never pushed a wagon again. He was killed. That was that. Lucky, we'd forced the Greek out of our neighborhood where the storekeepers knew us, or we'd a-been in dutch. It was all forgotten. A Greek on the west side in those years was nothing. It was winter, people forget easier in winter.

I had no trouble with Paddy. He and Bigthumb marched into the yard the next day. They'd been over to the market and offered me some apples they'd swiped. I wouldn't take them. Paddy stared at the shiny apples in his hand. "No more club," I said. "I'm out. Angelo's out, no more using my shed." Paddy clenched his fists and said for two bits he'd give me two socks, a pair of socks wrapped around my beak. Bigthumb was edging in on me. Another second and I'd have been sunk, but suddenly I remembered it was my backyard, my shed, the house was my old man's. I said I'd knock his ears into his big mouth. Bigthumb waited for Paddy to flatten me. Paddy edged away. "I'll see you when you ain't so hot," he said, walking out of the yard. I hollered after him, "Me, I'm no Greek, don't forget it."

If I hadn't kicked Paddy out, I might've ended the way he did. Luck was with me, because Bigthumb was neutral, because the shed was mine, because Paddy was yellow or didn't give a damn. Luck.

After that, Paddy went with a bunch up near Eighth Avenue, mostly wops. Then he was hanging out in a strange block altogether. Angelo and I locked the club up for keeps. We were graduating in a few months and thinking of high school. We were pals because we liked each other and were murderers. Angelo confessed, but I didn't. And it was all over . . .

I put down my cigar and read of Paddy going to the chair. I thought God rest you Paddy. He was so fair, so fine in complexion, slim, always on the go. And suddenly I was desperate, my throat dry, the juice of remembering leaving me, my heart bitter. I was sorry, not for the frankfurter man, but for something elusive and forgotten that I had held in fist and heart. It was gone. I laughed and thought: you poor fat slob, you're glad you helped kill that Greek. It makes you remember. It makes you feel good. It makes you recapture youth. That was the wonder. To hold youth when time had locked it out of heart for keeps. My confessional was almost over. I was sad, sighing, vaguely purged, but without wonder. I said to myself: it isn't environment. You bet it isn't. It's the will to murder in most of us, forgotten, covered over, faked up, and luck had been with me to steer me clear of the chair. I rang for the secretary and said I'd be in for other callers.

"Other callers?" she asked.

"Only the callers of this day and age," I said. Later she'd probably tell the officeboy the boss was getting woozy.

Tony Hillerman

"*First* Lead Gasser" grew out of my very vivid memory of an execution in New Mexico's then-new gas chamber, and an interview with the poor fellow who was about to die in it. Persons who have read People of Darkness will recognize in the background of a character I called Colton Wolf the same sad story of what turns a boy into a killer. When asked for a story by another author for this collection, "Goodbye, Pops" immediately leapt to mind. It is an excellent example of Joe Gores' superb skill at using human psychology as the core of his writing. In his usual tight style, and in only a few thousand words, he cuts to the heart of the ties that bind a family together, no matter how far apart they may grow.

First Lead Gasser

JOHN HARDIN WALKED into the bureau, glanced at the wall clock (which told him it was 12:22 A.M.), laid his overcoat over a chair, flicked the switch on the teletype to ON, tapped on the button marked BELL, and then punched on the keys with a stiff forefinger:

ALBUQUERQUE ... YOU TURNED ON? ... SANTA FE

He leaned heavily on the casing of the machine, waiting, feeling the coolness under his palms, noticing the glass panel was dusty, and hearing the words again and that high, soft voice. Then the teletype bumped tentatively and said:

SANTA FE ... AYE AYE GO WITH IT ... ALBUQUERQUE

And John Hardin punched:

ALBUQUERQUE ... WILL FILE LEAD SUBBING OUT GASSER ITEM IN MINUTE. PLEASE SEND SCHEDULE FOR 300 WORDS TO DENVER ... SANTA FE

The teletype was silent as Hardin removed the cover from the typewriter (dropping it to the floor). Then the teletype carriage bumped twice and said:

SANTA FE ... NO RUSH DENVER UNTHINKS GASSER WORTH FILING ON NATIONAL TRUNK DIXIE TORNADOES JAMMING WIRE AND HAVE DANDY HOTEL FIRE AT CHICAGO FOLKS OUTJUMPING WINDOWS ETC HOWEVER STATE OVERNIGHT FILE LUKS LIKE HOTBED OF TRANQUILITY CAN USE LOTS OF GORY DETAILS THERE ... ALBUQUERQUE

Their footsteps had echoed down the long concrete tube, passed the dark barred mouths of cell blocks, and Thompson had said, "Is it always this goddam quiet?" and the warden said, "The cons are always quiet on one of these nights."

Hardin sighed and said something under his breath and punched:

ALBUQUERQUE ... REMIND DENVER NITESIDE THAT DENVER DAYSIDE HAS REQUEST FOR 300 WORDS TO BE FILED FOR OHIO PM POINTS ... S F

He turned his back on the machine, put a carbon book in the typewriter, hit the carriage return twice, and stared at the clock, which now reported the time to be 12:26. While he stared, the second hand made the laborious climb toward 12 and something clicked and the clock said it was 12:27.

Hardin started typing, rapidly:

First Lead Gasser

Santa Fe, N.M., March 28—(UPI)—George Tobias Small, 38, slayer of a young Ohio couple who sought to befriend him, died a minute after midnight today in the gas chamber at the New Mexico State Penitentiary.

He examined the paragraph, pulled the paper from the typewriter, and dropped it. It slid from the top of the desk and planed to the floor, spilling its carbon insert. On a fresh carbon book Hardin typed:

First Lead Gasser

Santa Fe, N.M., March 28—(UPI)—George Tobias Small, 38, who

clubbed to death two young Ohio newlyweds last July 4, paid for his crime with his life early today in the New Mexico State Penitentiary gas chamber.

The hulking killer smiled nervously at execution witnesses as three guards pushed three unmarked buttons, one of which dropped cyanide pills into a container of acid under the chair in which he was strapped.

Hulking? Maybe tall, stooped killer: maybe gangling. Not really nervously. Better timidly: smiled timidly. But actually it was an embarrassed smile. Shy. Stepping from the elevator into that too-bright basement room, Small had blinked against the glare and squinted at them lined by the railing—the press corps and the official creeps in the role of "official witnesses." He looked surprised and then embarrassed and looked away, then down at his feet. The warden had one hand on his arm: the two of them walking fast toward the front of the chamber, hurrying, while a guard held the steel door open. Above their heads, cell block eight was utterly silent.

Hardin hit the carriage return.

The end came quickly for Small. He appeared to hold his breath for a moment and then breathed deeply of the deadly fumes. His head fell forward and his body slumped in death.

The room had been hot. Stuffy. Smelling of cleaning fluid. But under his hand, the steel railing was cold. "Looks like a big incinerator," Thompson said. "Or like one of those old wood stoves with the chimney out the top." And the man from the *Albuquerque Journal* said, "The cons call it the space capsule. Wonder why they put windows in it. There's not much to see." And Thompson said, with a sort of laugh, that it was the world's longest view. Then it was quiet. Father McKibbon had looked at them a long time when they came in, unsmiling, studying them. Then he had stood stiffly by the open hatch, looking at the floor.

Small, who said he had come to New Mexico from Colorado in search of work, was sentenced to death last November after a district court jury at Raton found him guilty of murder in the deaths of Mr. and Mrs. Robert M. Martin of Cleveland. The couple had been married only two days earlier and was en route to California on a honeymoon trip.

You could see Father McKibbon saying something to Small—talking rapidly—and Small nodded and then nodded again, and then the warden said something and Small looked up and licked his lips. Then he stepped through the hatch. He tripped on the sill, but McKibbon caught his arm and helped him sit in the little chair, and Small looked up at the priest. And smiled. How would you describe it? Shy, maybe, or grateful. Or maybe sick. Then the guard was reaching in, doing something out of sight. Buckling the straps probably, buckling leather around a warm ankle and a warm forearm which had MOTHER tattooed on it, inside a heart.

Small had served two previous prison terms. He had compiled a police record beginning with a Utah car theft when he was fifteen. Arresting officers testified that he confessed killing the two with a jack handle after Martin resisted Small's attempt at robbery. They said Small admitted flagging down the couple's car after raising the hood on his old-model truck to give the impression he was having trouble.

Should it be flagging down or just flagging? The wall clock inhaled electricity above Hardin's head with a brief buzzing sigh and said 12:32. How long had Small been dead now? Thirty minutes, probably, if cyanide worked as fast as they said. And how long had it been since yesterday, when he had stood outside Small's cell in death row? It was late afternoon, then. You could see the sunlight far down the corridor, slanting in and striped by the bars. Small had said, "How much time have I got left?" and Thompson looked at his watch and said, "Four-fifteen from midnight leaves seven hours and forty-five minutes," and Small's bony hands clenched and unclenched on the bars. Then he said, "Seven hours and forty-five minutes now," and Thompson said, "Well, my watch might be off a little."

BEHIND Hardin the teletype said *ding, ding, ding, dingding.*

SANTA FE . . . DENVER NOW SEZ WILL CALL IN 300 FOR OHIO PM WIRE SHORTLY. HOW BOUT LEADING SAD SLAYER SAMMY SMALL TODAY GRIMLY GULPED GAS. OR SOME SUCH???? . . . ALBUQUERQUE

The teletype lapsed into expectant silence, its electric motor purring. Outside, a car drove by with a rush of sound.

Hardin typed:

Small refuted the confession at his trial. He claimed that after Martin stopped to assist him the two men argued and that Martin struck him. He said he then "blacked out" and could remember nothing more of the incident. Small was arrested when two state policemen who happened by stopped to investigate the parked vehicles.

"The warden told me you was the two that work for the outfits that put things in the papers all over, and I thought maybe you could put something in about finding . . . about maybe . . . something about needing to know where my mother is. You know, so they can get the word to her." He walked back to his bunk, back into the darkness, and sat down and then got up again and walked back to the barred door, three steps. "It's about getting buried. I need someplace for that." And Thompson said, "What's her name?" and Small looked down at the floor. "That's part of the trouble. You see, this man she was living with when we were there in Salt Lake, well, she and him . . ."

Arresting officers and other witnesses testified there was nothing mechanically wrong with Small's truck, that there was no mark on Small to indicate he had been struck by Martin, and that Martin had been slain by repeated blows on the back of his head.

Small was standing by the bars now, gripping them so that the stub showed where the end of his ring finger had been cut off. Flexing his hands, talking fast. "The warden, well, he told me they'd send me wherever I said after it's over, back home, he said. They'd pay for it. But I won't know where to tell them unless somebody can find Mama. There was a place we stayed for a long time before we went to San Diego, and I went to school there some but I don't remember the name of it, and then we moved someplace up the coast where they grow figs and like that, and then I think it was Oregon next, and then I believe it was we moved on out to Salt Lake." Small stopped talking then, and let his hands rest while he looked at them, at Thompson and him, and said, "But I bet Mama would remember where I'm supposed to go."

Mrs. Martin's body was found in a field about forty yards from the highway. Officers said the pretty bride had apparently attempted to flee, had tripped and injured an ankle, and had then been beaten to death by Small.

Subject: George Tobias Small, alias Toby Small, alias G. T. Small. White male, about 38 (birth date, place unknown); weight, 188, height, 6'4"; eyes, brown; complexion, ruddy; distinguishing characteristics: noticeable stoop, carries right shoulder higher than left. Last two joints missing from left ring finger, deep scar on left upper lip, tattoo of heart with word MOTHER on inner right forearm.
Charge: Violation Section 12-2 (3) Criminal Code.
Disposition: Guilty of Murder, Colfax County District Court.
Sentence: Death.
Previous Record: July 28, 1941, sentenced Utah State Reformatory, car theft.
April 7, 1943, returned Utah State Reformatory, B&E and parole violation.
February 14, 1945, B&E, resisting arrest. Classified juvenile incorrigible.
August 3, 1949, armed robbery, 5-7 years at . . .

Small had been in trouble with the law since boyhood, starting his career with a car theft at twelve and then violating reformatory parole with a burglary. Before his twenty-first birthday he was serving the first of three prison terms.

Small had rested his hands on the brace between the bars, but they wouldn't rest. The fingers twisted tirelessly among themselves. Blind snakes, even the stub of the missing finger moving restlessly. "Rock fell on it when I was little. Think it was that. The warden said he sent the word around about Mama, but I guess nobody found her yet. Put it down that she might be living in Los Angeles. That man with us there in Salt Lake, he wanted to go out to the coast and maybe that's where they went."

It was then Thompson stopped him. "Wait a minute," Thompson said. "Where was she from, your mother? Why not . . ."

"I don't remember that," Small said. He was looking down at the floor.

And Thompson asked, "Didn't she tell you?" and Small said, still not looking at us, "Sure, but I was little."

"You don't remember the town or anything? How little were you?" And

Small sort of laughed and said, "Just exactly twelve," and laughed again, and said, "That's why I thought maybe I could come home, it was my birthday. We was living in a house trailer then, and Mama's man had been drinking. Her too. When he did that, he'd whip me and run me off. So I'd been staying with a boy I knew there at school, in the garage but his folks said I couldn't stay anymore and it was my birthday, so I thought I'd go by, maybe it would be all right."

Small had taken his hands off the bars then. He walked back to the bunk and sat down. And when he started talking again it was almost too low to hear it all.

"They was gone. The trailer was gone. The man at the office said they'd just took off in the night. Owed him rent, I guess," Small said. He was quiet again.

Thompson said, "Well," and then he cleared his throat, said, "Leave you a note or anything?"

And Small said, "No, sir. No note."

"That's when you stole the car, I guess," Thompson said. "The car theft you went to the reformatory for."

"Yes, sir," Small said. "I thought I'd go to California and find her. I thought she was going to Los Angeles, but I never knowed no place to write. You could write all the letters you wanted there at the reformatory, but I never knowed the place to send it to."

Thompson said, "Oh," and Small got up and came up to the bars and grabbed them.

"How much time have I got now?"

Small stepped through the oval hatch in the front of the gas chamber at two minutes before midnight, and the steel door was sealed behind him to prevent seepage of the deadly gas. The prison doctor said the first whiff of the cyanide fumes would render a human unconscious almost instantly.

"We believe Mr. Small's death will be almost painless," he said.

"The warden said they can keep my body a couple days but then they'll just have to go on ahead and bury me here at the pen unless somebody claims it. They don't have no place cold to keep it from spoiling on 'em. Anyway, I think a man oughta be put down around his kin if he has any. That's the way I feel about it."

And Thompson started to say something and cleared his throat and said,

"How does it feel to—I mean, about tonight?" and Small's hands tightened on the bars. "Oh, I won't say I'm not scared. I never said that but they say it don't hurt but I been hurt before, cut and all, and I never been scared of that so much."

Small's words stopped coming and then they came loud, and the guard reading at the door in the corridor looked around and then back at his book. "It's the not knowing," he said, and his hands disappeared from the bars and he walked back to the dark end of the cell and sat on the bunk and got up again and walked and said, "Oh, God, it's not knowing."

Small cooperated with his executioners. While the eight witnesses required by law watched, the slayer appeared to be helping a guard attach the straps which held his legs in place in the gas chamber. He leaned back while his forearms were strapped to the chair.

The clock clicked and sighed and the minute hand pointed at the eight partly hidden behind a tear-shaped dribble of paint on the glass, and the teletype, stirred by this, said *ding, ding, ding.*

SANTA FE . . . DENVER WILL INCALL GASSER AFTER SPORTS ROUNDUP NOW MOVING. YOU BOUT GOT SMALL WRAPPED UP? . . . ALBUQUERQUE

Hardin pulled the carbon book from the typewriter and marked out "down" after the verb "flagging." He penciled a line through "give the impression he was" and wrote in "simulate." He clipped the copy to the holder above the teletype keyboard, folding it to prevent obscuring the glass panel, switched the key from KEYBOARD to TAPE, and began punching. The thin yellow strip, lacy with perforations, looped downward toward the floor and built rapidly there into a loopy pile.

HE had seen Small wiping the back of his hand across his face. When he came back to the bars he had looked away.

"The padre's been talking to me about it every morning," Small had said. "That's Father McKibbon. He told me a lot I never knew before, mostly about Jesus, and I'd heard about that, of course. It was back when I was in that place at Logan, that chaplain there, he talked about Jesus some, and I remembered some of it. But that one there at Logan, he talked mostly about sin and about hell and things like that, and this McKibbon, the padre here, well, he talked different." Small's hands had been busy on the bars again and then Small had looked directly at him, directly into his face, and then at Thompson. He remembered the tense heavy face, sweaty, and the words and the voice too soft and high for the size of the man.

"I wanted to ask you to do what you could about finding my mama. I looked for her all the time. When they'd turn me loose, I'd hunt for her. But maybe you could find her. With the newspapers and all. And I want to hear what you think about it all," Small said. "About what happens to me after they take me out of that gas chamber. I wanted to see what you say about that." And then Small said into the long silence, "Well, whatever it's going to be, it won't be any worse than it's been." And he paused again, and looked back into the cell as if he expected to see someone there, and then back at us.

"But when I walk around in here and my foot hits the floor I feel it, you know, and I think that's Toby Small I'm feeling there with his foot on the cement. It's *me*. And I guess that don't sound like much, but after tonight I guess there won't be that for one thing. And I hope there's somebody there waiting for me. I hope there's not just me." And he sat down on the bunk.

"I was wondering what you thought about this Jesus and what McKibbon has been telling me." He had his head between his hands now, looking at the floor, and it made his voice muffled. "You reckon he was lying about it? I don't see any cause for it, but how can a man know all that and be sure about it?"

THE clatter of the transmission box joined the chatter of the perforator. Hardin marked his place in the copy and leaned over to fish a cigarette out of his overcoat. He lit it, took it out of his mouth, and turned back to the keyboard. Above him, above the duet chatter of tape and keyboard, he heard the clock strike again, and click, and when he looked up it was 12:46.

McKIBBON had his hand on Small's elbow, crushing the pressed prison jacket, talking to him, his face fierce and intent. And Small was listening, intent. Then he nodded and nodded again and when he stepped through the hatch he bumped his head on the steel hard enough so you could hear it back at the railing, and then Hardin could see his face through the round glass and it looked numb and pained.

McKibbon had stepped back, and while the guard was working with the straps, he began reading from a book. Loud, wanting Small to hear. Maybe wanting all of them to hear.

"Have mercy on me, O Lord; for unto thee have I cried all the day, for thou, O Lord, art sweet and mild: and plenteous in mercy unto all that call upon thee. Incline thine ear, O Lord, and hear me: for I am needy and poor. Preserve my soul; for I am holy: O thou my God, save thy servant that trusteth in thee."

THE pile of tape on the floor diminished and the final single loop climbed toward the stop bar and the machine was silent. Hardin looked through the dusty glass, reading the last paragraph for errors.

THERE was his face, there through the round window, and his brown eyes unnaturally wide, looking at something or looking for something. And then the pump made a sucking noise and the warden came over and said, "Well, I guess we can all go home now."

HE switched the machine back from TAPE to KEYBOARD and punched:

SMALL'S BODY WILL BE HELD UNTIL THURSDAY, THE WARDEN SAID, IN THE EVENT THE SLAYER'S MOTHER CAN BE LOCATED TO CLAIM IT. IF NOT, IT WILL BE BURIED IN THE PRISON LOT.

He switched off the machine. And in the room the only sound was the clock, which was buzzing again and saying it was 12:49.

GOODBYE, POPS

Joe Gores

I GOT OFF the Greyhound and stopped to draw icy Minnesota air into my lungs. A bus had brought me from Springfield, Illinois, to Chicago the day before; a second bus had brought me here. I caught my passing reflection in the window of the old-fashioned depot—a tall hard man with a white and savage face, wearing an ill-fitting overcoat. I caught another reflection, too, one that froze my guts: a cop in uniform. Could they already know it was someone else in that burned-out car?

Then the cop turned away, chafing his arms with gloved hands through his blue stormcoat, and I started breathing again. I went quickly over to the cab line. Only two hackies were waiting there; the front one rolled down his window as I came up.

"You know the Miller place north of town?" I asked. He looked me over. "I know it. Five bucks—now."

I paid him from the money I'd rolled a drunk for in Chicago and eased back against the rear seat. As he nursed the cab out ice-rimed Second Street, my fingers gradually relaxed from their rigid chopping position. I deserved to go back inside if I let a clown like this get to me.

"Old man Miller's pretty sick, I hear." He half turned to catch me with a corner of an eye. "You got business with him?"

"Yeah. My own."

That ended that conversation. It bothered me that Pops was sick enough for this clown to know about it; but maybe my brother Rod being vice-president at the bank would explain that. There was a lot of new construction and a freeway west of town with a tricky overpass to the old county road. A mile beyond a new subdivision were the two hundred wooded hilly acres I knew so well.

After my break from the federal pen at Terre Haute, Indiana, two days before, I'd gotten outside their cordon through woods like these. I'd gone out in a prison truck, in a pail of swill meant for the prison farm pigs, had headed straight west, across the Illinois line. I'm good in open country, even when I'm in prison condition, so by dawn I was in a hayloft near Paris, Illinois, some twenty miles from the pen. You can do what you have to do.

The cabby stopped at the foot of the private road, looking dubious. "Listen, buddy, I know that's been plowed, but it looks damned icy. If I try it and go into the ditch—"

"I'll walk from here."

I waited beside the road until he'd driven away, then let the north wind chase me up the hill and into the leafless hardwoods. The cedars that Pops and I had put in as a windbreak were taller and fuller; rabbit paths were pounded hard into the snow under the barbed-wire tangles of wild raspberry bushes. Under the oaks at the top of the hill was the old-fashioned, two-story house, but I detoured to the kennels first. The snow was deep and undisturbed inside them. No more foxhounds. No cracked corn in the bird feeder outside the kitchen window, either. I rang the front doorbell.

My sister-in-law Edwina, Rod's wife, answered it. She was three years younger than my thirty-five, and she'd started wearing a girdle.

"Good Lord! Chris!" Her mouth tightened. "We didn't—"

"Ma wrote that the old man was sick." She'd written, all right. *Your father is very ill. Not that you have ever cared if any of us lives or dies . . .* And then Edwina decided that my tone of voice had given her something to get righteous about.

"I'm amazed you'd have the nerve to come here, even if they did let you out on parole or something." So nobody had been around asking yet. "If you plan to drag the family name through the mud again—"

I pushed by her into the hallway. "What's wrong with the old man?" I called him Pops only inside myself, where no one could hear.

"He's dying, that's what's wrong with him."

She said it with a sort of baleful pleasure. It hit me, but I just grunted and went by into the living room. Then the old girl called down from the head of the stairs.

"Eddy? What—who is it?"

"Just—a salesman, Ma. He can wait until Doctor's gone."

Doctor. As if some damned croaker was generic physician all by himself. When he came downstairs Edwina tried to hustle him out before I could see him, but I caught his arm as he poked it into his overcoat sleeve.

"Like to see you a minute, Doc. About old man Miller."

He was nearly six feet, a couple of inches shorter than me, but out-weighing me forty pounds. He pulled his arm free.

"Now see here, fellow—"

I grabbed his lapels and shook him, just enough to pop a button off his coat and put his glasses awry on his nose. His face got red.

"Old family friend, Doc." I jerked a thumb at the stairs. "What's the story?"

It was dumb, dumb as hell, of course, asking him; at any second the cops would figure out that the farmer in the burned-out car wasn't me after all. I'd dumped enough gasoline before I struck the match so they couldn't lift prints off anything except the shoe I'd planted: but they'd make him through dental charts as soon as they found out he was missing. When they did they'd come here asking questions, and then the croaker would realize who I was. But I wanted to know whether Pops was as bad off as Edwina said he was, and I've never been a patient man.

The croaker straightened his suit coat, striving to regain lost dignity. "He—Judge Miller is very weak, too weak to move. He probably won't last out the week." His eyes searched my face for pain, but there's nothing like a federal pen to give you control. Disappointed, he said, "His lungs. I got to it much too late, of course. He's resting easily."

I jerked the thumb again. "You know your way out."

Edwina was at the head of the stairs, her face righteous again. It seems to run in the family, even with those who married in. Only Pops and I were short of it.

"Your father is very ill. I forbid you—"

"Save it for Rod; it might work on him."

In the room I could see the old man's arm hanging limply over the edge of the bed, with smoke from the cigarette between his fingers running up to the ceiling in a thin unwavering blue line. The upper arm, which once had measured an honest eighteen and had swung his small tight fist against the side of my head a score of times, could not even hold a cigarette up in the air. It gave me the same wrench as finding a good foxhound that's gotten mixed up with a bobcat.

The old girl came out of her chair by the foot of the bed, her face blanched. I put my arms around her. "Hi, Ma," I said. She was rigid inside my embrace, but I knew she wouldn't pull away. Not there in Pops's room.

He had turned his head at my voice. The light glinted from his silky white hair. His eyes, translucent with imminent death, were the pure, pale blue of birch shadows on fresh snow.

"Chris," he said in a weak voice. "Son of a biscuit, boy . . . I'm glad to see you."

"You ought to be, you lazy devil," I said heartily. I pulled off my suit jacket and hung it over the back of the chair, and tugged off my tie. "Getting so lazy that you let the foxhounds go!"

"That's enough, Chris." She tried to put steel into it.

"I'll just sit here a little, Ma," I said easily. Pops wouldn't have long, I knew, and any time I got with him would have to do me. She stood in the doorway, a dark indecisive shape; then she turned and went silently out, probably to phone Rod at the bank.

For the next couple of hours I did most of the talking; Pops just lay there with his eyes shut, like he was asleep. But then he started in, going way back, to the trapline he and I had run when I'd been a kid; to the big white-tail buck that followed him through the woods one rutting season until Pops whacked it on the nose with a tree branch. It was only after his law practice had ripened into a judgeship that we began to draw apart; I guess that in my twenties I was too wild, too much what he'd been himself thirty years before. Only I kept going in that direction.

About seven o'clock my brother Rod called from the doorway. I went out, shutting the door behind me. Rod was taller than me, broad and big-boned, with an athlete's frame—but with mush where his guts should have been. He had close-set pale eyes and not quite enough chin, and hadn't gone out for football in high school.

"My wife reported the vicious things you said to her." It was his best give-the-teller-hell voice. "We've talked this over with Mother and we want you out of here tonight. We want—"

"*You* want? Until he kicks off it's still the old man's house, isn't it?"

He swung at me then—being Rod, it was a right-hand lead—and I blocked it with an open palm. Then I back-handed him, hard, twice across the face each way, jerking his head from side to side with the slaps, and crowding him up against the wall. I could have fouled his groin to bend him over, then driven locked hands down on the back of his neck as I jerked a knee into his face; and I wanted to. The need to get away before they came after me was gnawing at my gut like a weasel in a trap gnawing off his own paw to get loose. But I merely stepped away from him.

"You—you murderous animal!" He had both hands up to his cheeks like a woman might have done. Then his eyes widened theatrically, as the realization struck him. I wondered why it had taken so long. "You've *broken out!*" he gasped. "*Escaped!* a fugitive from—from justice!"

"Yeah. And I'm staying that way. I know you, kid, all of you. The last thing any of you want is for the cops to take me here." I tried to put his tones into my voice. "*Oh! The scandal!*"

"But they'll be after you—"

"They think I'm dead," I said flatly. "I went off an icy road in a stolen car in down-state Illinois, and it rolled and burned with me inside."

His voice was hushed, almost horror-stricken. "You mean—that there *is* a body in the car?"

"Right."

I knew what he was thinking, but I didn't bother to tell him the truth—that the old farmer who was driving me to Springfield, because he thought my doubled-up fist in the overcoat pocket was a gun, hit a patch of ice and took the car right off the lonely country road. He was impaled on the steering post, so I took his shoes and put one of mine on his foot. The other I left, with my fingerprints on it, lying near enough so they'd find it but not so near that it'd burn along with the car. Rod wouldn't have believed the truth anyway. If they caught me, who would?

I said, "Bring me up a bottle of bourbon and a carton of cigarettes. And make sure Eddy and Ma keep their mouths shut if anyone asks about me." I opened the door so Pops could hear. "Well, thanks, Rod. It *is* nice to be home again."

Solitary in the pen makes you able to stay awake easily or snatch sleep easily, whichever is necessary. I stayed awake for the last thirty-seven hours that Pops had, leaving the chair by his bed only to go to the bathroom and to listen at the head of the stairs whenever I heard the phone or the doorbell ring. Each time I thought: *This is it*. But my luck held. If they'd just take long enough so I could stay until Pops went; the second that happened, I told myself, I'd be on my way.

Rod and Edwina and Ma were there at the end, with Doctor hovering in the background to make sure he got paid. Pops finally moved a pallid arm and Ma sat down quickly on the edge of the bed—a small, erect, rather indomitable woman with a face made for wearing a lorgnette. She wasn't crying yet; instead, she looked purely luminous in a way.

"Hold my hand, Eileen." Pops paused for the terrible strength to speak again. "Hold my hand. Then I won't be frightened."

She took his hand and he almost smiled, and shut his eyes. We waited, listening to his breathing get slower and slower and then just stop, like a grandfather clock running down. Nobody moved, nobody spoke. I looked around at them, so soft, so unused to death, and I felt like a marten in a brooding house. Then Ma began to sob.

IT was a blustery day with snow flurries. I parked the jeep in front of the funeral chapel and went up the slippery walk with wind plucking at my coat, telling myself for the hundredth time just how nuts I was to stay for the service. By now they *had* to know that the dead farmer wasn't me; by now some smart prison censor *had* to remember Ma's letter about Pops being sick. He was two days dead, and I should have been in Mexico by this time. But it didn't seem complete yet, somehow. Or maybe I was kidding myself, maybe it was just the old need to put down authority that always ruins guys like me.

From a distance it looked like Pops but up close you could see the cosmetics and that his collar was three sizes too big. I felt his hand: it was a statue's hand, unfamiliar except for the thick, slightly down-curved fingernails.

Rod came up behind me and said, in a voice meant only for me, "After today I want you to leave us alone. I want you out of my house."

"Shame on you, brother," I grinned. "Before the will is even read, too."

We followed the hearse through snowy streets at the proper funeral pace, lights burning. Pallbearers wheeled the heavy casket out smoothly on oiled tracks, then set it on belts over the open grave. Snow whipped and swirled from a gray sky, melting on the metal and forming rivulets down the sides.

I left when the preacher started his scam, impelled by the need to get moving, get away, yet impelled by another urgency, too. I wanted something out of the house before all the mourners arrived to eat and guzzle. The guns and ammo already had been banished to the garage, since Rod never had fired a round in his life; but it was easy to dig out the beautiful little .22 target pistol with the long barrel. Pops and I had spent hundreds of hours with that gun, so the grip was worn smooth and the blueing was gone from the metal that had been out in every sort of weather.

Putting the jeep on four-wheel I ran down through the trees to a cut between the hills, then went along on foot through the darkening hardwoods. I moved slowly, evoking memories of Korea to neutralize the icy bite of the snow through my worn shoes. There was a flash of brown as a cottontail streaked from under a deadfall toward a rotting woodpile I'd stacked years before. My slug took him in the spine, paralyzing the back legs. He jerked and thrashed until I broke his neck with the edge of my hand.

I left him there and moved out again, down into the small marshy triangle between the hills. It was darkening fast as I kicked at the frozen tussocks. Finally a ringneck in full plumage burst out, long tail fluttering and stubby pheasant wings beating to raise his heavy body. He was quartering up and just a bit to my right, and I had all the time in the world. I squeezed off in mid-swing, knowing it was perfect even before he took that heart-stopping pinwheel tumble.

I carried them back to the jeep; there was a tiny ruby of blood on the pheasant's beak, and the rabbit was still hot under the front legs. I was using headlights when I parked on the curving cemetery drive. They hadn't put the casket down yet, so the snow had laid a soft blanket over it. I put the rabbit and pheasant on top and stood without moving for a minute or two. The wind must have been strong, because I found that tears were burning on my cheeks.

Goodbye, Pops. Goodbye to deer-shining out of season in the hardwood belt across the creek. Goodbye to jump-shooting mallards down in the river bottoms. Goodbye to woodsmoke and mellow bourbon by firelight and all the things that made a part of you mine. The part they could never get at.

I turned away, toward the jeep—and stopped dead. I hadn't even heard them come up. Four of them, waiting patiently as if to pay their respects to the dead. In one sense they were: to them that dead farmer in the burned-out car was Murder One. I tensed, my mind going to the .22 pistol that they didn't know about in my overcoat pocket. Yeah. Except that it had all the stopping power of a fox's bark. If only Pops had run to hand guns of a little heavier caliber. But he hadn't.

Very slowly, as if my arms suddenly had grown very heavy, I raised my hands above my head.

LAWRENCE BLOCK

If I have a favorite writer, it's John O'Hara (1905–1970). While he's not by any stretch of the imagination a crime writer, some of his stories and novels concern crimes, and a few are genuinely crime fiction. "In a Grove" is one of these. I admired it enormously on first reading and immediately read it a second time in the hopes of figuring out how he made it work.

"How Far It Could Go" was written to order for The Plot Thickens, *a volume Mary Higgins Clark assembled as a fund-raiser in aid of literacy. Every story had to contain three elements—a thick fog, a thick steak, and a thick book. I thought the premise was a bit thick, frankly, and that the literary sleight of hand involved would preclude the possibility of the stories being any good. But how on earth could I say no to Mary?*

The story turned out to be a personal favorite. Rereading it later, I heard echoes of O'Hara in it, which makes it a nice companion piece for "In a Grove."

How Far It Could Go

SHE PICKED HIM out right away, the minute she walked into the restaurant. It was no great trick. There were only two men seated alone, and one was an elderly gentleman who already had a plate of food in front of him.

The other was thirty-five or forty, with a full head of dark hair and a strong jawline. He might have been an actor, she thought. An actor you'd cast as a thug. He was reading a book, though, which didn't entirely fit the picture.

Maybe it wasn't him, she thought. Maybe the weather had delayed him.

She checked her coat, then told the headwaiter she was meeting a Mr. Cutler. "Right this way," he said, and for an instant she fancied that he was going to show her to the elderly gentleman's table, but of course he led her over to the other man, who closed his book at her approach and got to his feet.

"Billy Cutler," he said. "And you're Dorothy Morgan. And you could probably use a drink. What would you like?"

"I don't know," she said. "What are you having?"

"Well," he said, touching his stemmed glass, "night like this, minute I sat down I ordered a martini, straight up and dry as a bone. And I'm about ready for another."

"Martinis are in, aren't they?"

"Far as I'm concerned, they were never out."

"I'll have one," she said.

While they waited for the drinks they talked about the weather. "It's treacherous out there," he said. "The main roads, the Jersey Turnpike and the Garden State, they get these chain collisions where fifty or a hundred cars slam into each other. Used to be a lawyer's dream before no-fault came in. I hope you didn't drive."

"No, I took the PATH train," she said, "and then a cab."

"Much better off."

"Well, I've been to Hoboken before," she said. "In fact, we looked at houses here about a year and a half ago."

"You bought anything then, you'd be way ahead now," he said. "Prices are through the roof."

"We decided to stay in Manhattan." And then we decided to go our separate ways, she thought but didn't say. And thank God we didn't buy a house, or he'd be trying to steal it from me.

"I drove," he said, "and the fog's terrible, no question, but I took my time and I didn't have any trouble. Matter of fact, I couldn't remember if we said seven or seven-thirty, so I made sure I was here by seven."

"Then I kept you waiting," she said. "I wrote down seven-thirty, but—"

"I figured it was probably seven-thirty," he said. "I also figured I'd rather do the waiting myself than keep you waiting. Anyway—" he tapped the book "—I had a book to read, and I ordered a drink, and what more does a man need? Ah, here's Joe with our drinks."

Her martini, straight up and bone dry, was crisp and cold and just what she needed. She took a sip and said as much.

"Well, there's nothing like a martini," he said, "and they make a good one here. Matter of fact, it's a good restaurant altogether. They serve a good steak, a strip sirloin."

"Also coming back in style," she said. "Along with the martini."

He looked at her. He said, "So? You want to be right up with the latest trends? Should I order us a couple of steaks?"

"Oh, I don't think so," she said. "I really shouldn't stay that long."

"Whatever you say."

"I just thought we'd have a drink and—"

"And handle what we have to handle."

"That's right."

"Sure," he said. "That'll be fine."

Except it was hard to find a way into the topic that had brought her to Hoboken, to this restaurant, to this man's table. They both knew why she was here, but that didn't relieve her of the need to broach the subject. Looking for a way in, she went back to the weather, the fog. Even if the weather had been good, she told him, she would have come by train and taxi. Because she didn't have a car.

He said, "No car? Didn't Tommy say you had a weekend place up near him? You can't go back and forth on the bus."

"It's his car," she said.

"His car. Oh, the fella's."

"Howard Bellamy's," she said. Why not say his name? "His car, his weekend place in the country. His loft on Greene Street, as far as that goes."

He nodded, his expression thoughtful. "But you're not still living there," he said.

"No, of course not. And I don't have any of my stuff at the house in the country. And I gave back my set of car keys. All my keys, the car and both houses. I kept my old apartment on West Tenth Street all this time. I didn't even sublet it because I figured I might need it in a hurry. And I was right, wasn't I?"

"What's your beef with him exactly, if you don't mind me asking?"

"My beef," she said. "I never had one, far as I was concerned. We lived together three years, and the first two weren't too bad. Trust me, it was never Romeo and Juliet, but it was all right. And then the third year was bad, and it was time to bail out."

She reached for her drink and found the glass empty. Odd—she didn't remember finishing it. She looked across the table at him and he was waiting patiently, nothing showing in his dark eyes.

After a moment she said, "He says I owe him ten thousand dollars."

"Ten large."

"He says."

"Do you?"

She shook her head. "But he's got a piece of paper," she said. "A note I signed."

"For ten thousand dollars."

"Right."

"Like he loaned you the money."

"Right." She toyed with her empty glass. "But he didn't. Oh, he's got the paper I signed, and he's got a canceled check made out to me and deposited to my account. But it wasn't a loan. He gave me the money and I used it to pay for a cruise the two of us took."

"Where? The Caribbean?"

"The Far East. We flew into Singapore and cruised down to Bali."

"That sounds pretty exotic."

"I guess it was," she said. "This was while things were still good between us, or as good as they ever were."

"This paper you signed," he prompted.

"Something with taxes. So he could write it off, don't ask me how. Look, all the time we lived together I paid my own way. We split expenses right down the middle. The cruise was something else, it was on him. If he wanted me to sign a piece of paper so the government would pick up part of the tab—"

"Why not?"

"Exactly. And now he says it's a debt, and I should pay it, and I got a letter from his lawyer. Can you believe it? A letter from a lawyer?"

"He's not going to sue you."

"Who knows? That's what the lawyer letter says he's going to do."

He frowned. "He goes into court and you start testifying about a tax dodge—"

"But how can I, if I was a party to it?"

"Still, the idea of him suing you after you were living with him. Usually it's the other way around, isn't it? They got a word for it."

"Palimony."

"That's it, palimony. You're not trying for any, are you?"

"Are you kidding? I said I paid my own way."

"That's right, you said that."

"I paid my own way before I met him, the son of a bitch, and I paid my own way while I was with him, and I'll go on paying my own way now that I'm rid of him. The last time I took money from a man was when my Uncle Ralph lent me bus fare to New York when I was eighteen years old. He didn't call it a loan, and he sure as hell didn't give me a piece of paper to sign, but I paid him back all the same. I saved up the money and sent him a money order. I didn't even have a bank account. I got a money order at the post office and sent it to him."

"That's when you came here? When you were eighteen?"

"Fresh out of high school," she said. "And I've been on my own ever since, and paying my own way. I would have paid my own way to Singapore, as far as that goes, but that wasn't the deal. It was supposed to be a present.

And he wants me to pay my way and his way, he wants the whole ten thousand plus interest, and—"

"He's looking to charge you interest?"

"Well, the note I signed. Ten thousand dollars plus interest at the rate of eight percent per annum."

"Interest," he said.

"He's pissed off," she said, "that I wanted to end the relationship. That's what this is about."

"I figured."

"And what *I* figured," she said, "is if a couple of the right sort of people had a talk with him, maybe he would change his mind."

"And that's what brings you here."

She nodded, toying with her empty glass. He pointed to the glass, raised his eyebrows questioningly. She nodded again, and he raised a hand and caught the waiter's eye and signaled for another round.

They were silent until the drinks came. Then he said, "A couple of boys could talk to him."

"That would be great. What would it cost me?"

"Five hundred dollars would do it."

"Well, that sounds good to me."

"The thing is, when you say talk, it'll have to be more than talk. You want to make an impression, situation like this, the implication is either he goes along with it or something physical is going to happen. Now, if you want to give that impression, you have to get physical at the beginning."

"So he knows you mean it?"

"So he's scared," he said. "Because otherwise what he gets is angry. Not right away, two tough-looking guys push him against a wall and tell him what he's gotta do. That makes him a little scared right away, but then they don't get physical and he goes home, and he starts to think about it, and he gets angry."

"I can see how that might happen."

"But if he gets knocked around a little the first time, enough so he's gonna feel it for the next four, five days, he's too scared to get angry. That's what you want."

"Okay."

He sipped his drink, looked at her over the brim. His eyes were appraising her, assessing her. "There's things I need to know about the guy."

"Like?"

"Like what kind of shape is he in?"

"He could stand to lose twenty pounds, but other than that he's okay."

"No heart condition, nothing like that?"

"No."

"He work out?"

"He belongs to a gym," she said, "and he went four times a week for the first month after he joined, and now if he goes twice a month it's a lot."

"Like everybody," he said. "That's how the gyms stay in business. If all their paid-up members showed up, you couldn't get in the door."

"You work out," she said.

"Well, yeah," he said. "Weights, mostly, a few times a week. I got in the habit. I won't tell you where I got in the habit."

"And I won't ask," she said, "but I could probably guess."

"You probably could," he said, grinning. He looked like a little boy for an instant, and then the grin faded and he was back to business.

"Martial arts," he said. "He ever get into any of that?"

"No."

"You're sure? Not lately, but maybe before the two of you started keeping company?"

"He never said anything," she said, "and he would. It's the kind of thing he'd brag about."

"Does he carry?"

"Carry?"

"A gun."

"God, no."

"You know this for a fact?"

"He doesn't even own a gun."

"Same question. Do you know this for a fact?"

She considered it. "Well, how would you know something like that for a fact? I mean, you could know for a fact that a person did own a gun, but how would you know that he didn't? I can say this much—I lived with him for three years and there was never anything I saw or heard that gave me the slightest reason to think he might own a gun. Until you asked the question just now it never entered my mind, and my guess is it never entered *his* mind, either."

"You'd be surprised how many people own guns," he said.

"I probably would."

"Sometimes it feels like half the country walks around strapped. There's more carrying than there are carry permits. A guy doesn't have a permit, he's likely to keep it to himself that he's carrying, or that he even owns a gun in the first place."

"I'm pretty sure he doesn't own a gun, let alone carry one."

"And you're probably right," he said, "but the thing is, you never know. What you got to prepare for is he *might* have a gun, and he *might* be carrying it."

She nodded, uncertain.

"Here's what I've got to ask you," he said. "What you got to ask yourself, and come up with an answer. How far are you prepared for this to go?"

"I'm not sure what you mean."

"We already said it's gonna be physical. Manhandling him, and a couple of shots he'll feel for the better part of a week. Work the rib cage, say."

"All right."

"Well," he said, "that's great, if that's how it goes. But you got to recognize it could go farther."

"What do you mean?"

He made a tent of his fingertips. "I mean you can't necessarily decide where it stops. I don't know if you ever heard the expression, but it's like, uh, having relations with a gorilla. You don't stop when you decide. You stop when the gorilla decides."

"I never heard that before," she said. "It's cute, and I sort of get the point, or maybe I don't. Is Howard Bellamy the gorilla?"

"He's not the gorilla. The violence is the gorilla."

"Oh."

"You start something, you don't know where it goes. Does he fight back? If he does, then it goes a little farther than you planned. Does he keep coming back for more? As long as he keeps coming back for it, you got to keep dishing it out. You got no choice."

"I see."

"Plus there's the human factor. The boys themselves, they don't have an emotional stake. So you figure they're cool and professional about it."

"That's what I figured."

"But it's only true up to a point," he went on, "because they're human, you know? So they start out angry with the guy, they tell themselves how he's a lowlife piece of garbage, so it's easier for them to shove him around. Part of it's an act but part of it's not, and say he mouths off, or he fights back and gets in a good lick. Now they're really angry, and maybe they do more damage than they intended to."

She thought about it. "I can see how that could happen," she said.

"So it could go farther than anybody had in mind. He could wind up in the hospital."

"You mean like broken bones?"

"Or worse. Like a ruptured spleen, which I've known of cases. Or as far as that goes, there's people who've died from a bare knuckle punch in the stomach."

"I saw a movie where that happened."

"Well, I saw a movie where a guy spreads his arms and flies, but dying from a punch in the stomach, they didn't just make that up for the movies. It can happen."

"Now you've got me thinking," she said.

"Well, it's something you got to think about. Because you have to be prepared for this to go all the way, and by all the way I mean all the way. It probably won't, ninety-five times out of a hundred it won't."

"But it could."

"Right. It could."

"Jesus," she said. "He's a son of a bitch, but I don't want him dead. I want to be done with the son of a bitch. I don't want him on my conscience for the rest of my life."

"That's what I figured."

"But I don't want to pay him ten thousand dollars, either, the son of a bitch. This is getting complicated, isn't it?"

"Let me excuse myself for a minute," he said, rising. "And you think about it, and then we'll talk some more."

WHILE he was away from the table she reached for his book and turned it so she could read the title. She looked at the author's photo, read a few lines of the flap copy, then put it as he had left it. She sipped her drink—she was nursing this one, making it last—and looked out the window. Cars rolled by, their headlights slightly eerie in the dense fog.

When he returned she said, "Well, I thought about it."

"And?"

"I think you just talked yourself out of five hundred dollars."

"That's what I figured."

"Because I certainly don't want him dead, and I don't even want him in the hospital. I have to admit I like the idea of him being scared, really scared bad. And hurt a little. But that's just because I'm angry."

"Anybody'd be angry."

"But when I get past the anger," she said, "all I really want is for him to forget this crap about ten thousand dollars. For Christ's sake, that's all the money I've got in the world. I don't want to give it to him."

"Maybe you don't have to."

"What do you mean?"

"I don't think it's about money," he said. "Not for him. It's about sticking it to you for dumping him, or whatever. So it's an emotional thing and it's easy for you to buy into it. But say it was a business thing. You're right and he's wrong, but it's more trouble than it's worth to fight it out. So you settle."

"Settle?"

"You always paid your own way," he said, "so it wouldn't be out of the question for you to pay half the cost of the cruise, would it?"

"No, but—"

"But it was supposed to be a present, from him to you. But forget that for the time being. You could pay half. Still, that's too much. What you do is you offer him two thousand dollars. I have a feeling he'll take it."

"God," she said. "I can't even talk to him. How am I going to offer him anything?"

"You'll have someone else make the offer."

"You mean like a lawyer?"

"Then you owe the lawyer. No, I was thinking I could do it."

"Are you serious?"

"I wouldn't have said it if I wasn't. I think if I was to make the offer he'd accept it. I wouldn't be threatening him, but there's a way to do it so a guy feels threatened."

"He'd feel threatened, all right."

"I'll have your check with me, two thousand dollars, payable to him. My guess is he'll take it, and if he does you won't hear any more from him on the subject of the ten grand."

"So I'm out of it for two thousand. And five hundred for you?"

"I wouldn't charge you anything."

"Why not?"

"All I'd be doing is having a conversation with a guy. I don't charge for conversations. I'm not a lawyer, I'm just a guy owns a couple of parking lots."

"And reads thick novels by young Indian writers."

"Oh, this? You read it?"

She shook her head.

"It's hard to keep the names straight," he said, "especially when you're not sure how to pronounce them in the first place. And it's like if you ask this guy what time it is he tells you how to make a watch. Or maybe a sundial. But it's pretty interesting."

"I never thought you'd be a reader."

"Billy Parking Lots," he said. "Guy who knows guys and can get things done. That's probably all Tommy said about me."

"Just about."

"Maybe that's all I am. Reading, well, it's an edge I got on just about everybody I know. It opens other worlds. I don't live in those worlds, but I get to visit them."

"And you just got in the habit of reading? The way you got in the habit of working out?"

He laughed. "Yeah, but reading's something I've done since I was a kid. I didn't have to go away to get in that particular habit."

"I was wondering about that."

"Anyway," he said, "it's hard to read there, harder than people think. It's noisy all the time."

"Really? I didn't realize. I always figured that's when I'd get to read *War and Peace*, when I got sent to prison. But if it's noisy, then the hell with it. I'm not going."

"You're something else," he said.

"Me?"

"Yeah, you. The way you look, of course, but beyond the looks. The only word I can think of is class, but it's a word that's mostly used by people that haven't got any themselves. Which is probably true enough."

"The hell with that," she said. "After the conversation we just had? Talking me out of doing something I could have regretted all my life, and figuring out how to get that son of a bitch off my back for two thousand dollars? I'd call that class."

"Well, you're seeing me at my best," he said.

"And you're seeing me at my worst," she said, "or close to it. Looking to hire a guy to beat up an ex-boyfriend. That's class, all right."

"That's not what I see. I see a woman who doesn't want to be pushed around. And if I can find a way that helps you get where you want to be, then

I'm glad to do it. But when all's said and done, you're a lady and I'm a wiseguy."

"I don't know what you mean."

"Yes, you do."

"Yes, I guess I do."

He nodded. "Drink up," he said. "I'll run you back to the city."

"You don't have to do that. I can take the PATH train."

"I've got to go into the city anyway. It's not out of my way to take you wherever you're going."

"If you're sure."

"I'm sure," he said. "Or here's another idea. We both have to eat, and I told you they serve a good steak here. Let me buy you dinner, and *then* I'll run you home."

"Dinner," she said.

"A shrimp cocktail, a salad, a steak, a baked potato—"

"You're tempting me."

"So let yourself be tempted," he said. "It's just a meal."

She looked at him levelly. "No," she said. "It's more than that."

"It's more than that if you want it to be. Or it's just a meal, if that's what you want."

"But you can't know how far it might go," she said. "We're back to that again, aren't we? Like what you said about the gorilla, and you stop when the gorilla wants to stop."

"I guess I'm the gorilla, huh?"

"You said the violence was the gorilla. Well, in this case it's not violence, but it's not either of us, either. It's what's going on between us, and it's already going on, isn't it?"

"You tell me."

She looked down at her hands, then up at him. "A person has to eat," she said.

"You said it."

"And it's still foggy outside."

"Like pea soup. And who knows? There's a good chance the fog'll lift by the time we've had our meal."

"I wouldn't be a bit surprised," she said. "I think it's lifting already."

In a Grove

John O'Hara

IN THIS OBSCURE little California town, far away from Hollywood and not even very close to the Saroyan-Steinbeck country, William Grant once again encountered Richard Warner, as he had always known he would.

Johnstown—to give it a name—was one of those towns that vaudevillians used to describe as "a wide place in the road" and that had owed its earliest existence to the gold strikes of more than a century ago. But in the intervening years it had been all but abandoned until irrigation began to help agriculture, and Johnstown got a second life; unspectacular, unromantic, unexciting, and obviously unprofitable—the last place Grant would expect to find Warner, and yet, since his disappearance had been so complete, the kind of place that was just made for a man who wanted to leave the world in which he had once been widely known.

Grant stopped his car at a filling station. "Fill it up, will you please? The oil is okay, but will you check the water and tires?"

"Right. What do you carry, twenty-six pounds, the tires?" said the attendant.

"Twenty-six, right."

"You been driving a distance, they'll all be a little high, you know. You want me to deflate to twenty-six?"

"Yes."

"Some don't, you know."

"Well, I'm one of those that do," said Grant. "What's the name of this town?"

"Johnstown. Johnstown, California."

"Is that a cigarette machine in there?"

"It's a cigarette machine that's out of order. The nearest place is the supermarket. You can see it there on the edge of town. They call it a supermarket, but nothing very super about it. It's only what used to be the Buick agency, that's all it is."

"But they have cigarettes there."

"Oh, they have cigarettes. They have most everything you find in a supermarket, but I don't know who they think they're kidding, calling it a supermarket. It's no bigger than when it was the Buick agency."

"What happened to the Buick agency?"

"What happened to it? This was never a town for Buicks. You wait here a few minutes and you'll see a couple Model-A Fords, still chugging away. Maybe some International trucks, been through various hands, one rancher to the other. Way back, when I was a kid, one family had a Locomobile. You ever hear of the Locomobile?"

"Yes."

"Another rancher had a big old Pierce-Arrow. Those big ritzy cars, but I'll tell you something. You look on the running-board of those cars and every one of them carried canteens. Ed Hughes, that owned the Locomobile, I remember he had like a saddle holster he had strapped to the right-hand door, to carry a 30-30 rifle in. They didn't buy those cars for show. They bought them because they stood up. That was before they thought up this planned obsolescence."

"Planned obsolescence. Uh-huh."

"You know, 'Here's this year's piece of junk, come back and see what I allow you on it two years from now.' That's where all the trouble lies. Now what you got here is a foreign car, and it ain't even broke in at forty-five thousand miles. This is an automobile. You don't mind if I take a look under the hood? I know, you said you don't need oil, but—"

"That, that just went by. That was no Model-A," said Grant.

The attendant had missed the passing Jaguar, but now waved to it. He smiled. "No, that was Dick Warner. He's a fellow lives here. You ever hear of the expression, as queer as Dick's hatband? I think that's who it originated with, Dick Warner."

"Dick Warner? How long has he lived here?"

"Oh—I guess fifteen, maybe twenty years by now. Why, do you know him?"

"Possibly. Where did this fellow come from?"

"Oh, well I'm not even sure about that."

"Is he a tall thin fellow? Brown hair? About my age?"

"Well, I guess he'd answer that description. What are you, the F.B.I. or something like that?"

"Hell, no. If I were the F.B.I. I'd go looking for the deputy sheriff, wouldn't I?"

"You found him. *I'm* the deputy sheriff, and I never had any bad reports on Dick, bad or good for that matter. He pays his bills, don't owe nobody, and his fingerprint's on his driver's license. Well, now he's making a U-turn. Maybe he recognized you."

"I doubt it."

"Heading back this way. Yeah. Moving slowly. Wants to get a good look at you. Mister, are you armed? You got a gun on you?"

"No."

"Well, Dick has, so get behind something. I am."

"There's not going to be anything like that."

"All the same I'm getting out of the way till I make sure. I'm going in and put my badge on. And my gun."

"Go ahead. I'll stand right here."

The Jaguar drove past slowly, the driver staring at William Grant. After the Jaguar had gone past the filling station it stopped, then backed up into the parking area. Dick Warner got out.

He was tall and thin and wore a planter's Panama with a band of feathers, a safari jacket with the sleeves rolled up, suntan slacks and leather sandals. "Is it you, Grant?"

"Yes it's me. Hello, Dick."

"Christ Almighty," said Warner. He put out his hand, and Grant shook it.

"No, just me," said Grant.

"What the hell are you doing here?"

"I was looking for a good place to hide out from the law."

"Then get going. There isn't room for two of us. Well, God damn it, Bill. Hey, Smitty, come on out and meet a friend of mine. This is Mr. Grant, Mr. Smith. See that you give him four quarts to the gallon."

"Now, Dick. Now, now."

"Mr. Smith thought you might be going to shoot me," said Grant.

"Now why'd you have to tell him that? I didn't know but you were some-body snooping around and Dick didn't want to see you."

"I hear you carry a gun, Dick," said Grant.

"Smitty, whose side are you on? You talk too much."

"This fellow started asking me questions. He's the one with the big mouth. That'll be four-eighty, Mister, and the next time you come here there's an-other filling station the other end of town."

"You decided not to check the air for me?"

"I decided if you wanted to check the air you can do it yourself, and there's the hose if you need water."

"All right, Sheriff. You owe me twenty cents," said Grant, handing Smitty a five-dollar bill.

"Mr. Grant's a nice fellow, Smitty. You shouldn't take that attitude."

"I know what attitude to take without any advice from you, Dick."

"I know. Your gums are bothering you again," said Warner. "Smitty has a new upper plate, and he won't give his gums a chance to get used to it."

"I don't think it's his gums. I think he's just a disagreeable guy."

"Move on, Mister, or I'll give you a ticket."

"What for?" said Grant.

"Obstructing traffic. Failure to pay for parking on my lot. I'll think of a few things."

"He will, too, and his brother-in-law's the mayor," said Warner. "Smitty, this is no way to treat a visitor to our fair city."

"We don't encourage tourists. If this fellow's a friend of yours, Dick, you get him off my property pronto."

"All right. Follow me, Bill. And don't go through any stop signs."

"I'll get out of here as quickly as I can."

"Thirty-mile zone," said Smitty.

"I think that dentist gave you the wrong plate, Smitty," said Warner. "Come on, Bill."

The built-up section was four blocks of one-story white stucco business buildings, which changed abruptly to a stretch of one-story frame dwellings, all badly in need of paint, and then there was country, bare in the rolling hills where the irrigation was not effective. Grant followed Warner for about a mile, until Warner blew his horn, slowed down, and made a right turn into a dirt road. A few hundred yards along that road Warner again slowed down and entered a dirt driveway that ended in a grove of various trees, in the center of which was a ranchhouse. Two horses in a small corral looked up as the cars approached, and a collie ignored Warner's car to run along beside Grant's, barking ferociously. Warner signaled to Grant to drive up alongside him.

"Stay in your car till I put Sonny away. He's liable to take a piece out of your leg," said Warner. He got out and the dog came to him, and he grasped the dog's collar and snapped a leash to it and attached the leash to a length of wire that ran between two trees. The dog could run only between the trees. "You're safe now."

"What do you feed this dog? People?"

"I don't have to. He helps himself. Particularly fond of Mexicans. Itinerant workers. Salesmen. Hollywood writers, he hasn't had any but I can tell he's willing to have a taste of you."

"I can tell that myself."

"Well, just stay out of reach."

"All right, Lassie," said Grant. "Maybe if I gave him a good swift kick."

"You'd never leave here alive if you did. Even if I let you get away with it my wife wouldn't."

"Oh, you're married."

"Good God, do you think I could live here if I wasn't?"

"Well, what the hell. Itinerant workers, Mexicans."

"Lay off the Mexican angle. My wife is half Mexican."

"What else do I have to look out for?"

"Well, at certain times of the day, down there near the ditch, rattlesnakes, but they don't come up here much. I've done a pretty good job of exterminating them around the house. Anyway, you won't be here that long. You're on your way somewhere, obviously. Come on in and meet my bride and have a cooling drink."

"And I forgot to get some cigarettes."

"We have plenty. The señora's a heavy smoker. There she is."

A girl, not readily identifiable as Mexican but wearing a multi-colored peasant blouse and skirt and huaraches, opened the door of a screened porch. "Hi," she said.

"I brought somebody out of my past. This is Bill Grant, used to be with me at Paramount. Bill, this is the present Mrs. Warner, Rita by name."

"Hi," she said. "And what's with that present Mrs. Warner bit?"

"We can only wait and see."

"You wait and see. Come on in, Bill. What would you like to drink? I got some cold beer."

"Thank you, that's just perfect."

"Where did the great Warner run across you? Or you across him? He never has any company. From Hollywood, anyway. Dick, you get the beer."

"All right," said Warner, and went to the kitchen.

"I'm working for TV now, and I came up this way scouting locations. Have you been in pictures?"

"No, but I know what scouting locations means. I went to high school in L.A. Fairfax."

"How did you stay out of pictures?"

"You think I'm pretty enough? I guess I'm prettier than some of those dogs, but I was never discovered. Except by his majesty."

"Where did he discover you?"

"You better ask him, he has a different story for everybody. He told a couple people in Johnstown I was his daughter. The son of a bitch. I *am* married to him though. You married?"

"Sure. I have a daughter around your age."

"Well, so has Dick, although I never saw her."

"I know. She lives back East."

"And he has a son. You don't have to be cagey about that side of him. Three ex-wives, a daughter and a son. A brother, a sister, a mother—all that I know. Did you know him a long time?"

"A long time ago I knew him pretty well. Then we had a falling-out. I can't remember what about."

"Well I remember," said Warner, bringing in a tray of bottles and glasses. "I fired you because you went on a three-day bender and never let me know where you were."

"I guess that was it."

"You made me look bad on my second picture as a producer."

"Yeah. You behaved like a jerk producer, that's right."

"Why do you say jerk producer? What other kind is there? You're one now, only in a worse medium. I've seen your name in the paper once in a while. The hell with that. What are you up here for?"

"What are you?"

"I asked you."

"I'm scouting locations."

"Stay away, will you? Go on up to Marin County. I don't want a bunch of those bastards coming to Johnstown. I went to a lot of trouble to get away from them, so don't spoil it for me, will you?"

"I won't promise. Anyway, I might make you a few dollars. I could rent this place for a couple of weeks."

"I don't need the money."

"Hey! Who don't need the money?" said Rita. "I could use a few bucks."

"On what? We have enough."

"I was wondering about that," said Grant. "You do have enough? This is a nice place and all that, but I remember when you were playing polo."

"I could still play polo if I wanted to, but who plays polo these days? For that matter, who makes pictures these days?"

"His majesty thinks the movies stink," said Rita. "That's why he never goes to them, and that's why he knows all about them."

"You don't smell with your eyes. The beautiful odor is wafted all the way from Culver City," said Warner.

"Culver City is where I work. I shoot a lot of stuff on the Metro lot," said Grant.

"Speaking of shooting, what was that conversation with Smitty?"

"He told me you carried a gun. Apparently he doesn't know anything about you, your background, where you came from."

"I've seen to that."

"But this is the strange part. He was willing to believe that you were ready to shoot it out with the first stranger that asked about you. That's an odd impression to leave after living here fifteen years."

"I've told Smitty what you might call conflicting stories. It's nobody's business what I did before I came here, or what I do now, if I stay within the law."

"What *do* you do now?"

Warner pointed to a wall that was completely covered with bookshelves containing paperback books and old magazines; western stories, detective stories, science fiction, popular delvings into the human mind.

"You write them?" said Grant.

"I steal from them and then write my own. I have five by-lines, and I make anywhere from five to fifteen thousand a year, turning out stories. I'm what we used to call a pulp writer."

"It must keep you busy, but do you need the money? I thought you left Hollywood with plenty of glue."

"Don't give this greedy little Mexican the wrong idea," said Warner. "We live on what I earn."

"Except when you want to buy a Jaguar, or send away to New York for some clothes," said Rita.

"My extravagances, my spirit-raising expenditures, they come out of my capital, the money I took out of Hollywood," said Warner.

"You let him get away with this, Rita?"

"She's devoted to me, you can see that. Sit on his lap," said Warner. "He's wondering if he can make you, so let him have a try at it."

"You want me to sit on your lap, Grant?"

"Of course. He's right."

She put down her glass and sat on Grant's lap. Grant took her in his arms and kissed her and felt her breasts.

"Cut!" said Warner. "Now go back to your chair."

The girl returned to her chair and picked up her glass.

"How do you feel, Chiquita? Would you have gone on?"

"What do you think, king? Of course I'd have gone on."

"Then why didn't you?"

"Because I knew you were going to say 'Cut.'"

"That isn't the answer you're supposed to give."

"That's the answer I gave, though. I told you I have a lot to learn."

"She has spirit, this girl," said Warner.

"Plenty."

"Oh, not only what you mean. She still has a mind of her own."

"I always will have. His majesty thinks he rules me, but he doesn't tell me to do anything I don't want to do. You can't hypnotize somebody against their will."

"Yes you can," said Grant. "But there's some theory that while they're under hypnosis they won't do anything they don't want to."

"I guess that's what I meant."

"Let me remind both of you that this has nothing to do with hypnosis. I am not a hypnotist."

"Maybe not, but you like to think you have hypnotic powers," said Grant.

"There you're perfectly correct."

"I'd like to know why you said 'Cut'? It wasn't just to show your power. It was because you were afraid."

"Nonsense," said Warner. "Afraid of what?"

"Ho! Afraid that Rita and I would get in the hay. She was willing to stop because she was getting embarrassed."

Warner gave a short laugh. "Embarrassed? Rita? Tell the man what you used to do for a living."

"I was a hooker," said the girl.

"A fifty-dollar girl that got tired of the grind," said Warner.

"And several other things," said Rita. "You don't only get tired of the grind."

"My wife doesn't embarrass easily, Grant."

"I guess not," he said.

"The complexities and deviations are all old stuff to her. What did you think of Grant when you first laid eyes on him?"

"Well, I knew by the car that he was probably some Hollywood friend of yours."

"Yes, but what else?"

"Well, he'd make a pass at me if he had a chance."

"So far nothing very complex," said Grant.

"Well, I knew he didn't like you."

"Now we're getting somewhere. Do you know why you thought that?" said Warner.

"That I couldn't tell you."

"All right, never mind. Tell us some other first impressions and reactions."

"I thought I wouldn't mind getting in bed with him."

"She doesn't see many men here," said Warner.

"Let her tell it," said Grant.

"But he wouldn't be much fun after a while. You're still the most fun, king."

"Why is he so much fun, Rita? Not just sex," said Grant.

"Don't knock sex. And it is sex. With this character everything is sex. Want to ask you a question, Grant. Did he lay all those picture stars?"

"He had his share, but not many of the big ones. He was afraid to go after the big ones. He was afraid he'd get a turn-down and it would get around that he'd made a pitch and was unsuccessful. In Hollywood, honey, that's losing face. No, your husband didn't score with the big ones."

"I knew you were lying about that," said Rita to Warner.

"Grant is only telling what he knows. There's a hell of a lot he doesn't know."

"What Academy Award winner did you ever lay? Now don't give me any best-supporting actress. I mean the Number One. Or what star that got top billing, her name over the main title? Or a hundred percent of the main title."

"What's that?"

"Your name in letters as big as the title of the picture," said Grant. "The only one was Ernesta Travers, and she was giving it out to projectionists. She actually laid a projectionist while he was running a picture for her."

"You've got the story wrong, but no matter. I even forgot about Ernesta."

"I didn't know she was ever a big star," said Rita. "Have some more beer, Grant."

"All right, fine," said Grant.

"You, king? You want another?"

"If you get it, yes," said Warner.

She left them.

"Yes, what you're wondering is true. She was a hooker."

"Well she was a damn pretty one. Is. I have to be careful of my tenses. Is damn pretty, whatever she was."

"Would you give her a hundred dollars now?"

"Sure."

In a loud voice Warner called out: "I've got you lined up for a fast hundred dollars."

"With Grant?" she responded from the kitchen.

"Yeah."

"All right," she said. She brought in three bottles of beer, clutching them by the neck. She put a bottle in front of Warner, then sat herself beside Grant and poured beer into his glass. "Do I get to keep the whole C-note?"

"Certainly," said Warner.

"Do I get shot in the back?" said Grant.

"That's the chance you take."

"Just so you don't shoot him while he's in the kip with me."

"That's the chance *you* take, señora."

She looked at her husband. "Listen, how much of this is kidding and how much is kidding on the square?"

"I'm not kidding at all. If you'd like to make yourself a quick hundred dollars, Grant and I made a deal. Ask Grant if I'm kidding."

"Just like old times, back in the Thirties," said Grant.

"I don't know," said the girl.

"What don't you know?" said Warner.

"Well, what the hell?" she said.

"It's how you used to earn your living," said her husband.

"I don't deny that. But the first friend of yours ever came to the house and you promote him into a party with me," she said.

"Don't you want the hundred dollars?" said Warner.

"I always want a hundred dollars."

"Well, you necked him, you let him give you a little feel."

"Yeah, but I thought that was—I was just playing along with the gag."

"Grant wasn't playing along with any gag, were you, Grant?"

"To tell you the truth I guess I wasn't."

"And it was no gag when you said you'd give her a hundred bucks."

"No, I'd give her a hundred bucks."

"Well, you son of a bitch, if you meant it, I'll level, too," said the girl to her husband. She reached out her hand. "Come on, Grant."

Grant stood up. "You'll excuse us, I'm sure," said Grant.

The girl looked at her husband. "You can't be on the level," she said.

"Why not?" said Warner.

"God damn you. God damn you!" She ripped off the peasant blouse and, naked to the waist, put her arms around Grant and kissed him. "Come on," she said, and led him by the hand.

She lay on the oversize bed, and Grant shed his clothes and got down beside her. She looked at him. "Don't worry, I won't welsh on it now," she said. She put her arms around him and began running her little hands up and down his spine, slowly, caressingly.

"Perfect." Warner's voice was cold and calm.

The girl saw her husband in the doorway, then she screamed. "No! No!" The first shots struck Grant in the spine, he shuddered and died. The girl tried to hide behind his body, but Warner grasped his hand and pulled him aside and took his time firing the remaining four shots. Then he went to the telephone and dialed.

"Smitty, come on out here. I've got something for you," he said.